Julia, Thank you for your support. I ho you enjoy the book. Emmy R. Bennett

Eyes of Wynter

Storm Bloodline Saga

Book One

Emmy R. Bennett

Published by Emmy R. Bennett

© 2018 Cover Artwork & Design: Consuelo Parra

Model: Maria Amanda

Edited by Helen Arnestad

Learn more about the author visit:

erbennettbooks.com

facebook.com/ERBennettbooks

twitter.com/emmyrbennett

instagram.com/e.r.bennettbooks

ISBN: 978-0-578-41122-4

DEDICATION

To my daughter: I finally finished

AUTHOR'S NOTE

This book has been 15 years in the making. I never thought I would ever get to this point. I've always had the dream to write stories. I have always told my kids, *'never give up.'* Last year I realized, it was time for me to live up to those words. What kind of example was I setting for them, by telling them to reach for the highest star, if I don't do that myself?

So, I decided to finish the book I started all those years ago for my daughter, Elly.

Fast forward to 2017, and I find myself in a dream. My late grandmother had a message for me.

"Why have you stopped writing?" she says.

"I don't know. Grams, I miss you. The passion wasn't there after you left."

"It's still there, my child. You must find it. It's time you stop this nonsense and get back to doing what you're meant to do." Then she hugged me. It was a real physical hug, not like the ones usually felt in a dream. She kissed my forehead. "I will always be here, watching over you. You may not see me, but I'm there."

And with that, she was gone...

Acknowledgements

First, thank you to God, my family and friends: you know who you are. If it wasn't for your continual support, this book might still be locked away on my computer. Thank you to my husband who has been my constant rock throughout this whole process, never once doubting, always pushing me to finish. And to my four kids, all asking in their own way, 'How's the book coming along?'

To my sister, Olivia thank you for dealing with my ups and downs, and Sharon, who has been like a mother, boosting me to keep moving forward. Honestly if it hadn't been for either of you, I'm not sure I would have ever finished. You gave me the motivation to keep going. I also would like to thank my mother for raising me to be the person I am today.

Then there is Lesley Donaldson-Reid. My coach, editor and teacher, what can I say? When you pulled me aside that first day, I had no idea how much my writing world would change. You helped me to shape my craft into something I never would have foreseen without your guidance. You were tough on me with critique, something I needed, and without it, this book would not be the same. You helped me see the potential it had.

To Helen Arnestad: I'm truly blessed to have you as my editor. I couldn't have thought of anyone better than you to entrust with my manuscript. You have done a wonderful job.

And to my beta readers: Sharon, Olivia, Denise, Samantha, Gracie, Chris, and Mel you all have been awesome giving me feedback. You played an important role, by taking the challenge and sorting through the awful rough drafts. Thank you so much for helping me make this book better than it would have been.

And finally, to those who read it: thank you, for giving me the opportunity to show you a new undiscovered story.

Enjoy...

Wynter's Thoughts

Time has a way of spinning out of control. It doesn't always go according to plan. One-minute life is beautiful, fast growing and in that moment, we feel alive.
Seasons bring change to that existence, making it a constant struggle.
In-between these two is my coexistent. Where reality becomes a choice, a path for the future. This presence is where my fate begins.
Time heals all wounds they say. I'd like to know who '*they*' are.
As for me, my wounds are clearly open…

Prologue

"Quick, she's coming," my sister calls out, as I glance over my new born child with fear. I never knew what pain could be like, until now, as it begins to dissipate. Gazing at her in my arms, I wonder how we will keep her safe from the evil that is about to be forced upon her. Dark hair, black as night, green eyes, bright as emeralds; a little image of me. Sarmira, the evil queen has me right where she wants me, or so she thinks; in her clutches, taking the last of our bloodline. Over my dead body. She will not win the battle this night.

My sister prepares our bags, while my husband stands guard at the door. "I hear the shadows of silence coming," he says. "We must hurry if we are all to get out of here in time."

"I'm too weak. I cannot go with you," I say, looking over at him. "Please, take this." I rip the chain from around my neck, handing it to him. "Give this to our daughter. Have her wear it always. It will protect her from Sarmira."

His blue eye's glow with fury and fear and I can see the rage inside him. I know he doesn't like my idea to stay behind, but what other choice do we have?

"I can hold her off, but only for a little while," I express with urgency.

"I can't take this," he says, holding the chain between his fingers. "She will destroy you without it."

"You must my love, to protect our daughter. It is the only way, to buy you time to the portal." I place the swaddled baby in a hand-woven basket beside the bed. "There is no time to waste. She's closing in," I voice with firmness, pushing the basket towards my sister to grab. "She will kill us all. It's the baby she's after."

"How do you know all this Isalora? I won't leave you," he protests. I see the pain written all over his face.

"My father came to me in a dream warning me of the prophecy. Our daughter is the key to Sarmira's destruction. You must go, now!"

"I sense her company getting near," my sister says. "We need to leave, if we are to escape her wrath."

Tears fall from my eyes and I feel the wetness cool my cheeks, from the crisp air. "Promise me you will protect them, my sweet sister," I say.

"With my life," she says, and she kisses my forehead.

Then gripping my husband's hand, I stand, saying, "Sarmira's presence is growing closer with each second that passes. Leave now, before it is too late."

He gently hands me the Elvin valiancium dagger crafted in labradorite. "Take this, for your protection," he persists, and not waiting a moment more, they leave. I hear my baby's whimpering cry echo down the hall and fade away.

I grab parchment from my nightstand along with a pen. *'Not much time to write a letter,'* I think to myself. I need to warn them about the secret I bear. Sarmira may think it ends with me, but little does she know what I have up my sleeve.

Chanting the spell aloud, I say;

On this full moon night, I claim what is right.
Binding them by three, one then they shall be.
When the super blue blood moon ascends,
The ties that bind, then amends.

I burn the handwritten letter in a leather-bound coffer, placing my spellbook over the ashes and close the lid.

Anticipating my time is short; I position the box behind the stone fireplace concealing it tight and wait for Sarmira. With my dagger in hand, I gently kiss the blade and chant another spell.

The full moon brightens the darkness in the room. The oil lamp flickers on my nightstand cluing me that she's near. So, I tuck the hilt behind my skirt and wait patiently.

Seconds later, the door bursts open in a vengeful thrust, forcing the kerosene light to blow out.

There, in the doorway she stands with her eyes glowing blue as usual, hiding under her hooded cloak.

"Well… well… how pathetic, do you look, Isalora," she says, slithering over to me. "There you are quivering like a frightened animal. You have no power here. There's no magical force that can protect you. Do you honestly think you can fool me with your façade?"

"You will not get away with the murderous evil you have bestowed on our family, Sarmira," I counter back to her.

She appears surprised I discovered her secret hidden away for centuries. What she doesn't count on, is my gift of vision. I can see what lies beneath the skin, of a human. "Yes, I see the innocent soul you suppress," I retort. "Talk about façades? Yours is in plain sight."

She laughs a wicked cackle: like a witch ready to cast a spell. "I see, and you dare cross me anyway? Fascinating."

"What is there to cross, Sarmira? I have known for a long time. We were planning the perfect getaway, until you decided to lock me in this room. You may think you have me where you want me but think again. Eyes and ears are watching, yes indeed, but that goes both ways." I keep my expression to her stern, not wavering to fear.

"Whatever have you done?" she says in a condescending tone. "Trying to turn my followers against me? It will never work. We both know you have no power here. You're no match for me. You will lose, should you try anything foolish." She paces forward, and I tighten my grip on the knife.

"Now, where is the little heathen you grew in that belly of yours?"

"She's long gone, Sarmira. You will never find her," I roar, hiding the dagger I hold tight in my hand ready to strike, if she dare come closer.

"Ah, so you had a girl?" Sarmira, raises an eyebrow and her eyes begin to grow a brighter blue than before. I know that look from the many times she tore through innocent souls. It's the look of possession. Avoiding her stare, I remind myself not to peer back. "Oh... Isalora please... do you honestly believe you can resist me...?"

I don't have the necklace to shield me, so I close my eyes and begin chanting the spell a second time holding ground against her will.

"No," she screams, as I feel the room saturate with light from my closed eyelids.

Sensing her maddened frustration, I chant my spell louder and shout, "You will never hurt them, Sarmira. I have bound them with a spell. You're finished. The prophecy will be fulfilled." What she doesn't know, by killing me she seals her fate.

"What have you done!" she screeches. My eyes still closed, I hear shattering from the window behind her explode into a million pieces. Fierce winds howl, blowing a cloud of dust my way.

I shield my face with my free arm, trying to avoid being stabbed by glass. Knowing full well, I'm weaker without my necklace, I bind my soul with the spirits, chanting a spell of immortality. It is the only way to protect the innocent and bring this prophecy to fruition.

"You cannot defeat me!" Sarmira roars. I peek out to see her lunge forward and before I have a chance to stab her with my dagger, she slides her hand into my chest grabbing my heart, ripping it from my body.

1

The Stranger

Hearing the locker door slam shut, jolts my drifting mind. Rory's voice calls from behind me, "Wynter, are you coming? Class is about to start."

"Um, yeah, I'll catch up," glancing back to her with a wave of my hand; still listening to the resonated sounds of slamming metal ringing in my ears. I grab my books from the locker shelf and quickly tail behind her, making it just in time before the bell rings for second period. The teacher eyes me a warning glance as I scamper to my seat.

Rory smirks with an *'I told you so'* look. Sneering back at her, I shake my head in response, along with a shrug. We've been best friends since tenth grade and she's like the sister I never had. Hard to believe this is our senior year. It's finals week before Christmas break, and our last day of grueling tests.

"What's gotten into you?" she whispers.

"Something is off," I say, and I straighten my posture, placing my fingers around my neck to grab the chain that isn't there. "My necklace," I whisper aloud. I strain to think where I last remember wearing it. My dad is going to kill me if he finds it not around my neck. I can't remember a time when I didn't see dad checking to see I wear it always. My cheeks flush and my head begins to fill with fear.

"Wynter, what's wrong?" Rory murmurs.

"My necklace. It's gone."

"Where did you last have it?"

I wrinkle my forehead and shake my head. "I don't remember," trying to think back, visualizing where it might be. I recall doing one more lap around the pool, when Sadie pulled at my legs dunking me under. I swear that girl is pure evil. The coach didn't see me floundering around in the water, like a fish, either.

Raising my hand, stretching it as far into the air as it will go, I call out, "Mr. Cadzek."

Feeling as though he pretends not to notice, I speak his name louder.

"What is it, Miss Storm?" he asks, still looking down at his notebook and continuing to write.

"I forgot something in last period, may I run and get it?"

He ignores my question, still focusing on what is in front of him.

"Please?"

He glances up at me. "Fine, go on. We're not doing much today in class anyway."

I see Rory out of the corner of my eye. Wiggling around in her seat like she's about to burst at the seams any moment. "Me too?" she blurts out.

Mr. Cadzek pulls off his glasses. "I suppose she needs you with her for emotional support, huh?"

I turn to look at Rory and mouth the word no. The teacher shakes his head, lets out a big sigh and pulls out a pen and pad. Writing us both hall passes, he hands them to us saying, "Now hurry up and go before I change my mind."

Rory giggles once the door shuts. "Did that just happen?" she exclaims and twirls around.

"It's the last day before break," I reply, holding my books tight to my chest. "I mean, we don't have a test today, remember? We had an essay as a final."

Skipping at my heels trying to keep up with my brisk pace, she ignores my comment, saying, "So, where are we going anyway?"

"I think I dropped my necklace somewhere around swim class."

Once we arrive at the entrance to the swimming pool, I test to see if the doors are unlocked and to my amazement, they are. "Thank you," I mouth to the gods above who may be listening.

Lucky for me there isn't a class set for second period. We look in corners, around the chairs lining the walls and along the bins where water sport items are stored, finding nothing. My worst fear finally arrives.

"It's gone forever," I say aloud. Thinking to myself, I'll never hear the end of it with my dad. *"What!? You should be more careful. That necklace was your late mother's."* The thoughts roll over and over in my mind as I begin to panic.

"Wynter, what's that?" Rory says, pointing towards the pool.

I walk over to her and peer down at the bottom of the floor to see something shiny, sparkling back at us.

"My necklace," I cry. Throwing my bookbag on the bench behind me, I begin to take off my shoes and jacket.

"What are you doing?" Rory says, looking startled. "You're not going to—"

"Jump in? Yes. That's precisely what I'm about to do," as I strip down to my underwear and dive to the bottom.

After getting out of the pool I realize there isn't a towel handy to dry off. "Well crap. You don't by chance see a towel lying around, do you?"

"Come on, let's go to the locker room," she says grabbing both our backpacks.

The bathroom is empty, and I find fresh towels. My hair is dripping wet, reminding me that I should have put on a swimming cap first, stored in my book bag. We find clean towels still folded in the linen area and I grab a couple of them.

"I'm going to look like I peed my pants," I say, as I shimmy my jeans back on. Looking down I see water from my underwear already seeping through the material.

Rory giggles at my predicament. "Laugh it up, small fry," I retort back at her.

"Hey, at least you got your chain back," Rory says.

I roll my eyes. "Yeah, well, it's either find the necklace or die by the hands of my father when I get home." Rory snickers more, and I push further saying, "I'm glad I can amuse you my dear friend. I assure you this is no laughing matter. While I can understand your jest, it's annoying to stand here watching you mock me."

"Okay, okay, I'll stop," she says, and proceeds to cover her mouth, hiding a grin.

"Unbelievable," I say, turning my back to her so as not to see her gawking at me. "I wonder if this will give me an excuse to skip school all together?"

"You wish," she says. "We are just in time for third period, though."

I look up at the clock to see the bell about to ring. "Isn't third period your math class?" I ask Rory, wondering if she has her final today.

"You're right. Crap, Wyn, I'm sorry I gotta' go." Grabbing her stuff, she darts out before I have a chance to ask if she plans on staying at school the whole day. With my next class being study hall, perhaps it's a good time to make myself presentable again after indulging in a quick swim.

My chain feels cold and wet against my skin, so I unclasp the locket, tucking it in my jeans for now. My bra is soaked, with the moisture becoming prevalent on my dark blue sweatshirt.

"Lovely," I say aloud, looking at my reflection in the mirror. Good thing I have a coat that will hide the watermarks. I'm going to look ridiculous. I put my hair in a ponytail just as the bell rings and within seconds, students begin to pile into the locker room.

"That's my cue," I say under my breath as I pick up my stuff.

After school I wait for Rory by the big fir tree as always, when ahead a seemingly familiar image stares back at me from one of the nearby buildings. I had seen this before in the past. A silhouette would appear, I would look away, taking a double take and it would disappear.

Well, not this time. I stare the figure down, as I step forward. Fixating on the voyeuristic imposter, I'm not about to let it get away from me this time. It stands there, smirking back at me. I ignore the urge to look away and keep a piercing eye on the individual, picking up my pace. A brown hooded cloak covers most of the face, and its hands are clasped gently against the abdomen, like a priest about to give a sermon. I kick it up to a fast walk crossing the parking lot, not paying attention to whether cars are coming or going. Probably a dumb move, but at this point, I don't care. I'm tired of seeing this onlooker, poking its happy little head in my business whenever it wants to.

The last time I saw this watcher was in Florida a few years ago. The next thing I know, my family uproots to Washington State. As I get closer, I see it grin, showing pearly whites, like it's trying to egg me on. That's when I begin a slight jog, tripping over the curb and falling to the ground.

My distraction gets the best of me and I look up to see that the stranger's gone. Many students see me on the ground and laugh and point.

"You should really watch where you are going klutz," I hear a teen boy say, as he steps over me.

"Hey Wyn, are you okay?" Madeline says, dropping her bag to come over and help me up. Another girl gets to me first, putting her hand out for me to grab and says, "That step can be a doozy. I've tripped over it many times."

"Yeah, thanks," I finally say, still distracted by the person I saw standing over by the building.

My hands are filthy, and I wipe them on my now-soaked jeans. At this point I can't wait to stand in a warm shower. Decembers are brutal here, with frigid air sweeping across faces and the rain that comes down is like ice pellets.

Madeline hands me back my bags and says, "Here you go. Have a good break. See you next year."

"Yeah, thanks. You too," I say, and reach for my pack.

Still feeling uneasy I peer over my shoulder, glancing around to see if the shadow figure is lurking somewhere. Instead Rory walks up to me.

"What happened to you?" she says, obviously seeing that I look like hell.

"Apparently there is a curb that divides the sidewalk from the parking lot," I say in a sarcastic tone, flipping my bag to my back. "As usual, I'm not watching where I'm going and took a nose dive."

"Well, are you hurt?" she asks, sounding concerned. It throws me for a loop. *'What's the deal with her being so nosey,'* I think to myself?

"Why are you heading in that direction when home is the other way?" she voices, pointing over her shoulder.

"It's nothing. I thought I saw someone I knew and the next moment I'm on the ground eating grass."

"Are they still lurking around?" she asks looking about. Her odd behavior strikes me.

"No, they're long gone," I reply stepping onto the pavement. "We'd better get going, the clouds up ahead look nasty, like it's about to snow."

Thankfully, our homes are located a few blocks from school, so we don't have far to walk. A cold wind begins to pick up, sending a wintry chill drifting across my face. I pull my wool scarf up over my nose and stick my hands in my pockets for warmth, but it still doesn't do the trick. I'm stone cold. The dunk in the pool during second period has kept me chilled all day, plus the fall on campus doesn't help any either.

Rory and I don't say much on the way home. The temperatures outside are uncomfortable, and the chattering of our teeth makes it difficult to speak. As we come to the edge of our block, I see the figure again. It stands there watching us both at the opposite corner.

"Rory," I say softly, without avoiding my glance at the figure up ahead. I stop and point. "Do you see that person standing there?"

She looks in my direction, but before she says a word the image flashes out of sight like a bolt of lightning. "Please tell me you saw that too?" I say, feeling a little overwhelmed that someone can move that fast.

"Yeah, I saw," she says still staring in the direction. "Wynter, what's going on? Is that who you saw back at the school?"

"Yeah. We better get home," I say. "I don't feel safe. Whomever it is has followed us."

We both approach our perspective houses; Rory lives next door. I watch her facial expression, as I'm sure she can hear yelling and screaming inside my household.

"Sounds like my dad and aunt are at it again," I say.

"I can hear from here. Are you going to be okay?"

"I think so. I'll see you around."

Rory waves at me as I watch her unlock the front door and go inside her house.

I turn the knob to open my front door, trying hard to be quiet, as I hear Aunt Fran yell from the upstairs hallway. "When is the right time to approach this Jeoffrey? I mean my word, she has us wrapped around her finger! At what point are we going to stand up to the wench?" There she goes, her old-world tongue is at it again. I swear she should have been born in the early 1600s. She sure talks like it sometimes, especially when she's mad.

"I don't have a choice, Francesca," Dad says, raising his voice. I can tell he's in the same room as her.

Do I dare sneak up the stairs? They will probably notice me. Perhaps I should hang out in the living room and wait out the family storm.

"Why must you go now; have you not seen the weather outside?" Aunt Francesca is sounding more like a frantic bird than a concerned sister. Whatever happened to the soft gentle qualities I remember? Normally, she has a spunky attitude, but this has gotten out of control. I hear clapping heels walk back and forth across the floor upstairs.

They squabble all the time like siblings do, I guess. I hear Dad's feet pace along the floor and stop. Then hangers tap against the wall from being pulled and seconds later, a drawer slams. *"What gives?"* I think to myself, hesitating to announce my arrival.

"Jeoffrey please… a blizzard is on the way, not to mention a holiday weekend." I hear Aunt Fran plead. "Flights are canceled. It's all over the news. You think the Cessna will fly in this weather? It's suicide."

I glance out the living room window and see the heavy snow begin falling outside, proving her worry. Perhaps I'll wait, to take my first step on our creaky staircase until I hear one of their voices raise. Old houses tend to make sounds.

"You're right Fran, but we both know what *she* is capable of."

She? Who are they talking about? Surely not me? I move to the next tread, easing my way up the steps slowly.

"Maybe it's time to use your super-human power on her." Fran chuckles sounding like she's trying to make light of the conversation.

"This is no time for jokes. Moyer means business. December 21st is in two weeks; she's coming for her. You and I both know it."

Who's Moyer? I've never heard of such a person before and from the sounds of it, I probably don't want to find out either. Not to mention my birthday being brought into the conversation.

I hear heels clicking on the hardwood floors again and incline up another step. "There must be something we can do. What did you see, Jeoffrey?" There's a long pause. I almost thought I'd been made.

"I saw her order *them*, to find us. It's only a matter of time. I'm sure you will see it soon, too." Then I hear dad slam another dresser drawer. "Besides, no amount of superhuman power will defeat her," he says in a low tone. "And even if there is such power, Wynter's not ready. We put her at risk the day we took her away."

This goes deeper than a little family quarrel and it has me curious. In all my seventeen years, I have yet to feel any sense of belonging. We seem to not stay in one place for more than a few years. I've seen this before: Dad packs, they argue, we relocate. I never discovered why. When I ask, both quickly change the subject. Well it's time I find out the truth.

By this time, I've reached the top step. "Who's not ready?" I interrupt. My voice carries down the hollow hall.

The look on both their faces is priceless. I step out into the open, so they can see me. "Why are you two discussing my birthday and what are you arguing about? And don't tell me it's nothing. I'm sick of hearing you guys brush me off like I'm just a kid who doesn't know anything."

2

Untold Stories

I hear dad let out a deep sigh, while Fran folds her arms and raises a brow glaring at him.

"Sweetheart I have something to go do," he says turning in my direction.

Glancing at the bed behind him, I say, "And it requires a suitcase?"

Nodding in agreement and looking like he's been put on the spot, he says, "Come, sit down. Now is as good time as any to talk."

There's a long pause before Aunt Fran speaks, "I should start supper. We are going to need it," and heads for the stairs.

"We?" I blurt out, staring at her as she ignores my question continuing to descend to the level below. Her cooking is rare, sending me signals we are about to run again. Walking over to Dad's room, I hear the wind kick up outside, and the sounds of ice rain pellets hit the windows. Living here in Washington State, it can get icy and when the rain mixes with the snowflakes; it has a different sound, like hail only less intrusive. "Storms brewing outside Dad, what's going on?

He gives a teetering smile. "Please sit," he says, motioning to a chair in the room. "How much did you hear?" I see him hesitate to say more, as he looks at me with his blue eyes that seem bluer than normal. Almost like they are glowing.

Brushing off my thoughts and scowling, I say, "Just that Fran is worried you are about to fly in conditions that will bring a plane down. I mean Dad, you're an excellent pilot, but come on, no one can fly in this, no matter how good they are."

"Yeah about that, we don't have much time to talk. And you're right. It sounds like I'm going to have to leave in this weather. I have some unfinished business to attend to back east. Don't worry, I won't fly until it lets up."

"What business Dad, and how far east are you going?"

"New York."

"What? But you said—"

"Never mind what I said before, none of that matters now," as he folds a shirt and lays it in his bag.

"Dad, I don't understand?"

"I know, and that's my fault for never explaining—" he diverts his attention to my throat. "Where is your necklace?"

"Relax, dad—" and before I have time to finish, he dashes to my room in a sprint. I've never seen him move so fast.

"My gosh, Dad… What… is…up…?" I say, running after him.

"Where is it? Why don't you have it on?" he says, looking around my room as if in a panic.

I reach into my front jeans pocket. "Dad chill, it's right here," I say, and I pull out the necklace, as it dangles in-between my fingers.

He takes hold of the charm, with gentle fervor, his eyes giving an impression of pain and fear, not seen before. The chain loops around his fingertips and he touches it to his lips. I see a tear cascade down his cheek. "How many times have I told you never to take this off?" His tone is angry, but soft at the same time. It's a tone that puts fear in my gut yet makes me understand its significance.

"It came off my neck today in the pool, during swim class. I tucked it in the pocket of my pants, so it would dry faster. Kind of cold outside, ya' know? Cold weather, wet water; not the perfect combination, Dad. If I wore it, I would be colder than I already am right now."

"I guess so. Do you mean to tell me that you have always taken this off during swim class?"

"Of course, why? Dad, what is it...? What's wrong?"

Moving toward him, I touch his arm, but he says nothing, as if I am not there. Gazing at the necklace in his hands, I watch his eyes as they seem to glow with a slight blue hue. After a few more seconds he says, "There are some important things that you need to know about our family and waiting so long to tell you them might have been a poor choice on my part."

"What sort of thing's?" He doesn't talk much about the death of my mother, only that she died trying to save us. Aunt Fran raised me like any mom would. I remember her making it perfectly clear that she would be referred to as Aunt Fran. Keeping the memory of her sister alive was important to her and nobody had the right to take that title but my mother.

Smiling at me and kissing my forehead, Dad says, "Nugget, I wish we had more time. I fear it is too late."

"What's too late? Dad, you're not making any sense," as I stand here watching him twirl the chain through his fingers.

"Soon…you will discover that things are not what they appear to be. The life you thought you knew, is a mere lie, and it's my fault keeping it from you."

"What do you mean a lie?" If I wasn't confused before, I'm really baffled now.

"You will uncover that there are hidden places in this world. Evil places I hope you never have to see, where demons live among the shadows."

Oh, boy, he's completely lost it, "Dad, really? C'mon, you hear yourself talking right now? I don't believe in that hocus pocus demonic stuff. It's what fiction books are made of."

"There is no time for logistics. What you need to recognize is this necklace is to be worn always. You're to never take it off, under any circumstances." Placing it into my hand, and tightening his grip he says, "Do you understand?"

I nod in agreement, "But Dad, I thought it's just a piece of jewelry. You've never explained why that is."

He walks over to my window looking out at the falling snow. "Your head must be swimming with questions. I love you more than life itself and I will do everything within my power to save you from harm. Your mother died to protect you," he says, turning back to face me.

"Now, you're scaring me," I say to him, starting to feel my heart race.

"Shhh, now - no need to be scared." Reaching for the locket, he says smiling, "Let me tell the story of its creation."

It's a silver chain holding a silver locket with a sculpted dragon on one side, while on the other lies a rose, with a single sword in the center.

"This locket belonged to your mother, and she wanted you to wear it always," he pauses to open the ornament. "Perhaps when I get back, I'll tell you about the ancient stories my father told of our family belonging to a long line of sired knights. There is old history I have never shared. It's time for you to know your roots."

I peek inside with him as he explains the two pictures. "I don't think I have ever told you who these people are, have I?"

"No, I assumed it was you and mom," I say shaking my head.

"Dear heavens no, although I can see why you would think that," he says, smiling at me.

"The pictures are painted on with gold. It was a gift from Ailbert to Sara, your great-grandparents. He was a jewelry maker's apprentice, one of three brothers, and the only one to carry on the jewelry making traditions. His older brother, Gavin, and younger brother, Bram, took after their father, Bryce, a knight, protector of the king and queen. During Ailbert's apprenticeship, he fell in love with the most beautiful woman, a man could set eyes on, named Sara. She didn't feel the same or so Ailbert thought at first. One day in the meadow near their home, he caught a glimpse of her admiring the roses in his family's garden. So, he quietly went to the orchard nearby, cutting one rose with his dagger, but not before pricking his finger with its thorns. He removed each spike gently, before surprising her with the delicate flower. Once their eyes met, fate sealed them together forever. The love they shared was forbidden by both their families, yet their affection endured no matter the cost. To prove his devotion, he made this necklace for her. Hand carved each delicate detail with his own hands. He had quite a talent, indeed."

Dad pauses, gazing back out the window. "Ailbert made three lockets, the other two he gifted to his brothers, to give to their betrothed."

"What happened to them? The lockets, I mean?" Listening to the history makes me want to know more.

"Bram's wife, Clarice, died giving birth to their second son. He ended up giving her necklace to Eleena, your grandmother. He felt that it would be in good hands for his two nieces. When the time came, both this necklace and the other were passed down."

"So, Aunt Fran has one of them?" I say, gazing back into the mirror.

"Yes," he nods.

"And the third?" I ask curiously.

"No one knows. Lost perhaps, maybe hidden somewhere in a junky old attic." He looks up, glancing at my crystal gem hanging on the edge of the window trim as it begins to sparkle from the dim sun, coming through the stormy clouds. "Labradorite?"

"Yes, how do you know that?"

He turns to me and smiles. "You see the dragon on that locket? It's made of stone that hangs here on your window."

"Really? It's my favorite type of gem."

"It is said that the dragon symbolizes strength, power and magic. Sara's family crest is the dragon symbol. Ailbert's family is the sword. The rose represents the garden, where they met. The Storm lineage pledged their loyalty to the king and in return were given protection under the crown. The sword represents bravery, courage, and loyalty; by giving Sara the locket it essentially promised her protection, and any future line. You see, thousands of years ago the Storms and Deagons fought a war of honor and pride. Family legends were passed down so when Ailbert fell in love with Sara, it opened old wounds."

He beams, stepping towards me, and says, "I shall tell you the whole story, someday," as he takes the chain from my hand and places it around my neck.

I look at my reflection, observing the beautiful white gold trinket. Hues of light coming from the window sent a prism of sparkly flecks bouncing off the walls of my room. "Thank you, I'll never take it off again, I promise."

Kissing my forehead, a second time, he says, "Wear it always, as it holds the key to your future. It's a symbol of my protection to you as a Storm. I will never let anything happen to you. You have no idea how much you mean to me, Wynter."

There is much more he needs to say, I know it in my heart.

"Dad, I love you so much," hugging him tight, and feeling his heartbeat racing, I sense his fear, which is heavier than ever before. Something bad is about to happen, and I can't quite put my finger on it.

"I need to finish packing, there isn't much time to waste," he says breaking away.

"Dad, you haven't told me why you have to leave?"

"I have revealed to you a lot of information, perhaps Fran can fill you in later. For now, I must finish getting ready." With that, he kisses the top of my head, darting out the door and down the hall, leaving me with still many questions.

I touch the delicate charm with my fingertips once more, staring back in the mirror. Thinking about the story dad shared, I'm captivated and want to know more.

"Supper is ready," I hear my aunt call from downstairs. Bringing me back from my thoughts.

"Be right down," I shout

I make my way to the kitchen where I see Fran placing a table setting for four.

"Everything okay?" she asks, placing silverware at the fourth-place setting.

"Fine, Aunt Fran, thanks. Um…who's coming for dinner?"

"Rory."

"Wait, what? Are her parents not home?"

Aunt Fran pauses for a minute. "It seems her father has had a slight accident and is in the hospital. Mrs. Jenkins is there with him and asked if we would look out for their daughter. She doesn't know how long she will be."

"I need to call Rory, and see if she is okay," and reach for my cell tucked in the back pocket of my jeans.

"Wynter no. Stop," she says, holding a hot pad. "Rory doesn't know anything is wrong. She thinks her dad is stranded from the car being stolen from the airport." Fran then proceeds to take a casserole from the oven and places it on the table. "Mrs. Jenkins prefers Rory not to know yet. At least until she has all the facts. The police don't have much to go on. All they told her is that he was found, in an empty stall of the parking garage, the car gone, along with his wallet. He was identified by his luggage tag." Aunt Fran grabs a utensil from the stove top. "The high jackers managed to leave that."

"Well, is he going to be okay?" My thoughts immediately go to Rory. How is it fair to keep this from her? If it was me, I would want to know. Now I have to bear the secret? When Rory finds out I held this from her she is going to flip on me.

I change the subject, "So, what's for dinner?"

"Spaghetti casserole, garlic bread, and broccoli spears," she says smiling. I know she is doing it out of jest, because I absolutely despise broccoli.

"Oh, come now, broccoli is good for the body," she teases. "Don't be rude, you will eat some. For Rory's sake. It's her favorite vegetable."

"You never cook, Aunt Fran. This isn't like you. If this is all for Rory's benefit, why not just order a pizza?" She hums as I stand there watching her finish setting the table, ignoring me. "Unless we are about to bolt again?" It seems family discussion works best when we all sit down at the table for a meal. "Is that what we are doing, leaving again?" Her silence confirms my instinct. "I see," sitting down in one of the chairs.

"We leave first thing in the morning, so after dinner, you must pack your things," as she puts an empty glass in front of me.

A knock at the door, interrupts my thoughts. "I'll answer it. It's probably Rory," I say getting up. But my dad already beat me to it.

"Look who I found hanging out at the front door?" He says with Rory standing next to him.

The first thought that comes to my mind is, *'How in the hell did he answer the door so fast?'*

"Hey all," Rory says, waving.

"Hi girl, come sit down, by me," I say. "You're just in time for Aunt Frans awesome baked spaghetti."

"Thank you for inviting me," she responds. "This is very kind of you." Rory sounds as though she's unsure about what to say.

"Oh, please, it's no bother. And you can call me Fran. Jeoffrey over there is sometimes called, Jeff."

I curve a smile. "It's kind of weird that this is the first time we had you for dinner. But I'm excited it finally happened."

While sitting around the dinner table I can't help but feel something is off. There's not the normal family discussions we usually have, probably because Rory is here with us, so I burst into conversation.

"What kind of plans have we made for Christmas?" Well, that certainly grabbed the attention of my folks. They eyed each other, ignoring my comment. Aunt Fran put her fork down. "Excuse me a minute," she says, and gets up from the table.

"Was it something I said?" I look at them both and wonder what else are they hiding from me. Rory seems to not notice the awkwardness and continues to eat her food. Like she's somehow turned into a zombie.

Aunt Fran must have seen the look of concern on my face, and says, "Don't worry she will be fine."

"What do you mean she *will* be fine?" I ask, glancing over at Rory.

"Your father is going to buy us time."

"Is this about the people who chased us from Florida? Did they find us again?" I already know the answer. "I'm tired of moving, feeling like we are running all the time. Why can't we stay here?"

My aunt ignores my question. "I know we haven't told you much about your past, but you need to understand one thing. Your mother sacrificed her life to save all three of us from something that is so evil, that without her, we would all be dead." She grabs an empty glass from the cupboard and fills it with water, drinking the entire cup full.

"Aunt Fran, does that mean whatever killed my mother is still after us?"

"Yes," Dad says. "Her name is Moyer, and she jailed your mother in a room, waiting for her to give birth to you."

"Me, but why? I don't understand." All the while, Rory keeps eating, looking unaffected by our deep family discussion.

Dad takes a deep breath, pausing to take a sip of coffee that is set in front of him. Looking at Fran, he smiles. She nods, smiling back. "Go on Jeoffrey, it's time she knows the truth. Besides keeping this from her may put us in more danger."

"What are you two talking about? What truth?"

"Wynter, remember upstairs, when I explained about demons?" Dad answers.

"Dad, you're losing it again. There is no such thing as magic and demons." He is talking crap again, and I don't want to hear any more.

"Okay, do you believe in ghosts?" Fran expresses calmly, sitting back in her chair folding her arms.

"Um, I guess so? I mean, I feel the occasional cold chill when it's eighty degrees outside, or the flicker of lights, when they are not in use. It's all merely psychological really, but okay I'll play along. Now you're talking about demons and monsters and I can't bring myself to believe such fabrications."

Dad sighs in frustration, "She isn't buying it, Fran." Talking to her as if I am not sitting at the table. As if Rory isn't here as well.

"Okay, just stop. Say for a split second, I believe you, and that is a *big* if, why can't we all just stick together? Why buy time at all? I mean, if what you say is true, that this *'evil person'* is coming for us, then am I not safer with you both together than split apart?"

"She has a point, Jeff," Aunt Fran says, taking a bite of food.

"Okay, but first she needs to see," eyeing Fran with intent.

"Well, I suppose you're right." She shrugs, grinning as she finishes chewing. Grabbing her glass of milk and taking a huge swig, she beams, as if in preparedness of something about to happen.

"Hello? I'm right here. I can hear you. Stop talking in third person. It's so annoying!"

"Crash course, or ease in gently?" Dad questions.

"Crash course, we don't have time to take the band aid off her gently," she says.

'These two have seriously gone bonkers.' I feel like I have been put in an audience watching a stage performance. Before I have a chance to react, Aunt Fran gets up from the table, takes a knife from the counter and slices her hand open. Blood gushes everywhere.

"What are you doing? Aunt Fran, are you crazy?" Running to help stop the bleeding, I quickly grab a towel hanging from the stove. Only by the time my reaction caught up with my actions, Aunt Frans hand heals, right before my eyes. The cut is now merely a scar, in the place where the injury was moments ago.

Not able to grasp the concept, I stutter "H—how did you…I mean…w—what was that?" I glance to Rory and see she doesn't even flinch from what occurred in front of her.

"Beginning to understand now, Wynter? Are you ready to know the truth?" Dad says, comfortably sitting in his chair, still eating his dinner and immune to the events that just transpired.

I feel like I'm in some alternate reality at this point or a dream, wishing to wake up.

Aunt Fran comes back to her chair and sits, smirking as she pours another cup of coffee in Dad's mug. "Please be seated Wynter, let us explain."

"That's your second cup of coffee." I say, stunned that he's drinking so much caffeine.

"Going to need to stay awake somehow tonight," he rambles.

"I'm trying to wrap my head around this. I don't understand. This doesn't happen. This isn't normal," I voice, as I still stand in the middle of the kitchen, looking at the pool of blood on the floor as evidence. "One question…" stepping around the mess, "if Aunt Fran can heal in an instant, then that means you can too?"

They both stare at me silent and smile. "Does that mean I can, too? Is this what you both are implying?" I ask.

"That's three questions, but who's counting? Please, Wynter, come sit down so we can explain," Dad says.

"And what's with Rory? Did you put a hex on her or something? It's like she is unaffected to any of this."

"No, we didn't cast any spell on Rory. She will be fine. Come sit down, we will explain everything," Fran says with a slightly humorous tone.

Pulling my chair back to the table, I say, "What other surprises do you have in store for me? This explains that strange remark you made earlier."

"What remark?" Dad asks.

"When you said they are coming, and it hasn't happened yet, but soon Fran would see it, too. Does this have anything to do with the stranger I saw twice today? Once at school, and once outside our home?"

"What stranger?" Now Dad looks concerned, like he did when he saw me not wearing my necklace.

"I don't know. Hard to describe. It wore a hooded cloak and ran very fast. Doesn't fit the modern description of society."

He glances back to Fran, "Are you thinking what I'm thinking?"

She nods. "Sounds like we'd better get a move on."

"Wait, wait, wait. Please don't leave me hanging. You said you would explain."

"And we will. But for now, we need to leave. Before it's too late," Dad says with urgency.

"What about Rory?" I ask, looking over at her as she smiles back at me with a mouth full of food.

Aunt Fran shrugs, wrinkling her forehead, hiding behind her glass of milk. "Hey, I already did the crash course -your turn," she chortles in response.

3

Secrets Hidden

Dad takes a deep sigh, pushes his chair back, and picks up his plate and walks to the kitchen sink. "Your aunt and I were born with gifts. I can see the future. Fran? Well, she can explain hers."

"How is that possible? You mean like having a dream and waking to find a few minutes later it comes true?"

"Similar to that, yes. Except I'm awake when it happens, and it only works on people I am close to. Not like predicting the stock market, although once I was able to do that. It's dangerous and stupid, but the side effect weighs heavy on the mind. Most days, I ignore the frequency waves."

"What do you mean side effects?" I ask, watching him scrub off his plate.

"Migraines that last for days. Leaving the body weak," Aunt Fran interrupts. "I can see the present. What's happening in the *now*." She gets up and follows dad's lead with her dish.

"What do you mean?" I ask.

"I mean, I can see when someone is near, or on their way. Actions that are currently in the present." She takes her plate and begins to rinse it. "Usually I push the clamor out. It takes practice at first. It's like fishing through the white noise, to find the object on which you're trying to concentrate on. Although this stranger you speak about, if it's who we think it is, I'm surprised I didn't feel them coming."

"Are you implying I will have a gift too?" I ask.

Dad comes back and grabs his coffee cup in his hands. "Yes," he says, "but not until you reach eighteen. It will be a powerful gift." Then points to his head, after I stare at him with a naïve expression. "I know it's a strong gift because I have seen you use it in the future."

"Okay, that's just plain weird to hear you say out loud, Dad." I squint my eyes, trying to avoid the headache I feel coming on. "If what you say is true, why am I so important? What makes my gift so unique?"

"Because you have the blood of a Storm," Dad says, in a tranquil voice. "You, Fran, and I are the last in this powerful bloodline, and Moyer wants us dead."

"Dead? What are you talking about?" My heart begins to race, and I feel my body temperature rise a bit with panic.

"Honey, don't worry, we will protect you. Nothing is going to happen to you as long as we are here, and you follow our instructions." He points with his eyes, and nods. "If all else fails, keep that necklace on whatever you do. Do not take it off. And I mean ever. Not even for an indulging swim."

I swallow hard and touch the chain. The mystery around the 'why,' intrigues me but I know I must be patient.

"We must help you prepare, first though," he continues. "The closer your birthday approaches, the more powerful your gifts will become. In fact, you may experience some odd differences in this coming week. Past history from other Storm family members, has been known that the week before transition, one's senses become enhanced."

Fran walks over to me glancing down at my half-eaten plate of spaghetti. "Finished?"

Nodding in response, I ask, "Okay, I have loads of questions and obviously not enough time for them all. However, one resonates with me the most. Why am I just learning this now? Shouldn't I have not been raised to know all this before the eleventh hour? And furthermore, how on earth is Rory not aware of our conversation? It's like she is here, but she's not *'there.'*

"Rory is in what is called a catatonic state. Don't worry. It's only temporary. She will not remember any of this, "Aunt Fran answers.

"W-what are you saying?" I stutter, backing away from the table. Now a little scared. "Is that why I have all these déjà vu episodes? So, that you have me in a catatonic state, too?"

"No, Wynter. I have never done that to you," Dad says, setting his coffee down. "The déjà vu is because you are close to turning eighteen." He slowly moves in my direction, "Don't be frightened. Look at who you are talking to? Come on sweetheart. It's me, your dad. Don't you think if I wanted to harm you, I would have done it already?"

I can feel my heart pound within my chest. The blood in my veins begin to feel hot. I'm so flustered at the moment I don't know how to calm my nerves. All this supernatural phenomena is beginning to go to my head and I feel like I want to scream at the top of my lungs. "Why have you waited so long to tell me all of this?" and I back up a little more with nothing behind me but a wall.

"It's a regret that we must live with moving forward, but our focus has shifted now, to keep you from being captured by Moyer," Dad conveys. "You see she can tap into one's thoughts. With you *'not knowing'* makes it easy for you to hide from her. A lot like looking at a blank page, when really there is invisible ink on the paper." He glides around the table walking toward me, putting out his hand. "Please, don't be afraid. It's still me. I haven't changed: I'm still your dad. What's changed is your age. And we all need to stick together."

"When you know nothing of your past," Fran adds, "it helps with the necklace you wear, in shielding you. Essentially preventing Moyer from locating us."

"You mean it protects my thoughts?" I watch them both smile, then nod in unison. "And when I took the necklace off, it was like a beacon, leading directly to us?"

"Exactly," Fran blurts out.

"So, the stranger; is that why I saw him today?"

"Perhaps," Dad answers. "But you said you always took it off during swim class. That leads me to believe that they have been planning the right moment to make their move."

"You see, Wynter," Fran cuts in. "Each time the necklace is removed, it opens the door for Moyer's mind to find you. When the chain is clasped around your neck, it forms an invisible circle of protection."

"And I broke the circle when I tucked it into the pocket of my jeans. I think I understand now."

"Look at it this way," Dad interjects. "It's like what you would see in the movies, when someone makes a phone call, and the police try and trace the location before the caller hangs up; your swim class is an hour long, not enough time for her to fully find our location, but you had the necklace in your jeans—"

"All day," I interrupt. Realizing I've unknowingly lead Moyer right to us.

"Precisely," Fran replies.

"So, you're telling me she knows our location now?" I ask, with a slight fear in my tone.

"Quite possibly. It's only a matter of time, though I haven't any warning that she's near. But if what you say is true and that this stranger you saw is one of her minions, then she has already found us."

"Dad, are your premonitions ever wrong? I mean does the present alter the future?"

"Yes, but as it stands now, if we do nothing, the future path is inevitable, we die, and you're kidnapped."

"Kidnapped?"

"To Storm River Manor, where you were born," Dad says softly. "Where we escaped, and your mother died."

He veers toward Fran, with a stern eye. "We must leave within the hour. We can't take any chances on waiting until the morning."

"We? Does that mean you're coming with us? What about Rory?" I glance back at her, sitting there staring off at the wall in a vegetative state. It's like looking at someone dreaming, with their eyes open.

Dad takes a deep breath, "I'll take care of Rory."

"You mean, compel her again?" I say in a sarcastic and irritated tone.

"You have a better plan, Wynter?" Dad replies, in a sarcastic tone.

Realizing, it's better she not remember any of this, I bow my head, looking at my feet. "No."

"Go upstairs and pack your belongings," he says.

"Where are we going, this time?"

"To the cabin, where it will be more difficult to find us among the heavy fir trees and snow. Mountains have a way of blocking the airways of the supernatural mind."

"That means us as well, though, doesn't it?"

"To a degree, yes," he replies. "Now go get packing." I find myself stepping halfway up the stairs when I hear my dad say to Rory, "Go home, close all your blinds, and forget you ever met

Wynter. No matter what happens, do not look outside until tomorrow."

"Okay, Mr. Storm," she says, and I hear her get up from the table and walk out the front door.

Realizing I have lost my best friend I run to my room, slamming the door behind me, with tears streaming down my cheeks.

4

Escape

I spend the next hour packing my two suitcases, deciding on which items of importance to take with me, realizing I'm not going to be able to take everything. Staring at my bookshelf, *"only a few selective things,"* I say aloud. Dumping my school work on my bed, I fill my book bag with exactly that: books. Only my favorite things, I keep reminding myself, trying to forget dad telling Rory to forget me. The more I wipe my face the more the tears fall. I'm angry, but I know Dad doesn't have a choice. It's for her protection and ours. I pause a moment to see the illuminating crystal hanging from my window. I'm not leaving it behind, nor Charlie, my stuffed rabbit. He has one eye missing along with not being washed in years, but he's my comfort when I feel terrible or sad.

After stashing a few more items in my sack, I put on jeans, and a sweater. Making one last attempt through the bathroom, I grab my pillow off the bed, tucking it under my arm, and grip the two packed suitcases in the corner, and head downstairs.

I find Aunt Fran in the living room chanting a foreign speech. The smell of sage fills the room along with other odors I don't recognize.

"What's all this?" I question, giving Dad a perplexing stare.

"Change of plans. It seems *they* are here already," he answers.

"What do you mean? Like, here… here?"

"Like outside our window… here," he says. I watch him take a shotgun lying on the table and load it.

"Dad! Where did you get that?"

"What?" He seems oblivious to my obvious question. "You're not living in a dream world, sweetheart. The strategy has changed, and we need to improvise."

"With that?" pointing to his gun powder blowing object.

"Yes, with this. Don't act surprised. It's not like you haven't seen a gun before."

"Well, yeah on television, but with my own two eyes. Seriously Dad, put that away before you hurt someone."

"Precisely," he chortles, "That's exactly what I intend to do with it; hurt someone."

I hear Fran continue to chant over and over the same words, as she walks from room to room, holding a book in one hand and burning sage in the other.

"What exactly is Aunt Fran doing anyway?" I say to him.

"Fran is casting a protection spell. For now, it's keeping those outside from coming in. It won't hold long."

"Okay, so what's the plan now? Wait until the protection breaks, be killed or worse - kidnapped by demons?" I ask, in a worry tone.

I hear Fran stop chanting and she turns around staring at both dad and me. "Grab me the grimmroot!" she yells.

I begin to smell a very odd odor. "What's that smell?" I ask, as I watch dad bring her a stalk-like plant, that's brown in color, with white flowers and looks like wisteria.

"Gasoline," she says. "They plan to smoke us out by setting the house on fire." She grabs the stalk from him, placing the petals in a bowl sitting on the dining room table.

"What!?" I scream, watching, as Aunt Fran adds in the burned sage. Then she opens the locket hanging from her neck, pulls out a small green bottle filled with liquid, and squeezes one drop into the container. The smoke from the burning sage intensifies. It's then that she begins a different chant.

I begin to smell smoke from a fire. And I can see the flames grow higher as it consumes the living room window.

"Wynter, come. We all need to stick together near the bowl," Dad coaxes.

We huddle around the table as Fran continues to chant; then suddenly without warning, I feel myself lift from my body, while my form falls to the ground. As my spirit rises above me, I see Dad and Fran mimicking the same experience. We watch, as the fire consumes the house like a vacuum. Pictures burn, the furniture goes up in flames. Our bodies charcoaled from where we left them. *'I'm dead. Just peachy.'*

I hear Aunt Fran's voice in my head, *"No, it's all an illusion. Patience, it will all be over soon."*

I look toward the burning living room window to see four figures standing outside observing; unmoving to the event unfolding. Two of them are cloaked in hooded garb. Looking much like the image I saw at school, except this time, peeking out from the darkness of their cowls, are glowing blue eyes. The other two figures I don't recognize. They wore black suits, with their hands cupped in front of them, and legs straddled apart, like they were enjoying the chaos.

Soon the fire department comes rushing to put out the flames. We float above our bodies undetected, waiting for our audience to leave. The officials push people back who are watching, waving at everyone to keep a distance. Hours pass before the fire comes to a smolder.

It's early in the morning before we are finally alone in the house. Aunt Fran says telepathically, *"Moyer's men appear to be gone, for now. Let's get cleaned up and move out."*

I watch as Aunt Fran and Dad, float back down to their charcoaled bodies and fill back into them. Shedding off black flakes of dust, I follow their lead, standing in the exact spot I had left hours ago, and I do the same. It's like having sand all over the body from the beach and brushing off the grit from the skin.

The house looks to be intact and not a scratch, nor a scorched wall in sight. It's back to the exact appearance it was, before I watched with my own eyes, as it burned to the ground.

"What was that, Aunt Fran?"

"A preservation spell," she says, as I witness her stretching back into her skin.

"What about the firemen, and the investigators? All the witnesses who saw the house burn?"

"All memory of the past twenty-four hours will be erased from anyone who witnessed it, leaving everything intact, as if nothing happened. To us the house is still standing, to the outside world it's a pile of dust."

"We should hurry. Now would be a good time to pack the car," Dad interrupts, as he begins to pile our bags, at the front door.

Fran smiles, picking up a suitcase in each hand. "You ready?" she says, looking at me.

All I could do is shrug a smile. Outside is cold and I feel the ice crunch beneath my feet, treading carefully toward the car.

Dad greets us at the trunk, and we throw all our belongings in together, climb into the car and fasten our seatbelts.

"Adventure awaits," he says, and pulls away from the curb. "When was the last time we went up to Mt. Rainer? We should be safe at the cabin."

Aunt Fran has her arm folded across her chest, looking out the window, ignoring his question. Dad looks in the rear-view mirror back at me and says, "Well aren't you all just a cheerful bunch? Come on you guys, we will get through this."

"We're running again," I cry out. "When are we going to stop fleeing from the strangers that chase us? Am I not allowed to have a normal teenage life?" I don't wait for his answer. "Oh wait, that's right, I'm almost eighteen. Just a few more days, and I'm out of here."

Dad swerves the car slightly, pulling it over. He turns around to face me pointing his finger. "Now you listen to me, young lady. You're not too old for me to pull you out of this car and put you over my knee. You know exactly why we are leaving Blaine. They are close on our tail, and the mountains are the only place where we can hide from the telepathy, they have so strongly perfected."

I roll my eyes at him. All my life I remember us running. We would get settled into a new place and live there for a year, sometimes two, and bam! Uprooted again, away from the 'demons' Dad so passionately believes are after us. Until today, I hadn't seen so much as a ghost, let alone a monster in the dark. I'm not so sure those people after us today were demons, rather they were more like evil people with a purpose. I straighten my back, folding my arms, and look out the window watching the snow begin to fall from the sky. After a moment's pause, dad pulls out onto the road again. "Here we go."

We reach the foothills of Mt Rainier, after a long quiet ride. Frans says, "It will be harder for Moyer to detect us once we reach—" She stops in mid-sentence, bringing attention to us all.

"What is it Fran, what do you see?" Dad says, sounding anxious.

"We are too late. They found us again," Aunt Fran announces.

"How is that possible?" he questions, keeping his eyes on the road.

"I don't know! I see them now, and they're gaining on us fast." She shakes her head and gathers her composure. "The roads are really icy, Jeff, please be careful."

"Aunt Fran, Dad, what does this mean?"

"It means, that I hadn't any forewarning of them coming," she says. "I don't understand why, because usually, I can give us a head start by a minimum of three hours. They were off my radar when we left the house."

"It means, Moyer has probably come into a new power," Dad says, appearing nervous.

"So, this Moyer, she can gain powers?" I ask, trying to increase as much information as I can. This new-found secret has me curious. My brain is a sponge, absorbing it all in detail, hoping I'll remember everything.

"It appears so. Seems she broke through my distance barrier and I have no idea how," Aunt Fran exclaims sounding irritated.

She half turns, putting her left arm over dad's seat, looking back towards me. "You see, Moyer has an uncanny way of tracking people and never stops until she finds what she's after. However, this is new to me and I am not sure how to process it yet." She pauses as if to be channeling a thought, then says, "Remember when Jeoffrey and I said the world is not as it appears to be? Well, you are about to be thrust into a reality that has never been bestowed upon you before. Your first clue should have been back at the house. That's a pinch of the world you will soon come to know. It is hard for us to explain everything, right now."

My mind's in chaos, trying to think of the right words to articulate. "The move from Florida to Washington,"- as I begin to put two and two together, slowly, "-is that a time when Moyer found us? Those men who chased us at the beach that day. They were her men? Is that why we move around a lot?"

She answered with a nod. "Yes, she found us. It's you she wants. We've raised you from the very hour you were born. There are things much worse to come. Our job, is to protect you, prepare you—"

"Prepare me for what?"

"War."

Aunt Fran must have sensed my urge of panic. Such a strong word to use; *war.*

"Not the same battle you're thinking of, not a war between nations. Rather, a battle of competitions. Magical races between the worlds of the universe. Where deities strive to rule and be more powerful than the house of their neighbor. Things that are going to change your life forever. No going back to the existence you used to have. Once you learn your true history, life as you know it, will be gone."

My thoughts ramble in my head as I gently grab the charm on my neck, intertwining it with my fingertips.

"Your eighteenth birthday is near. She will stop at nothing to bring you back to the mansion," Dad says, trying to keep his eyes on the road.

"They are very near, Jeff. We must go faster."

"The road is icy, any faster and we will crash."

"How much further to the freeway exit?" she asks.

"About a mile," he replies and excels, stepping down on the gas. "How did they catch up to us so fast?"

"I don't know." Fran has a worried look on her face, and I sense that this outcome may not turn out good for any of us. "They're less than a mile away, now."

"Hang on, our turn is coming up," dad says as he decreases his acceleration.

"Jeff you're going too fast we will never make the turn. It's too icy."

"What does this mean? Are they gaining on us?" I ask, feeling nervous that we might crash.

"It means if we do not make it to the mountains soon, your dad and I are dead, and you're enslaved like the others. Never to see the world outside Storm River Manor again."

"Like the others? What others?" I question.

But, before she can answer, we're bumped from behind, spinning the car out of control. I cling to the handle above my door, beginning to feel dizzy as we skid across the road. My heart sinks to my stomach, and my head throbs with pain. I see a car in oncoming traffic and brace for a second impact. When the car hits, it sends us reeling down a ravine, end over end. Sounds of glass breaking and metal twisting, sang through my ears. I feel the weightless air beneath us, then a tumbling end over end again before landing upside down.

When we finally stop spinning on the icy ground beneath us, I glance toward dad and Fran, both unconscious and looking dead. Dad's head is at an odd angle, and one arm is aimed in the wrong direction, while Aunt Fran's face is unrecognizable, with blood gushing everywhere. Their bodies are nearly crushed from the dashboard.

"Dad!" I scream. Panicked, I tried to reach my seatbelt, but my arm is pinned against the passenger door. I can't move.

"Aunt Fran!" I scream again, "Wake up!" Tears overflow onto my face. I try to free myself from the seatbelt, as I'm hanging upside down. With hair in my face, and my necklace disrupting the line of sight, my choices limit me to see. Not realizing I'm hurt until I feel the dripping of blood onto my chest, do I see the bone protruding from my knee. It's then I scream in pain. Throbbing aches shoot up my leg when I try to move it.

I hear a car pull up in the distance, wondering if it's the same vehicle that rammed our bumper. My hanging hair skews my vision a bit, while I watch two men in black suits, wearing gloves and sunglasses, approach our mangled car. They look like the same men, that were watching our house as it burned to the ground. One man appears bald, wearing a hat and scarf, while the other a long coat with blonde hair slicked back; the kind of men you see in the movies, hiding lethal items.

"Well, look who we have here?" the bald man says. "Looks as if someone may have been driving too fast in icy conditions. Shall we help them?" As they loom, snow crunches under their feet. He then bends down to investigate through the now broken passenger window.

"Hello, my dear," he smiles. "Seems we haven't been properly introduced. The gentleman behind me, is Chad. I am Dexter. We are here to take you home."

I feel a sharp pain in my neck, like a needle, along with pressure, and that's all I remember.

5

The Ride Home

"Wynter, you're in danger," I hear a whisper in my ear.

"Who's there?" I ask, looking around. But all I see is darkness.

"There's no time," the voice says.

A faint image emerges, in the distance. It's white, with a grey tint. It creeps closer to me, along with a humming noise.

"Never take off the necklace. It's for your protection," it whispers, as it howls before me.

"Who are you?" I ask.

The figure comes closer bringing with it, more ear-piercing noise.

The sound of whining becomes louder, while the ghost slams through my body; waking me to the buzzing of an engine running. Hums flood my senses, canceling my thought process. My brain drifts into a million conversations going at once, along with ringing through my ears as my unfolding mind becomes coherent. It is comparable to being in a room full of people who are talking and trying to focus on one voice. It drains my thoughts, leaving me with a pounding headache when I try to concentrate. I attempt to open my eyes, only to find my vision blurry and not able to focus.

Noticing my pillow under my head, I turn slightly to look around. Bright glows radiate through the window next to me. The shimmer hurts my eyes, and they water, making me think it's mid-afternoon. Sitting up, I observe, my backpack sitting to the left of me and Charlie lying by my feet. Bending over to pick him up, I whisper to myself, *"Where am I?"*

I see white empty seats in front and beside me, while a man sleeps in the next aisle with his head down and a hat over his face. Immediately I recognize him as Dexter, the man that stuck me with a needle. It brings me to remember the awful car accident. Flashbacks of dad and Aunt Fran hanging upside down in our battered car with Fran's head bleeding, dad's body looking broken in every possible spot, fills my eyes with tears.

I distinctively remember a bone sticking out of my knee with blood seeping through my jeans. Now there's no evidence that there had been a tragic accident. I look down to see my clothes changed. I cannot check the damage, as the slacks I wear are too tight to roll up. More memories kick in, and I remember gathering my things in my room. With Charlie in my hands it brings me a slight comfort of home. *'So, they thought to bring my things along? What kind of person would do that?'*

I try to concentrate on where I am, straining to hear through the engine noise. I listen to the clanging of dishes in the background and faint conversations going in the distance. It isn't until I feel the swift turbulence that I realize I'm on a plane.

'How long have I been out?' I think to myself. Rambling thoughts parade through my mind, as I realize I've been kidnapped. There is nothing I can do about it, either. High in the sky doesn't give a person a lot of options.

My mind dashes through more memories making its way to the forefront. The thought of my necklace comes to the surface, and I touch my neck, thankful it is still there.

What is this secret that seems to have everyone either protecting me, or seeking me out?

"Seems someone is awake." Hearing an unfamiliar voice, brings me back from memory lane.

I see a blonde woman, with blue eyes coming up the aisle slowly, hair tightly bound in a bun. She wears a red suit, black heels and a bell-shaped hat. It's like eyeing a person from the 1920's.

"Who are you?" Thinking I've warped through time, glancing from her to Dexter, who is still snoring away.

She smiles, an evil but quiet grin. "Your worst nightmare my dear." She turns to Dexter, sleeping the aisle over, and knocks the hat off his face, reeling it to the floor.

He fumbles a bit, coming out of his slumbering stupor and sees her glaring at him. Jumping from his seat, he says, "Ah, ma'am, sorry ma'am. S-seems I fell asleep."

"I see… It appears to be a human flaw. Dexter, she's awake!" Pointing in my direction, "And don't call me Ma'am. I'm not my mother!"

"Yes, Ma- I mean Miss. Storm," he says, picking his hat up from the floor.

'Storm,' I think, *'perhaps a cousin I never knew about? How oddly inappropriate. A Storm kidnapping a Storm.'*

She looks back in my direction, "It appears you have caused quite a stir at the house of Storm River Manor. Moyer will be pleased that you have finally come home." Smiling, content like a cat, she says, "I see you have grown some, since last I saw you."

Moyer? Last saw me? What? I don't ever remember seeing someone like her.

She bends down to my level reaching for my chin with her right hand. Looking into my eyes. "Aqua green. Guess we shall see if Moyer's plans played out as intended."

'What plans?' I think, while I peer back at her.

She appears to be intensely looking at me, as if to be searching for something. A few seconds later, she forcibly pushes away my chin, lashing back at me with her words. "What the hell?" Stiffening her body and turning to see Dexter who steps backwards towards his seat, she barks, "Clearly, she's had influence." Her body language flares in frustration, like she is ready to strike him.

Dexter glances toward me. "Influence?" Squinting, he holds his hat between his fingers, comparable to what a squirrel does grasping food; only he appeared to be waiting for a whack at the head.

She glares at him as if to begin to speak but changes course and targets back on me. "I want to know why you cannot be compelled." And, like a slithering snake, she creeps up, eyes on me, a second time. Her face smooth, her eyes bright blue, glowing just like Dad's when he's upset. "Jeoffrey!" she seethes through her clenching teeth. "He did something. Or Fran." She smiles wickedly. "Tell me my dear, what do you know? What… did he tell you!?"

"I-I don't understand." Stumbling with my words, scooting back in my chair, without anywhere to go. I don't dare tell her what was said in the car or back at the house.

"Enough! Leave her alone," a voice says, appearing in a doorway from the back of the plane.

A snarl comes from the woman's mouth, ignoring him, and about to say something else to me.

"Blair! Leave. Her. Alone." He comes closer to us where I can now see his face. I recognize him immediately as the second man with Dexter, the day of the accident.

She stands up, brushing herself off. Stiffening her posture and stepping aside for him to pass. She glowers at him with piercing eyes. He nods with a smile. "Always so uptight, my dear sis."

I don't know what to think. This woman who calls herself Blair is not someone I want to cross paths with alone.

"You're both dismissed, I will take it from here," he reprimands them. Dexter took off quickly, but Blair hesitates, pursing her lips tightly, hand over her hip.

He scowls at her. "Go!"

Her body language shows pure irritation, and she stalks off, hissing under her breath, without muttering loud enough for anyone to hear.

"Hi there, Wynter. You will have to excuse Blair, she is not one to do well with introductions. I don't think we have properly been introduced. I'm Chad. Jeoffrey's brother, and your uncle," he says, as he puts out a hand to shake.

I sink back in my chair recoiling from reaching. *Uncle? So, dad had a brother? One he managed not to ever tell me about?*

He chortles a smile. "Ah yes, I see. You're upset," he mocks, retracting the good gesture. "May I sit with you?" looking at the vacant seat next to me.

I nod with a half shrug. Wondering what's the catch, plus I don't have much of a choice, now do I?

Taking a seat, he smiles along with a deep breath. "Where to begin," he taunts, crossing his right ankle to his left knee.

Twirling his finger pointing at me he says, "I'll bet you're loaded with questions. I imagine they're floating around up there in that brain of yours, just itching to come out, huh?"

Silence comes from my end, as I just stare at him. I hold Charlie tighter to my chest, still smelling home on him. I'm not sure what to say. Part of me is afraid to say anything, for fear of yelling and screaming at anyone who will listen. *'You idiot. You kidnapped me. And you think this level-headed talk is going to calm me?'* No, I wanted nothing more, than to have him go away. I know deep down, the real reason I'm here. Dad warned me enough to know, I'm in danger. So, how am I going to get out of this mess?

He shakes his head and snickers. "My apologies, I haven't asked if you're thirsty. Would you like some water? Soda, or tea?" He pauses with a smile. "Bourbon, perhaps? ...Oh, heaven's no, you're too young for that yet, although I presume you will hit the bottle before you're twenty-one... I know I did." He raises his arm snapping his fingers in the air. "Dexter!" he yells.

I just sat there soaking up his comments, while dissecting his involvement. First shock, he's my dad's brother. Who is Blair? He said sis earlier, and she caved to his direction, so he's obviously her equal. He spoke to her as a sibling would.

"Is that woman your sister?" I finally inquire. I at least want to know that much. The more information I can muster, the better odds I can plan an escape.

"Ah, she speaks," retorting back a smile. He reminds me of a sarcastic jester who pretends to be serious, then plants some dry humor.

When I don't react to his response, he huffs. "Yes, Blair is Jeoffrey's sister, your aunt, and a royal pain in my ass."

He makes me giggle. Not sure if it is intentional on his part, but it's funny just the same. It gives me a visual of what it must be like with sibling rivalry. I didn't have such luxury raised as an only child. I watched movies though and understood the crazy bond siblings have.

He smiles back at me. "What would you like to drink? You must be parched."

"Water is fine, thank you," I finally say to him.

In seconds, Dexter is next to us. "Yes, sir?" Nodding in compliance.

"Would you bring the young lady a bottle of water?"

Dexter glances at me, and nods again. "Right away sir," and begins to turn around.

"And fetch me a scotch on the rocks, too, please."

"Certainly sir." Dexter bows, with poise, and walks away.

"So, tell me, what you want to know?" he urges, folding his hands in his lap, staring back at me with a half grin.

"Where's my father and Aunt Fran?"

"Hmmm, somehow I anticipated that would be your first question," he says in a sarcastic tone. "I'm thinking the better question to ask would be where am I going?"

"That, too, but I assume you are taking me to Storm River Manor."

"Seems Jeff has already prepared you somewhat," he says sounding pleased. "It is true we are heading there. When we took you from that horrendous accident, there wasn't time to check on Francesca or your dad. Quite literally, the moment we got you and your things, the car exploded. No amount of healing power can fix a supernatural after they have been burned to a crisp."

"What do you know about the supernatural?" I snap, glaring at him. "They died protecting me." I try to hold back my feelings, but I know any second, I will lose control. "Such a lack of emotion coming from a person, who has just lost a brother" I add, wrestling back the tears.

Before he can answer, Dexter is back with my water and Chad's scotch.

"Dexter, do you happen to know when the plane will land?" Chad asks, passing my bottle water to me.

"Thirty minutes sir," Dexter replies, handing him, his drink.

"Thank you. That is all," Chad says, and takes his first sip.

"You honestly do not know do you?" shaking his head in disbelief. "I do say, astonishing," he sneers.

"Know what? You kidnap me from the only home I know and claim to be a rescuer. The irony." I can tell he's beginning to lose patience as he swirls his glass of scotch, with his finger, before taking a second swig, and setting it in the holder next to him.

"I see my brother and Francesca have kept you well protected and in the dark, or more like unprotected." His eyes glow blue, staring me down. "I'll show you what I know about the supernatural."

"What's with everyone and these glowing eyes?" I blurt out. "It baffles me beyond belief." This must have been his catapulting weapon of choice. To scare me into thinking his glowing blue eyes would have me cave into him with fear. He hasn't a clue what he's up against. Dad may have kept me in the dark, but I know full well Chad's up to something.

His attempted glower must have been thwarted, because I see rage in his eyes, as he darts out of his seat. "Seems, my sister is right," he says, stiffening up to iron out his suit with his hands and buttoning his jacket. "There must be a protection spell about you. Compelling you is impossible." Pacing back and forth, hands in his pockets, he walks the aisle.

My thoughts are confused, trying to work out the puzzle in my mind. Suddenly I remember what both my Aunt Fran and Dad said about the necklace. I don't want to draw attention to it, so I quietly tuck it under my shirt. This must be what they meant when they mentioned to never take it off. That's preposterous. Something as simple as this. After all that I have witnessed so far, I'm not going to take anything else for granted. I'll sit here quietly acting innocent, pretending I'm not catching on.

He comes back for his glass, grabbing it in his hand and taking a gulp. Again, occupying his seat, he murmurs, "We will be on the ground soon," and glances up to see Blair eying us both, like daggers to a future kill. Then he leans in, speaking softly, "I know my sister isn't the kindest person, you've met so far, and she wouldn't dream of telling you this, for pure fear of our mother, but I'm not afraid of *her*. Remember one thing: if you remember anything at all Wynter Storm. Not all things in life, appear as they truly are. Where we are going; what you are about to discover will leave you perhaps scarred for life. You will be entering a very dangerous place. Especially since you have no clue what you are up against. If Jeff wasn't already dead, I would kill him myself."

Chad seems angry, shaking his head, creasing a scowl between his eyes. "Do not trust anyone and stay true to yourself. Whatever is protecting you, has reason to. Eyes will be watching you, always. The good, as well as the bad." Chad pauses a few minutes as if trying to find the right words. "The blue eyes, you mentioned?" he hesitates to say more, glimpsing a moment at Blair.

"Yes?" I inquire.

"It's a power that comes from the Storm family line. All Storms have it."

"Except me." I say, looking out the oval window of the plane with agitation.

He slightly nods, as if to imply yes, tilts his head to the side and says, "Well no, not exactly. You're not yet eighteen. Storms do not get their power until they reach this age."

'So, this must be the power that Dad and Fran talked about,' I think to myself while staring at Chad in surprise.

"Yeah, let that sink in a minute," as he squints at me with pursed lips.

I begin to feel annoyed, at the thought of both my so-called aunt and uncle trying to compel me, blurting out, "I want answers. If I'm truly your blood, why the performance stunts? It's not something one does out of the pure kindness of their heart. Why chase us down?"

Chad swigs what is left of his drink, then puts it back in the holder. Peering at me, carefully weighing his thoughts before answering, he scans my direction a few times, with scowling bright eyes.

"Blair and I don't want you influenced by her. You see, our mother is the epitome of evil. If the devil himself had a sister, she would be it. The only way to protect you, would be to compel you. If you were compelled by one of us, the spell could not be broken unless one of us died. And, ...well, we know she wouldn't do that, as we are needed for her little soiree of evil plans. If you are compelled, then she would not gain the power to control you. Simple as that."

"Ah, I understand now. You're her puppets." I smirk, folding my arms in front of my chest.

He ignores my remark, smiling down at his feet and says, "But it seems Jeoffrey was already one step ahead of us, with his *seeing the future and all.*" He puts his hands up in the air and spreads out his fingers for a dramatic effect. "Our brother, had it in his head that Blair and I somehow turned to the dark side of evil."

His eyes widen, and he wrinkles his forehead as he gets up, taking his empty glass, saying, "Since we are puppets, I'll leave you to stew on all your remaining questions alone."

The pilot comes over the speaker as Chad walks away. "We will be arriving in New York about ten minutes. Please put your seatbelts on. You may feel rough turbulence. It seems the state is covered with storm clouds this late afternoon."

Adjusting my pillow, I lay my head back, Charlie in my lap, and deliberate the last twenty-four hours. How does something so perfect in life, go completely wrong in a matter of seconds? Thinking about meeting this Moyer character terrifies me, and now I'm about to live under her roof? For how long? I turn eighteen in a couple weeks. Surely that will give me enough time to plan an escape? The secrets continue to pile. Finding out I have more family throws in further questions.

I feel the plane hit the ground minutes later, pulling me from my thoughts. The view outside shows a white airport with huge flakes coming down. Plows seem to not be able to keep up with Father Winter. Only one runway is clear of snow.

"How soon do you think we will arrive at Storm River?" Blair asks Chad, as we depart off the plane.

"About an hour," he says, glancing at his watch. "Maybe more with the heavy snow coming down."

My mind starts to race again. Fresh memories surface of Dad in the driver's seat, head turned in the wrong direction, and Aunt Fran looking mangled. Knowing now that I will never see them again, according to Chad. A tear falls from my eye and I quickly wipe it away before anyone can see my sorrow. I'm not about to give them that satisfaction.

Not too far from the private plane a limousine waits for us. The driver has the door open already, and Chad gestures Blair and I to hop in, with Dexter riding shotgun.

Inside is glamour galore, nothing subtle in the slightest. Lights are inlayed around the floor, trimmed in wood. The seats are a soft black leather with white pillow accents. There's room to fit well over fifteen people. To the side is a wet bar, with empty crystal glasses, waiting for them to be filled. A half empty decanter bottle holds what I imagine is whiskey. My father has an identical set that he would bring out when holding rare business meetings at our house. Next to the wet bar nestles a small fridge. Chad reaches for the door. "A drink ladies?"

Blair stares at me and smirks a smile. "The strong kind, I am not in the mood for a juvenile beverage," she states.

Chad huffs a smile, shaking his head slightly. "Nothing but the best for my sis." Then glances my way, asking, "And you?"

"A soda is fine, thank you," I reply graciously, wishing my manners would rub off to Blair.

Drinks of everything imaginable stocked the fridge, including food and snacks.

"Sandwich?" he asks, wrinkling his forehead.

"Yes, please." I hadn't eaten since we left the house.

Tossing me the double-decker, he looks over at Blair.

"None for me, thanks. I'm hungry for something a little more tangible," she says, then eyes me with a smirk.

Chad chuckles at her remark. "Seems mother has only supplied us with whiskey," he retorts. "On the rocks?"

"Fine, it will do," she says, rolling her eyes and looking out the window.

The windshield wipers fiercely race back and forth making a swishing sound, in the front cab. Snow melts as it hits the glass. Soon the limousine picks up speed and we are on the freeway.

Blair keeps quiet most of the way, with periodic glances toward me. Her arms fold across her chest, looking like a child in time out, rather than the venomous snake I met earlier on the plane.

"If you don't stop staring at me, I am going to gouge your eyes out with a stake," she says, looking out the window.

I look over at Chad, we both smile, and I take my sandwich and begin unwrapping it.

Soon we approach a turn off, leading down a dark muddy road. Through the trees, in the distance, are wrought iron gates that can be seen, with pillars on either side. Gargoyle statues decorate the tops. As the car creeps closer to the gate, it automatically opens, inviting us in.

6

Family Reunion

Frozen tree branches overhang at the opening, with green ivy intertwining between layers of brick, while gargoyle statues sit upon pillars at either side of the gate.

"Home sweet home," Blair sneers under her breath, still looking out her window.

Stone fencing trail beyond what the naked eye can see, and foliage glisten in the headlights as we travel down the dark gravel road.

To my right lies a snow-covered orchard that can barely be seen in the dusk, with hedges looking nearly six feet tall. Giving an impression of a once beautiful garden. I catch a quick glimpse of the inside as we pass its arched gate.

"Sara's garden," Chad whispers with a smile, eyes going soft. As if bringing back a pleasant memory.

"Who is she?" I ask, charmed by intrigue.

"Was," he replies. "She died many years ago. My Aunt and your great-grandmother Sara built this garden along with her sister Isobel. The sisters, left Scotland with their husbands to build a new life here. The garden is a replica of the one they had at home. It was their sanctuary."

"Until Maura, destroyed them both," Blair blurts with a snarl.

"Don't." Chad glowers at her. "Not now."

"What does she mean? Who is Maura?"

"Nothing, Blair likes to act dramatic. Maura Moyer, our mother, merely didn't help Sara or Isobel when they fell ill, allowing them to die, without treatment."

"Sounds awful," I say, thinking if this would have been one of dad's future stories to tell.

Blair's eyes scowl with rage. "Yes, it seems both were poisoned by a venomous snake, yet nobody could find bites anywhere on their bodies. Moyer is no mother of mine."

'This Moyer must be unforgivably evil to have her children hate her so much,' I think to myself.

We continue driving slowly down the frozen dirt road, turning to the left, then to the right, and then to the left one more time before passing tall cypress trees. I spy through falling sprinkles of snow a gigantic gothic-like mansion in the distance. More like a castle with three levels. The rather large courtyard could quite possibly fit twenty cars or more and the closer we approach, the more details I see. Ivy covers the stone wall façade while the moonlight bounces off the stained-glass windows, and more gargoyle statues sit atop the roof. The car turns to the right one last time before rounding the edge of the driveway. I notice a female fountain statue in the center of the square that has a look of elegance, with a pitcher in her left hand. Her eyes are carved to look frightened and there is much detail in her wavy hair, giving the impression she had once been human.

"Beautiful, isn't she?" Chad says near my ear, startling me from my trance.

Turning toward him, I say, "Yes, she looks sad."

"There are many more statues like her inside. Each unique in its own way," he says, smirking.

"What do you mean?"

He nods with a smile, "There are more made of the same marble as here."

The limousine comes to a full stop before the castle. Scuffed gothic French doors reveal old world charm and beauty. Dragon symbols on both doors, with a gold ring through the mouths accessorize each flap. Moss covers the massive grey jagged stones, while dark wood trim encases all the windows with a gothic era feel.

"This place looks like a castle or palace," saying aloud. Not expecting anyone to answer.

"It is another replica of the home in Scotland," Chad replies. "Only bigger."

The castle's height has me flinching with fear. How can something look so terrifying, yet be so stunning at the same time?

"Listen, before we go inside there are three rules you must remember," Chad says.

"Rules?" I question, blankly staring at him.

Both Blair and Chad glare at me. "Don't be so ignorant," she hisses.

Ignoring her remark and putting a hand up, Chad interrupts, "First, avoid eye contact as much as possible. Just because my sister and I can't compel you, doesn't mean you're immune to the others inside."

"You mean there are more that can do what you two can?"

"More, and much worse than either of us."

Blair takes off her seatbelt. I bet she can't wait to get out of this car and away from me.

"Second, Maura prefers to be called Madame Moyer. Don't get caught calling her anything else."

It took me this moment to realize that, if Chad is dad's brother, then that means Maura is my grandmother. Somehow, I feel deep in my gut something isn't right: that I'm about to enter the depths of hell with no way out.

I shake my head. "Aren't grandmothers supposed to be soft, warm and loving?"

"Not this one," Blair blurts out with an annoying grimace and she scooted to the other door of the limo, not waiting for us to get out.

"And the third?" I ask.

"Do not be caught out after nine in the evening. She has a curfew set in place. If you go against her rules, you will quickly learn about her wrath. She is not one you want to cross."

I nod, and lower my eyes, realizing my old life is over and the new one is about to begin.

"Here we go," he says, as the driver comes to his side and opens the door. "Remember, don't ask questions, do as you're told, and all will be well." And we scoot out of the car.

The winds begin to pick up, making the air sing to my cheeks.

"Here, put this on your head. It will help you stay warm." Chad gestures, handing me a knitted beanie.

"Where did you get this? It looks handmade?"

"It was Sara's. She had intended for you to have it. Made it long ago, right before her death."

I pull it over my head while walking up the magnificent steps to the front door, half hoping the gales would take me away.

The door creaks open before any of us has a chance to knock.

"Now, that's just plain creepy," I whisper to Chad.

He chuckles with a smile. "You haven't seen nothing yet, my dear."

Standing beside the door is a tall man in a black suit, with light blonde hair. Perhaps grey, it's very hard to tell, with his pale white skin. He stares at me long and hard, but without expression as if he is a statue fixed to the floor. His piercing blue eyes, staring at me, as if desperately trying to put me in a hypnotic trance. Again, with the compelling willfulness. I smile at him, impervious by his glare.

"Good evening Daniel," Chad interrupts, "are you just going to stand there, or will you let us in, out of this wretched weather?"

His faux interlude breaks, as he shrewdly steps out of the way, slightly bowing, as we enter.

Chad grabs my elbow and whispers in my ear, "Remember to avoid the eyes."

"I didn't feel a thing," I say, smiling back at him.

Sitting my luggage and pillow on the floor beside me, Dexter darts past us. "Take these, will you Daniel, up to the girl's room?" Then he looks back at me, glancing to see that I still hold Charlie. "Your rabbit, miss. It mustn't be with you when you meet *her*. She may throw it out. I can tell you're attached."

Chad nods with approval, and I hand Charlie to him.

With the snap of Daniel's fingers, a servant comes to grab my belongings sitting on the floor. Daniel whispers something to him, eyeing my direction, the bell boy nods, carting the luggage away.

The house radiates with heat throughout, welcoming my cheeks with warmth, reminding me of stepping into a five-star hotel.

"May I take your coat and hat, miss?" Daniel says, still trying to stare me down, to no avail.

"Yes, thank you," I reply, smiling back at him, smirking my own glare in response. *'Give it up,'* I say on the inside, gathering he's dangerous and perhaps one not to cross in a dark hall at night.

"I'll get Madame Moyer at once, sir. Shall I escort you all to the parlor?" he questions, still staring me down not giving in to the interlude. It makes me want to laugh out loud at his childish persistence to glare me down with fervor.

"Give it up Daniel, she cannot be compelled. And no, we know the way." Chad smiles. "Follow me, Wynter." The shocking look on Daniel's face, is priceless. I hear a smirking undertone come from Blair. I bet she, too, is laughing on the inside, but not in the same way, more like, 'yeah dude, I already tried.'

I shadow Chad's lead, looking around at the impressive castle made of marble, and feeling like I stepped through a time warp to the medieval era. The foyer entrance presents a high colossal ceiling, with marble stone floors and walls. Grand portraits hang about on all sides. In the center of the room, stands an impressive staircase to the upper levels, splitting to left and right at the top, with balconies on either side. *'There must be at least twenty doors upstairs,'* I think to myself. Red velvet carpet blankets beautifully detailed steps, accenting dragon statues on either side of the staircase. As we walk toward the parlor, the clapping sounds of our feet echo throughout the large hall. Some servants dusting off the front windows stop to see who is making such a clatter. It all feels a bit intimidating.

"Nothing to see here. Get back to work before I report back to Moyer," Blair exclaims, walking ahead of us.

I hear scurrying feet behind me, along with whispers, as we continue pacing towards the parlor.

Is this what Chad meant - eyes watching everywhere? The hired help? I mean, servants, talk right? I've seen it played in the movies and read about it in books.

As we move closer to the parlor, I am drawn to a portrait hanging to my right. It's a couple on their wedding day, showing a man very much like my father, dressed in royal attire and a lady in a white dress. Her hair is black, her cheeks red, and she has lips of rose. Her eyes are the same green as Francesca's. She has a slight smile and her hands lay gently in her lap. They look a lot like the couple in my locket, and I can't help but stare, she's mesmerizing.

"That's Sara and Ailbert on their wedding day," I hear Blair say. "Keep moving, we are late. There will be plenty of time for introductions. Can't leave her highness waiting," she says in a sarcastic tone. Seconds later we enter the parlor.

"Have a seat." Chad says, gesturing to a Victorian chair. Pastel colors of pink, yellow, blue, with heavy green accents decorate the room. Next to my seat is a tray of coffee cups, a French press and crumb cake.

"Hungry? Do you drink coffee?" Chad asks, gesturing to the display.

"No, thank you."

More portraits hang along the walls and a gigantic fireplace warms the space. This place feels inviting, unlike walking through the foyer a moment ago. I sit down along with Blair and Chad who are opposite of me, waiting.

Soon I hear clicking of heels against the marble floor, with whispers following, and a pattering of feet that seem to scatter quickly. Suddenly the door to the parlor bursts open as if to have a mind of its own, revealing a woman in black. She appears callous, with eyes sunken in, high cheekbones and tight pursing lips. She's carrying with her a black wand, with a tassel hanging on one end. Her black dress flows to the floor and gloves cover her hands. A bun like Blair's is tightly wound in the back of her head with not a strand of gray hair in sight.

Goosebumps prickle my arms, and I immediately feel a sensation of nausea.

Chad motions me to stand quickly, along with him and Blair.

"So, you come bearing gifts I see," she expresses, looking at me. She glides in my direction, smacking a leather stick against her garment, filling the parlor air with echoing slaps.

"Why on earth did you take so incredibly long, dear son?" Piercing her eyes in his direction, she voices, "I have a schedule to keep."

"I know, but it seems Francesca caught on, she knew we were coming. They had a good head start on us." He appears nervous, as he stands his ground and I sense him stiffen.

"Francesca had a special talent, didn't she? I thought we took care of that." Turning her dagger eyes towards Blair, she says, "The shield was supposed to work. What happened?"

Chad must have sensed my fear and held me steady by the elbow.

"I don't know Mother," Blair begins, "the spell said it would hold for twenty-four hours." Hearing the quiver in her voice makes me feel nervous. If someone can intimidate someone like her, I don't want to think how this woman would be with me.

Twice she slithers around the chaise lounge and chairs before stopping directly in front of me.

"You have caused quite the commotion here at Storm River." She says coldly. Her eyes, black as coal, are not the same icy blue as my dad's, nor green like mine. She doesn't look old either, like a grandmother is supposed to look, with grey hair. She can easily pass for a woman in her thirties. It left me confused. Come to think of it, Chad and Blair both look no older than twenty-five. How do they stay so young looking?"

"She is so frail and small; definitely has her mother's eyes," Moyer blurts. "I am Madame Moyer, you will address me as such. Not Grandmother, not Maura, not Moyer. Strictly Madame Moyer. Do I make myself clear, Wynter?"

Chad nudges me with his elbow. "Yes." I say in a raspy voice.

"Not yet eighteen. What shall we do with you my dear child," she says, staring at me.

Her eyes beginning to glow blue, like Chad and Blair's did on the airplane. Is she trying to compel me as well? I watch impassively as the black coals of her eyes turn sapphire blue, becoming lighter and lighter, until they glow bright and illuminating.

There, I see someone's face, peering back at me in Moyer's irises as *she* stares me down. It isn't me in her reflection though, rather a face that looks trapped in fear. An appearance looking like hers, but slightly different. The image in Moyer's eyes look older, middle age.

Madame Moyer hisses unexpectedly, turning around and scowling at Blair. "What did you do!?"

"Nothing, I swear. I didn't do anything. She can't be compelled Mother. Chad and I both tried already." A pleading look in Blair's eyes, gave way to her fear. The tension can be cut with a knife and still it would not alleviate the pressure in the atmosphere.

"I see. I don't know whether to chastise you two for trying to undermine my authority or thank you for the forewarning." I watch Moyer's face, as muscles in her jaw move while clenching her teeth. She looks back into my eyes, "So it appears my first-born son has detoured my plan slightly. How reckless, he should've known it wouldn't stop me. For when you turn eighteen, my dear, that's when the real fun will begin." She cackles a cool vindictive sound.

Turning towards Chad, she says, "Seems we are temporarily at an impasse," and then peers back at Blair. "You will find out a way to fix this problem. Do you hear me child? We have less than two weeks left. Find a solution!" she yells. "Now go!" Blair half curtsies and leaves the room.

I feel hot on the inside, cold sweat running across my forehead, and heart racing. What just happened? Panic sets in, '*Breathe Wynter, breathe,*' I say to myself. I'm Petrified.

She roams the room, wand still in her hand, this time slapping it against her hands and she says, "What to do with you now?" She walks around the sofa a third time, before saying, "You have brought a great burden on me today. A temporary issue, no matter," looking directly at Chad. He stands there like a warrior. Inert by her tone.

Her pitch is foul, saying, "Jeoffrey seems to have played me for a fool. I do not forgive easily. If he weren't already dead, I would have killed him myself, while you watched. However, seeing that we are forced to an alternate plan, I have no other choice but to wait."

Looking back, remembering the argument that Aunt Fran and Dad had, I can see now why they wanted to flee so quickly. I want to cry, but I'm not about to give her that satisfaction.

She adds, "You will, of course, earn your keep for the next week, by working alongside the maids, and be paid like the others. I have no interest in buying you things for your enjoyment. We go off the point system here and are tallied daily by the house bookkeeper. Introductions shall be arranged tomorrow."

Looking back at Chad, she says, "I want her fully briefed before I leave this next week for Scotland. Coolly, she looks back at me with glaring eyes. "See to it that she knows all the rules.

We wouldn't want an accident before her grand ballroom debut."

"Yes, Madame Moyer, is there anything else?" he says.

Pivoting her stare. "Make sure Wynter here has a room, near the west tower. I don't want her mingling with the others. Her influence will give them hope." She turns towards the door and stops. "Perhaps the room her mother died in would suffice."

Chad nods, acknowledging her instructions. Then glancing towards me and raising his eyebrows, he half tilts his head as if to imply, *'welcome to hell.'*

The parlor doors swoop open without Madame Moyer touching the handle, and Dexter waits on the other side for orders. He bows slightly as she passes him, and she says, "Please see to it, that Rosie has Wynter supplied with uniforms. I want her fully ready for next week."

Chad, still by my side, murmurs, "And the adventure begins." He smiles, trying to lighten my mood. "C'mon, I'll show you to your room."

7

The Manor

The atmosphere feels cold as I observe servants murmuring amongst each other as they work. An unsettling breeze sweeps across my face, sending chills down my spine as we pass through the foyer heading toward the staircase. I feel cold, to the point that I want my jacket. For a brief second, I swear I saw my own breath exhale from my lungs.

"I'm with you," I hear a whisper in my ear.

"Do you hear that?" I say to Chad, as we approach the staircase.

"Hear what, the echo of heels clicking upon the marble floors?" he asks, chuckling back.

"I'm inside your head. No one can hear me but you," a voice says to me.

I try to ignore it, pretending it's my imagination talking to me.

Beyond the staircase, I can see French doors opened wide, displaying countless shelves of books, past the threshold.

"Is that a library?" I ask as we begin to ascend onto the grand stairs.

Looking over to my direction, he says, "Yes. When the doors are open, all are welcome to enter. If the doors are closed, one must wait until they are not. Perhaps, I can find Cory and he can show you around, tomorrow afternoon."

"Cory?"

"He would be your cousin." Then, extending an arm, gesturing to the steps leading to the level above, he says, "Shall we?"

As we approach the top of the stairs, I peek to my left to see a girl standing near the balcony, looking at me curiously. Her eyes gaunt, face pale, clothes wrinkled and dirty, wearing black laced ankle boots that are partly covering her white dress. She stands there frozen like a statue.

"Get back to work, Stella," Chad says. "You don't want Madame Moyer to see you standing there doing nothing." Her expression of fear gives way, as she bolts to a room behind her, shutting the door.

"Do all the hired help dress in such old-world attire?" I wonder aloud.

"You mean the uniforms? Yes, well, you see… Moyer is fixated on old fashioned styles. A rather eclectic design, dating from medieval era to early twentieth century. She prefers everyone to act old school. Thus, you do not see much in the way of heat, hence all the lit fireplaces. She prefers the most minimum amount of modern technology used. Oil lamps at night, fires lit in the evenings, and reading by candlelight. Of course, some exceptions are made, like the lower level is lit with bulbs, and there are computers in the library for the school curriculum."

Chad turns to me with concern. "Wait, do you have a cell phone, electronics, laptop, anything that may connect you to the outside world?"

"Yes, in my suitcase, why?"

"If Moyer catches you, she will destroy them. Never, and I mean never, be caught with any of it."

"No, please. I'll be careful."

"I'm almost tempted to take the items myself." With hesitation and taking a deep breath, he says, "I won't, but if she catches you, I can't save you from her wrath."

"Understood. I promise to be cautious. Does Moyer not have internet… television? Are you saying that those who live here do not have access to those items?"

"No, not really. There's hint of it, such as computers set up in the library, like I mentioned, or the television in the community room, but you will never see a telephone in sight. The staff live here too, with no family for them to go home to." He gives a hopeless looking smile, "They do not go beyond the gates; nobody does."

"Like, ever?" This must be what Aunt Fran meant, by never having contact with the outside world.

"No, never. Did you not observe the ten-foot stone walls at the gates when we arrived? It's to keep *them* out, and us in. You stand within the most luxurious jail of all time."

"Them?" I interrupt him.

"The real world beyond the gates. Everyday people, they are who Moyer keeps out." I can tell he's on the verge of a tangent, as he is giving the impression we are embarking on a sore subject. His eyes begin to glow blue, and he quickly changes the topic.

We reach the top of the stairs, going in the opposite direction, from where the girl, Stella, stood, and stopping at French doors that automatically open before us.

"This is one of the few times you will ever go this way. Of course, the week of your birthday, when she throws a welcoming party, you will come back through this door."

"Why is that? She clearly hates me. She seems to have her own agenda, forget what anyone else thinks."

"Careful, my little one, ears wait for gossip, then report back to her."

We pass through a dark hallway lit with oil lamps hanging on the walls, along with more paintings. A plethora of stained-glass windows hedge the corridor while doors line the other side. Far in the distance a second set of French doors wait for us to approach.

"You see, Wynter, you're a Storm and a Storm must be introduced properly. She will throw a party of introduction. It's already in the plans. Something I think they call now a days, a house warming, wrapped in a bow. It's a disguise really, to cover something bigger. Your coming here, it gives her a perfect opportunity…an excuse if you will, to cover her real scheme. She brought you back here for a reason. You have something she wants, and she's gone to great lengths to get it."

"What might that be?" I know he's not going to tell me, and I blurt out my words without even thinking.

He laughs loudly. "Oh my dear, if I told you that, it wouldn't be a surprise, now would it?" He appears to hesitate, then I hear him say more. "My dear niece, this place must display much mystery to you. I can see it in your eye's, the wonder you have that lies hiding behind that head of yours… don't go poking around, you may not like what you find."

He adds, "As for the girl back there, clinging to the banister as we passed, her name is Stella, and she came to us a few years ago. Blair found her one day, while out on an errand for Madame Moyer."

"What do you mean found her? Like she was up walking around alone?"

He huffs a grin. "In a matter of speaking, yes."

"So, Madame Moyer adopted her?"

"Adopted? Oh heavens, no. Madame Moyer runs an adoption agency, and a home for homeless, unwanted or orphaned children."

"An orphanage? So, there are other children?"

"Yes, many. Storm River has been an institution for over one hundred years. I imagine they are already down in the cafeteria."

"That explains the many doors."

"And the many more ahead of us," he comments, opening the second entrance, to another long corridor.

"With the numerous orphans living here, we need many rooms to house them all. The rooms we are passing now are for the staff. It might take a while to get used to everything, but I'm confident you will figure it out. If I am around, you're free to come and ask me or Blair. Avoid Madame Moyer, obviously, but there are others you can talk to."

"Blair? She hates me. Daniel, well you told me to stay away from him already."

"Indeed, I did," he says, with a nod of approval. "Blair on the other hand, doesn't hate you. She's annoyed to be stuck here. Hates being under Moyer's thumb. She tried to convince me to run away with her, while out finding you, in fact. She thinks she's as smart as Jeoffrey and can get away with it… like he did. She fails to remember she has no leverage. Well, we did, back when we kidnapped you, but that didn't go as planned, now did it?" He smiles in a snide manner.

"That's why you tried to compel me isn't it?" I ask, remembering back on the plane, both so angry I thought they would kill me.

"Ding, ding, ding… the girl catches on quickly," he says, sounding sarcastic. "It was our chance to escape." He rolls his eyes and I can see his frustration. "I blame your dad, not you, of course. Let me be very clear," – pointing his finger at me. "Trust no one. Not even me. You are the only person you can count on."

"That's what my dad always taught me."

Chad smiles. "Where do you think I learned it from?"

"Why do you say I can't trust you? I mean, you obviously are trapped here like me."

"I'm not protected like you are, Wynter." He peers down at my neck. "If you haven't noticed Moyer, lives under this same roof," he says. "We are stuck here forever." His attempt at dry humor fizzles, when I don't smile back.

He shakes his head. "Soon, dear niece, you will know everything, and wish you hadn't. Remember that bourbon I teased about earlier? Yeah, I wasn't being flippant, I give you six weeks." Then he laughs as if humor will fix it all.

We come to a third door, at the end of the second corridor, and grabbing the knob, he says, "This is the staff's community room, where one may rest, read, talk, play games. And as I mentioned before, no electronics, so choices are limited, except of course television. And even then, Moyer has the channels regulated."

Two ladies in a corner space play a game of chess, trying not to act nosey when we walk in. They whisper to each other, peering at us, giggle, then go back to the board game, one of them making a move with a pawn. Another person I see on the opposite side of the area, sits in a chair, reading, not seeming to notice us intrude into the quiet room. The social zone is enormous, with a pool table, foosball, and shuffle board set up in another location.

Chad strides to a bay window and looks out. "You see, this house stands over a thousand acres. Come," he says, gesturing to me, "see for yourself."

I peer out the window to view lampposts lit among the vastness of the snow-covered ground.

"Stone fencing encases the whole property," he says, as he points outward to the faint skyline. The moonlight above gives way to silhouettes in the far distance.

"At night, the guards release dogs; Moyer has the place fully secured. One never leaves unless under strict authority, of course." He turns to me and smiles. "Like finding you, for example, *she* allowed it." Forming a smug expression, he adds, "Otherwise you are killed on-site if caught escaping. The only way off the grounds, I suppose, is death."

"The horror," I think to myself. Madame Moyer sounds like a monster, with control issues. I patiently listen more, as Chad continues his tale.

"Unless, of course, she invites you as a guest. You will meet more family members at the party she has planned." He guides me to yet another door. "There are many cousins, in the House of Storm. Daniel is Madame Moyer's eyes and ears and can hypnotize anyone without even realizing it. Although, you seem to be unaffected by his gaze," he remarks.

I snicker, remembering when we first arrived at the front door.

"Yes, well, he's wasting his time. Rather amusing at any rate," Chad says, stopping before the next door, to open.

"Is Moyer a Storm too?"

"Oh, my dear no, she married into the Storm family. She hasn't always been so controlling and callous. Something changed in her years ago, when Jeoffrey and I were still boys, before Blair was born."

"What happened?" Oddly enough, it intrigued me.

"No one knows," as he opens another door, exposing a spiral staircase.

"But her eyes glow blue, like you and Blair?"

"Oh, that's easy, she studies witchcraft."

That explains the glowing eyes I thought, remembering her anger. She's not pleased that Jeoffrey foiled her plans. I let out a light giggle at the thought. He indeed beat her at her own game, and it thrills me to no end, that he is still watching over me, even though he is not of this world any longer.

"What is so funny?" Chad asks, as we climb the twisting stairs. "This way my dear, the tower awaits you."

"Nothing, thinking of my dad, and the past. The power of mind control, seeing the future, being able to project what's approaching. Madame Moyer didn't see any of it coming."

"Don't get too caught up in the moment, she can easily take you down with one strike. You are on her turf now. You're much more vulnerable than you were hundreds of miles away." He pauses to change the subject, as we wined around the turret. "Of course, you will still need an education and will be participating in school curriculum."

"Where is the school? In town?"

"We don't leave the grounds, remember? All the children are homeschooled, of course. The classrooms are downstairs off the kitchen. A whole wing is dedicated to school. There you will find a gym, pool, and the outside courtyard."

As we climb, step by step I feel my knees begin to tire, especially the one I broke a little while ago. It must have been written all over my face, because I hear Chad sigh, "You will get used to it. There are no elevators, just dumbbell chutes, allowing large objects to cart to the upper levels. If you have legs, you walk." He pauses a second. "Besides, it's great exercise," he says, turning to look at me with a grin.

We finally reach the top and come to yet another corridor. "This is your wing. Not much farther now, just to the end of the hall."

"Such a long trek, to get to a bedroom," I say almost out of breath.

The cold becomes more apparent as we wander the last hall. The wind outside is fierce, giving dramatic tones to whistles coming through the cracks of the window casings. Faint sounds of icy snowflakes splatter upon the glass, sounding as if it might be turning to an icy rain. Floors appear to be made of the same marble as the foyer and parlor, with the same jagged brick stone surrounding the walls, downstairs.

"Is it always this cold and noisy up here?"

"Yes, or so I have heard. My living quarters are downstairs. Sounds like the storm has arrived."

We continue sauntering, passing door after door until we stop at the end of the passageway, to see someone standing among the shadows. A blue glow comes from the dark.

"Who is that," I whisper?

He ignores my question, and asks one of his own, to the person in the darkened cove, peering back at us.

"Hello Nora, hope you haven't waited too long for us?" he asks, smiling.

A young girl with dark hair and eyes in maid attire, rests on a bench near another turret tower, holding a folded dress, apron, tights, and black boots. As we come closer, the blue hues of light fades.

"Not at all, Your Lordship. Her room is stocked for the week, a fire is lit so the room should be warm soon. There are fresh sheets, blankets and water in the basin," she says softly.

He nods. "Well done. Nora, I would like you to meet Miss Wynter. She is the granddaughter of Madame Moyer. Please make her feel comfortable and show her around, will you?"

"Wynter you say? It's like I am seeing a ghost. Welcome home, Milady." And she curtsies. "You look just like your mother."

Not used to such a formal introduction, I smile back with a slight nod. Nora seems to stiffen, and glares at Chad, as if she wants to speak.

"No need to worry, Nora, she's real. Not a spirit, I assure you." He coaxes.

"I hope not, the last time we had the like of her, it brought chaos to this household."

Is she referring to my mother? I glance at Chad, wondering what she means.

He smiles, and as if he can read my thoughts, says, "When your mother was alive, she tried to keep the peace among the houses. Moyer and she butted heads. When she died, it divided factions. Soon you will find out who loved her and who did not. Moyer sees you as a threat to her. Seeing how this place belonged to your mother, it automatically passes on to you."

"Then why did she even bring me here if all she wants is my inheritance?"

Nora's eyes widen, and she raises her brow. As if to be waiting to hear Chad's reply.

"For your power, my dear," he chortles. Then he looks at Nora, "I've disclosed too much in front of staff," and paces toward her, with his back to me, as he stares into her eyes. Blue glowing hues permeate the shadowy hall. "You will show Wynter around and forget what's been revealed here today."

She repeats him word for word, and the glowing stops. Chad turns around and smiles. "Now, where were we?"

He must have seen the shocking glare on my face. "Don't worry, she doesn't feel a thing, and won't remember what happened here, only that you are Her Ladyship, she will not remember our conversation."

"What just happened?" I ask. Astonishment isn't the word I can find as to what I witnessed.

"Shhh, details later." Brushing me off, he pats my shoulder smiling. "Nora will you please show Wynter to her room. I must be on my way, I have business to attend to."

"Wynter, my dear niece," he adds, taking my hand and giving a gentleman's kiss, "it's been a pleasure. I must be on my way, as duty calls." And before I can respond, he disappears like a ghost.

Turning around making a complete 180 degree turn, I stare back at Nora, who seems to be in a daze, staring at nothing but the air in front of her. Not at all shaken by the vanishing act, instead she smiles. "This way."

Moving forward, towards a round dark hallway with three doors before us. Nora beams. "We are in one of the largest turrets of the house: big enough for three bedrooms. Try the middle one. Go ahead, open the door."

8

The Lady's Maid

Walking into a room big enough for a bed, dresser, and night stand, I stare at the small space with curiosity. Flames from a handcrafted fireplace flicker in the hearth, a mirror hangs above the dresser, and a chair sits in a corner. My luggage and backpack lay on my bed along with Charlie and my pillow.

"This will be your room; the door over there leads to a small closet where I have hung up your school uniform," her voice bland as she spoke.

"Uniforms?"

"Moyer prefers all children wear the appropriate clothes."

Nora has a strange look to her. I can't quite put my finger on it. Although she has this monotone body language, I can't help but sense beneath that skin of hers is something else. Like she, too, has a secret to hide.

"Outside, in the hall to your left is a washroom," she says. "You're in the family wing now. Rosie will be here in the morning to introduce you to staff."

She points, continuing her blank stare, avoiding my eye contact. "Behind this door, is a daily schedule. It should help you with being organized. Breakfast is eight sharp; if you miss a meal, you will have to wait until next serving."

Still in an automaton state, Nora moves her arms out to hand me the items in her clutches. "Rosie wishes you to have these and be ready for tomorrow. This is the maid attire."

"Thanks," as I take the items and lay them across the bed.

"It gets cold up here," Nora replies. "So, it's important to be fully stocked with kindling. The firewood closet is in the hall, a few steps from your room. A chart on the back door must be filled out should you take what you need. Casey, the estate's errands boy, keeps it fully stocked."

With a sigh, Nora moves to the fireplace, that seems to have lost its flare. Is this an indication that whatever Chad did to her is wearing off? I watch as she pokes the fire, with sparks flying up the chimney.

"How long have you lived here?" I ask, wondering if there are more like her living under such a controlling thumb.

Nora smiles, hesitating to reply, "A long time," and changes the subject quickly. "Do you know how to start a fire?" She moves charcoal logs to make room for another. This time her voice sounds a little more human, instead of the drone-like manner moments before.

"Yes, my father taught me. We went on many family camping trips, training me in survival." I wonder if preparing me for the future was the plan all along, knowing what I know now, thinking back.

"Good, grab me another log from that shelf over there, will you?" she questions, pointing in its direction.

Tossing her more timber, I ask, "Are you an orphan, too?"

"You are a nosey one, aren't you?" Her eyes watching the fire as she pitches the lumber… "No," she says, and she drops the poker back in its chamber.

I can tell the spell or compelling of whatever it is, is wearing off. She gets up and brushes her hands on her apron, "My mother is Rosie, the head maid who you will meet tomorrow. I don't know who my father is. I was born and raised in this house."

"I-I don't mean to pry," I stutter, feeling a little meddlesome, now.

"It's no bother, really." She walks around my bed toward the door as if to get ready to leave, stopping at the nightstand, "I almost forgot. If you need to order anything, simply put it on the form here," and she pulls a notepad from the drawer. "All requests are picked up once a week, on Fridays, and all deliveries made on Monday mornings. You happen to already be stocked up, until next week… if you last that long," she murmurs. Her monotone inducing stature becoming more aggressive now, appearing to be completely coherent and it seems as if she doesn't particularly like me.

"What's that supposed to mean?"

"Nothing," she retorts. "Merely that people tend to disappear the first week if they do not follow the rules." Her eyes glare a blue hint of warning. "Something tells me you like to go against the grain."

I watch as she curves a mischievous smile, adding, "So, make sure you anticipate what you may need beforehand. Else you will do without until the following week. Careful what you order, too, as it will be deducted from your pay." And, as if she forgot having intentions to leave, she moves forward to the window, glancing out to see icy rain replace the snow. Drops melt to the window making pelting sounds that echo in the room. "Looks like temperatures may drop tonight through the week, creating dangerous conditions outside."

She turns to look at me. "There is a movie theatre downstairs, that is open on Friday and Saturday evenings, only. Another avenue to entertain a growing crowd of broods."

I gasp at the thought. This place is like a compound. Free to roam the grounds, but not beyond the gates.

"The classrooms are downstairs near the parlor, through a hallway," she says. "It's there that Mr. Derek Storm will teach everyone."

"Derek Storm?" Another cousin, or uncle I wonder?

Nora nods at me, and pursues to finish her spiel, "Class is at nine sharp. Moyer is very good at keeping all the little heathens in line. Make sure never to be late. You will see many children here working as hard as you would an adult."

"Does Madame Moyer work them all to the bone?"

"Yes, of course. Miss Wynter all the children have strict chores. Play is on the weekend."

"That's dreadful. Doesn't this woman have a soul?"

"Now you sound like Gabrielle."

"Who is she?"

"Who is? You mean… was?" She pauses to wait for my reaction I imagine, and simply smirks. "Lord Chad's betrothed. Daniel put an end to that, turning her to stone. You may remember her when you passed the courtyard fountain this late afternoon?" she states. Sneering a grin, I can see from her expression that she is waiting for me to be alarmed.

So, I play along. "Nora, come now, do you expect me to believe that?" Trying to find the core of her vindictive attitude, I wonder, is this why Chad had compelled her? She has a mischievous side?

"Believe what you will, Daniel can turn people to stone if one antagonizes him enough, but who am I? A mere pawn like the rest of us here." Nora sucks a breath in so deep I thought she would faint. "Never call Madame Moyer anything but Madame Moyer. If she hears you say her name, she will send you to the chambers below, if not strike you down first with one blow of her wrath." Nora cowers after saying the words aloud, as if what she says is forbidden.

"She really has you wrapped around her finger, doesn't she?" I say, watching her change from hostile demeanor back to timid, from the mere mention of Moyer's name.

Nora stops to glare at me. "Don't say I didn't warn you. Besides, you will soon learn the truth, anyway."

As if to be done with this conversation, she darts for the door, only to stop and say, "Wynter, I know you must have some sort of judgement already floating around in that head of yours and I am willing to bet it isn't happiness and sunshine. But get one thing straight... be careful what you say out loud. I am sure you have already been told that ears are listening, and eyes are watching." And with that, she closes the door behind her.

I look around, finally having a moment to exhale and reflect on my day. Memories of crunching metal, tumbling car, and hanging upside down, comes to the surface again. Visions of Dad and Aunt Fran dangling unconscious, bleeding; it all keeps playing over and over in my mind and tears begin to fall down my cheeks.

I put away my maid's uniform and begin to unpack my first suitcase. Fresh clean clothes bring me to realize, I haven't bathed in almost two days. Changing course, I gather my things, hoping to find the washroom. With all the doors in the hall, Nora didn't show me which one it is.

Opening the first entry on my right leads to another long corridor.

Pacing down the hall, I see a plethora of more doors before me. *"Which one is it?"* I say under my breath. Against my better judgement, I try the first one I come to, moving the knob, finding out it's locked. I hear noises on the other side, like someone whimpering in pain. Gently I press my ear to the door, listening for any signs of movement. A deafening thud comes from behind it, then screams. "Let me out of here!" The screams are faint but the pounding fists against the steel door from the other side, are loud.

My instinct is to back away, and I bump into Nora who appears out of nowhere. She looks different, not like a few minutes ago back in my room. Blankly she stares at me, with gaunt eye sockets, unaffected by my stumble. I see her irises switch from yellow back to brown.

"Whatever are you looking for Wynter? Snooping around where you don't belong?" This time she has a tone of malevolence.

I back away, overcome by her dramatic appearance, I say, "Looking for the bathroom, that you never showed me." I know full well she probably won't believe me. A white lie perhaps, deep down I know the bathroom isn't in this corridor, yet the curiosity got the best of me. Something tells me she's on the other team. I watch her skin change from a grey, to yellow scales, then back to a human skin.

'Okay Wynter, you know how to act from drama class…at least a little.' I say to myself.

Not expecting a reply, I hear a voice inside my head say, *"Play 'the dumb lassie.' Fake it!"*

"The door seems to be locked," I say, and I move backwards toward the French doors behind me. "I haven't bathed in days."

"Good, That's it. Act it out," the voice says.

"You don't listen very well, do you?" Nora says, her eyes changing to a blue glow. "I told you the washroom is outside your room to the left." She motions with her hand, as she points to the opened doorway behind me.

Passing through the threshold to the other hall, not taking my eyes off her for a second, I say, "Ah, yes. Makes sense now. I took a right, didn't I?"

Nora doesn't look well, or should I say human? For all I know some demon possesses her. She has a hissing tone when she speaks, gliding her way towards me like Madame Moyer.

"I—I'm all turned around in this place. Thank you, Nora. However do you keep up in this maze is beyond me? I mean, it's my first day here, I can't possibly know my way around this quickly."

Her stance holds. "We will let Madame Moyer decide that."

"C'mon Nora, it's an honest mistake," I plead, knowing full well I didn't want to see the punishment that is about to be inflicted upon me.

Nora ignores my comment. "Behind you is the door you seek," and she glides off, stiff and unmoving.

Without veering my stare from her, as she slithers away like a snake, I search with one of my hands for the doorknob and quickly enter the bathroom. Shutting the door and locking it behind me, I take a deep breath, sinking my body to the floor, holding my knees. The tile is cold and the only lighting in the room is a window high above my head. Same mason stone like the rest of the manor. A claw foot tub sits in the corner sharing its space with a shower head above. It's a large basic bathroom, set in a 1920's style.

I huddle for a minute to collect my thoughts, to dissect what I saw. Is this place for real?

"Yes," says the voice in my head.

"Who are you, and why do you keep infringing on me?"

The voice doesn't reply. I wait a few more minutes sulking, feeling sorry for myself. *"Suck it up Wynter,"* I say aloud. Beginning to realize crying isn't going to do me any good.

I start the bath before slipping off my clothes. Looking at myself in the mirror, reminds me of the broken leg I had, as I trace my fingers over the knee that bled. A scar like Aunt Fran's hand, leaves an impression of what was once a bone sticking through my leg. No bruising, on my chest from the seatbelt, nor a scar from the gash on the side of my head. What is happening to me? Injuries to a normal human being doesn't disappear, but then again, I'm beginning to discover I'm not the average human. Perhaps what Dad, Fran and Chad say is true? I am soon to be like them.

I'm not entirely sure my mind can handle this unexplained phenomenon, even though Dad and Fran clearly showed proof of it earlier. Apparently, it isn't a theory at all: I too, must have that ability. Absolutely nothing hurt on my entire body. It partly clarifies why the change of clothes—blood must have been everywhere. But the injury was so severe it would have taken a cast. Having had a broken arm before, from jumping off a rock at school when I was around five, could corroborate that. I don't remember much, just that it was painful, and dad took me to the hospital where the doctor plastered my arm. I wore it for about three weeks, Doc stated my arm healed too quickly and wanted to run tests on me. The next day we moved, again.

I turn to slide in the warm bath and it's so therapeutic my eyes begin to feel heavy, and I fight to stay awake.

Screams coming from the front of the car pierce my ears as we tumble down the hill. Everything is flying around inside the sedan. Suddenly we roll to a stop, with the sound of nothing but quiet. "Dad…Fran?"

Looking around I see fog, and in the distance a figure comes out from the mist, beckoning me, with open arms, moving its hands for me to come forth. "Come Wynter, come to me."

"Don't go," A whisper sounds off in my ear.

"Why? Who is it?" I murmur, "Who are you?"

"Trust me, don't go. All she will bring is destruction to all."

"Don't listen to her, Wynter," the image ahead says. "She is trying to confuse you. I can show you the truth. I can show you what you have been looking for. Don't let her cloud your mind."

"How do you know my name?"

"See, she is doing it now. Giving you reason not to trust your inner voice. If you go to her, she will destroy you," the voice inside my head says.

"It is you, she shouldn't trust, Sarmira. Trying to control her dreams. You brought her here. Sought her out, because you know she has the strength to destroy you. Now you have managed to get inside her head. It's the only place you can manipulate her… for now. I will teach her how to block you out. Make no mistake of that."

The voice which I cannot see, laughs out loud, "My child you cannot reach me. Wynter is with me now. It is only a matter of time."

"Go with your gut, Wynter. Isn't that what you have always been taught?" The image comes closer, "It's what we have always told you."

"Isalora, you cannot defeat me so easily." The voice laughs louder.

"No, it will not be me, that will destroy you," Isalora says, "Wynter will do that. Don't you see Sarmira, the prophecy has already started."

Loud noises begin to pound through my ears. Screeching sounds ring out, making my head throb and wake to the sounds of banging. At first, I think it's the door, but realize a branch is tapping the window above me, making a scratching sound from the forceful winds outside.

By this time the water is cold. I quickly finish up and go back to my room.

When I round the corner, I see a note attached to the door:

Eyes are watching, ears are listening.

Tearing the paper off the nail I crush it into a ball and go inside.

I turn to my luggage sitting untouched on my bed and begin to search for my night clothes. Random thoughts continue to play out in my mind, as I get dressed. Bringing to the front, are happy times with Fran and Dad. Camping trips in the summer, raking leaves in the fall, Christmas tree cutting in the winter:

these memories all play with my emotions. Tears fall again down my cheeks. Time seems to slip away, as I pull my second suitcase, and unzip it, bringing out my favorite throw blanket, along with slippers, sandals, and my running shoes, evoking a smile of me sprinting on the tracks back home.

Finally, I lift my school bag full of random books. The nightstand next to the bed has just enough room on the bottom shelf for all my paperbacks. As I pull to unzip the large compartment, I notice a crinkle sound coming from the small zipper pocket on the outer side.

I find two envelopes stuffed inside. One is addressed to me, and one to another. *"Why them?"* I think.

My approach is now thwarted from everything that has happened. Trying hard to hold back my anger from the second letter, I tuck it into my pocket robe, for safe keeping. A part of me is curious and perhaps I will have a chance to confront them tomorrow. How do they know my dad? I rip open the letter addressed to me.

Dearest Wynter,

If you are reading this letter, then it means, you are in the clutches of Madame Maura Moyer, Fran and I are dead, and you are in danger.

I am sorry it came to be this way, but do not give up hope. A few things you must remember:

One, never take the necklace off.

Two, find the person I addressed on the second envelope. They will have the answers. Keep it safe until then. Tell no one. Trust no one.

Three, destroy this letter. She mustn't see it.

I love you with all my heart.

Dad

My heart sank. The whole world is caving in on me and I have no clue how to stop it. I try to hold back the tears, but the anguish keeps coming. I grab my bookbag and send it sailing through the air, hitting the opposite wall, while books fly everywhere, scattering on the floor. I throw the letter in the fire and grabbing Charlie, I lay back against my pillow sobbing until I fall asleep.

9

Shadow Walkers

Scampering footsteps outside my bedroom door jolt me awake. Looking at my clock, I see it's three in the morning, and realize I must have sobbed myself to sleep. The thought occurs to me, to check outside my door, but leaving the warm comforts of my bed doesn't sound inviting enough. Drifting back to sleep, I hear sounds of a baby cry, followed by screams. My head spins out of my dream for a second time.

"This is nuts." I glance around in the dark trying to focus and see Charlie had fallen to the floor during the night. Catching up on my thoughts, more screams beyond my door, bring me to consciousness. Grasping that the shrieks are real and not delusions of sleeping, I roll out of bed inquisitive as to what it is. Whoever is squealing it sounds like they are in agonizing discomfort. The torture of pain rips through my ears. Another screech rings out through the walls, and then cries of a baby again. Finding my way to the door I listen intently pressing my ear against it. I need to prove my ears are playing tricks on me. Silence at first, then what sounds like new born cries start again.

My interest has the best of me, knowing full well by opening this door I'm putting myself in danger. *'It's three in the morning and well after midnight,'* I think to myself. Some people would surely be stirring in an hour, anyway.

Talking myself out of a rational decision, I turn the knob slowly, cracking it ajar to listen more, hoping the door wouldn't squeak. An icy breeze swifts past me, fanning through my hair from the pressure release. Voices fill the hollow barren halls, followed by moans of pain from a young woman. Echoing sounds bounce off the stone walls. My mind racing, with curiosity, I step forward, careful not to make a sound. The hallway is very dark, and my eyes are wide open, trying to find a speck of light as they focus. Ahead of me is a window, allowing the moon to illuminate the dim halls. The stone floor is cold beneath my feet, and I realize I have forgotten my slippers. Ignoring the numbness in my toes, I continue forward to the noise with curiosity.

I hear muffling voices, along with more painful sounding moans.

Moving closer to the end of the hall, I try to listen. The corridor smells musty and any light from the moon doesn't give enough brightness to see much farther than what's in front of me. Against my better judgement, I step closer to the corner wall, near a window, anticipating better leverage with seeing in the dark, however it makes vision worse. I stop for a moment to observe how far I should go.

More cries echo as I tiptoe slowly, inching my way further down the corridor. Sliding against the wall, keeping in the shadows and away from the moonlight, I ignore the inner voice warning me to stay back, continuing to follow the noise down the passageway. I know the French doors are locked, so once I arrive to where the sounds are, I place my ear to the door.

I hear whispers sounding like Blair, "Hurry go quickly, before you're seen."

"You can't take my baby," cries a woman. An infant wails following its mother's shrieking scream. Random whispering of voices continue to speak.

Transferring to an adjacent wall, I hide out in a small nook, trying to be as still as possible. Voices sound like they are right behind the French doors. I would be caught for sure if I dart back to my room right now.

"Someone is coming, quick hide!"

Scuffling footsteps slowly dissipate…

I see a shadowy figure up ahead coming from the direction of my room. It holds still, as if it sees me. Glowing blue eye's pierce through its cowl, lighting the path ahead.

Holding as still as possible I can feel the beating of my heart pound beneath my chest and I fear this creature, gliding down the corridor can hear it, too.

Spouting cries break its approach toward me, drawing its attention to the French doors, and it follows the wails instead.

The doors fling open, as the cold air brushes my face from the force. I try not to take a breath, keeping as still as possible.

The shadow moves closer to the curious sounds. Voices beyond intensify.

"Shhh" … says one voice, "I hear something."

"What is it," says the other?

"Shhh, Shhh" the first voice says again. "We need to go, someone is here, we can't take any chances. Let's move now!" and shuffling feet dissipate through the cold passageway.

The shadowy figure bolsters through the threshold past me with eye's glowing bright.

"He's here, we're too late… quick, run!" I hear screams, then the sound of someone choking. Blue hues bounce off the shadowy stone wall, displaying two figures. One shape flinging around trying to break free while the creature grasps its neck, until soon all movement is still.

I want to run as fast as I can back to my room, but do I dare? Will it catch me? It's now or never. So, I dart to my room, as fast as I can, but before I can make it half-way, I see another figure with glowing eyes ahead of me. It's a figure that looks the same as the one behind me, and it's moving towards me quickly. I turn around to see the first shadow moving towards me just as fast.

Both shadows are gliding in my direction looking directly at me with glowing blue eyes, and I haven't anywhere to run. Fear rushes through my veins, I'm caught, and I know it. Why didn't I listen?

I can't budge my feet, and I can barely breathe. Somehow my body is frozen in place. It's like I'm paralyzed, pinned to the floor beneath my feet. Even my fingers, are immobile. My whole body is fixated in time and I feel faint, like I'm going to lose consciousness at any moment. Then it all goes black.

I awake in the morning with piercing pain behind my eyes and at first, I can't focus. I find my window slightly open, with the cold brisk air awaking my senses.

Did I dream a nightmare? Remembering the intense blue eyes, I try to center myself, ignoring my throbbing head as I sit up to examine the goose egg on the back of my skull. Barely turning my chin, I see it's nearly seven in the morning, I don't care at this point if I missed breakfast, the pain is too horrible. I doze in and out of sleep.

"Stay strong," I hear a voice say.

"Who is that? Is someone there?" Sitting back up from my bed, I look around my room, hearing only the echoes of my own voice.

"Don't give up, stay the course," it whispers again.

"Who are you?" Am I losing my mind? I swear someone is present in my room, yet I see no one.

"She has plans set. You must hurry," it persists. It's as if someone is right here in the room with me.

Rapid knocks on my door wakes me from my reverie. A little drowsy I stumble from my bed tripping over a book, forgetting for a moment where I am.

"Good morning, you must be Wynter," the woman standing before me says, smiling. "I'm Rosie. Did you sleep well, I hope?" She has a friendly, but tired face with pink cheeks and brown eyes. Salt and pepper hair is bound up in a bun. Her dress is a crème color with a white apron.

I nod in gesture, and she scoots into my room. "Oh my, what happened here? I do hope you don't do this to all your books?" As she peers around the room at the mess I caused from the night before.

"I—am sorry. Had a little temper tantrum last night," not knowing what else to say. *'Hey Rosie, I came across these letters,'* doesn't seem to be a proper introduction to a stranger I just met. Besides, she isn't to whom the letter is addressed.

"Aww, my dear I am so sorry for your loss. It must be awful to have to be ripped from a life you had and plopped into a new one such as this." She looks me up and down, noticing I'm still in my nightgown. "I see you are not prepared for the day yet. I presume Nora brought you your uniform?"

"Yes, I put them away in the dresser last night."

"Is the room warm and cozy? Did Nora show you around yet?" Peering over my shoulder then around my room, she moves to my newly filled closet looking inside, then dips downward at the fireplace checking out the hearth. "Did she show you the wood store room?"

"Yes, and the washroom." I nodded. I don't want to let on about the encounter in the next corridor.

"Ah, well, that's good. I worry about her. She can appear a bit odd to strangers." Then she pulls a silver lighter from her pocket. "I brought you this my dear. Might help on these cold nights ahead." Handing me the small object, I exam it, noticing it's much like the necklace I wear.

It has the same carved dragon and it wraps from one side of the heirloom to the other with its mouth flicking out a flame when open. Instinctively, I motion my hand to the hidden jewel beneath my nightgown.

"It was your mother's, dear," Rosie adds, smiling, with a look of sadness in her eyes. "Passed down from her mother, and so on. Dating back to early 1800's."

"It's so beautiful. The dragon on the front reminds me of something."

"Well, it should. It's your family symbol."

"My family's symbol? I thought it's the sword?"

"Yes, indeed you are a Storm after all. Now, there will be more time to explain it all later." Moyer has strict instructions that you're to be introduced to staff today.

"Scoot and get dressed. We mustn't be late," she says, stepping back out into the hall.

"Yes, ma'am. Do I wear the uniform?" I ask.

"No need today my dear. You're going on a tour. But perhaps wear the school blazer. It should be hanging in the closet. This way you're recognized by curious minds of others you may pass."

I dress as quickly as I can. Remembering that I stuck the letter in my robe, I grab it, and stuff it in the pocket of my jeans. I don't want to take a chance in leaving it in my room, where someone can go snooping around. Glancing at the mess of books, still not cleaned up, I leave and meet Rosie, out in the hall.

"Does the jacket fit, dear?"

"Yes." I nod.

"Very well, then. Follow me. Keeping Madame Moyer waiting will send us both to the basement."

"Basement? You mean the chambers' below?"

"Yes, have you been told of stories already?" Rosie sounds restless.

"Oh, no, it was brought up in passing by Nora. She wouldn't elaborate and quickly changed the subject."

"Interesting ..." She hesitates a moment as if trying to find the right words to explain. "If you're caught not following the rules... some people have been sent to the lashing chamber's below—"

"Or turned to stone?" I interrupt.

I think I took Rosie by surprise. "My dear whoever told you that?"

"Nora stated, to stay away from Daniel."

"Well, she's right. Not sure how he does it, but he can put one in a trance, if given enough time, turning them to mere granite like you see on kitchen counters these days."

"Rosie, that's horrible! And people are whipped too?"

She nods. "Tied by their wrists, arms over their heads, and hung by the ceiling, stripped to the skin and whipped. Sometimes I think being turned to stone is the better punishment. I don't know how else to explain it to you, dear."

I follow her through the halls, showing me along the way the different doors, and for what and whom they all represent, until finally we reach the back stairs leading downward to the foyer. She stops on the mid steps. "I strongly recommend that you learn the rules very quickly, Wynter. This is not a safe place for someone such as yourself. There are hidden secrets..."

"You mean ghosts?"

"Heavens no," she chuckles. "If only, it was that easy... no, my dear, terrible things happen here. Please, I warn you, whatever you do, do not ever go out within these halls at night after nine pm. If you are caught...well, let's say you would be wishing ten lashings as your only punishment."

"If only she knew," I think to myself.

As we walk the corridor to the kitchen, Rosie comments about rules and gossip, including the library being open daily until five, and the one place I most want to be.

"Come, Wynter, I'll introduce you to Stella and the others. You probably have many questions as to why you're here. I wish I had all the answers, but sadly I do not. I'm so sorry to hear of your father's untimely death, and your Aunt Fran's."

"Thank you," I say, trying to ignore my feelings, as the pain of losing them both is still fresh. I try to concentrate on Rosie's chatter rather than memories.

She must have seen my sorrowful face. "Ah dear, there, there," she says, hugging my shoulders before we enter the kitchen. "Time will heal your pain. We will drop the subject." Squeezing me tight like a grandmother would. "I see it causes you too much discomfort. We mustn't let *her* know how you feel. People gossip. The tears you shed will get back to Madame Moyer, and she will see this as a weakness using it against you. Be strong, be brave; never show her your fear, as she feeds on it." Taking a kerchief from her pocket, she wipes tears from my eyes.

"Ok." Grabbing both my shoulders and looking straight into my eyes, she says, "Ready?"

"Ready." Nodding with a smile and sucking in a huge breath. And as if our conversation never happened, she swiftly opens the kitchen door.

10

A New Friend

Maids chat and giggle among themselves, while peeling vegetables around a large kitchen island. I recognize one of them as Nora.

"Ladies, I would like you to meet, Wynter Storm. She will be staying with us for a while," Rosie interrupts.

"More like indefinitely," I hear one maid from the table say, not making eye contact looking down at the vegetables she's peeling. She gives a brief glance in my direction, enough for me to see her amber eyes. The smirk on her face tells me she is not amused in Rosie's introduction.

"I met her last night, Victoria," Nora exclaims. "She's not all that bad." They talk among themselves as if I'm not standing there listening.

"Come now, girls. Be pleasant," Rosie says. "She is after all a Storm. Give Wynter the courtesy she's entitled." Then Rosie glances around the kitchen, saying, "I don't see Stella. Has anyone seen her?"

"We haven't seen her all morning," Nora answers.

"No bother. It's Sunday after all." Rosie smiles, and with the gesture of her hand, says, "Carry on, ladies. Wynter, this way." And I follow her through the kitchen to a pantry.

"During your stay, you will be partnered with Stella. She's younger than you, but don't let that fool your opinion of her. She's very smart; an old soul in a little girl's body. Stella's team-up partner had an unfortunate accident a little while back. She will be happy to have another again," Rosie says.

"Accident? What happened?" I ask, afraid of receiving an answer.

"Oh, never mind my dear, it's nothing you need to worry about. Just a little misunderstanding between she and Madame Moyer." Rosie gives me a look as if to imply that's a good enough response, dropping the subject entirely.

We go by a room, filled with white towels, linens and folded uniforms. Through the next door a small girl, maybe thirteen, prepares a cleaning cart. I hear her humming a beautiful melody. Sounding much like a lullaby. Her back is to us, so she doesn't hear anyone walk in. The room is small, with shelves of cleaning supplies and cleaning rags in bins. A wash sink next to a laundry hamper, is filled with water, with what appears to contain dirty rags.

"Good morning Stella," Rosie says, startling her from humming. "This is Wynter Storm. Please show her around. She will be working with you during the week."

Stella looks towards me and nods. "Yes, ma'am, thank you ma'am. I will do my best." She has a timid aura about her, and she seems to have a surprising look on her face.

It seems whenever my last name is thrown into the mix, people's demeanors change. It's written all over their body language.

"I'll be back after lunch. Will you please show Wynter around, Stella?" Rosie instructs. "She arrived last night and hasn't gotten a tour."

Stella nods. "Yes, ma'am. She's in good hands."

We both watch Rosie leave the washing quarters, hearing her steps echo through the back hall.

"I'll show you our daily duties," Stella begins, pointing to the clipboard hanging on the door opposite to where she's standing. Then says, "This is where we keep our list. I'm preparing this cart, for tomorrow. It cuts my time down in the morning."

I half smile, not knowing what to think. Wondering if this is what I'll be doing from now on. Earning my keep, so to speak.

"Come help me, will you? It might be faster if two people stock this trolley. Since we are going to be partner's and all," she says grinning. Nodding to the clipboard on the door. "I already have that list memorized."

As she tucks soaps and other essentials in the drawers, she questions, "So, you're a Storm?"

"That's right. Guess the secrets out," I say trying to act funny, in a not so funny situation.

"Storms don't do maid work, yet, here you are."

"What do you mean?"

Stella grabs the cart and pulls it to what looks to be an elevator. "I mean, you're a Storm. *She* has you doing maids work. All the Storms around here have other jobs."

"Like, what do they do?" I figure this is my opportunity to get as much information about this place as possible.

"Well, Miss Blair, and Mr. Derek are our teachers. Sir Daniel is the butler. Chad is the second in command. He takes care of matters when Madame Moyer is gone. Then there are Cory and Cole, the twins."

"The twins?"

She giggles at me. "Cory oversees the library duties, and then there's Cole. He roams the halls and monitors inside and outside the compound. We call him the ticket wizard."

"Ticket wizard?" I snicker at the name.

"Yes, because he's a wizard at giving out tickets. Cole writes down a violation, for those who are caught breaking the rules and then we are forced to report to Madame Moyer. Sometimes, he doesn't play fair. If someone makes him mad, he will make up allegations, and frame you, making it look like you broke a rule, when you didn't."

"How disheartening. So, he's like a security guard?"

"Yes. With a whole team that are assigned areas to monitor, under his command. Nora is one of them. Have you met her yet?"

"In a matter of speaking yes," I reply.

It all makes sense now. That's probably why she caught me in the next hall over, from my room.

"Interesting," she says. "Usually Nora is one of the last people you would meet." I watch Stella shove the cart next to the boxed elevator compartment. "There, it's all set to go for tomorrow. This is where you will meet me in the morning."

"Do I dress in uniform like you?"

"Oh yes, you don't want to get your school clothes dirty. What I do is slip my cleaning uniform over my school outfit, do the morning chores, then I slip off the maid attire, throwing it in the hamper behind you to be washed," she says. "Follow me, I'll show you around. You're probably hungry."

Stella shows me the dining room where I see children sitting around tables, chatting amongst themselves, eating breakfast. "On the weekends, during breakfast and lunch a buffet is set up front and we select what we would like to eat. It's the only time we have the freedom to sit where we want. Most of the time we are assigned seating." Then Stella points to a table up ahead off to a corner near the front of the room. "That table over there is your seating area. You will sit there tonight during dinner."

"It looks like a table for one," I reply.

"Oh, it is. Rosie said she has it under strict instruction from Madame Moyer that you're to have your own space."

"Is that normal? Why am I to have a table of my own?"

Stella shrugs her shoulder, as if she doesn't want to answer. "It's what has been requested. We don't question the authority of Madame Moyers instructions."

I line up behind Stella following her lead and begin to plate my food at the buffet. Breakfast sandwiches lay across the table along with bananas, oranges and apples. Pitchers of water are set on either side of the spread along with empty glasses. I'm so hungry, that I instantly grab some fruit and start eating, before Stella even has a chance to finish plating her food.

"I guess someone's a little hungry?" Stella snickers as she moves the water pitcher towards me.

"Sorry, just a little," I say with a mouth full of food. "Haven't really eaten in the last couple of days. On the car ride here, I had a snack. Nothing like this, though."

Stella shakes her head at me and says, "You're a nut." She pauses, as if wanting to say more.

"So, how long have you been here?" I ask, trying to strike conversation.

"About five years." I can tell I struck a nerve with her, and not sure whether to press the subject, however Stella volunteered more information, so I listen intently to her story. "My parents died in a train accident. It took me a long time to get through the pain. Blair found me and brought me here."

"I'm sorry. My dad and Aunt died in a car crash. Seems I am officially an orphan now, like you."

"Ah, I get it now," Stella begins, sounding like a light bulb went on. "The maids you see around here, are all orphans. Once you are twelve, Madame Moyer puts you to work. She figures if you haven't been adopted by then, you won't be."

"But I'm her granddaughter."

"I don't think that matters. She still sees you without parents and can do to you as she sees fit."

Emotions begin to swell as I allow my mind to wander around the room. "My new home," I say in a sarcastic tone.

Perhaps my voice carries too far, and I notice glances towards me, followed by whispering. Giggling stares bounced back at the far end of the table.

Stella took the hint. "Hey, you want to get out of here?" With an apple in her hand, she doesn't wait for my response, and grabs my hand, taking me to a bench outside the kitchen in the foyer area.

She fills me in on more gossip and what to expect come Monday. Apparently, Madame Moyer has a strict rule that all students dress in uniform attire.

Stella begins, "Madame Moyer insists that each child have an education, otherwise we would not be adoptable should the opportunity arise. Occasionally a party is held, a few times a year, but they are not your standard run of the mill parties. She invites people from all over the world. With hors d'oeuvres, dinner and cocktails. Always a black-tie event. Then all the guests go to the theatre room, where the grand occasion takes place."

"What kind of occasions?" I ask, thinking this might be what Chad warned me about yesterday evening.

"The kind that make for great gossip and future stories to tell others," she giggles.

Suddenly I remember the room that is filled with books. "Chad mentioned there's a library?"

"Um, yes. Do you like to read?"

Making hand gestures to implement a movie camera, I say, "I do. Nothing more exciting than watching a movie play out in your head, don't you agree?"

I look at her, to see wide eyes staring back at me, as she smiles at my emotional theatrics.

"Do you not like to read, Stella?"

"No, but I like bugs." Raising her eyebrows, face filling with excitement like a kid opening presents, exclaims, "I would rather be outside exploring the woods, looking for worms, bugs and strange undiscovered creatures."

"Um eww." Wrinkling my nose and shivering at the thought of creepy crawlers on me, I ask, "So, do you explore the woods often?"

"No, not exactly. We are only allowed to venture to the courtyard. The woods are off limits most of the time. Although Miss Blair, takes us on nature walks now and then, for a science credit."

"Miss Blair?"

"Our math and science teacher, of course. You will meet her tomorrow too, I'm sure."

'I already have,' I say to myself. "Tell me about school, Stella. Chad mentioned that all the children are homeschooled."

"Well, yes. Can you imagine if all of us hundred or more orphans went to a public school?"

"A hundred?"

Stella laughs at my remark. "A hundred and five, I think...plus one, on Monday," she adds, with a smile.

"I see, and these children are of all ages I suppose?"

"Indeed. We have the kids split in two groups. Children under eleven in one group, twelve and up in another," as she finishes the apple, she crunches on. "Here you will find everything you would in a small town. A movie theatre, store, gym, snack shop, even an ice cream parlor."

"Sounds like Madame Moyer has thought of everything."

Stella ignores my remark. "On Sunday afternoon's the younger kids have reading time and the older kids usually play in the gym. Some venture out and find other activities of course, but during the school week we start early at nine and end at four, leaving Friday as chore day. The older ones, like us, have daily chores before school."

I watch with fervor as she tells her story with such detail. I feel like, *'Have a question? Ask Stella.'*

"If we get our list done early, we have the weekend to do what we please." Stella takes one last bite of her apple, then continues, "Bottom floor of the south wing is entirely made for the children."

Stella laughs and grabs my hand, pulling me to my feet. "Come, I'll show you," she says, trashing the apple core.

I begin to follow, and ask, "Where are we going?"

"To the south wing silly. You don't want to be lost tomorrow, do you?"

We creep down a hallway, where Stella gestures with her finger to be quiet. Stopping at the first door she points to the window for a peep where I find young students sitting at their desks reading quietly. In the back corner of the room a woman looks up from her seat and I immediately recognize her as Blair. Going sheet white, I back away from view in hopes she doesn't see me. Giving a stare at Stella, she knows I want to say something, but we remain quiet. Walking further down the hall, we pass four more doors until we reach the end, opening to a large gym. I see balls bouncing and children laughing, playing as if no one watches them. I hear a whistle blow as all the kids begin to scamper together and get in line.

"It's their snack time," Stella says as we continue observing silently, but for some eerie reason, I feel like we were not supposed to be in this area.

Pulling on Stella's shoulder, I urge us to go. She watches intently as teenage boys play basketball at the other end of the gym; away from the younger ones who lined up.

"Let's go," I whisper, pulling her hand this time. I lose my grip and fall backwards, but instead of hitting the floor I fall into something soft and plush. I turn to see Blair staring back at me. "Having fun, are we ladies?" she smirks.

Well, that got Stella's attention, cringing as she turns around. "Miss Blair," she says.

"Another one of Stella's mischievous moves I suppose," Blair says clinching her mouth. "What shall we do with you?"

"No, Miss Blair. Please, I was showing Wynter around, so she isn't completely lost come Monday." Stella looks terrified. Like she is about to lose all sensibility.

"It's my fault Blair. I asked her about school and where to go." A white lie never hurt right? "Blame me, not her."

"Nice try, Wynter. You fail to see one small point," her eyes beginning to glow. "She knows better." And as if my words don't mean a thing, Blair grabs Stella by the front of her clothes, looking directly in her eyes saying, "You will forget that you were ever in this hallway today. You will take Wynter to the library, then you will wait in your room and not leave until I release you. Do you understand?"

Stella's eyes transfix on Blair, repeating her word for word. I can't believe what I'm seeing. I mean I suspected Dad did something like this to Rory, but he was at least discreet about it. It's so crazy that my brain can't keep up with rationalization. Wanting to shout to the roof tops with anger, my confusion, and overwhelming assessment of what's happening right in front of me, I cry out, "What did you do to her?"

"Nothing. Nothing at all, I merely made her forget a smidgen of memory." Blair looks at me as if to dare challenge her. "What do you think will happen if Moyer sees you here?" She points behind me. "See that door? It leads to the basement. I did this for your protection. Since I can't compel you, you will have to keep your mouth shut and hope Moyer will not catch onto your little field trip today."

She smiles a wicked grin. "Stella, on the other hand, has no choice. She isn't protected like you are. Moyer will read her thoughts and know you were with her."

"So, wait. Are you saying Madame Moyer can read minds?"

"Most of the people here, yes, but not all." She stares at me a minute, as if to imply Moyer can read mine. "No, she can't read your thoughts." Then she focuses on the chain around my neck, giving me a hint that she knows, what I wear.

"Remember those secrets you want to know so much about, Wynter...? This is a drop in the bucket. Please tread lightly."

I glance at Stella, looking onward, as if she is a statue of flesh and bone.

"Who am I?" I ask aloud, realizing that I too may have the same powers as the others.

"You will soon find out, but now is not the moment to discuss this."

"Is she going to be ok? Her mind seems absent. Like you scrambled her brain or something."

Blair scoffs, "Oh, Wynter you have much to learn about this family." Pausing to look at the girl in a daze. "She will be fine, her stagger will wear off in about three more minutes, so you might want to get her out of here. I don't care to have to repeat my pacifying words to her again." Stiffening her stance, she barks, "Now, scoot."

'Who's guiding whom?' I think to myself, taking Stella's hand and walking back to the foyer.

I sit Stella back on the bench outside the kitchen where we were earlier and wait for the real Stella to come back to reality.

Seconds later she says, "Where is my apple?" I watch as Stella gets off the bench and checks if it dropped to the floor.

"You threw it away, remember?" I answer, trying to play the part as best I can.

"Ah, yes that's right," she says. "Perhaps I should show you the library and what it has to offer to a bookworm such as yourself," and grabs my hand, pulling me to my feet as déjà vu sets in.

11

Library Encounter

A few minutes later we find the doors leading into the library wide open. The room is a grand and magnificent sight. Before me, books galore, from floor to ceiling, with every spine labeled. In the center is a card catalog station, with tables and chairs surrounding it. Along one wall, study desks sit against stained glass windows, while off to one corner at the other end of the library, two plush chairs are placed in a cove. The opposites side of that, is a large desk attached to a counter, in front of a locked iron door. Stairs in the back lead to a loft, housing more books. It's there that I see a few people engrossed in reading.

"Stella, it's like looking at a slice of heaven."

She covers her mouth and giggles. "I guess I'll leave you now." Stepping backwards out the door. "I see that you two need a moment, to bond," laughing at her silly remark. "Besides, I should head to my room."

"Okay," I say, eyes, still bulging from my head. "I'll see you later, thank you."

A fireplace is set off to the far left, giving warmth to the already cozy feel. I'm ready to find a book, that will take me away from this place, if only for a brief time. Thumbing through the classics, I find something to read, *"Perfect,"* whispering under my breath and making my way to the two plush chairs in the cove.

About the time I'm through the first few pages I see *him* walk in. A tall good-looking, teenage boy with white blonde hair much like my dad's. Having a glide in his walk, he makes his way to a corner bookcase. My eyes sneak glances, as he looks intently at the section. His beautiful features catch me by surprise. I mean, there were cute boys at my former school, but not as good looking as *him*. So as not to be caught as a voyeur, an occasional look back at my book, becomes a temporary practice. Now, of course I haven't the pleasure to look into his eyes yet, but, if by the pure chance I do, well I will gladly give up being compelled by him any day.

I watch as his finger trails along the shelf studying each spine. His infrequent grabbing of a book, reading the back then flipping to a page inside becomes a ritual; with every book, ending up sliding back into place. Finally, one speaks to him as he reads one page, then another, before shutting the book, and turning my way. There, he stops dead in his tracks, staring directly at me and I see a lopsided smile appear from the corner of his mouth.

Quickly I scan back to my book, hoping he doesn't notice my rogue glances. I feel his eyes study me. A sensation of butterflies coats my stomach. The sway in his stride, as he approaches, melts me to the chair. *'Where are the sunglasses when one needs them,'* I think to myself?

As he gaits closer and closer with ease, my heart pounds harder and harder. I feel my cheeks begin to flush. *'Okay, Wynter,'* I think, *'stay cool.' He sees an empty chair, that's all.'* What am I thinking? There are all kinds of places to sit. Why does he have to come my direction? I aim my book closer to my face as if to send signals I'm reading.

I can hear his movement getting closer, until he stops right before me. "Hello," he says politely.

Ignoring the fact that I'm intently reading my book, upside down, I pretend not to notice him, as I look up. My tongue apparently at a loss for words, I charmingly nod in response. He is even more gorgeous than at first glance, and now I have the full pleasure of looking at his features. How is it possible that someone like him can look so good?

My silence must have been a clue. "Pardon me. I'm Cory. You must be Wynter Storm," he says, smiling, offering a hand shake. His formal introduction makes me blush.

"Hi," I reply, half getting up to welcome his hand gesture, while feeling my knees buckle beneath me.

"No, please sit. May I?" he asks, signaling to the chair next to me.

A gentleman to add to beauty. "Yes, please sit," and I settle back in my chair, half glancing at my book trying hard not to stare at his beautiful face.

"Do you…ah…always read upside down?" he asks sounding confused.

Noticing that I'm a complete idiot, I move the book right side up, "No…um… I'm studying how the words look different." *'Is that the excuse I just gave him? Really Wynter? Come on girl you can do better than that,'* I think to myself.

"Good read," he says. "Do you like the author?"

"Yeah, she's not bad - it's my second time reading the book," I say, trying to avoid eye contact. I know, if I give into his gaze I would be toast instantaneously. Shoot me now and write love-sick on my forehead.

"Twice?" He smiles. "You like historical fiction? Have you read other classics?"

I raise the books from my selection of the three for him to see. He smiles.

"I guess that's a yes," he says with a grin. "Looks like you enjoy reading. We just might get along," he laughs in jest.

'Get along?' My head burns at the thought of being friends. "Yes, it's a favorite pastime. Good book on a cold afternoon, snuggled someplace warm," I say, as I glance over toward the fireplace. "What about you, I see you like to read too?"

Then I mistakenly fix on his blue eyes forgetting the subject at hand. I remember Chads words, *'Do not make eye contact with anyone.'* Too late, put a fork in me, I'm done. The necklace clearly does not work on gorgeous young men. I bet all sort of female's collapse over him. He must know I'm blushing. My eyes lock on him, and although I try looking away, he keeps them there. A sweet sensation comes over me and I feel more at ease suddenly, like someone is taking my emotions and calming my fears. I can't quite explain it. I feel my heart start to slow, my flushing cheeks dissipate. Is he stealthily compelling me?

"So, when did you arrive?" he asks with a joyful chuckle, that suddenly broke the trance.

"What?" I question, still in a fixated daze.

He laughs louder, shaking his head. "When did you arrive to Storm River Manor?"

"Oh, ah…last night." I reply, taking a gulp of air, realizing I'm still staring at him. "I met Stella, and she guided me to here."

"Well, it's finally nice to put a face to the name Wynter. People have been frantically trying to prepare for your arrival. So glad I came in here today. There's an English class assignment due tomorrow. I'm really good at procrastination."

"Ah, and here I thought you came to read the classics." I smile, feeling way more at ease now, than a moment ago.

"They're ok, I prefer science fiction, horror, a little mystery is always good, too." He changes the subject, "So, have you been shown the place yet?"

"Not much. Chad showed me the community hall, and how to get to my room. Nora gave a great speech, as to what not to do, when she brought my uniform, and Rosie introduced me to some staff in the kitchen. However, Chad says you are the one to seek out for a tour."

"Yes, *'The Tour.'*" He laughs. "Well, where would you like to start? Seems the library and you, have already met," he jokes.

I shook my head at him, smiling. "Lead the way." Grabbing my books and getting up from the chair, we exit the reading room.

I see Madame Moyer talking with Rosie, along with Daniel and a man I don't recognize. He's tall and thin. Has white hair and a mustache, wearing a brown suit. He must have sensed our presence because he looks our way, smiles and does a small wave.

"Who's that?" I ask curiously.

"Hmm...?" Cory turns in the direction to view what I see, and says, "Oh, he's Mr. Derek." Tilting his chin as if to be discreet, adding, "our language arts teacher. You will meet him tomorrow. We call people by their first names, giving the appropriate title first. Seems everyone is a Storm," Cory says in a mocking tone. "See, over there…" glancing towards Daniel, "whom I presume you met yesterday? Sir Daniel is his proper title. He usually answers the door, takes coats, lugs suitcases, does much what a butler would do and is Madame Moyer's puppet."

"So, he's a knight, doing butler duties?" I ask raising more confusion.

Cory elevates one eyebrow, and cocks his head slightly, "In a matter of speaking, yes…sad really, he was once a great soldier. Rumors spread that he sired a bastard son. Now he sulks in the past."

"How miserable." And Mr. Derek, he's a Storm too?"

"Aye, that he is. Daniel and he are cousins. Also, a Sir. However, he wishes not to be associated with such a title until things change. You see, he doesn't quite agree with Madame Moyer's way of running the orphanage."

We walk further through the foyer and come upon many portraits on the wall stopping in front of a painting, with mesmerizing bright colors, of purple, pink, green and blues. "Beautiful, who is she?" I ask.

Cory blusters a grin. "Look closely, what do you see?"

"I don't know. Should I be looking for something?"

"You really don't know do you?"

"She looks like me in a way…I guess? Same color hair, same features. Very young, maybe sixteen? Her eyes are brown color. She's…" Then it hit me, "No, it can't be?" I back away a little.

Cory chuckles at my reaction, "Yes, Wynter, your grandmother Madame Moyer."

"What happened to such a beautiful girl?" I say in a soft tone.

"Evil is what happened," Cory says with repulsion. I know he saw my look of dismay. "She is not the same as she once was."

"Is there no humanity left in her at all?" I ask.

"Humanity?" Looking at me as if something horrific has come out of my mouth. "Heaven's no. There isn't a human bone left in that woman's body. I mean, she looks human enough." Then he whispers, "I have my suspicions she is not who she claims to be."

I want to change the subject, the thought of looking like Moyer as a young girl repulses me. "Can we go now?"

"Go? But to where?" in a muddle voice. Reminding me that we are standing on the grounds of a fortress.

I roll my eyes at him. "I mean move on. Next subject matter. Thinking of being related to such a revolting creature disgusts me."

"Ah, yes. Well, I presume it will be something to get used to," he says, as we step onward. "Can't change who you are Wynter, only what you become. I do believe in free will, however. People always have a choice, no matter how dire things may get."

"And if they make the wrong choice?" I ask.

"Well, of course they must live with it, but it doesn't mean that they can't change the future. We may all be stuck here, in this evil forsaken place, but it's who we are on the inside that counts. Isn't that what it boils down to?"

"Wow, Cory. Is speech class in the curriculum?" I say in a teasing tone.

"Ha! Well, if the spiel works, I would say I accomplished my goal," he taunts.

We roam to another set of French doors, where Cory takes me inside a now empty movie theatre with a hundred seats or more. He smiles, knowing full well I'm in awe. Red plush velvet seats cascade upward toward the back wall. Corner balconies sit on either side of the grand cinema, allowing for an audience to peer out from the alcove above, for a better view.

"The screen shares the stage, turning this place in a theatre playhouse should Madame Moyer choose to do so. Most of the time it's only for movies shown over the weekend. It will be filled with many kids of all ages come Friday. One of many sources of entertainment."

"Entertainment?" I question, reminding me of the other activities this place has to offer, from remarks Stella made earlier.

"We do, in fact have a mall, if you will. You might find it odd, but when one is not allowed to leave, there are limited resources available. One receives points which are traded for tokens every Friday."

"You mean like play money?"

Cory nods. "Mmm, in a manner of speaking, yes, but quite real within the realms of here." Gesturing with his hands, to follow back out to the foyer, he says, "You see, everything bought from the outside world is resold in here. There is a dress shop, grocery store, or rather a mini store, filled with snacks, a supply shop, even an ice cream parlor, believe it or not."

"Stella mentioned there's a place such as that."

Cory snickers. "See for yourself," he says, opening the next door. Inside sits kids of all ages, mostly teenagers, at tables talking and sipping on soda, or reading.

'Finally, civilization,' I think. *'So, this is the hang out spot.'*

"Would you like something?" he asks as we approach the counter.

"No, thank you," I reply, shaking my head.

"You sure? Because I am ready for a root beer float," he says, as I watch him work the pocket of his jeans to get out his wallet. "Seriously my treat."

"Ok, a vanilla shake please." I say to the lady who waits behind the counter.

"You heard her," Cory says, talking to the clerk. "And I'll have my usual please, Gloria. Thank you."

Pulling out his *'fake'* money, I smile. "Unbelievable."

He smirks back, as if to agree, but doesn't say anything.

Once our beverages are ready, we take a seat in the back of the parlor. Candy colored pink and white stripes decorate walls, while a black and white checker design covers the floor, giving one the feel of being in a 1950's diner.

"So, tell me," I begin, as I take my first sip of sweet vanilla, "Stella says you're a twin?"

I think I took him by surprise, for he pauses a few seconds before answering, "Indeed I am. Stella has quite a mouth on her, doesn't she?" Adding nothing else he takes a drink from his float, prompting me to ask another question.

"What's your brother's name?"

"Cole." And he takes another sip.

"Are you identical?"

"Yes." And as before, takes yet another swig.

I give him a raised eyebrow, and he clearly knows I want more than one-word answers. At the rate this is going, it'll be a game of twenty questions.

He sighs, looking around as if to imply the place we are at is not an ideal spot for this type of conversation. Then he leans forward in a light whisper, barely enough for me to hear. "We don't talk about him. At least not here, where eyes and ears are observing; too dangerous." Sitting straight, back in his chair, looking at me intently with a pursed smile he probes, "So, how's your vanilla shake?"

"Good." I nod.

"Good." He smiles folding his arms and glaring at me with slanting brows, that emphasize concern.

I can tell I've struck a nerve, and it intrigues me to know more. Obviously pressing the issue wouldn't get me anywhere right now.

We finish our drinks and go back to walking the estate. Cory shows me the grand ballroom where Madame Moyer holds two dances a year. Guests from all over come to enjoy the celebrations. Hard to believe such a callous person can throw such elaborate, lavish parties. We continue onward roaming the halls and rooms throughout the castle.

We pass through the hall where classes are held during the week, making our way to the gym at the end of the wing, giving me a slight memory of earlier this morning. This time the courts are vacant. At the other end of the gymnasium, he shows me the entrance to an indoor pool and Jacuzzi where many people often stay to pass the time.

"Perhaps when it stops snowing, I can show you the grounds outside as well."

Being up close I can tell Cory has a good physique. The muscles mold to his clothes. Even his smile sparks pearly whites. As the hours pass, it becomes easier to be around him without having my knees quake beneath me. If I avoid his eyes, I'm good, however his face continues to give me the butterflies.

"Wynter, I'm a bit confused. May I ask you a personal question?"

"Sure, I guess so."

"Has no one ever told you, about your true family line?"

"Told me what?"

Cory pauses, as if to try to find the right words.

"Cory, just say it. What's the question?"

He glances at me, pulling from his concentration. "Wynter, I'm curious, what exactly do you know about your mother?"

"Oh, um. Wow...um, let's see. Well, according to my dad, Moyer wanted me behind these walls. He was planning to tell me more about my true past, but he and Aunt Fran died before I found anything out."

"So, you know nothing? You have no idea about this place existing at all?"

"Know what exactly? I mean I have witnessed strange things..."

"Like?" he coaxes.

Trying to find the words, "Well, for example... I don't feel any pain from the car accident and I swear I broke my leg. Aunt Fran has this... rather... 'had' this ability to heal. Dad told me he could see the future..."

"Interesting. Have you ever thought that perhaps you did break your leg and it healed?"

"Yes, of course. Clearly it did." I think I would have been more alarmed by my healed knee, if I hadn't witnessed the healing proof Fran showed me the other day at the kitchen table.

"If you would have asked me this question last week, I would insist you have your head checked, but now, I'm not so sure. Earlier I saw Blair compel Stella before my eyes. Cory, she was completely under Blair's control. Nothing is beginning to phase me anymore."

Opening yet another door, as we walk and talk. "Yes, the compelling phenomenon," he says, grinning at me. "That must have been a real eye opener."

"It's not funny, Cory. What's going on? I mean, I'm starting to believe I'm in an alternate reality or something."

"It's not something I can explain to you, and poof you know everything. Time will tell, once you have been here a while."

"That's it? That's all you have to say?" I ask, looking at him.

"It's hard for me to explain it all to you now, but perhaps I might be able to help next weekend? There is a garden."

"You mean, Sara's Garden?" I ask.

"Yes, how do you know?"

"Chad told me briefly about it as we passed it on our way down the driveway."

"Ah, I see, well, I'm sure we'll have a chance soon. But it must be discreet, because if Moyer finds out I've shown you, she will flip."

We trailed back to one side of the house and to the other, showing me more halls, and doors.

"This place is an utter maze," I say to him.

All he does is smile. Finally walking back into the foyer, he says, "The front bedrooms, above either balcony is for guests that visit Madame Moyer and her lavish parties. I'm sure we will have one soon, as you are the new prize, she has recovered."

"Recovered? Sounds so possessive, like I'm property or something."

Tipping his head to the side, he says, "Mmm. In a matter of speaking you are."

"What's that supposed to mean?"

"You are family, and she keeps her household under lock and key…if you haven't noticed?"

Cory looks at his watch. "It's close to five, I can't believe the time has gone so fast, dinner is in an hour. We'd better not be late. We can finish this conversation later, I suppose," and he walks me to the end of the corridor, leading to my living quarters, and says goodbye.

When I come to the entrance of my room a note is tacked to the door reading: *Eyes are watching; ears are listening.*

Is this supposed to scare me? First person coming to mind is Moyer. I grab the note crumbling it in my hand and enter my bedroom.

12

Redmae

Because it's dark already, it takes me a moment to search for the light switch by the door. It's pitch black and not even the light from the moon sheds any help. After a few seconds, I reach the lever, and to my surprise the room doesn't show much brightness from the bulb. However, in the corner near my dresser I see a shadow move. I realize then, I'm not alone.

"Who's there?" I ask. Peering into the shadowed corner.

Stepping out from within the darkness, "Come with me Wynter, I want to show you something."

It's evil herself and I can see she has on a black hooded cape, as she moves away from the shaded wall into the moonlight, holding a lantern in her hand. She lights it with a match, bringing the dark room into an auburn hue.

My perplexing expression must have shown through, for she smiles with a grim satisfaction on her face. She seems to gloat in the fact that I'm feeling unsure of where we are going.

Seeing she wore a warm garment over her clothes I clue in, and grab my coat hanging in the closet and put it on.

Closing the door behind me I follow her down the hall corridor through the mahogany French doors at the end of the hall; going the exact route I came yesterday.

She guides me through the dark castle with an oil lamp held in her hand. As the days become shorter, night falls earlier in the evening. We make our way out in the frigid cold to a barn nestled not far from the manor, where horses are found in stalls, and a few mooing cows are eating hay.

"As you can see," she finally says, "this is our stable, or barn as modern folks call it. Casey, our stable boy, takes care of the place quite nicely, don't you think?" She lights another lantern near the barn door entrance before we go inside.

I give her a blank stare, wondering why she brought me here, thinking to myself, *'Casey? The errand boy Nora talked about?'*

Inside, the chickens roam free, clucking, and many Dutch doors are half open revealing all types of animals, such as horses, cows, goats and sheep. The barn is larger than any I have ever seen. A mansion size barn to go with the mansion size house, I suppose.

I hear a loud thud come from behind, startling me to move aside. The banging grows louder and louder as muffling sounds behind a door intensify. The more I ignore it, the noisier it becomes. Moyer grins from my anxiety.

"Yes, do stand back. They're anxious to hunt."

"They?" I ask. Feeling uneasy, as the pounding continues, and snarls escalate.

"The pack of dogs of course." She smiles, like a proud mama about to introduce her children. Then she releases the latch, expressing evil joy, "They guard the grounds at night, to keep outsiders, out, and insiders in." And before I have a chance to blink, five wolves dart out of their cell, knocking me to the ground. They circle around me, and the heat from their breath burns my neck as drool falls from their mouths. The dogs saliva pierces holes through my jacket; burning my skin like acid on metal. Razor sharp canine teeth appear, all of them snapping at me, as if to taunt my fear. The burning I feel from my skin, searing beneath my coat sleeve, is temporarily forgotten from the sheer horror that I'm about to be eaten.

"Avoid the eyes," I hear the voice say in my head. *"The necklace does not protect you against the dire wolves."*

I have nowhere to go but backwards. Scooting myself up against the wall behind me, I look away. A paw pins my leg, preventing me from moving. I try to scream but nothing comes out.

One dog lunges forward and I brace for impact, putting my arm up over my face for protection, terrified my life is over. I'm not going to let her see me cry, so I cover my face and wait for them to take their first meal of the evening.

"Redmae!" A male's voice behind the gang of dogs, yells firm, "Stand down!"

Immediately the mongrels release their defensive stance, sit up and stare at me, no longer growling.

"Madame Moyer, what are you doing?" He snaps his fingers. "Redmae, come." And the beast moves to his side with the others following behind. "Go outside." And flinging his arm in command he points to the entrance of the barn. Before I have a chance to catch a breath, they are gone into the darkness.

"Oh, Casey, I didn't harm them. They saw food is all, I merely tried to feed them," Moyer says in a demonic tone of voice.

His glare gives a different account, "By serving her to them? Have you gone completely mad?"

'Of course, she has, isn't it obvious,' I think to myself. Thankful neither of them can read my mind.

"Relax. Wynter, must understand what can happen to those who roam the grounds at night," she implies, smirking a glare directly towards me. "I think she gets the point."

The mysterious looking man comes in my direction, towering over me like a giant and says, "Hi, I'm Casey, also known to folks around here as the errand boy. I live in this barn with my animal friends. They haven't seen people in a while." He extends a gesture of help. "Please accept my apologies from Redmae, she's not used to seeing anyone but Moyer or me."

I graciously take his hand, as he pulls me from the ground. "Thank you," I stutter, wiping the dirt from my clothes, trying not to stare at his peculiar features.

"You must be Wynter, I'd recognize that face anywhere," he says with a gruff tone, but a mild pitch.

Casey's face is askew, with his forehead jutting down over a 'hog like' nose. He has a lopsided diagonal grin and when he speaks, only one side of his mouth moves, appearing that he may have had a brain injury at one point.

"Enough of this," Madame Moyer shouts, slapping her wand against her garment. "We must go and leave you to the livestock." I can tell she's annoyed that her plan is foiled.

Casey bows, moving aside allowing me to pass, but not without his large body bumping against a trough full of oats and dumping it. Animals stampede towards the food, distracting from the moment as we leave the barn.

I follow Moyer back to the house, while hearing echoing howls in the darkness. "Perhaps the idea of leaving the grounds no longer exists in that little head of yours," she says whisking the back entrance open without the use of her hands. Before I can reply, she disappears, leaving me alone in the doorway.

The clanging of dishes can be heard in the room next to me, along with many voices. Aromas coming from the kitchen sent sensations through my nose, and my stomach begins to growl. Not knowing where to go at first, I make my way to the smell of food.

"There you are!" Blair, shouts in front of me. "Where have you been? Rosie came to escort you down to dinner to find your room empty. The house has been searching all over for you."

"Ask your mother, perhaps she will tell you," I assert, glaring at Blair. After what I witnessed moments ago, I have become numb from the glowers of this evil place. To give her credit, she does legitimately seem concerned.

"What did she do?" she asks, peering past my shoulders to the outside doors behind me. Her eyes become big, showing clear indication she knows where I've been. "Did she—"

"Take me to see Casey and his brood of pets?" I say cutting her off. "Why, yes Blair, she did. I've never been more terrified in all my life. What is this place? Some sort of hell hole you've brought me to?"

Stalking off to leave Blair stewing in her juices, I peer down at the hole in my coat, that the beast's saliva burned through; to see my arm already healed, with only a scar remaining. Another memory etched in my brain. Moyer is out for blood, I know it and I think Blair does too.

Blair must have found Chad. I see him strolling down the hallway with an angry look on his face. "Are you okay?"

"Yes, I'm fine. A little shaken up, but other than that, I'm alright."

"My apologies Wynter, I had no idea she would ever do something like this. Come with me and I'll have Doc look at you."

"I'm fine, really I am. See?" I protest, pulling up my sleeve to prove it.

He hesitates, before replying, "Did she bite you?"

"Who?"

"Redmae. Did she bite you anywhere? You must tell me."

His look of concern concerned me. I'm taken aback by his approaching questions and answer, "No Chad, she didn't bite me. Her saliva burnt my skin, and perhaps bruised my leg, but other than that, not a scratch." What is so detrimental, if I had been bitten, I thought? "Chad, what's wrong?"

"Nothing," he pauses, "Come with me."

We push open the French doors leading to the grand dining room full of kids talking among themselves.

"Let me show you to your seat. It's your first night having dinner here. People are going to question who you are. Rather, they already know, but an introduction is still in order," he states, as we make our way to the front of the dining room. A table is set off to one side already waiting for me. Chad gestures with an arm. "Here you go."

My blank stare prompted him to say, "Moyer requests you be sat apart from others, but near the rest of the Storm family. I look beyond his shoulders to see many faces I already identify along with others that I don't.

"They are going to make a big announcement before dinner. You're just in time," Chad says, quietly.

"What announcement—" and a chime of a glass rings through the atmosphere, interrupting Chad, working its way through the room to quiet all the voices. Chad removes himself and takes a seat at the other table while everyone begins to veer their heads to the front of the room. I notice Cory sitting at the same table, along with his twin. They are hard to tell apart, except the eyes. One showed kindness, while the other scowled. They both stared at me ignoring the attention bell.

"May I have your attention, please?" Daniel speaks, sounding like a nobleman for the first time. "Quiet voices, please." And as if it's her cue, Madame Moyer glides to the front of the tables.

The room becomes quiet as all eyes stare, as if waiting for her to speak. Daniel nods at her and takes his seat.

"As you know I will be leaving Wednesday for a week," she begins saying. "And while I am gone, Sir Chad will be in charge." She points in his direction, acknowledging him as he stands up giving a bow.

All the kids look around, filling the room with whispers. "Silence," she screams, skating in and out of each table as she speaks. "During this time, you will be courteous, listen, and obey him. When I return, I will be bringing guests back with me, from all over the world, to celebrate the return of our long-lost family member: Wynter Storm." She smiles wickedly, implying underlying plans behind her face. I can see right through it. "They will begin to arrive this coming weekend. See to it that you welcome them appropriately."

'She's gone completely mad,' I think to myself.

The voice inside my head rears its thoughts to me once more. *"Not entirely, Wynter.* Then the voice says, *"stand up, dear."*

I hesitate, *"Why?"*

"Just do it. Everyone is watching. Moyer just introduced you."

Moyer glowers at me, as I rise. "Children I would like to introduce to you, my granddaughter. You will give her respect, by not speaking to her, unless she speaks to you first. Is that clear?"

Huge gasps ring out, children scream, and panic shoots through the atmosphere.

"Silence," she shouts again, whipping her wand against her garment. "Is that clear?" This time her voice sounds more imperious.

"Yes, Madame Moyer," they all say together.

I glance around the room, surprised at all the new faces staring back at me, including Stella, who's grinning wide.

I can feel my body become warm as a cold brush of air crosses my skin, sending chills up my spine. It's as if I'm looking at a bunch of people who've been brainwashed. I feel a burning sensation run through my veins, yet I don't feel hot.

"Now that introductions are done, we can carry on," she cries out, twirling around, slithering back to the front. "Children please… calm yourselves!"

The excitement grows in the room and the children keep whispering in awe, even after Moyer shouted to be quiet. It's then I see a blue light scan across the room. Not realizing what it is at first, as the room becomes eerie silent, do I recognize then she has pacified everyone into a tranquil state of peace. As if all is forgotten. Like what Chad did to Nora, and Blair did to Stella.

Each orphan begins to pick up their fork, all eating in unison, comparable to robots being programmed. I begin to grasp the kind of hell I have been brought into. Now, I understand that the depths of the underworld do exist. It's right here, and Moyer is their queen.

Prompting my mind with ways to escape, I ponder how much time I really have. My birthday is in ten days. Why is this day so important to her? Thinking back, I remember the warning Dad and Fran told me. Is this what the necklace is for? To protect me from her?

"Yes," the voice answers. *"It's one of many reasons to never take it off."*

A slap on the table jolts me from my reverie, "Something wrong with the food?" She glares at me, like a cat does at prey. The other Storms seem to overlook her aggression. Periodic glances come from most of them. Except from one of the twins – he grins widely, watching with fervor.

Shaking my head, I take a bite of food, not expressing a sound from my lips. At this point no amount of words will encompass her injustice. The other children tabled in front of us fixate on their food, not talking, just silently eating with the occasional clanging of silverware on plates.

For the rest of the evening I sit there quietly trying to ignore any glances people make toward me. Blair announces the school schedule for the week, Chad announces the rewards kids did for the month of November, and Mr. Derek talks about the Christmas program.

Chad instructs Cory to walk me back to my room. When we come to my door, it's ajar with another note attached:

Eyes and ears are watching you.

13

Ransacked

Pushing the door open more, Cory and I stand in the threshold gazing around at the clutter before us. The place is ransacked. My clothes are scattered across the room along with the books I had yet to pick up. My mattress is on the floor, the sheets and blankets thrown in a corner. The place looks like a big hot mess.

"What in the world happened here?" Cory finally says. "It appears someone was looking for something." I think he saw the panicked look on my face, as the tears begin to well up, and fear take hold.

"Wynter, look at me."

"No." I shake my head. "I can't let you see me cry. I won't allow it."

"Nonsense," he says, turning me towards him and peering directly in my eyes. "You're going to be fine. We will get to the bottom of this, okay?"

Tears begin to fall down my cheeks. I don't know what to do, I can't even sit on my bed. *'Where's Charlie?'* And I begin hunting for him.

"Look under the mattress," Cory says, "perhaps he's there."

"Who?" I reply, as my mind tries to catch up with my thoughts, looking around at the disaster before us.

"Your rabbit. I mean that is what you are looking for, right?"

"H—how do you—"

He cuts me off, saying, "Here, let me help you." And begins assisting me, by picking up the mattress off the floor, where I find my stuffed animal, smashed.

A quick look over him, and to my relief he isn't torn. I hold him tight, for a few minutes, from the over-stimulating moment. "It's silly really, but he's the only thing I have left of my mother." Looking back over to Cory, I ask, "How did you know where he was?"

"I sort of have these gifts," he says. Seeming to shy away from my question, he fixes my bed frame. I watch him place back the sheets, pillow, and blanket. "There, good as new. No indication of any disruption." He smiles back at me.

"What?" he says, looking at me with a dumbfounded.

"You haven't answered my question. How did you know Charlie was under the mattress?"

His body language relaxes a bit, "Ok, promise me, you won't freak out?"

I roll my eyes at him. "As if I can't be more surprised than I am already?"

He laughs and bends down to pick up a few books that lay a bit too close to the fireplace. "I can read minds, but not in the way, you might think," he sighs.

"What do you mean?"

He hands me the literature, to put away. "You don't at all seem surprised by this."

I smile on the inside and turn away, to place the books on my nightstand, so he can't see any expression I may have, and say, "My dad could see the future, and my aunt Fran, the present. Your reading minds, doesn't exactly phase me." I get up and step over tossed clothes to grab more paperbacks and put them away on the shelf. "Isn't that kind of the same thing?"

"Sort of, but not exactly. When I concentrate on the person at hand, I can see what they see. I can't hear thoughts, but I can read pictures they see in their mind. Along with sensing emotions, allowing me to understand what they are saying."

"Well, that explains how you saw Charlie, I guess."

He walks to the fire and begins to crumble paper. "I can also calm one's soul."

"What do you mean? Like what Moyer does to those kids down there?" Beginning to feel upset. I work to push back the anger and pick up thrown clothing from the floor, folding it.

"No, no. Nothing like that." Grabbing a few pieces of kindling he stacks it on the hearth, over the pile of paper. "Do you have a lighter?"

"A what?" I say, diverting my thought process.

"You know, a flame thrower, to light the fireplace."

"Oh yeah, sorry." Pulling from my pocket I hand him the heirloom Rosie gave me.

"Nice," he says, holding the object in his hand, admiring the craftsmanship. "Where did you get this?"

"Apparently, it used to be my mother's. Rosie kept it safe until she had the opportunity to give it to me, I guess."

"It's beautiful." He uses it to light the fire and places the lighter on the mantel. "As I was saying; I can hear the pumping of heartbeats, much like what's coming from you. I can feel your anger, your confusion, and right now, your doubt about who I am."

I take a step back, not knowing what to think. Is he another one of Madame Moyer's experiments?

Cory flashes to my side before I can blink, staring into my eyes. "Do not be scared."

I feel the heart in my chest calming down and a mild warm sensation flutter through my veins. The anger, although still present doesn't want to jump out to claw someone any longer.

"To answer your question, no not exactly," he says. Releasing his hands from my shoulders.

"Wait what? I didn't say anything." Confused for a moment, by what he's implying.

"Your thoughts. I'm not one of Madame Moyer's experiments. But I was born into this maddening hell hole." He smiles. "You pictured Moyer, with scientific beakers in her hand. That's how I can read one's mind."

"I understand now," touching the necklace around my neck. "What is that, you do with your eyes? Calming emotions - isn't that mind control?"

He grins, saying, "I don't need to say anything. I merely think it and a person calms down. What Moyer does is different. She controls people with spells. Changes their thought processes into making choices different than what a person may have intended to do." He pauses a minute, grabbing a couple logs from the corner, placing in the fire. "I soothe people, but they never lose control of their minds."

"But isn't that pacification like what everyone else does around here?" To his credit, I feel more at ease and not in an angry panic. I think he saw the concern on my face, as I gaze at a blank body of air.

Standing up, he turns to me and I notice him looking at my neck. "Let me help you finish cleaning this place up," and he bends down to pick up more scattered books. "What were they looking for, do you suppose?"

"This, perhaps?" And I pull out the second letter, addressed: Cory, from my pocket, to hand to him.

With a concern on his face, I ask, "Cory, what's wrong?"

"Where did you get this?" he asks, taking the letter from my hand.

"I found it tucked away in a side pocket of my backpack. I'm not even sure how it got there, or even when."

"I don't understand," he turns the letter over and flips it around a couple times, before sliding a finger in the corner to open it.

I wonder if he is thinking the same thing I am right now. That life is about to change, and we're both connected.

"Wynter, I need to say something, first. No matter what happens, we are in this together. Deal?"

"Deal," I say back to him.

He fumbles a bit with his words, hesitating, like he's hiding something. Looking up at me, he smiles. "I guess here goes nothing… right?"

"Go on, open it." I coax, waiting impatiently for him to pull out the letter and read it.

He stands there a few minutes, as if stunned by what he's read, then begins to pace back and forth across the floor, with the letter still between his fingers, before sitting in the corner chair. Placing his hands over his forehead, he takes a deep breath. "I need ventilation in this tiny room, to process this. Would you mind?" he asks, pointing to the window.

I shift over to open the room up with fresh air; stepping over the scattered clothes and books that still remain on the floor. Cory's face gives way to worry, prompting me to ask, "Is everything okay, what is it?"

"Seems time is not on our side, after all. What exactly do you know about your past?" he asks in a calm but firm tone, stretching his arm out, handing me the letter.

"Nothing. I'm still trying to figure it all out. Why?" I question, glancing at him before taking the parchment and reading it.

"Because you are about to take a crash course in family history," he says, walking to the window next to me to breathe in the cold air. "Go on, read for yourself," he urges.

Cory,

If you are reading this, then the prophecy has begun. There is a hard task ahead, for you. Wynter is the key to putting an end to Sarmira once and for all.

You must find the others before the super blood moon rises, else all is lost. You know what to do. Cole is not gone forever to her grasp. Only you, can bring him back.

Memorize this riddle. Then burn this letter. Moyer and the others must not know, for if they do, all will be lost.

Behind the roses you will find…
Something hidden from behind…
There's a second one about, but not in soot...
It is, after all, under foot...
But before you go there look to the fire...
Hidden inside, a box you desire...

Jeoffrey

I look at Cory in puzzlement. No words can express the chaos flowing through my thoughts, as I read the letter over and over. It must have been fifty times or more. Each time, the same reaction. Bewilderment, anxiety, skepticism, and every other kind of emotion imaginable. Good thing I'm near the window, else I might have made a bigger mess from my queasy stomach. I hand the paper back to him.

"You must have many questions," Cory says, taking the letter from my hand. "Unfortunately, I only have some of your answers."

"Perhaps…" breathing in the cool air from outside, "…try from the beginning. Though, I do have one question that resonates with me, Cory. Why did Dad say, 'only you' can save Cole? What did he mean by that?"

Cory paces back to the chair and sits. "About a month before I turned eighteen, I found myself walking the grounds as I always do. Rather running the perimeter, I should say with my brother, Cole. You see, we were jogging buddies, something we used to do every day."

Cory seems to get lost in a memory and it's quiet for a few minutes. Only the splashes of the rain mixed with snow are heard, from outside.

"And then what happened?" I inquire, interrupting his thoughts.

"Hmmm? Oh yes, sorry. Where was I?"

"You were about to tell me, a story right before you turned eighteen?"

"Ah, yes. Only on this day, I veered off the path. I saw an image in the woods that distracted my attention. It was a ball of yellow light floating about, in the air."

Cory seems to get lost in more memories, as he acts out a conversation:

'What are you looking at, little brother?' I heard Cole say, to me.

'It's a bulb of light of some sort,' responding to him.'

"He proceeded to tell me to leave it alone and we should move on. Of course, I didn't listen; ignoring his gesture. Instead, I took off after it, losing Cole behind me. I ran so fast, I found myself at the river. I could hear my brother calling out, but I disregarded him, fixated on the image."

"What was it?" I probe, sitting down on the edge of my bed, as he continues his tale.

"A wisp of some sort. Like a ball of buzzing light, floating in the air making whisper sounds. It glowed so bright, I had to squint. Behind the wisp stood your father…"

"Wait, what?" The shocking tone in my voice must have hinted a sign of panic, because the next thing I know, Cory's calming me with his eyes again. I begin to feel tranquil vibrations flow through my veins.

"How do you do that?" I demand. "I mean I have seen Blair compel Stella, and Chad do it to Nora, neither of them could make any headway, yet here you are, able to do that to me?"

"I'm not compelling you. It's merely an aura to help you control emotions. It's the gift I received when I turned eighteen. Along with seeing other people's images in their head, like I mentioned before."

I watch Cory grin at me, as I can tell he sees me working out the puzzle in my mind. "So, you saw me picturing my father, and heard my heartbeat, and felt the panic of a revealed truth I wasn't sure about?"

"Precisely," he affirms, just like when I saw Charlie under your bed."

"Wow! I wonder what mine will be?"

"We will find out soon enough, but first we must burn the letter. Do you have it memorized?"

I nod. "Yes, it's memorized from reading it over and over a thousand times in disbelief."

Taking the letter from my hands, he throws the paper on the burning logs. There we watch it char to ash.

"And you?" I ask, looking back at him, "memorized?"

"Yes, I have a photographic memory, remember?" he articulates, pointing to his head.

"Of course it is," I express, shaking my head. As we stand here gazing at the flames burning the paper, I ask, "You didn't finish. What happened that day you saw my father by the river?"

"Jeoffrey stated, my brother and I were in danger and that Moyer had immoral plans, and not to trust her." Cory turns to sit back in the corner chair. "Then, your father showed me two watches." He raises his arm to show me one on his wrist. "One for me and one for my brother. I didn't take him seriously at first, until I caught back up to Cole, where I find him with Moyer. She was angry, and I heard her shouting in a gruff whisper. It's then I saw her do the unthinkable." I watch Cory's face become somber, going quiet for a few seconds.

Then he continues, "I hid behind a tree, out of view, but close enough to hear her say, 'you will bring your brother to the chambers below, once you find him,' and I watched her disappear into thin air right before my eyes. After what I witnessed, I clued in quickly and put on the watch, but it was too late for my brother, or so I thought at the time."

"So, you never gave him the watch?" I ask.

"No, and I feel somewhat responsible for the way things have turned out thus far. If I had given him the watch that day, perhaps it would have protected him - his powers even."

"Cory, you can't blame yourself. You couldn't have known."

"Oh, but I did. You see, Jeoffrey instructed me to give the watch to Cole no matter what happens. It would protect him from Moyer gaining his power."

I see Cory's eyes glaze over as if he is trying to control his emotions.

"What I didn't know at the time; had I given it to him, while he was compelled, Moyer would not have known he had it on anyway. Evil cannot see the watch. And because he was compelled, his coherency put him in a daze, he wouldn't have noticed I put it on him."

Instinctively I touch the charm hanging from my neck.

"Yes, I know about your necklace. So, do Chad and Blair."

"But you told me evil cannot see it," I argue.

Smirking at me, he says, "I just gave you, your first clue. Only good magic auras can see our amulets. It's how we know who is good and who is evil." He pauses a moment, watching me soak up the information.

"Amulet? But clearly, you're wearing a watch?

"It's an amulet made to look like a watch, I guess. According to Jeoffrey, it does other things besides protecting us by acting like costume jewelry. If you haven't noticed, Chad wears a ring on the right hand, what some refer to nowadays as a class ring. Blair wears a necklace, much like yours."

"Blair? The same person you refer to as being good, tried to compel me before I got here. Chad, too. Are you telling me they are good?" The annoyance begins to cloud my mind, as I rumble through my thoughts of the last couple days.

"It's a façade. They must maintain undercover, else *she* will discover that they are not as they appear to really be." He takes in a deep breath, "Wynter, have either of them seen you wearing your necklace? Or better yet, have you seen Chad's ring, or Blair's chain?"

I instinctively grab my necklace again, remembering back looking for clues to jewelry that Fran and dad wore. Dad sported a class ring on his left hand. Told me he bought it, his senior year. Fran didn't have a ring, rather always had on an emerald necklace. Never did I see either of them, take off the items.

"Yes, you're beginning to see now," he blurts out loud, coming to the fireplace to stand next to me.

"See what?" I say, squinting at him.

Cory takes his first two fingers of his right hand and taps his temple.

"I see. Get out of my mind, will you?" I announce.

He laughs. "Okay, but don't kill the messenger please."

We stand there a minute, watching as the fire chars the paper with the last words being consumed in the flames.

"Sorry, it's all just too overwhelming," I whisper.

As we stand here watching the fire with blazes of orange, red and yellow, I think about what my father wrote. Clearly, he didn't want anyone else to see it but Cory and me. Eyes are watching all right, good as well as the bad. I glance in his direction, to ask another question, when out of the corner of my eye I see something sparkle on the mantel. Cory turns in the same path as me. Light is coming from a hole in the grout of brick, and we both look at each other, saying out loud together, *"look to the fire."*

He moves a candle out of the way above our heads. Disrupted mortar comes crumbling down off the mantel and we duck out of the way.

"Cory, what's that?"

"I don't know, but whatever I did, left a hole in the stone." And he takes his finger digging out more grout.

"What is it?" I asked with curiosity.

"Wait a sec, Wyn. One of the bricks shifted slightly."

"You mean it's loose?"

"See, look," and he lightly rubbed the mortar with his finger, watching some of it crumble to the wood mantel. "It shouldn't be loose like this. I wonder if this is what your father meant by the riddle, 'soot and fire'?"

"Do you have a pocket knife maybe?" I ask.

"Hey, yeah, I do. Duh." And he dug it out of his jeans.

I laugh and shake my head. "I was joking, I didn't actually think you had something like that on you."

Cory sneers a look, huffing a laugh. "She has no faith in you Cory, just face it bro," talking in third person to himself.

"Ha-ha, very funny," I say aloud.

Digging feverishly in the grout, he says, "Almost got it." It took a couple more scrapes before he has a full grip on one stone block. "Well, well, look at what we have here." Taking my lighter he flicks a flame to see inside the hole. "Jackpot," he says. "Wynter come look."

"I don't think I can," hoping he would recognize the obvious and see that the hole is clearly a few inches above my head.

"Oh...yeah, hang on," and grabs the chair in the corner.

I climb up, peeking inside the hole, where a black box covered in soot and dust lay.

"Can you reach it?" he asks, spotting my back so I wouldn't fall backwards.

"I don't know, I can try." Reaching for the treasure, I say, "It's too far back, my hands can't grasp it."

"Here, let me try, I'm a bit taller, perhaps I can bring it closer to the opening. I won't be able to pull it through; the combination of my hand and the box together will be too big to fit through the opening."

Stepping back on the chair, I reach a second time for the box, my fingertips barely touching the edge. I manage to work it forward, finally getting a good grip. "I think I got it," as I manipulate the box and pull it through the hole.

Bringing it out of the chamber, together we blow off years of soot and dust. The box isn't large, it's leather-bound with gold trim, and has an engraving carved on all four sides. Each etched with a symbol. We look for an opening and try the clasp, with no success.

"It appears locked," he says. "Did you see a key while you were pulling this out?"

Shaking my head, I return to the chamber behind the fireplace, looking to find the key. "No such luck," I say.

I shake the delicate coffer, hoping to hear any sign of noise within its hollow case, but no sounds come from it. My mind wanders, remembering the jewelry box my dad gave me. He said it wasn't just any box, but a place to hold memories and stash my deepest secrets. How ironic that here is one very similar. The bottom of the small chest has an engraving that is hard to make out. The "W" is worn, along with other letters, but I can read the faint words, "*Where secrets are kept.*"

"May I?" Cory asks as he reaches out his hand.

"Sure. Have you seen anything like this before?"

"No, never."

"Any clue as to where to find the key?"

"No," he says, shaking his head.

I sigh, "All in a day's work I suppose? Shall we add this to the list of mysteries hanging over the house of Storm?" I joke.

He laughs in response and places the container on the mantel. Together we look down at the ashes that leave a skeleton of the note we burned. I take a poker and scramble the dust, so no clue is left of its existence, then Cory adds another log to conceal our small crime.

"Guess I should finish picking up this mess." Making my way to the window as the cool air clears the stuffiness, Cory, begins to help me pick up the last of my books. Luckily, none of them appeared to be damaged from my earlier tantrum. I finish gathering up the remaining clothes on the floor, and hang them in my closet, while Cory stacks the rest of the books on the shelf of my nightstand.

"So, what now? How do we find the key?" I finally say.

Cory shakes his head. "I don't know. But for now, we should keep this box hidden." Once the room is nearly back in order, we hear footsteps approach my door.

"The box," I whisper. He glances above the fireplace, taking the coffer and racing to my closet to hide.

Expecting a knock to come at any moment, I rush to pick up the remaining books. Moments later a couple wraps come to my door.

"Come in, please," I say, trying to sound busy.

14

Who are you?

It's Nora, with a smirk on her face, standing there with folded towels, in the doorway. "Good evening, Wynter, I bring you these," handing over the items in her hands. "Did you have anything to order?"

"You said I'm completely stocked for the week. Remember?"

"Yes, of course. It must have slipped my mind." I watch as her brown eyes, turn a blue hue. "It's nearly nine, I must be going." She turns away, leaving me standing there, in the doorway, speculating her intentions other than to drop off towels.

Shutting the door, I say, "You can come out now. It's all clear."

Cory slides from the closet. "It's getting late. I should get back to my room before I'm missed. I think we should put everything back for now, and revisit this in the morning."

"You're right, we should get some sleep."

I watch Cory place the box back to its home, and then say goodbye.

The rain hitting the windows sings against the glass, reminding me of home, as I make my way to bed. I feel tears start to well around my eyes yet again and decide to open a book. Perhaps reading will put me to sleep. Outside, eerie sounds from the wind, whistle through the cracks of the window pane, sending haunting chills through my frame. I try to ignore the vibrating screeches, pulling my comforter up over my shoulders. At least if I get lost in a book, I will be in my room, comfortable in front of a fire…

"Wynter, darling, you're in danger," I hear a voice whisper to me.

Cold sweat beads across my face, as I sit up in bed. Looking around, I find my book has fallen to the floor and Charlie stuffed behind my pillow. Apparently, I'd fallen asleep. I peer towards the fireplace to see hints of burning coals left in the ashes.

"Who's there?" I ask, gazing around, seeing nothing. Lying back down, thinking it a dream, I hear the voice again.

"Wynter, wake up. Come with me." This time the voice isn't in my head. Someone is in the room with me.

I cover my ears, pretending not to hear anything, turning over, and burying my face in the pillow, thinking it's all in my mind. "It's just a dream," I say, and I will it to go away.

"You must know the truth," it whispers.

I sit up again, glancing around not seeing evidence of anyone in sight.

"Who are you?" I ask again, almost screaming.

An image in the corner near the dresser, comes away from the darkness, like Moyer from earlier, but this time it's a shadow, forming into a silhouette ghost-like figure. "I have been waiting for you, for a long time," it says.

I rub my eyes. "Again, I ask, who are you?" Hoping it's just an illusion of my imagination.

Putting out a hand it says, "Come with me. I have something to show you. You must know the truth, before you're sent on a quest to fight '*her*." The figure comes closer, eyes glowing green, and I can see a partial resemblance of a woman. She extends her hand out further, for me to grasp. "Don't be afraid…, there is no harm that will come to you, as long as you are with me," she smiles. "Come, there is much work to be done, before your birthday."

I feel a sense of peace surround me as my body lifts out of bed and glides toward her, beyond my control.

"You must accept your fate, I'm here to show you how to fulfill your destiny," the image says.

She takes my hand and we instantly appear on the shore of a riverbed, watching, as the event plays out like a movie screen.

I see a child throwing pebbles in the water, laughing and having fun.

"Isalora, darling come, it's time for your nap," a woman says, and the toddler runs to her open arms, where they walk into a cabin.

Then I see a dark force across the river; a wraith peering through the trees, as they go inside the chalet. A black hooded robe covers its face, and blue eyes peer out beneath the darkness of its cowl. It reminded me of the same shadow figure I saw that day at school. This one floats above the ground unmoving, hiding, among the shade.

"Eleena," I hear a woman's voice call out from beyond the trees away from the hidden specter. She knocks on the door and walks inside.

"Ian is asking for you back at the house," the woman says. "Seems Drelanda has a fever that's coming on suddenly and is quite ill. You must go, I'll look after Isalora."

When Eleena leaves the small house, the phantom appears in front of her without warning, casting an aura that surrounds her, denying movement. She has no time to react and lets out a scream of dying pain. Her feet dangle above the ground, as she chokes for air. Desperately trying to catch her breath, she flashes beams from her eyes, thwarting the banshees grasp, allowing Eleena to fall to the ground.

The other woman comes from the lodge and flings her arm in motion with sonic power, pushing the force backwards. Then chants out loud, as she forms in her fist, a ball of fire, hurling the flame towards the spirit. Before the intruder has a chance to foray back, the woman casts another spell, creating a shield; dividing the river from the land, keeping the shadow from penetrating. Screeching sounds are heard with each attempt that the wraith strikes at the invisible safeguard.

"Can you walk?" she asks Eleena, grabbing her hand, as she pulls her from the ground. "We must get Isalora out of here. The spell will not hold Sarmira for long."

'Sarmira?' I question, to the shadow by my side.

"I can walk," Eleena says tottering to the front door.

"Wait here, I'll get her," the woman says, running for the child that sleeps inside.

Sharp sounds continue to scrape, like nails on a chalkboard from the direction of the force field. "Hurry, Isobel, she's angry. The screen won't hold much longer," Eleena screams out.

The woman comes running with the baby. Then Eleena pulls from her hand a stone-like crystal. Auras shine brightly around the gem.

'Is that labradorite,' I ask the ghost next to me.

She nods, with delight. *"Indeed, it is,"* as she gestures to continue observing the enactment play out in front of us.

Eleena unfolds her hand, placing a crystal in the center of her palm. I watch as a swirl of dust spins around the gem, like a mini tornado, and they disappear right before our eyes.

'Where did they go?' I ask still reeling from what I saw.

The ghost, gazes at me and smiles, moving her arm in a circular motion, as she erases all images before us, and suddenly we emerge in a room, much like mine. There a child sleeps, appearing sick. A man comes in with a woman looking much like Rosie, only younger. She holds a cloth and bowl of water. I watch her wring it out and put it on the girl's forehead. "This should help with the fever, sir," she says sounding concerned.

"I don't understand, why has the family fallen so ill?" he quizzes.

"I don't know, my lord, but whatever it is, has most of the château plagued. Eleena brought the baby back here. It appears Sarmira tried to kill her this afternoon."

"We must plan for escape now. There is no time to wait," the gentleman says, holding the child's hand.

"But sir, Drelanda is too weak to travel. Whatever are we to do?" she asks sounding worried. "

He stands up turning to the woman, saying, "Stay with the child. We must prepare for travel. Ladorielle is no longer safe."

"But where are we to go my lord?" she says in a low tone. "Sarmira has us surrounded."

"Only place we can go," he instructs, "Through the portal where magic does not exist."

Seconds later another servant comes bursting through the girl's room. "My Lord, the cottage in the woods is on fire! The trees are burning. What do we do?"

"Gather the family together, in the foyer. Find Genevieve, we must port at once, before it's too late." I watch him pick up the sick little girl and run out of the room.

Minutes later, people gather in the center entrance hall.

"We can only take ten at a time, my lord," says a woman with wavy red hair.

"Take women and children first, Genevieve," he orders. "Arik, you must go with them." Kissing Drelanda on the cheek the man puts his precious daughter in Arik's arms. Then he says,

"Someone must take care of the women and children, dear cousin. Derek, you go too."

"I will not leave you, Ian!" Arik shouts, with anger.

"Cousin, Arik is right," Derek says. "We must fight! Sarmira will kill you, and all our men. You're no match for her alone."

Loud thuds, pound at the door, echoing through the grand hall. "We don't have time to argue, go now!" Ian yells. "Hurry Genevieve there is not much time."

Genevieve takes a rock from her pocket that is etched with a symbol, bringing a glowing light of yellow surrounding the room. A bubble encloses her, and the others, and they disappear into thin air.

Ian looks at Eleena; tears fill her face. "You will be right behind us my love. I will come back for you."

He smiles, then kisses her forehead. I see Moyer among the faces in the crowd huddled together. She looks beautiful, and not the evil creature she is now.

"Eleena my love, take care of our precious babes. Teach them to never forget who they are. Promise me." And he kisses her again, this time on the lips.

"I promise," she says. I watch Eleena hand the baby to a woman who looks like the one in the painting hanging in the foyer, back at Storm River Manor. "My Queen, will you please take, Isalora?" she says. "I will cast the port now. Everyone hold onto each other tight."

Another thud pounds at the door, electric bolts of light sear the edges of the frame. "The shield is weakening, you must all go now," Ian yells.

Two small boys stand close to the huddling women and the many servants. Screams of panic sound off with each screeching blow from outside the walls.

Eleena pulls from her pocket a rock, much like the one Genevieve had, only this time it's a green hue forming a bubble around them. And like the others before, they too disappear, leaving the men alone.

The doors pound louder, and the noise increases with every strike, until I find myself waking in my room, disoriented, hearing a knock come from my door.

15

Stella's Story

Another knock comes, and I force myself out of my warm bed to answer.

"Hello there, Stella, what brings you here?" looking over her, checking to see if anyone else is there.

"Did you forget about something perhaps?" she replies, stepping into my room.

"Oh Stella, I'm sorry. I slept right through my alarm apparently," looking back at the clock. "Oh, the horror!" I say, sprinting to the closet, grabbing my school clothes. I'm two hours late, and completely bailed on Stella with the daily chores.

Throwing off my gown in front of her and pulling my jumper over my head, I hear Stella say, "Wynter relax, Moyer doesn't know. I made sure all the chores were done. Everything was already pretty clean, anyway." She looks down at her feet. "Although, Rosie knows I covered for you. She's not who I'm worried about though. It's Nora. She noticed you were missing.

"I'm fine Stella, thank you for coming to get me. Please come sit down," motioning with my hand to the chair.

"It's really cold in here, is the radiator on, Wynter?"

"I don't know, I haven't ever checked. Here, take this," and I toss her my throw blanket. "I usually light a fire.

"Thank you," taking the cover in her hands.

"Stella, maybe you can tell me something," wincing slightly, as I brush the tangles from my hair.

"Have you ever heard screams at night or babies crying? Strange things are happening."

Stella went white as a ghost. "Stel, what is it?"

It took her a minute before I finally hear her articulate the words: "Never repeat that you hear a baby. Never." She moves around to my bed. "I mean we all know they are here, but we do not ever admit we hear them," she says softly.

Nodding in acknowledgement at her, I reply, "So, I'm not imagining the strange occurrences?"

"No, I hear them too. Now, stop talking about it," she whispers, placing her fingers over her lips.

I figure I should change the subject. "Stella, you never told me the details of how your parents died. I don't mean to pry, but I have these memories of my dad and aunt, in the accident. The pictures of seeing them like that, they won't go away."

"I don't think they ever will," she says, "I wish I could tell you it does, but it only gets pushed to the back of the mind. I'm not sure one can ever heal from witnessing their parents' deaths."

Tears well up in my eyes as I put the brush down, and say, "I want to break this mirror and shatter it into a million little pieces. I want to yell at the top of my lungs until my voice cracks. I want to run as fast as I can until my sides hurt and then run some more until I collapse to make the pain go away!"

Stella jumps up to hug me tight and says, "When my parents died five years ago, I roamed the streets alone for a couple years before Blair found me, as I mentioned yesterday. Some idiot jumped the tracks, thought they could beat the train."

"How dreadful Stella," my heart goes out to her.

"The train tried to stop, but the impact derailed the locomotive. When the cars lifted off the tracks, one train car fell down a steep slope. My parents ended up being in that car."

She stared at me a long while, as if not seeing me at all, deep in thought. "We were on our way back from shopping. It was Christmas Eve. I wanted to give a gift to my baby cousin. So, together we took the train into town."

"When the train went down the embankment another coach came crashing on top. Somehow, I was flung under a seat." She pauses, a minute as if to catch a breath, then whispering so soft, that I can barely hear her. "I can still see their faces, eyes staring at me. They were dead."

"Oh Stella, I am so sorry. That's just awful."

She continues, "I try to remember the way it used to be, but it's starting to become a blur. I mean I was eight. My memory of them dulls more and more every year." She takes the throw, putting it around her shoulders, walking to the chair to sit. "This time of year, is really hard for me and I try not to think about it." Her eye's well up with tears, full of sadness and I want to change the topic.

"Stella, do you run? I find that running helps with my pain."

"Me?" and she shook her head. "Dear heavens no. I love to go into the woods though and- "

"Yes, catch creepy crawly things. I know," interrupting her. "Thinking about it gives me heebie-jeebies. I think I might go for a run. What do you think, Stella? Want to go running with me?"

"In this cold weather? Are you crazy?" Stella exclaims, with wide eye's looking back at me.

"Yeah, it is a bit cold. But it's good to wake the body up sometimes."

"Go take a cold shower then. It's right around the corner, here I'll show you," voicing a sarcastic tone. "You know it snowed again last night, don't you? Besides, school starts in an hour, anyway."

"Right, school. Ha! I almost forgot. Well, in that case a shower it is. I'll see you downstairs, Stella, and thank you for checking up on me."

After Stella leaves, I gather my things for a shower, quickly dress and head downstairs, not knowing what to expect for the day.

I'm a little relieved that I'll at least know Stella and Cory. It's been a long weekend and I'm not particularly looking forward to a long week as well.

My thoughts wander again, about my odd dream, as I move closer to the kitchen hall. The secrets behind these walls have me curious. Why does Madame Moyer want the sounds hidden of a baby crying in the night? Thoughts of home come flooding to the forefront. "Push them back Wynter," I say aloud.

"Push what back?" a voice behind me says, sounding patronizing and familiar.

I glance over my shoulder and notice Nora. "None of your business," I say as I continue towards the kitchen.

"Oh, come now, Wynter. You know there are no secrets among friends."

"So, you're my friend now huh? Apparently, you have short-term memory. Last I checked you tried to intimidate me. Who are you, some sort of snitch for Madame Moyer?"

I can see her unblinking glare as she becomes flush with anger, shoving me up against the wall. Placing her hand up around my neck, her eyes slant yellow, in the shape of a reptile's. Her skin changes, scales begin to appear around her sockets. *'She's stronger than she looks,'* I think to myself.

"You better learn to watch that mouth of yours, Miss-ss Wynter...." She pauses, sticking her snake-like tongue out, licking the side of my cheek. "I might request to have you for breakfast," hissing again, as she stares me down. Then she drops her hand, allowing my feet to touch the floor, "You're late for mealtime. I suggest you go before I carry out my will to kill you right here."

While I try to rationalize this all in my head, my thoughts are scrambling with fear, confusion, and horror that such a creature as her exists at all. I back away, not allowing my eyes to veer from her. At this point I don't trust her, nor anyone else for that matter. Memories of what Dad expressed to me the last day he was alive, *"Demons live among the shadows."* Is this what he meant? Is Nora a demon? I see it as plain as day now. Does Rosie know, I wonder? Oh no, is Rosie this snake creature too?

When I reach the kitchen, maids appear to be busy cooking, completely unaware of what happened right outside the hall. Nora, soon follows behind me, smiling saying hello to everyone, then smirking at me as she lifts her chin. She appears satisfied that she literally penetrated fear under my skin.

I don't stick around, I want to be as far away as possible from her. When I arrive in the dining room, there must have been more than fifty children already filing in for breakfast.

Kids are chatting and laughing, happily. It seems louder than usual, as I fight the crowd to my table in the corner.

Deep in the dining room I see Stella waving at me, so I go her way, before taking a seat. Her eyes are wide with excitement.

"I see you finally made it, uniform and all," she says.

"Ha-ha very funny. There are so many children of all ages and loud too!"

"It will calm down, soon. When Madame Moyer enters, you will be able to hear a pin drop, it gets so quiet," and as if that is a cue, the villain herself enters, and the entire room dissipates in silence, like Stella warned. I take my seat as fast as I can, hoping she doesn't catch me out of place.

When we finish eating, Stella leads me to the foyer where I see children sitting on the floor.

"What now?" I ask, eager to get to know the routine.

"Shush, Madame Moyer is about to do the opening prayer."

"We do open prayer?" I wrinkle my nose and raise a brow.

Stella snickers loudly, drawing attention. Everyone stares us down, as if to say, *'shut the hell up before you get us all in trouble.'*

I recoil. *'Well that's embarrassing,'* I think to myself.

As I look around, I see the twins leaning against a wall, staring at us both. I'm not able to tell which one Cory is, then I remember he wears a watch. I should have taken a clue, when I see him give me a smile.

Stella nudged my elbow and says, "Don't waste your time. They're bad news. If she catches you flirting with either of them, she'll send you to the basement. Other girls have had the same punishment."

"You can't be serious, Stella."

"Trust me, you want to steer clear from both of them."

"I'll keep that in mind," as I remember the nice tour, I had with Cory yesterday. Not hard to guess why. There're both gorgeous.

"Mr. Derek teaches us language arts, history, and reading," Stella begins softly, nodding her head towards him. "Then there is Miss. Blair and she teaches math, and science."

"Good morning, everyone, it's time for us to line up," I hear Mr. Derek call out. The smaller children run to hug his legs. They laugh and giggle as he picks a few of them up and cheers with them. "Shall we get the day started?"

"Here we go! You ready?" Stella says enthusiastically.

"They must really love him," I say. "It's like watching an old classic movie when the father comes through the door from being away a long time."

"Yes, he's probably the most loved person in this whole manor," Stella says, smiling.

"Quick, follow behind me," then presses her fingers to her lips to suggest we be quiet.

When we reach the classroom, the children file to their respective seats, leaving me there to stand alone.

Mr. Derek stands behind a large desk in the back of the room, not yet noticing me standing there. Behind it hangs a chalkboard with cursive writing up in the corner stating today's lesson. There are no windows for anyone to look outside or artwork hanging on the walls. Names are labeled over hooks on the back border, with coats and hats hung underneath them.

The teacher begins to speak, when he looks up, seeing me.

"Well, hello there, Wynter Storm. My apologies, I didn't see you standing there."

I smile slightly, feeling a little uncomfortable with all eyes looking at me.

"Class, this is Wynter, she has come from very far away. Please make her feel welcome."

"Welcome Wynter." The class all says together.

"I am Mr. Derek, please, come sit down at the empty desk in the third row there. Inside the desk should be a book and supplies. You're fully stocked up." His gentle smile makes the situation easier. He looks too young to be a teacher, much like everyone else I have come across so far. I've yet to see one older looking person, except perhaps Daniel.

I hurry to take a seat, then realize I will be sitting directly in front of Cory. It's hard to take my eyes off him and he gazes directly back at me, smiling. I notice he wears a watch on his wrist, which clues me in that Cole is the one sitting off in the corner, glowering. Much of the class is staring at me as I take my seat. Chills race through my body, and I try to focus on the front.

Stella nudges me with her elbow, and smiles. "Glad you're sitting next to me."

"Now then, class," Mr. Derek says, "Take out your English books, we will start on page twenty-two this morning."

Cory whispers, "Don't worry, our cousin won't bite, he's like that with all the new students." Then he sits back into his chair.

For the duration of the morning we are taught language arts. Soon lunch comes, and Stella leads me to the kitchen. Students form a line that trails out into the foyer. As we wait our turn she says, "During the week, we line up and go through the kitchen, grabbing our choices of food that spreads out along the kitchen island and then take our lunches to the dining room. In the spring, Moyer opens the courtyard."

"I see some are eating out here in the foyer?"

"Yes, as long as Madame Moyer hasn't any guests staying, we are allowed."

"Guests? But I thought no one from the outside enters?"

Stella seems to backtrack on her words, as if she said something she shouldn't, "Well…I mean, she sometimes has her extended family come to visit." Stella looks around as if to imply someone somewhere is watching our every move. She cowers, as I veer in her direction to see one of the twins' scowl at her. When we move up the line and out of his view, Stella begins again, finishing her story. "Sometimes I get so excited I forget I can't talk as freely as I would like," she whispers.

After we have a chance to grab our food I ask, "Where are all the other kids?" I notice the line dying down and not one kid sitting in the foyer.

"In the dining room, I suppose," she says, with a mouth full of food.

Looking back at Nora and watching her laugh among the girls opposite of where we are, I say in a low tone, "Nora makes it sound like the children here are worked to the bone."

Stella peeks in my direction, "Don't let her fool you. She may be Rosie's daughter, but she is nothing like her mother. As for her claims, she's partially right, kids older than twelve are put to work. Once you have reached that age, Madame Moyer thinks you're a lost cause for adoption."

"That's so sad," I say softly.

"It is what it is, right? I mean, we don't choose our parents. We can't help the hand, that fate deals us, can we?"

"I don't know Stella. What about free will? What about having control of your own destiny? You always have a choice."

"If you say so." She seems to shrug off my optimism, and slightly changes the subject.

Finally, the bell rings for the second half of the day and we line up for the afternoon classes, waiting for Blairs cue to open the door.

"I feel like an outsider, like they all know who I am already," whispering to Stella, as we walk in the classroom.

"You will get used to it. They know you're the granddaughter of Madame Moyer. Rumors get around fast, regardless of how evil this place is. Gossip is everyone's source of entertainment these days since televisions are not allowed. Well, that leaves you as the new guinea pig," she giggles.

"Glad I can easily amuse you, Stel."

16

Class Bully

Time passes fast with the second half of the day, and the bell rings for our last break. "Grab your coat, I want to show you the courtyard. Moyer has it open right now," Stella says with excitement. "Most days, it's closed."

"How do you know?"

"I heard some girls whispering about it. Come on." Taking my hand, as she leads me outside.

"So, this is where they have all been hiding?" I whisper, following Stella, while weaving in and out of other kids running about playing. A basketball can be heard, pounding the pavement, not too far away, and I watch Stella stop and gaze at the boys playing hoops.

"Do you like basketball?" I ask.

"No, not in particular," she comments, glancing back at me. "I enjoy watching the cute boys play ball."

"Stella," I whisper, nudging her side. "You're going to get caught flirting." I can see girls playing tetherball in the distance, occasionally glancing in our direction and laugh amongst themselves.

"Relax," Stella says, "I'm not hurting anyone by looking." I watch the expression on Stella's face change, when she looks over my shoulder, staring at something behind me.

I turn to see Cory standing against the outbuilding that holds sports equipment, with a warm hooded cowl, and gloves, folding his arms, peering back at both of us.

"I see one of the twins is staring," she mumbles, as she too eyes him standing alone in the corner. "Somehow we have grabbed his attention. Have you already met them?"

"Well, I met Cory in the library yesterday," I confess.

"I told you before, do not associate with either of them. We do not talk or socialize for fear of backlash from Madame Moyer. Remember I told you earlier, about a girl who flirted with one of them once?"

I nod in acknowledgement.

"Well, both boys flirted back. I think one of them claimed she was their girlfriend. Madame Moyer caught wind of it and the next thing we know she disappeared: never to be seen again."

I don't want to believe Stella, but somehow, I won't put past the possibility that Moyer has ways of solving 'a problem.'

"Why? He was incredibly kind when I met him yesterday. That doesn't sound right," I dispute, trying very hard to push back her words.

"Cory and Cole are Madame Moyer's *'adoptive sons,'* Stella, counters. "Much like you being her granddaughter. Which I'm slightly confused by, because she doesn't allow the Storm family to mingle with the rest of the house."

"I see. Your guess is as good as mine. Seems one of them is gone. Do you know which one is against the wall?"

"I don't know," she says, and I watch as she peers around as if to be searching for something.

"Who are you looking for?"

"Um, no one really. It's just that…the twins are always together. When they split up, it means something bad is about to happen."

"Well, maybe one is sick or had something to do?"

"No, Wynter, something is off. They are like the hall monitors. Their job is to observe while we are outside."

The bell rings, signaling that our break is over. I glance back at who I *'think'* is Cory, to see he's still staring at us. I smile at him, and wave. He grins back, then scowls at Stella, leaving me to question if he can hear us.

I observe her cower, saying, "Come on, we better file into line."

I can tell he's sensing something. Beginning to wonder if his gifts are stronger than he's leading on. Although Stella says they are adopted. It does leave an open-ended question.

Stella whispers in my ear, "There's deep hidden secrets here. Secrets I don't even know. What I do know is don't go snooping around, or you can end up disappearing, much like the children who have in the past. So, when I say, do not get close to the twins, I mean it. They are trouble, with a capitol T."

Just then a scream lets out in the courtyard and Miss Blair comes running out of the building.

"It hurts! I think it's coming!" a girl says, as she sinks to the ground, looking to be in pain.

Cory races to the girl's side. "Nora, help her to her room immediately," he instructs. "Stella, run and get Rosie, tell her Shanna is ready to go!" I see Stella hesitate, as she looks at me, then back at him.

"Quickly now, no time to waste! Get going," raising his voice.

By this time, I see Derek running to the scene. "Line up guys and gals, nothing to see here. Let's go," he cries out, clapping his hands. Blair helps Nora with the girl, and I watch the two of them pick her up, carrying her off as if she's light as air.

I turn to Cory, wrinkling my forehead in surprise at all the excitement, when without warning I fall hard onto the icy pavement. Cory dashes to me before my head hits the ground. I hear something crack and know immediately I re-broke my leg.

"Guess you should watch where you're going," says a voice from behind me. I look up to see a large girl about sixteen, in braids, with a round face. She giggles, not the least bit apologetic. The ice is cold underneath me and my lower body begins to go numb. I clench my teeth and suffer through the pain.

"You tripped me," yelling at her. "If I didn't know any better you did it on purpose."

"Prove it," she bellows, laughing back at me.

I see Cory glare at her and fear begins to form in the girl's eyes. "You never make yourself look good, trying to pick on others, JC," he says.

He takes his attention off her and says to me, "Hi, seems you took a little tumble," then glares back up at JC."

"I can't move my knee," seeing my leg swell before my eyes. *'Could use that healing ability about now,'* I think to myself.

"Can you walk?" he asks.

"I don't know. I can try."

Mr. Derek comes over to check on the additional excitement playing out. "What happened here?"

"Wynter had a little fall. Nothing to worry about." He begins to wrap his arms around my waist, explaining to me, "What I am going to do is lift you up. Lean against me, okay?"

All I can do is nod. The pain is so bad, I feel I may pass out at any moment.

He glares at JC once more, as he begins to help me up. With all the lies, mystery and secrets I have experienced, I feel the need to ask him, "Are you Cory or Cole?"

"Wynter, it's me," he answers. "Let's get you to the nurse's office. Now tell me, can you put pressure on either foot?" He looks directly at JC and as if to imply a hidden communication, between him and Mr. Derek, he says, "I wonder what Madame Moyer will say about this?"

JC goes sheet white. "No please, it's all a misunderstanding." She backs up slowly.

"Tell me what exactly, is the misunderstanding?" The tone of Cory's voice sent a shrill up my spine.

"What seems to be the problem?" Appearing from thin air, Moyer emerges next to me, scrutinizing directly at JC, then my way. "Wynter, what happened here?"

Stuttering out my words, I say, "It seems I have two left feet." No matter how angry I am at JC, I don't want to witness the wrath of Madame Moyer and what she can do.

"Yes. I imagine, it's impossible to walk when you're tripped too," glaring towards JC as she speaks.

"I—I it was an accident," JC stammers, backing up.

"This is Wynter's first day at a new school, and here you are, JC, the first opportunity you get, to bully your way in. Thinking no one is watching. Ah, you forget. Forget that I am still here in the back of it all. Observing. Just because you do not see, does not mean I'm not here hiding. You, of all people, should know eyes and ears are always watching, always listening."

JC has a look of panic. She backs up a nudge more. "Come with me child, I have someone I want you to meet," Moyer calls.

"No, please not the basement. Anything but that." She shakes her head, continuing to back away.

Seconds later, I witness Moyer's eyes glow, as she seems to herd JC away from the rest of the crowd, and it isn't long before she succumbs to Moyer's commands, like a sheep going to slaughter.

"Everyone else get back to class!" I hear Mr. Derek yell. Raising his voice, he has the rest of the children scurrying back in line.

"I presume you know where to take Wynter?" he says looking directly at Cory.

"Yes, Sir. I'll take care of her, sir," nodding his head.

"What is Madame Moyer going to do to her?" I ask, as I hobble on one foot.

He takes a deep breath. "This is going to take forever to get to the medical center," and he swoops me up like I'm a family pet, cradling me in his arms.

Cory looks ahead and keeps quiet, as if he doesn't have the words to formulate. I don't know if he's angry or if he's thinking.

Finally, he says, "Our cousin must follow protocol in reference to JC. However, with Moyer there, he won't need to file a report.

We soon arrive to a small room. Cory opens the door. "This is the resident doctor's office. "I am sorry to say, I am not very good at being a nurse, but I will try." And he sets me down on the examination table.

The room smells clean and sterile. Twin cots sit under windows, while at the opposite side there's a counter and sink. To the left of the door, is a supply cabinet and next to it a small desk.

"Looks like something one would see in a clinic."

"Well, Moyer tries her best to keep this place as normal as possible."

"What? Normal, in her time, maybe."

Cory snickers. "Let's just say, not all areas of this house are behind the times. You may need to take off your shoes and tights. I'll look for a bandage, so we can wrap your leg up."

"Do you think we will have to set the break? I mean I can't move it."

"I don't know. We will have to wait until Blair gets back."

He must have seen the look of concern on my face. "Don't worry, I won't look," he says.

I feel flushed and embarrassed as I prepared to take off my shoes. Here is one of the most beautiful creatures on the face of the earth, telling me to take my clothes off. I'm surprised I haven't fainted yet.

My breath burns against my lips as I breathe through my mouth. My cheeks feel hot, and my mind roams to forbidden thoughts.

Cory turns to look at me prematurely, as I'm taking off my tights, and turns his head away. "Um sorry. I didn't mean…" Quickly changing the subject. "You can bet I'll find out why she did this, and if Nora is behind it..."

"Nora? But why?"

"Because she's jealous."

"Of what? I've barely been here two days."

"She feels threatened by you somehow. She and Cole are…um…well, you know… an item. She thinks you will ruin what they have together."

"That's preposterous. I'm not even interested."

"Really?" Cory still has his back to me.

"All set. You're in the clear. I'm fully decent," I say to him. My knees are bruised and tattered as I look down at them. "Amazing the damage ice can do," I add.

Finding a towel on the shelf, he dampens it with cold water, and brings it to me, along with some ice. "This should help with the swelling, and tide you over until Blair can see you," he says.

His hands are soft and gentle, and I close my eyes as he cleans around my knee. I don't dare look at him, for fear of losing my emotions again, only this time it would be frivolous passion. I'm falling for him, and I know it. I refuse to believe that there is such a thing as love at first sight. Twenty-four hours is not enough time. I've read books on love that exist in fairytales, but not in real life.

Every touch of his fingertips tingles my skin, and my stomach is tied in knots, as I begin to imagine what it would be like to have my first kiss be with his lips. Is this another one of Cory's emotional powers trying to make me lose all sense of resolve? I feel my cheeks become warm, my arms become weak, when Blair bursts through the door. "So, what the hell happened to you?"

"I made new friends apparently," I say in a light but sarcastic tone.

"So, I've heard. Let me take a look," as she moves her fingers around my knee. "It appears you have re-broken your leg in the exact spot as before, from the accident. I'm going to have to set it." She looks up at Cory, then to me. "This is going to hurt a little—" and before she finishes her sentence, I bellow in pain. "Thanks for the warning," falling backwards against the cot.

17

Eyes Are Watching

"What did you do to her?" The female voice says, sounding angry.

My mind sings through voices in my head between images of people talking. Eyes watching me. Half awake, half dreaming I float to a flashback of home where I am swinging on the tire in my front yard. Autumn leaves on the ground.

"Nothing, I didn't do anything to her. One moment she's awake, the next she's out. I swear! Blair set her leg. She broke it good."

"And you saw it all happen?" she asks.

"Aye, I did."

His charming voice brings me closer to consciousness. Vision of snowflakes flash across my face as I swing. The feel of cold air hits my nose and cheeks.

"Leave her, she will wake soon, I do not want you to be here when she is conscious. This is the second time I have had to place a memory stamp. We need to be careful. She is not ready for the truth yet."

His handsome face flashes before me. His blue eyes piercing my memory, standing there in front of me. Waiting. Smiling. He walks closer to me.

"I am drawn to her mother. I can't control it much longer."

He smiles at me as he comes closer, stopping the swing. His tender strong hands reaching out. Cupping the nap of my neck, he takes his other hand and pulls me close.

"It will be fine, son. She will have a small headache is all. When she awakes, she will have no memory of our conversation. She hears us but thinks it to be a dream. I will sweep her mind before she comes around. She is having a dream of you right now, my dear. Your feelings might very well be mutual. I will send Blair in before she awakens. Let her think your relationship is coming natural."

"I think it is natural, mother. I can't seem to get her out of my head. Her scent, aura, I can't get it out of my mind. I feel her as though she belongs to me."

His hands are warm and loving. His breath against mine, hot, smelling sweet, as he ascends to my lips.

"And so, it shall be, but you must go now. She is coming to."

A shut of the door wakes me from my pleasant sleep. I look around to see that I'm still in the examination room. The windows are wide open, allowing fresh air in. My whole-body shivers, and my head throbs with piercing pain, just like the night before. It's now quite dark and I look for a clock to know the time. I find my leg is in a brace, not allowing me to bend my knee.

A light knock at the door startles me. "Wynter, are you okay?" says a familiar voice.

My mind races to collect my thoughts. "I'm fine, come in."

Blair opens the door. "Hey there, how are you feeling? You've been out of it for a few hours." Coming over she checks my leg. "Looks like your break is nearly healed." She takes in a deep sigh, "You're going to have to wear this for the next twenty-four hours, I'm afraid. I think it's the only way to ensure your bones heal properly."

"Blair, do you know why I heal so fast? Dad and Fran never had the chance to explain it to me."

She smiles. "Yes, it has to do with your gift. The closer you get to eighteen the more your powers will be developed. Have you experienced your hair turning color yet?"

"My hair? What do you mean?"

"Well, your hair's a medium brown now, not black as it was this morning. Each day it will become lighter and lighter, until your birthday. Soon, you will have the same color as mine. If you haven't noticed where there is a Storm, there is white hair. Your green eyes will change to blue, too."

"Why is that?"

"It's who you are as a Storm, but now is not the time to discuss this. Eyes watching and ears listening if you know what I mean."

Changing the subject, knowing that is probably all I will get out of her I ask, "Where's Cory?" trying not to sound nosey.

"He's right outside." Would you like me to get him?"

"Okay," I nod.

Moments later Cory walks in. "You rang?" he jokes.

"Ha-ha. I wanted to say thank you for helping me today."

"You don't have to thank me. I did what was necessary."

I look at Blair. "So, um. How long do I need to stay here?"

"You're free to go," she asserts .

Looking down at my leg, I groan, "It's going to be a long walk to my room."

They both chuckle, and Cory remarks, "I have time. "He grabs the crutches laying against the wall near the doorframe, handing them to me. "You can lean beside me if you need to."

Time drags on, and it feels like an eternity before we finally reach the hall corridor to my room. There, a fire has already been lit, with the warmth inviting me in.

I see Stella standing there, in a servant stature with pursed lips. "Good evening, my lady, I've warmed your room and brought you food, by order of Rosie."

I look back at Cory, confused, when he says, "If you will excuse me, ladies. I must be on my way." Bowing in formality, he closes the door behind him.

"What's that all about, and what is all this?" objecting to her formality. "And why do you act like that Stella? Please, sit down. Take a load off girlfriend."

"Wynter, I must act accordingly when in the presence of a Storm."

"Well, you're in my room now, so act yourself please. I like you much better that way."

She smiles, adding, "I see you met JC. Most people avoid her like the plague." Stella draws closer to me, and glances at my knee brace.

"Rosie says to come check on you. She's concerned you may want something to eat, since you missed supper and has permission, to bring you food this evening."

"I'm fine, Stella thank you." And I sit on the bed, with my head still throbbing.

Stella pulls the tray in, next to my bed. "Do you remember anything? I heard you passed out after Blair set your leg."

"How do you know that?"

"Gossip carries through the halls, my friend."

Another, *'eyes watching and ears listening,'* I think. "I don't remember a lot, only that Blair set the bone, and I passed out."

On the cart is a glass of milk and full dinner plate. A feast for a king. "Eat before you shrivel up into a prune and tell me all about the juicy gossip I missed today," Stella says with excited enthusiasm.

Avoiding her comment, I answered her with a different one. I really don't want to get into the drama, rather I would like to forget it forever.

"How is that girl doing? You know the girl who screamed this afternoon. She said it's coming and looked to be in real pain, like she was terrified."

Stella's eyes widen and then she says, as if trying to think quickly of words that will satisfy my curiosity. "I think she had the stomach flu or something, but Miss Blair is a great doctor. I'm sure Shanna will be fine".

"But she looked to be in so much pain."

"Shush, Wynter, remember the house has ears?"

Her comment reminds me, that the house has eyes watching and ears listening, leaving me to wonder if what Cory and I discussed earlier had been heard.

"Well I don't know how much pain she was in Wynter, but Miss Blair said it was a stomach flu. So, I believe her," she dictates, trying to sound convincing.

Stella's scared, I can see it in her eyes. There is a mystery about her. On the outside she looks sweet and innocent, but on the inside, she leaves me to wonder what she's seen from the past, what jaded her thirteen-year-old body at such a young age. Has Moyer completely taken the child part of her? I don't know if it's something I should bring up, but as I look into her bright eyes, I know the only option is to press the issue.

"Stella, why does it seem like there are so many secrets in this place?" I ask, with eager curiosity.

Instead of speaking, Stella takes out a pad and pen. Not in note form, but letter length, as I watch her write the words down.

"Everyone here who resides in this castle watches with eagle eyes. Ears can hear through closed doors. There are bizarre unexplained phenomena that surround this place. I cannot speak to them aloud. Should I get caught, I shall be severely punished. Madame Moyer has killed for less. You will soon discover on your own, but I caution you to tread lightly. The babies you hear are real, the agony of screams are real.

Rumors have it, that this is not only an adoption agency, but Madame Moyer brings in young unwed mothers. Once they give birth, the girls are on their way, and Madame Moyer adopts the babies out."

After I pick my jaw up off the floor, I take the pen from Stella's hand, and I quickly write back, *"Do you know why I am here?"*

Stella shakes her head, no, and then writes, *"we need to keep talking aloud or they will suspect something."*

Once I read the note, Stella takes the letter from my hand and throws it into the burning flames. "It's getting warm in here," she says, and she walks to the window, opening it. "I guess I should get back to my room. It's getting late and I don't want to be caught out after nine. I'll see you tomorrow." As I watch Stella leave, I see a shadow waiting in the hallway. Stella cowers, looking over her shoulder towards me, with worry. What does Stella know? The shadow figure stands in the corner waiting in silence until Stella is down the hall and out of sight before approaching me.

Déjà vu kicks in when I realize it's the evil Spawn of Satan herself coming to my door. "Good evening Wynter, how's the leg?" Looking down she gives a half grin. "I feel the need to show you where one goes when breaking the rules at Storm River Manor.

18

The basement

Deep down, I know where we're going. She's taking me to a place from which I may never return. What happened today isn't my fault. Why is she punishing me for it?

"There is no need for a coat. Don't worry, I will bring you back unscathed... this time." She has a cackle to her tone. An eerie sound and one I don't care to hear ring through my ears.

Willingly, I follow behind her. What choice do I have?

Closing the door behind me she leads me downstairs through the hall to the classrooms, where we end up at the threshold of the basement below. This isn't going to be easy with my leg brace. The stone staircase, spirals downward endlessly it seems, until we finally hit bottom; where Moyer lights an oil lamp hanging on the wall next to the door frame.

The smell is grotesque, flaring my nostrils, while trying hard not to breathe in the odor, making my stomach churn in knots. Cries can be heard to the left of me, but I can't see through the darkness of the damp, musty crypt. Amber hues hit the wall behind Moyer where I can see water drizzle down the stone.

She glares at me, see these cells? This is where people go when one doesn't obey the rules. I feel it important to show you, what happens when breaking them."

She guides me further into the darkened chamber, where only the lamp she holds is visible. "You see, I have splendid hearing, and excellent eye sight. I see in the dark like a predator hunting for prey at night. It's a gift really. And I use it to my full potential. You, my dear, will soon find out your gift...but in due time. It usually matures around eighteen years of age." I can tell she is enjoying my nervousness, as I continue to listen to her.

"I've found some have come to their power early, like the twins. Their powers rendered very useful indeed. I'm betting yours will strike at midnight on your birthday. Which is why I will be hosting a lavish party for you next Wednesday."

She stops and turns around to face me. Her eyes glow blue, beginning to light the walls around us and I can see a bit more. "I do love such lavish parties. Birthday's such as yours give me an excuse to throw one."

To the left of us, I can make out images of wrought iron bars, behind a large locked gate. It's there, that I hear moans of pain, and rustling movements.

She smiles, giving an impression of conniving preparation. I don't trust what she's up to and I remember Dad voicing, she wants my power. What's Moyer's grand plan?

"You will soon discover the inevitable. You are after all, *'family.'* I will do whatever I can to protect that, even if it means to bring you here. A choice I would have rather you wait to see until later. However, such incidents like today, makes my job a tad bit harder."

We start walking again, further down the dank room, to red stain benches butted against walls and tools hanging from hooks. The filth, the stench, crawls on my skin like a million spiders, giving me chilling goosebumps all over my body. I feel the heavy cloud of evil surround me like a blanket of dread. My eyes fill with disgust when I realize she's taken me to a torture chamber. I want to scream, knowing I can't. I don't think anything will come out anyway. This place leaves my senses in absolute shock.

"You may not understand now, but when the time is right, the truth will come out." Then she laughs a malicious cackle, pointing to the center of the room.

I don't understand, why she's telling me this. Trying to absorb it all hurt my brain. I veer in the direction she gestures, and see a figure hanging in the center of the room, a few feet from where we stand.

"Please dear child, do take a closer look. Go on, don't be afraid," she coaxes. Her eyes begin to glow brighter, surrounding the whole room with blue light. Giving me the advantage to see what image hung from the restraints before me. I know it's a person, but who? They are stripped naked, with wrists bound by chains, hanging above their head. Feet barely touch the ground, as I see blood drip from their toes. Lashes appear in the front and back of the body. As Moyer forces me to step closer, I can see the person is female. Her head hangs down partially covering her breasts. Her mouth is split wide open, with blood still oozing from her lip.

She must have noticed my presence, and moves her head to the side, opening her eyes. "Help me."

To my horror, it's JC. She's alive, but just barely. I cup my mouth to avoid screaming and back away, right into Moyer. I turn around to see her satisfied grin. "You see, my granddaughter, this is what happens to those who mess with family. I thought it appropriate to show you the acts of discipline. JC, I'm sure has learned her lesson."

Tears begin to swell. Madame Moyer is much eviler than I originally thought. A monster created by the Devil himself. I realize now, there is no escaping this. She would hunt me down and kill me first, before ever letting me go. The thought of being her lifelong prisoner terrifies me. My inner soul, although I don't know how I'll pull it off, has declared war on Madame Moyer. Right now, my grandmother clearly doesn't care about the life of a human soul. Thankfully, she can't read my thoughts, or can she? Dad and others never mentioned if one can read minds. Cory can see pictures. Does that mean it's possible? Is the necklaces sole purpose only to protect me from being compelled?

No, there is no escaping this inferno. But I will fight to the bitter end. Even if it kills me. She can't have my power, my soul. I'll die fighting before letting her have that.

"I don't feel so good," I say. "I want to go back to my room." It's all I can say to her.

As if to approve of our little field trip, she says with a curve of her smile, "Very well, we can go. I think you understand your roll now. Perhaps you have learned a little lesson at the expense of JC. Can you imagine what happens to the ones who try to escape?" Cackling another laugh, as if what she's about to say is amusing. "Well, you saw Redmae and her pack."

"What?" I say, looking at her with alarm.

"Oh, my dear child, hasn't anyone told you?" She paces back toward the door to the upstairs. "Those who even think about escaping are fed to the dogs." She turns around, cupping my chin. "But you wouldn't dream of doing that, now would you? You are, after all, family. And one never turns their back on family. Oh, my dear Wynter, do I ever have plans for you." She releases my chin from her hard grasp, scorning a foul tone, "You will not foil them either. For if you do, I will scar that pretty little body of yours. Do I make myself clear dear?"

"Crystal," I say. Wanting so much to shove her back to the hell hole she came from. I had not shared with anyone my thoughts of escape. Is it true? Can she read minds after all? I take this as a warning that she can.

Moyer startles me out of my thoughts, "Casey, you may take JC down. I think both she and Wynter here, understand their places now."

The basement is so dark and dingy I hadn't noticed anyone else there but us. I hear Casey reply, "yes, Madame Moyer."

By this time, tears are streaming down my face, with my cheeks feeling hot. My heart rate pounds with sheer anxiety.

"You're a smart girl and I predict we can begin fresh tomorrow," she jeers.

My heart went to JC. No amount of bullying on her part deserves what she went through. It makes me ill and I feel nauseous thinking about it.

When I got back to my room, I feel the instinctive need to shower or bathe to scrape every bit of smell from my nose, stench from my hair and odor off my skin. The basement's horrifying, and I know I never want to go there again.

I make a warm fire before grabbing my clothes and heading to the washroom. The bath is the perfect element to relax the restlessness inside my body. The brace poses to be difficult taking off, and I'm hoping it won't be a problem putting it back on. Besides, my leg feels fine and I can bend it without pain. I'll be careful.

Outside I can hear the wind, blow again. Another storm is on the rise I imagine, though I can't be sure from the lack of televisions in this place.

Something that I discovered as odd, is the mention of my gift. *She* knows it's coming. Perhaps dad was right when he and Fran stated Moyer wants me for my powers. Cory says it should happen at eighteen. But what if it doesn't come at all? It feels strange hearing it from her. Moyer has plans. I want to know why.

Almost an hour passes before I decide to get out of the bath and dry off. I want the day to be over, and the quickest way for that to happen is to go to bed. Not that I would get a good night sleep anyway. Heading back to my room I see the coals remain in the hearth, so I add another log, when I step on what feels like sharp rocks. Looking down at my feet, I see crumbled flecks of mortar, reminding me of the hidden box behind the mantel. Digging out the brick I find that it isn't there. But why? Why would you steal it? My anger begins to get the best of me.

"Do not stress it is safe," the voice comes to the front of my mind.

"Where have you been? Staying quiet while I hash it out with Moyer alone? You could have warned me you know?" The voice doesn't reply. Staying silent.

At breakfast Stella looks cheerful. Her eyes wide with excitement. Although my table sat off on its own, Stella managed to make a deal with another kid, so she can be closer to me. It's a sweet gesture.

"Good morning Wynter," she says. "How's the knees?"

"You're chipper this morning. What gives?" I question, and add, "They don't hurt nearly as much as yesterday."

"I see you finally made it to breakfast?"

"Ha-ha very funny. Is that to imply I am slow at the moment?"

Stella giggles. "Sorry," and comes to give me a hug.

"It's so loud in here today. What's with all the excitement?"

"It will calm down soon. Once Madame Moyer enters. I hear rumors that we are getting visitors today," she says in an enthusiastic whisper.

"Visitors?" I say, taking a bite of food. "I thought visitors weren't allowed?"

Stella rolls her eyes at me, putting her hand on my shoulder, as if I'm not understanding the sheer importance of it all. "Yes, visitors," she whispers in my ear. "There is a couple coming today from far away, Transylvania or something like that. Every now and then, prospective parents come to adopt one of the orphans."

"Transylvania?" I raise my brow. "What, like *Vampires* or something?" I snort, nearly choking on my food.

Again, I receive a disapproving look from Stella. Better yet a scowl. She wrinkles her forehead, and sighs in what appears as frustration, then walks to her seat and sits. "Really Wynter, you shouldn't joke about this. It's serious. It's been at least six months since someone has entered these doors. It's very rare the guests even come here."

"Ok, ok, I'll try to be more serious," snickering back. It's then, I realize perhaps not a permanent place to live after all.

A thud comes from the entrance of the dining room as the doors swing open, grabbing all the children's attention, when Madame Moyer walks in. Children scramble to their respective seats.

I watch Moyer's callous black eyes scan the room as if to be looking for someone in particular.

She glides across the floor with ease, weaving in and out of each table, glaring intently at each child. Her black leather covered hand pats lightly against the side of her dark navy-blue satin dress. Suddenly she stops directly across from Stella. Looking over her head she eyes me closely, as if she's trying to reach inside my mind. I stare back at her black eyes that turn a glowing blue. I feel her try to attempt yet another trance, but nothing falters, and she ends the interlude. I sit there feeling frozen, perhaps it's because of the terror I went through. At last she speaks, jarring me from my meditation.

"How's your leg Wynter"? she says coolly. "You had quite the adventure last night. I imagine you might be sore from walking so many stairs."

"Fine", I manage to mutter.

Stella glances at me, creasing her brows. I can sense she is wondering what Madame Moyer is talking about.

Eyeing me up and down, *she* adds, "Seems Nora and you have become fairly close these last couple days. She's quite fond of you."

'We have? What has she been smoking?' I think. While on the outside; I pretend to listen to her demeaning words of hate.

"I promised her I wouldn't send you to the basement yet. She prefers her meals unscathed.... Although it may pose easier for her, if you're in chains and cannot move." She gives a cold smirk.

I recoil from Moyer's comments, fighting back the panic festering inside. Then I remember Rosie saying she feeds on the fear, it's how she gains power. I wonder if that's why it feels like her hypnotic actions are beginning to penetrate my mind?

"Hold the fear back," I hear the voice again inside my head. *"Stand your ground. The more you allow trepidation, the weaker the necklace becomes."*

"So, it's what I wear that protects me?" Replying to the voice in my mind.

"Yes, it protects you for only so long before the magic wears off. You must find a way to be brave. Face your fear. Bravery fuels the amulet."

I stare back at Moyer, straightening my posture, knowing I will not cave as one of her puppets. I challenge such evil. *'Bring it on,'* wanting her to know I'm not afraid.

Moyer changes her position, veering to the girl sitting opposite of Stella, not much older than maybe eight. She sits there watching Moyer with sweat beading across her forehead.

"Esmerelda dear, someone has come a long way to see you, child." Moyer's words suddenly sound kind, and not cold like they were second's ago. "Come with me, my sweetness. You must get ready for their arrival."

Esmerelda gets up from the table, making not a sound from her lips. Rosie falls beside her taking a hand, and they both follow Moyer out the door.

"Where is she going?" I ask in a whisper.

"Remember the couple I told you about from Transylvania? Well, Esmerelda fits the description apparently. Madame Moyer is going to have her cleaned and prepped for a visit. If they like her, she will leave with them today. Should they not like her, Madame Moyer will throw her in the basement for the rest of the afternoon. A debriefing, so to speak."

"That's horrid, Stella. She's a monster. Why would you debrief a child?"

"To keep an orphan in line. Bring them back from the hope they had moments earlier. Adoption day is exciting yet horrendous in the same breath."

The vile I feel for Madame Moyer continues to boil. *"That's it. Bring the anger to the front of your mind."* The voice speaks again.

'The necklace is weakened by fear? Is that the secret?' I say on the inside.

"Yes," not expecting an answer. *'And Moyer feeds on it.'*

"We should line up for class before we're late," I hear Stella say, as she steps away from the table, grabbing her plate in the process.

"Right," pulling back from my deep thoughts.

I follow Stella back to the kitchen where we wash our plates and put them away, then enter the foyer where kids are already in line and following Blair to class.

19

School Lessons

Each student trails into the classroom one by one. Right away I noticed JC isn't present. I take my seat, while waiting for the rest of the students to file in. I'm wondering why Moyer hasn't brought her back from the depths of the abyss. I see Cory walk in and smile at Blair. His black sweater tunic makes his flaxen hair and ice blue eyes stand out. Why does he affect me this way? I look up before he fades by, taking his seat behind me.

"Hello," he says with a smile. "How are you feeling?"

I pretend not to notice him, but it's too late. I ponder if he can see the anger, I have of the image of the coffer missing in my room. "Fine. Thank you," I pout. I can feel him watching me with intentions. If I turn around, he will fixate on my eyes to calm my emotions. There's something about him that makes me feel all jello-like inside.

Blair begins speaking, waking me from my daze, "Class take out your science books and begin reading pages one hundred and two, to one hundred and fifty. We will have a pop quiz afterwards. Those who do not pass will be sent to the reading room with Madame Moyer."

Everyone takes out their books and begins reading. Still I can't concentrate as I can feel him stare at me. I don't need eyes in the back of my head to know that. *'Grow a pair Wynter, tell him to stop, you can do this!'* With some hesitation, I half turn, to see him smiling at me and chuckle.

"Is there something you would like to say to me?" I ask in an annoying tone.

He shook his head. "No, not yet, continuing to stare.

"Look, I don't know what your hex is Cory," I whisper, "But I am pretty sure I do not want to fail this quiz, so if you don't mind, I would like to get some work done. Your staring at me, makes me nervous."

He leans forward whispering in my ear, "So, I make you nervous, huh?"

"Cory what has gotten into you today?" I turn back around in frustration.

He breathes in deep, taking out his book, then exhaling like I just spoiled his fun.

His breath reaches my senses. Blowing my concentration again with his sweet scent. I stiffen to brush it off, but it keeps clouding my thoughts. My mind wanders as I read and soon, I'm through the whole segment, without knowing exactly what I read.

Anticipating a failed pop quiz, I turn to glare at the gorgeous being behind me. His stunning lopsided grin blows my plans up in my face, and my stern stare turns into a soft gaze.

He leans over to me and says, "Don't worry, I will fail too. It's all your fault, I can't concentrate."

"You can't concentrate?" I snap at him. Now I'm annoyed, but I keep my head, nonetheless. "Perhaps take a picture next time?"

He smiles as if to awaken his inner mischievous side, not seen before, murmuring, "So, it seems we both have concentration issues."

My glaring at him doesn't seem to work. I turn back around and try my best to ignore him.

"Besides," he says softly, "I don't have a camera, or I would have done that already."

'Really Cory?' I think. Responding to him is going to add fuel to the fire so I ignore him. Perhaps if I skim over the material I can squeak by with a passing grade.

Stella, sitting next to me, jabs my elbow scowling; her bugged out eyes tells me all I need to know. Cory is going to get me in trouble. Thirty seconds later Miss Blair stands in front of the class, going over key points of the section, splitting us up in groups of three. As luck would have it, I'm paired with Stella and Cory. It probably makes for a perfect recipe, because I'm able to focus with a third wheel in the group. Cory doesn't give me the seductive stares, or the gentle scented breaths as before, and Stella's totally engrossed on the task at hand. It makes for a better second half of the two hours we have of science.

Miraculously I pass the pop quiz and throughout the rest of the day I do my best to avoid Cory. While I had come to terms that I'm attracted to him, I'm still upset that he took the leather-bound box from my room.

By the last hour we had endured a heavy study time with history.

"Is it always like this on Tuesdays?" I ask Stella as we left for the day and headed to the dining room for our dinner hour.

"What do you mean? I don't understand."

"I mean, the two classes divided, from morning and afternoon? It's nearly five.

"Oh, I see, well yes. I guess you can say that. Monday Wednesday is English and Math, while Tuesday, Thursdays are Science and History. Friday after our chores, is Geography then Independent Study in the afternoon."

"Independent Study?"

"Yes, after geography we are free to either go to our room to finish out any homework from the week, study for a test, or go to the library and work on lessons there."

"What about the weekend?"

"The weekend is filled with extra chores that didn't get done during the week. Once that is finished, we are free to walk the courtyard outside, with weather permitting or roam the manor in areas allowed." Then Stella looks at me, "Kind of ironic that such a cruel and evil place allows such freedom huh?"

"I noticed the grounds had an overgrown garden, as we entered through the gates the other day?" I ask, trying to play off that I don't know anything about its history.

"That garden used to be the most beautiful place years ago, I hear. Though we have never seen it as the potential it should be. Apparently long ago when Lady Sara was still alive, she kept it up. A gardener would come, once a week to clean it. There was a huge tragedy, and the garden has been locked up ever since."

"What happened?"

"Not now, perhaps another time," and with that Stella walks off as if to have said too much. I don't get it. Sometimes she talks freely and other times she's as tight lipped as a clam. It's then, that I turn to see evil herself glaring back at me.

After dinner I make my way to my room and find my door open a gap with the flickering of golden amber, reflecting off the walls from a lit fire. I find no one present, but there is a mound of wood along with kindling loaded up in the corner and neatly stacked newspaper. I add another log, so the room will be warm. Its then, I see a note folded on the mantle.

Wynter,

Meet me in the library tomorrow, after school. Bring your coat.

Cory

The next day I avoid Stella, for fear that Madame Moyer will blame her for talking to me yesterday. Cory too, for that matter, I'm still upset with him and I may just ignore his little note he wrote.

My chores are done early, and I sit at my table eating quietly. In class I confine myself in my own world. Once lunchtime gathers, I simply eat my sandwich in the corner of the kitchen on the floor, bringing something to read for pastime. I nearly go unnoticed too, until he walks in on me. I glance up to see a lopsided smile hook the side of his cheek.

"What are you doing sitting on the floor all alone?" he inquires. His hair looks tossed, like he had been outside. But he's still striking as ever. He can be muddy from head to toe, and still melt my heart.

"May I sit with you?"

"I'm not much in the mood for company today," sneering at him. I am sure he saw the pictures in my head. Besides the tone in my voice should be a clue.

He invites himself to sit down next to me anyway.

"You haven't wanted much company all day."

"Yeah, well, a girl needs space sometimes you know?"

"Yeah, I know."- Glancing at my leg- "I see your brace is off?"

"Blair took it off this morning. It's good as new."

"Well that is good news."

There is a long silence before he finally says, "You know, I hadn't any idea that she would take you there."

"Yeah, well, it wasn't a pleasant experience that's for sure.

"Cheer up," he says. "She's gone. Won't be back until next week."

"Yeah, right before my birthday."

"I know." Then he takes a pencil from the kitchen drawer, and writes: *'I have a plan.'*

"Hey, that's my book!" I protest, glaring at him.

"Shh," he softly laughs, and erases the words without ever knowing the page had been violated.

"Remember the note I left you in your room?" he asks.

I nod. Thinking, *'I'm still mad at you, Cory.'*

"Meet me there after class, Okay?"

"Sure, I can do that."

Cory pulls me to my feet. "The day will get better, I promise."

"You shouldn't make promises you can't keep," I debate.

"Oh, but I can keep this one."

When we enter the room, I see JC. She has been gone since Monday, and now moved to the front of the classroom for all to see. Her eyes are bloodshot, and her face distorted. A few bruises sweep across her cheeks. She has a split lip and a vivid scar on the side of her neck that clearly shows a healed gash. Her eyes fixate on the desk in front ignoring her surroundings. Welts surface across her arms, and her wrist looks raw from being tied up in chains. Watching her, gives me a sudden reminder of that night. My eyes well up, as I try to control the emotions. Then anger begins to fill my mind. Why did she do it? I'm angry at the fact that she must have known she wouldn't get away with it. Yet she gambled her thrill anyway and lost. But why? Is it that horrible here that she thinks death is the better answer? Clearly, she must have known, by hurting me it would end badly.

As if Cory can see the images in my mind, he gently put his hand on my shoulder to move me forward quickly so as not to torture myself by JC's appearance any longer.

The entire two hours of class I see JC flinch in pain. Red blood stains already bleed through her clothes, and it appears that Casey hadn't wrapped up her wounds. Every movement she makes, seems to open a fresh scar all over again. The gruesome sight renders me ill, and the entire class hour a moot point, for concentration. All my hopes of ever escaping are gone. My stomach continues to churn with empty bile within its walls. The heartburn hits with vengeance, and I force it back down. I will be glad when class is over, but it won't be soon enough.

Every so often I can feel Cory's hand brush against my back. It's a temporary solution comforting my pain, but it doesn't ease my mind knowing what I saw in the depths below the castle grounds. I can't help but think part of JC's pain is his fault. He must have told Mr. Derek everything. I can't see the students saying one word. That thought makes me angry. How dare he try to sooth my pain, knowing full well he's the cause of her going to the depths of misery. I shrug off Cory's hand, as it caresses my shoulder, cluing him in, *'don't touch me,'* and he pulls it back where it stays for the rest of class.

After the final bell, I can't get out of there fast enough, and I think I'm the first person to exit the doors. I ran immediately to the kitchen to grab a glass of water. I feel like I'm going to choke. Cory follows shortly behind me.

"You ok, can I do anything?" he says, looking at me with concern in his eyes.

"I don't know," starting to get angry. "You tell me Cory. Why was JC sent to the basement? You seem to know more than

I do. Why did you tell Mr. Derek what JC did to me, why couldn't you just let it go?"

I'd obviously caught Cory by surprise, from my cold response. He takes a step back to adjust himself for a rebuttal I gather, but I'm prepared, comparable to a cougar ready to pounce on their prey. At this moment it doesn't matter how attracted I am to him; how beautiful he is. Nothing will equal an excuse I'm about to hear from him. How can anyone have the calm as he does to stand there, as if the pain JC went through is a mere afterthought.

Finally, after a few seconds, as if Cory decisively finds his voice he says, "I didn't tell Mr. Derek anything."

I can see his eyes begin to glow, but I look away too quickly for him to latch on.

"Why are you lying to me. Do you think I'm stupid? I saw the look in Mr. Derek's eyes that day when he looked at you. As if he read your mind."

A slight chuckle came from Cory just then and I'm in no mood for the games. Ignoring my inner fire, I begin to stalk off, before Cory grabs my arm, "Wynter, let me explain before you make hasty assumptions....Please?"

As if my glare isn't enough warning, he drops my arm as quickly as he grabbed it, continuing. "I didn't tell Mr. Derek, and contrary to what you believe about mind reading, it's more like... video reading."

"What?" I say confused.

"The classroom, it's secretly recorded daily. There is a hidden camera in class and the courtyard. Madame Moyer saw the whole thing. I didn't need to say a word. My theatrics Monday was that, theatrics to keep everyone thinking I'm the watcher for Madame Moyer. The other kids and staff do not know about the hidden cameras. They are everywhere. Even in here, and you can bet she will know about this, now too."

I froze in shock. I didn't see that coming. At that moment I feel like a horrible buffoon. Fear crosses my face at the thought of Madame Moyer seeing us together, talking. I'm at a loss for words, and Cory caught on, as the images started passing across my brain.

He pulls me to him, hugging me tight. "It's going to be fine.

He holds me there a few minutes, then whispers "Come on, I know where we can go. You can let it all out and no one can hear you. But you need a coat, dress warm."

He looks at his watch. "Meet you in an hour?"

"Sure okay, I can use some free time."

20

Imposter

I quickly rush to my room, changing into jeans and a sweater, along with warm socks and my hiking boots, before meeting up with Cory in the library. I wonder if Nora went snooping around and saw the note last night. I'm really wishing I had a lock right now. I trust no one, except maybe Stella and Cory.

Inviting me with open doors, the library is already warm from the cold day. There, I find Cory standing near the horror section reading a book, deep in expression. I can tell by the look on his face, he's reading an exciting part, off in another world.

"You're late," I hear coming from the beautiful mouth of the one reading before me. *'So much for sneaking in,'* I think.

"Yeah, well, I ran to my room to change," I say.

"What do you think of this place so far?" he questions, "I mean with it being your fourth day and all?"

"School is school, I guess. Most of the kids don't talk to me. Stella seems to be my only friend, except for you of course."

"So, I saw," he snaps, continuing to read his book.

"What do you mean, you saw?" I ask, pulling at his sleeve lightly. Ignoring my question, he turns to the next page.

"Oh, stop it," I cry, becoming annoyed at his teasing. He knows it too. I can tell by his smirking smile. "How can you stand there reading, and talk to me at the same time? Don't we have things to do today?"

He glances up at me. "Just a second. Let me finish this paragraph. Besides, you seem to think we have all day."

"Really?" I stomp to the corner chair and pout, like a child. He's beginning to frustrate me. But why? "You know, if it wasn't for being in the library, I would leave right now."

"Oh, come, now. Is that the way a lady such as yourself should act?" he lectures, grinning as he still reads.

Looking at him closer, I notice his hair is different. It seems shorter and I quiz, "Did you get a haircut?"

He glances over at me. "Oh, the hair, yes well. Seems I needed a trim. Can't disappoint the ladies by having it grow too long," he teases, as I watch him pat down the back of his hair.

Something is off, folding my arms I watch him. Still gorgeous as ever. "You may want to take a picture," he remarks, turning yet another page.

"What?"

"You're staring. It seems you can't take your eyes off me Wynter. Is there something else you prefer to do other than read in the library? We can go somewhere private, I can show much more than my pretty face."

"Cory, you're insane. What has gotten into you?"

He closes his book with a loud thud and faces me. "I'm insane?" And in a blink of an eye, he's sitting right next to me. Wow, Cory mentioned he can move quick, but this is lightning fast.

Staring at me intently, he counters, "You have no idea how insane I can be." A blue hue of light begins to take hold in his eyes. This isn't the Cory I know, as I begin to put the pieces together. Thinking back earlier in the week when Stella alluded that something felt off, I saw Cory's glower. It had to be Cole, that day standing against the wall, glaring back at Stella. It had to be, why else would he be trying to compel me right now? The watches come to mind, as I look down at his wrist, to see he wears the watch Dad gave him. But that's impossible, I know in my gut this isn't Cory. It leaves me to question where the good twin is. To test my theory I play along.

I smile inwardly, thinking how to act the part. Giving the assumption, it's Cory who hasn't been present all week, I think back to when he sat behind me in class, and consoling me on the kitchen floor. It's Cole, who's coaxed me to the library today. Did he leave the note in my room, too? And what about the box? His glowing eyes continue to try and compel me.

My immediate thoughts race, wanting to know where Cory is. *'What have you done with him Cole? Okay, Wynter think. You must have a plan. Where is that voice of reason when I want her to pop up?'* But silence stays on the ghost end of this conversation.

Coles glowing eyes continue to try and coerce me. "You will come with me Wynter," he says, in a melancholy voice.

"I will come with you," I reply, trying hard not to giggle. Oh, this is going to be rich.

He grabs my hand. "You will forget about everything you have learned, you will become mine. Do with as I please."

'Really,' must I repeat *'that'*? So, I humor him, but when he stands, pulling me to follow, I root my feet to the floor. The confusion on his face is priceless. It takes every ounce of will power in me, to not burst out laughing. I must keep composure and avoid pissing off this evil twin. Who knows what he would do, if he knew I'm playing him for a fool.

"Why do you not follow me, my love? Please, I have much to show you," he soothes.

"My heart belongs to another," I confess. Standing ground, I laugh on the inside from his amazement, of my response.

"Impossible my dear, nothing can stand between us. I have made you mine. Come with me now," he insists.

"As I indicated before, my heart belongs to another. I cannot go with you." I can see the anger build in his eyes, and a brighter glow begins to appear.

He moves back to me, glowering a stance. "You will come with me, now."

I shake my head no, making him angrier. "Give it up, Cole. I know it's you."

He pauses a few minutes blinking, as he steps backwards, "Wait, I had you in my line of sight, I saw your pupils dilating back at me." Changing his body language, in what looks to be frustration. "You can't be compelled, can you?" he sneers, shoving his hands in his pockets.

I smile shaking my head. "No, but you put forth a great effort, though," I giggle.

He staggers back to me with swag. "So what was it? Where did I go wrong? I know I had you fooled at some point," he prods, squinting at me with displeasure. Then he begins to peer intently into my eye's once again, as if to try a third time.

"Probably when you started to stare at her with those glowing eyes of yours, brother," I hear Cory say from behind him.

"I see," Cole smirks, turning around to Cory. "It seems you have escaped your cage. I'll have to make a mental note. Next time, it will not be so easy."

"A little conceded are we, thinking there will be a next time? If someone hadn't tied me up for two days, locking my door from the outside," - Cory peers at Cole in an accusation, - "Perhaps I would have been here much sooner."

"In the nurse's office, and the walk to my room? That was you?" I inquire in surprise, with my suspicions confirmed. How is he able to see the amulets? I look a Cory, and he shrugs, as though he can see the pictures in my mind. "But you wear a watch?" I finally ask. My eyes widen as I back away. "You know…?" I glance back at Cory to see he's just as surprised as me. "That means Mad—"

"No, I'm keeping that to myself for now," Cole confesses. "I purchased one, at the little shop here on the grounds. Seems Moyer doesn't know Cory wears a watch. I thought I would test my theory." Cole glares at Cory, contemptuously, "Why do you where a watch that no one else can see, little brother?"

"Surprise…surprise bro," Cory sneers. "Guess the secret's out."

"Secrets. Seems this house is full of them. Mind telling me yours?" Cole asks.

Cory simpers, as if he seems to enjoy, Cole's mystified speculation. "Some things are best left in reserve, until proper timing."

I hear a low growl come from Cole's throat, like his inner animal cannot be contained much longer. Ignoring Cory's remark, he says, "Seems you have already told her about us. How convenient little brother." Sauntering back to face him. "I can see why you like her. Tell your little girlfriend, to stay in her room at night, and I wouldn't have to intervene on your behalf."

"My behalf?" Cory bellows, straightening his stance. "Like I said, if you hadn't locked my door—"

"Oh please, you know as well as I do, it's Moyer's doing. I'm merely following orders. You know what she does when one doesn't obey." Cole paces back and forth across the floor.

"You will never change, will you, Cole?" Cory sounds irritated.

"Change? What's there to change? We are all stuck here under *her* thumb. We all might as well get used to it! I, for one, am not going to get on her bad side. Need I remind you what happened the last time?"

Cory shuts his eyes, breathes in deep, as if to be controlling his temper. "I won't use my ability to control others for evil. I am not you, brother. You do not intimidate me like you do everyone else. Leave Wynter alone, she is not your new toy."

Cole raises his eyebrow. "Au contraire, that went null and void when she stepped out into the dark when Shadow Walkers roam while the moon is out.

'Shadow Walkers?' Is that what the glowing eyes are? The shadows that roam the halls?

"There haven't been arrangements made to say otherwise," Cory says. "Moyer has given strict instructions to keep her untouched. You dare cross her? Besides, if you want to challenge who saw her first, you lose, Cole."

"Arrangements? You think I will easily forget the guidelines?" And he scans my direction.

Another hiss whistles through Cole's teeth. "She will submit, and you will not stop me."

"Think again. This will not end well, Cole. It doesn't have to be this way." A low growl comes from Cory's mouth.

The two brothers circle the room, arms extended outward, with their legs bent, like they are about to start a wrestling match. The twins' eyes glow blue and fixate on each other as their appearances begin to turn grey. Black bulging veins appear translucent beneath their skin.

"First in sight, first in right, little brother," Cole gnarls a hiss of dominance.

"True, but you did not see her first, if this is where you're going," Cory rebuttals.

"You fail to remember. All is void if a border runs the halls at night," Cole argues. "She's mine. I will have her, and you will not stop me."

"That's where you're wrong, Cole! Do you forget you are not the only one to guard the halls in darkness?"

I run for cover behind a counter in the back, in time to hear both men clash and hiss. Punches sounding like rumbling thunder crashing, against one another. Peeking through a hole behind the library desk, I watch as they fly through the air across the room with each blowing hit. They dash from one corner to the other at lightning speed. Knocking down books, turning tables and chairs, light bulbs burst, with glass shattering everywhere.

I watch as Cole puts Cory in a headlock, and fear sets in as thoughts flash across my mind of Cory being decapitated. Then they quickly switch positions, with Cole now in a chokehold. His eyes pulsate outward from his skull, veins protrude from his neck as his body heaves trying to maneuver out of Cory's grasp. Cole manages to push backwards, slamming Cory into the lit fireplace and sparks shoot from the hearth, forcing him to lose his grip on his brother, giving Cole his opportunity to regroup.

"Enough!" I hear from a woman's voice, that sounds a lot like Blair. I can't see her, from where I am but I can hear both men hiss at each other like slithering lizards fighting for prey.

I peek over the counter peering out to see, all three standing together in the distance. Both men looking gaunt, like risen dead zombies. Black veins trailed along their face and arms as they continue to stare each other down, circling like they are about to pounce each other again.

Blair centers herself between them ready to strike the first one who makes a move. "If I didn't know any better, it would seem you two are fighting over a girl," she hisses back at them. "Calm the pheromones boys. She's not an option."

"She broke the rules," Cole sneers, still circling with his brother. "Moyer says anyone caught after nine, is mine as I please. To keep or kill. Isn't that right brother." His words slide from his tongue, cutting like a knife. So, is this what Rosie meant when she referred to those who go beyond the doors after nine prefer to be whipped? Is that why I'm alive. He wanted me for himself?

Cory's back is to me, when I see him tilt his head slightly toward my direction. "She's not yours, for the taking, Cole. I will fight to the death before I will let you steal her. She is no one's property. You have no rights to her. Like I said, back the hell off!"

Blair sees his reaction, and glances at me, stiffening her stance, "Moyer, is not here to make that decision Cole. She is with some prospective, *'guests.'* Do not alarm her with this nonsense right now. Do you two honestly want Madame Moyer getting involved? You know what happened the last time. Besides, do you truly think she is going to hand her over to you? Her only granddaughter? Think very wisely, son. You take her, and Moyer may take you."

Son? Blair is their mother? And like Moyer really cares about me? Is this her way of calming the situation? I see Cole relax. His skin going back to normal, then Cory.

"You keep your distance Cory. You hear me? This isn't over by a long shot!" Cole glowers at me from behind the counter. "And you,"-pointing directly at me, - "may not be so lucky next time." With that, he disappears.

Cory puts out his hand, for me to come from hiding. "Sorry you had to see that."

"Brings new meaning to following the rules," I say.

"You may not be so lucky next time," Blair warns. "What were you thinking? Haven't you heard a word anyone has told you?" Her tone is angry, looking directly at me.

"I see now. You will not catch me breaking the rules again," I say.

"Yes, well…it's not over. You have been marked, Wynter." Scowling back to Cory, "He won't stop. You do know that, right?" She folds her arms, shaking her head. "You must find a way to put an end to this once and for all, Cory. Get her away from here today." Blair glances around the room at the mess the boys created. "Let Cole calm down. And clean this mess up!" Then she flashes out of the library.

"A little warning would be great next time, Cory," I hint.

"My brother? Yeah, sorry. I think it would have been quite a different experience if someone stayed in their room," he replies in a low voice, hinting that he too is a bit miffed.

"You're mad." Honestly, he has a right to be. I made such a mess of things with no clue how to fix it.

"Mad, no...annoyed maybe, but not mad," he assures, as he picks up the table and chairs and places them back where they belong. "It's only been your first few nights here. Someone should have locked your door. That way none of this would have happened. You're not the first person to have disobeyed the rules, nor will you be the last."

"What did Blair mean about me being marked? And ...she's your mom?" I ask, grabbing the last remaining books from the floor and placing them on the shelves. "I thought Madame Moyer adopted you?"

"Yes, Blair is my mother. And Madame Moyer has the whole house thinking we were adopted, like any other orphan."

"I don't understand, this is all so confusing."

"I'll explain later. Now is not the time, we need to get you out of here. In Cole's eyes, you belong to him. He will stop at nothing to consummate it.

"Consummate? You mean—"

"Mate...? Yes, that's exactly what I mean." Cory picks up the remaining big pieces of glass, throwing it in the trash. "Wynter, when you went out that first night; you know into the halls...?" I'm stunned that he knows. He smiles. "Remember when you clung to the walls as the shadow slid past you?"

"Yes, h—how do you know that?" I feel panic flare on the inside.

"No, no Wyn, stay with me, look at me…it's okay. Focus." His eyes glow and I begin to feel myself again. "That's right, no fear, remember?"

"How do you know, I was in the halls?" I ask, once calm.

"I'll explain later. Not here, but first, where is your coat?"

"This place is still a mess," I reply.

"Don't worry. Blair will have someone here soon to— " and before he has a chance to finish his sentence, a couple of maids come walking in.

"Come on, let's get out of here," he urges, and grabs my jacket laying on the chair, handing it to me to put on.

"What are you up to, Cory Storm?"

"Nothing, just a walk," he replies, and guides me to the back door of the Library.

Which reminds me, as I picture the coffer in my head, and I begin to say, "Where's the— "

Cory puts two fingers to my lips, shaking his head, no. Then points to his ears, and I realize now isn't the time to ask about it. I feel at ease however, that he's keeping it safe. I don't press the issue. Not yet anyhow. But he'd better have a good reason why.

21

Field Trip

We stroll out of the manor to a field where snow-covered ice, crunches beneath our feet. Clear skies still present, for now. The sun peeks out through the trees, giving a hint that daylight will be over in a few hours.

"I have a feeling it will freeze again tonight," Cory says looking up at the sky.

"Do you think it will snow, too?"

"Most likely. We are very far north."

After we're a few yards from the house, Cory says, "There are hidden cameras everywhere in the house, and outside on the grounds. We are distant enough now to talk freely, but I would talk in a low voice."

"Yeah, I know. You told me this morning already," I laugh.

"Oh, I did, did I? What else did I tell you?" he plays along.

"He's on to us, Cory. I think he knows you have your gift too. He did really good at fooling me, posing as you. And I think he might have the coffer." I say in a worried tone.

"No, it's safe. Come, I'll show you where it is."

"You?" and I stop in my tracks.

Cory looks at me, coolly with a hint of sparkle in his eyes, squinting from the glare of the sun reflecting off the snow. "Trust me," he coaxes, putting out his hand to take.

"So, the cameras; they are outside the grounds as well?"

"Yeah, Moyer uses them along with the rest of the supernatural creatures in the house," he confirms, pursing his lips. "She had them installed years ago. Only people that know about them, are Blair, Chad, Cole and me. Now you of course. I am sure she will be pretty angry that you know, but sooner or later you would have found out, anyway."

"She doesn't have to know, unless your brother says something."

Cory looks up at the cumulus clouds surrounding the sun, as if to check what time it is without looking at a watch, then looks at me and smiles. "Only family are to know. It's her way of staying 'in control.' Keeps the humans into thinking the place is haunted," he laughs.

"Back there," I begin; turning my body as I point, "what was that all about?"

"Yeah, about that. Hmm, where to start."

"The beginning?" I suggest.

Cory grins and says, "It's never ending, actually. I don't mean to scoff, but it's almost a daily occurrence now; my brother and I..." He glances down to pick up a rock and throws it. "Sunday night when you stepped out into the hall, I was behind you, watching. I had walked in from the other hall, to see you slide your way to the notched nook near the doorway."

"You were watching me?"

"Well, no, not you, per se, but watching the halls. You see, I am one of the Shadow Walkers that roams at night making sure people stay in their rooms."

"You're one of them?" I question, releasing his hand and backing away feeling betrayed.

"Wyn, it's not like that. Please...." He steps closer to me as I move backwards some more. "Let me explain before you get all judgmental on me. I'm not like the others, remember?" he says, holding up his wrist to reveal the watch. "If I'm evil, would I be able to see your necklace?"

I clutch the heirloom with my fingers. My heart races, and I know he can feel it pounding. "It seems your brother can, too."

"No, I don't think so. He only mentioned that he can see my watch. Which makes me believe that there is still good in him somewhere. Can't see these enchanted items, otherwise."

I can see hurt in his eyes, as he raises an eyebrow, holding out his hand. "Are you afraid of me now? Is that it? After all we have been through so far. After the letter, and the box? You're going to allow fear to get in the way? Come on Wyn, if you do that then *she's* already won!"

"Why didn't you stop me?" saying aloud the first words that come to mind.

"Honestly, I was too late, you had already gone too far for me to save you. When Cole saw you hiding, he was making his way to pounce, until he heard the screams. That's when he opened the doors to catch the others doing a far worse crime than you. He knew he could come back for you later, you had already broken *'the rule."*

"The Rule?" I exclaim, shaking my head. "I'm mean, who does that Cory?"

"What do you want me to say?" he rebukes, continuing to pace towards me, as I keep backing away. "You think I like it? Do you think I want to be this way? A monster that hides within the halls of Storm River Manor?"

I stop. "I don't think you're a monster Cory… I'm confused is all. I don't understand any of this. One day, I'm at school, about to embark on Christmas break and the next minute my family dies and I'm thrust into a new world filled with demons, and supernatural beings." I look at him staring at me, speechless, with sympathetic eyes, like he wishes it would all go away. "It's a little hard for one human to take, in a short amount of time ya know?" Tears begin to well in my eyes again.

He nods, "I know…well, not really. I'm born into this life, but I know what you mean about having your world turned upside-down."

"So, is Cole the one, who killed that poor soul on Sunday night?"

"Yes, by the time it was done, he heard you racing to your room, I was the eye's in front of you, he was the eye's behind, knocking you unconscious." He moves closer to me, this time I don't back away.

"I'm the one who put you back in your bed…We, of course, argued about who saw you first; had a minor scuffle."

"So, what…you're a shadow walker when the moon is out or something?"

"Something like that." Smiling back at me, he says, "Rumors started long ago, about someone escaping the glowing blue-eyed shadow. It's stuck ever since. We, as guardians, roam the halls and grounds. Anyone caught after nine, is either food or property."

"You make it sound like I am a fish to be caught."

"In some ways, you are. At least behind these walls."

Anger begins to fill my head. Thoughts come to my tongue to lash out at him, and I say, "A fish to be caught?"

"Please Wynter, allow me to explain before you go all halfcocked again. Has anyone ever told you, that you have your mother's attitude?"

"You knew my mother too?"

"I did," he confirms. "Long before you were ever born of course."

"Wait, what?" I stare in bewilderment. My head hurts trying to figure out what he just revealed. "Cory Storm, how old are you?"

"Are you sure you are ready to hear that answer?"

"Would it really make a difference, Cory? I mean seriously? I've lost my family, so I'm an orphan. I've been told I have an evil grandmother—that I never knew existed in the first place—who's after my *'power'* - which I didn't even know I had— when I turn eighteen. Apparently, I can heal myself from a compound fracture, too. Try figuring this out, when you're a human. Wait, that's right…I'm not even human!" By this time my irritation begins growing again.

"Such a temper," he teases shaking his head. "Jeoffrey didn't have it nearly as bad as you. Although your wrath may come in handy later."

"Jokes? So, you have jokes, now?" I want to smack him, but can't, as I'd feel guilty later.

"No, no. Stop, okay? Hang on. Bear with me, I'm a slow storyteller."

"Speed it up, I'm losing patience."

He takes a deep breath, as if to regroup his mind before speaking. "You have so much to learn and so little time to explain it all. Technically, if we were playing by *'the rules,'* you are mine before his, anyway," he says, softly.

I don't know how to respond to that. A part of me likes that I can be his anyway. Like wearing the quarterback's letterman jacket.

After a long awkward pause, I finally say, "So, when Blair mentioned I'm marked…?"

"She means you now have a target on your back. Cole will stop at nothing to get what he wants."

"Wait, so, you both were fighting over who marked me first?"

Grinning, he says, "Essentially yes, but you are not one to be caged like an animal, a possession to have. I would want someone to love me because it is their will to do so, not because they are forced."

If he only knew how I truly felt. "Why not tell Cole the truth?" I say. The feeling of butterflies seem to dance in my stomach, making me sense that my cheeks are becoming hot.

"So, tell him the truth then," the voice replies to me. I ignore it, taking a few more steps away from Cory, to give some distance between us and to catch my breath.

"Stay out of this." I say back to the ghost that seems to pop in and out at its convenience.

Cory laughs, "Do you honestly think Cole cares about the truth? It doesn't matter if I tell him or not. He's convinced he saw you first and no amount of reasoning will stop him." He shakes his head, bends over grabbing snow and balls it up. "No, only death will come of it I am afraid." Then he throws the snowball through the air lightning fast. "Unless, of course, you have an idea on how to bring my brother back from the dead?"

Ignoring his sarcastic remark, I say, "Then I'll tell him I don't want him. I'll tell him my heart belongs to another."

"Does it?" he asks, looking at me as though I may have broken his heart.

Gulping back a breath and flushing cheeks, I say, "Yes. The first day I saw him, I knew." Thinking of the day in the library as he looked over the countless books until finally picking the one, he liked.

Cory tilts his head and smiles, as he paces closer to me. I know he can see my thoughts. "It appears one man's loss, is another man's gain," he says, our faces becoming inches apart.

"You see, I cannot belong to Cole, when I'm destined to another. I fear he does not know though," I confess.

"Perhaps it wise, that he not know yet." Our fingers touch, but we do not hold hands. Our lips so close, I can smell his sweet breath of exhale.

"If he knew, it would make such a mess of things wouldn't it?" I say, barely able to breathe.

"He's very lucky to have grabbed such a beautiful heart indeed," Cory whispers. His breath is warm against the cold winter air, signaling sensations through my whole body. I can feel my heart pound within my chest.

"Your heart beats so fast. Do I frighten you?" he asks.

"No… Cole maybe, but not you," I concede, holding onto the moment, hoping it wouldn't end.

"He won't stop until you're in his grasp. I can handle Cole. It's Madame Moyer we have to worry about." Then as though shutting off a faucet, he backs away saying, "Come on, I want to show you something." Taking my hand, he guides me towards the trees. "This way, I think I solved another part of the riddle."

We come upon a wrought iron decorative arched gate. Rose branches hibernate within the winters season, entwining themselves throughout the black decorative fencing which is very similar in detail from the fencing we passed on the way into the compound.

"This looks like the same garden I saw the day I arrived," I observe.

"Indeed, it is: the back entrance. We all call this Lady Sara's garden. It's supposed to be a replica of the one in Scotland."

"Scotland?"

"It's where the story all began, really."

"What story?" He has my full attention now and watches me touch my necklace, as I think about who Lady Sara is.

"She's your great-grandmother."

I sigh and roll my eyes at his remark.

"What was that for?"

"Nothing. Just something I'm going to have to get used to I suppose."

He smiles. "You mean being inside your thoughts. Sorry. It's unintentional, I hope you know that."

"I'm sure it is. It's not something a person can just overcome, overnight, ya' know."

"I'll try to remember that." He smiles, and continues, "Lady Sara was the baroness of this estate. She and Ailbert, along with the others, Isobel, Gavin, Clarice and Bram, fled Scotland in 1534. They made a deal with an explorer who was setting sail for

North America, and so it is told, that they later settled here: laying claim to the land, building this compound."

I watch Cory work on unlocking the ancient handle, as rust falls to the ground, turning the snow at our feet orange. "Rumor has it Moyer poisoned Sara. Sadly, there is no proof. When she died, so did her garden. This became her place of solitude when she was alive. She would come here to get away. To gather her thoughts."

"How do you know all this?" I ask.

He smiles. "If I can get this gate to open, I'll show you how I know."

Thorny vines intertwine the lock as Cory tries to pry it lose. "Normally, I come down the river, but I wanted to show you the garden."

The garden is so badly overgrown, that once Cory has the lock free, weeds break and fall to our feet before we enter.

Stepping inside, I gasp, "It's beautiful." Icicles hang from the hibernating tree branches, while snow illuminates millions of crystal reflections, that bounce off from the sun's rays. It's like looking at a winter wonderland. I can hear snow birds chirp from the tree tops, alarming the world that the garden has guests. "This was all Sara's?" I ask. "It's so enchanting."

"This is nothing, compared to what else lies ahead," he whispers.

Cory leads me deeper into the heart of the garden. I imagine during spring time the flowers, bring fragrances of all sorts to the senses. I look forward to what this place will bring.

"There's also another way, to the garden from inside the manor," Cory says. "But, no one can find the key to unlock the doors. Moyer has been searching for it for years."

"A portal?" I stop in my tracks. "You mean like in the movies where people travel in other dimensions; portal?"

"Something like that yes," he says, turning to me and smiling. "Now come on, we haven't much light, before Casey sets the dogs out to guard the grounds."

"The dogs. I almost forgot about that."

Eventually, we come upon a small trail hidden behind an overgrown cedar tree. Although winter has long shown itself to the world, the grand fir still lets out its magnificent aroma. Bringing my senses to remember Christmas Holiday. Memories are cut short, though, with the thoughts of my birthday around the corner. Are we going to solve this riddle in time, find a way to escape Moyers grasp, and be free of this wretched place? Racing thoughts begin to take hold of my emotions. I think Cory feels my panicked heartbeat because we stop.

"Wynter, look at me," he says turning around. My head's still in a foggy daze with thought. "Look at me!" This time shaking my shoulders a bit, until I snap out of it. "Right here, at my eyes, look at me," he whispers.

I gaze back at him. His calming face and blue eyes like the color of the ocean, stare back at me; bringing me back to calmness. The panic within my soul dissipates.

"I'm not going to let anything happen to you," he says. "We will find out how to destroy her. I promise you that."

I bite my lower lip, wondering how he can possibly promise me something he hasn't any control over, but I nod at him anyway in agreement.

"That's better, it's going to be fine." Grabbing my hand, he pulls me through the woods along the overgrown trail.

"How did you know? I mean, back there." Turning my head slightly to point. "You had your back to me, focused on finding whatever this is you are looking for, to show me."

"I'm always focusing on you," he says, grinning. "Have you not figured that out by now. Come on, it's not much farther now."

"Cory, you didn't answer my question," blushing from his remark. "How did you know the panic I felt a moment ago without seeing my facial expressions?"

"I can hear your heartbeat, remember?" he replies, stepping further down the path, not faltering on his mission, with each persisting question I ask him.

"How? You stated you don't read minds. Didn't you say you just see pictures?"

He stops and turns towards me, laughing quietly. "No, I don't read minds only pictures, like I told you before... at least not yet."

"Not yet?"

He moves some branches away, that are hanging over the pathway, allowing me to pass by him. Then he continues, "Well at first when I got my power; it started out as intuition. Like... I could feel something was wrong but couldn't put my finger on it. I could read people's emotions at first, then it grew to feeling them. Soon I could hear heartbeats. At first it was overwhelming, but I learned to control it."

"That's what my dad and my aunt Fran said when they came into their powers. Referring to it as white noise, you learn to block out."

"Yes, that's right. It's easy to narrow your heart beat because it's just us. But if we were around a group of people, I would have to study whose heartbeat is whose. Everybody's beats differently."

"That's kind of disturbing Cory, and cool I guess, too... and weird."

Down a small trail, and in the distance, I can barely hear a stream flowing. As we continue to walk down the path, I ask, "So, what's with the *'eyes'*? And, you mentioned *'not yet,'* about reading minds. What do you mean?"

He smiles at me, giving a teasing look, not answering a word, leading me closer to the sounds of water.

As we get closer to the creek, I can see a cabin through the thick fir trees.

"Is that what I think it is?" Gazing directly at Cory, I don't believe what I'm seeing. "How does Moyer not know this is here?"

His smile grew wide with delight and grabs my hand with excitement. "Come," he says, and pulls me faster down the trail toward the little cottage in the woods. The outside of the little house is made of logs, and in between them grows bright green moss, with the roof having a light dusting of snow.

"Remember the riddle?" Cory says with enthusiasm, *"Behind the roses you will find. Something hidden from behind."*

He gently turns the handle of the front door, opening it. "It has to be this cottage.

22

Cottage in the Woods

Inside the small cabin dusty sheets cover furniture, and a sooty river rock fireplace butts up against the back wall with windows on either side, overlooking the river below. A water wheel can be seen partially beneath the cabin, appearing not to be working. I perceive that the fireplace hasn't been lit in years. Cobwebs cover the hearth and dust lies everywhere. To the left of us is a tiny kitchen and to the right a hallway to what I imagine are bedrooms. Stairs to the side of the living room leads to a loft. Although this small house is quite old and probably hadn't been lived in for years, it gives an amazing, magical feel.

"Cory, it's simply breathtaking." I look upward and see a bannister, and faint glimpse of books shelved against a wall. "What's up there?" I point to the small balcony that overhangs to the living space.

"It's Sara's Library. A lot of literature is up there."

I turn to him with curiosity. "How many times have you been here?"

He comes to stand next to me and peers up. "I've come to this place more times than I can count. Most of the time during the day and I usually stay outside. If I do come inside, it's to go up there, and read."

"You come at night? But the dogs, won't they see you?"

"No, not at all. You see, this cottage is hidden from those who wish harm to others; those with darkness in their soul." He looks around us and begins taking sheets off the furniture. Shaking the fabric, prompts us both to cough. "Guess I should have done that outside," he says.

After sneezing, I say, "Suppose you're right."

"I'm sorry, are you allergic?"

"No, I'm fine really." He gestures with his hand for me to sit down on a settee that looks Victorian, with almond cover cushions. The back of the lounge is in the shape of a throne, having lion claws as feet. "This place is remarkable. How do you know of its existence?" I ask.

"Remember when I told you of that day, I saw my brother become hexed from Moyer?"

"Yes," I say, nodding with intrigue.

He pauses for a long time while folding the sheet in his hands, then walks toward the window that still revealed a hint of late afternoon light coming through the shaded trees. The rays sparkle through the stained glass, and he sits, as if finding a way to begin a story, he started back in my room when we found the leather box.

"Well, I didn't finish telling you the whole story, now, did I? That day I received the watch from your father, I ran back to the river, seeking him, but he was gone. I can still hear Cole calling my name, as if it happened yesterday. He sounded so different. Like Moyer had planted the evil in him already. When I reached the river, I ran all the way down until I came to this cottage. Smoke escaped the chimney stack, so I figured this must be where Jeoffrey would hide. It doesn't occur to me until later what this place truly is."

I squint at him. "What is this place, if it's not a cabin?"

"It's so much more than a cottage in the woods, Wynter." He smiles.

I can tell he's hiding something, like he doesn't feel it's the right time to give me everything all at once. "You said you thought this place belonged to my father, what happened?"

"That day…I knocked to see if anyone was home." He peers outside as he speaks. "When the door creaked open, I hesitated before coming inside."

"That's kind of spooky, Cory. What did you do?"

"Went in, of course," he says, grinning back at me. "The fire was lit and the place warm. Something was cooking on the stove, right over there." He Points to the now black and grimy cast iron metal oven, sitting in the kitchen.

"Yet I didn't see anyone around. I sat at the fire for a few minutes, wondering what to do with the watch, I held in my hands. Fiddling with it in my fingers. I decided to walk the home inside and out, thinking of a good hiding spot to place the watch. But nothing felt right, no matter where I looked. Then, from the corner of my eye I see the wisp again. The same one near your dad that day I saw him. It was a bright white bulb of light, singing an almost mesmerizing spell. I follow it back inside the cottage. It moves around me as though to be searching my thoughts. Then, right before my eyes appears a woman, looking much like you, only older."

"Who was she?"

"She called herself Isalora. 'Protector of Life'. It's then, that I learned a great deal about Madame Moyer and her plans. She indicated the prophecy is coming soon and would know it when a girl arrived by the name of Wynter."

"My arrival? You mean, you knew I was coming?"

"I did. And she prepared me for what is to come."

"What is to come, Cory? Have you been privy to this information all along and didn't tell me?"

"I had to be sure," he says. "I mean, let's face it. Not too many people are named Wynter. So, I waited for the letter she stated would follow. That's why when you saw me so distraught; I didn't know how to tell you right there. I had to think of a way to get you to here. To show you."

"To show me what? This house? Does this mean you know what to do about the prophecy? My mind is full of questions, I want to know everything. I want to know it all. Cory, do you know why I am here?"

He veers my questions with a different subject. "This house is a portal hub to our world back home. Where we as Storms all come from."

He looks at me with solemn eyes and nods. "Yes, I know about the prophecy. Not all of course…like the clues to the riddle, and how the prophecy is to be filled. But I do know you are the key to stopping it. That loft up there?" he continues, pointing with his eyes. "It's the gateway to other places, other worlds, other dimensions."

"Cory, if this place leads to other worlds, then why are you still here? I mean… why are we still here, even? Why has the Storms not fled the cruelty of Madame Moyer?"

"Because the portal is locked. It can't be opened. I've tried since I found this place. I've read nearly all the books shelved up there, hoping one would give me a clue."

"And apparently you have come to a dead end?" I say, lowering my eyes. *'If Cory doesn't know, why can't you tell me,'* I say to the silent voice that hides in my mind." I get nothing from the other end.

"So, where is the box? I assume you still have it? It was not in the chamber behind the fireplace in my room."

"I have it hidden, in the same place as the watch." Cory stands and smiles at me, as if he's about to show me something exciting. Walking over to a corner of the living space, he moves a shelf that houses books and a draping plant.

I give him a perplexing glance, as he grabs a toolbox from the closet, and begins pulling up planks within the floorboards.

"You've hidden it in the floor?" I ask, looking at him in surprise.

He smiles at me. "Sunday night, when we received the riddle, I thought about it deeply. The only roses I know of, is the garden. This cottage is so far off the beaten path it must be what the letter meant. *'Behind the roses you will find. Something hidden from behind.'* Then I thought about the next riddle, *'There is second one about, but not in soot. It is after all, under foot.'* It's then I clued in; remembering the hiding place I put the watch."

"Is that where you have hidden the box, too?"

"Yes. Monday morning during lunch I slipped up to your room and snuck the box, hiding it within my cowl. I wrote you a note to meet me in the library. It didn't occur to me that Cole would find it before you. When I came back to the mansion, I'd heard you had fallen. Cole guided me to where you were; I should have known it was a trick. He teamed up with Nora, and she slipped a cloth over my mouth, and the next thing I know, I'm locked in my room."

"How did you finally escape?"

"Well, it appears, I'd been out for two days. Casey found me tied up. He's the only other person beside Moyer that has a key to all the doors. If it wasn't for him, stocking the wood pile in my room today, I might have still been there."

"I don't want to even think about what could have happened. I'm glad to be safe here with you. So, how do you know about this hiding spot in the first place?" I ask.

"Isalora showed me the day we met. Told me it would be safe here. That when the time came, I could grab it."

"Unbelievable, Cory." Looking at him, I say, "I normally would think someone is off their rocker for ripping up a floor like you have, but somehow, I know you must have a plan."

"Indeed, I do." He grins.

So, I wait, watching him struggle at each plank as he pulls them out one by one. Once the last slat is pulled, he reaches into the floor hauling out the box we discovered in my room, Sunday.

"Any clue how to open it yet?" I ask wondering how on earth we would ever find such a tiny item, like a key."

"No, but I did find this." He reaches in, pulls out another box, like the same one found behind the fireplace in my room.

"Another coffer?" I ask, in surprise.

"I didn't see it in there before; when I placed the watch all those years ago. Probably because it was pushed farther back from view, but it wasn't until I tried to place the leather box we found on Monday, did I notice the second chest here in the hole."

"Is the watch still in there?" I ask.

"Yes, untouched. Still wedged in the corner where I left it."

"Who else knows of this secret spot?"

"Only the dead, and me."

"Dead?"

"Isalora is a spirit. She told me that day, only the dead can see this cottage, and those who serve good magic. You see, Wynter, this is how I know you are the one to fulfill the prophecy. Otherwise, you would not see this cabin on the river."

"And that's why Moyer will never see it either?" I ask, trying to grasp the mystery of it all.

"Precisely. There is much more I need to tell you, but the sun is going down quickly, and you must not be out after dark."

"Right, the dogs." I say, remembering that awful night meeting up with the dire beast and her pack.

"Meet me in the library after class tomorrow, we can come back here, then. We have the whole weekend to figure this all out, before Moyer comes back next week. Besides it's too much risk to talk freely with cameras everywhere, and if Moyer catches wind that this cabin still exists, she can do magic to fight the shield protecting it."

"Do you think she may know this cabin might still exist?"

"No, I don't think so. To her knowledge it burned down many years ago, when the Storm family first arrived here on the land. But that is for another time. We must prepare to leave now." And he stashes the items back in the hole beneath, replacing the floorboards back as carefully as he pulled them apart.

"At this rate we will have to run back, and it still won't be enough, will it Cory? It already looks dark within the shadow of the trees."

He gives me a grin. "Did I mention I run fast too?"

"Huh?" I smile at him, wondering what he means, saying, "I did get a taste of your speed back in the library when you were 'debating' with your brother."

"Right," he says, as he gets up, placing the shelf back in the spot it was before. "Ready to go?" And he walks to the front door, opening it.

I follow him outside and he shuts the door behind us. Turning to me he says, "Climb on my back."

"Cory you're nuts," I say, shaking my head at him.

"Seriously, climb on my back. I'm not joking."

Thinking he's gone completely mad, I begin to protest. "Cory—"

"Do you trust me?"

"Yes." Looking at him blankly.

"So, humor me." He nudges my arm and turns his back towards me.

Reluctant, I climb up, and before I have time to catch a breath, he says, "Hang on tight."

We glide like lightening across the snow. So fast that what took a good thirty-minute walk, ends up being three minutes tops and my feet touch the back steps of the library.

"Look at my eyes, how do you feel," Cory says.

"Cory, I'm fine, it's ok. You will explain when you can, I trust you." Then I hear the first howl of the dogs being released.

"Quick, let's get inside." He places his arm across my back and guides me through the door.

It isn't too long after that, I see a pack of dogs pass the French doors. One stops, and peers directly at me, giving me chills. I know it's Redmae. Her eyes glowing a bright crimson.

"They don't waste any time releasing them, do they?"

"Not at all," he replies.

It's about dinner time, when we walk through the back doors. Trying hard to not be noticed, we do our best to sneak through the library undetected. Luckily Cory knows the blind spots on all the cameras, however the front doors to the Library are found locked.

"This means it's after five," he says, and he stops. Appearing to be thinking on what to do next. I watch Cory whip out his cell phone from his jeans and dial.

The look on my face must have been priceless because he chuckles a second before speaking into the phone.

"Hey yeah, it's me. Where are you right now?"

Then a pause, while Cory listens. "Yeah, I seem to have been locked in the library again. Do you think you can come down and unlock it...? Yes, I know…she won't find out. Besides you know the blind spots… Right, I forgot about that…What about Derek? Tell him I fell asleep in the library again ... Of course, it will work… Okay see you soon. Then he hangs up.

You could have knocked me down with a feather. "Cell phone huh? And when were you going to tell me about this?" I say in a tone of irritation.

"Need to know basis, now that you know, I suppose I need to tell you, but not now."

"Really?"

"Yes, really, because Chad is already at the door."

"What?"

I can see Cory is quite amused leaving me hanging. I want to thump him in the arm, but that would only prolong the teasing.

"Well, that was fast," I say.

"He was outside the back porch, taking a smoke break."

"Outside? But the dogs."

"I suppose another thing to clear up later, right?" He says, I witness the knob of the door wiggle.

"Chad, hey there, thanks I owe you big time, dude." Cory says.

I watch Chad give a lopsided grin of irritation. Then says, to me, "Good to see you again Wynter, how are you fairing around the castle?"

"I'm managing I guess." Thinking to myself, *'What other surprises are in store for me?'*

"Quick! Get out of here. Derek said he can only hold the illusion for about five minutes tops." Chad says, and then appears to look around to see if anyone else may be watching.

"Illusion? What illusion?" I ask.

Cory grabs my hand. "This way. Follow me. No time to explain right now," he says, as we slide across the hall undetected and making our way close to the theatre room. "If anyone catches us together, they will for sure say something to Madame Moyer. Here's what we will do, give me your coat, and go into the kitchen, as if you are coming down to dinner. I will sneak your coat and hat to your room."

"But Cory—"

"Go! I don't have time to explain it now." I shrug off my jacket, handing it to him, and before I can protest, he's gone.

23

Hidden Scars

I make my way to the kitchen, trying to rehearse my whereabouts for the afternoon, knowing full well Stella would probably wonder where I've been all day.

When I enter the kitchen, the maids are busy cooking and prepping for dinner. It must not be six yet, that's a good sign.

At the far end of the table I see Stella peeling vegetables. Once she glances up and sees me, her cheery face turns to anger.

"Hi there Stella," I say, grabbing another peeler to help.

"You surprise me Wynter, showing up here at the last minute. Where have you been all day? I looked for you in the library, knocked on your door to your room, I even checked the grounds to see if you dared to venture outside in this wretched weather."

"Wow, Stella miss me today?" I retort, acting like she's overreacting, although I know she's right. I'd been gone all afternoon. I can't wait to get back to the cabin and learn more from the stories that Isalora told Cory.

"It's odd you show your face now, right before dinner time," Stella says. Her look of discontent shows all over her face.

"Well, if you did in fact come to my room, I simply didn't hear you. I fell asleep." I know my excuse isn't going to work.

She raises an eyebrow. "Mmm." And begins peeling the potato in her hand, harder and faster.

I sigh, knowing I've been caught in a lie, and I try to dig myself out. "Fine, I'll tell you later, but not here. After dinner, we can girl talk in my room."

A slight curve comes from the corner of Stella's mouth, giving me the impression that I'm temporarily pardoned. "Okay, I forgive you, but just this once, on one condition. You promise to go to the movies with me Friday night."

"Wait, I thought we had to be in our rooms by nine?"

"When Moyer is gone, Mr. Derek breaks the rules and gives the kids a treat, by doing movie nights," Stella says.

"Okay sure. Do you know what movie will be playing?"

"No, not yet. Usually they announce the movie, Friday afternoon."

After dinner Stella and I walk together to our rooms. I didn't realize until now, that we could have been doing the girl talk this whole time; knowing that her door is down the hall from mine. Once we reached my room, we both look at each other confused to see that my door is ajar.

The moonlight illuminates the hallway, but inside my room an orange flicker of light permeates in the shadows, and it can only mean one thing. Cory started a fire, waiting for me, and didn't anticipate Stella joining us. I wonder if he's inside now. Stella's surprised and hesitant, to enter. So, to ease her indecision I say, "I started a fire before leaving for dinner. Thought it would be a great idea to have a warm room when I got back." Hoping that will satisfy as an answer, I look over to see my closet open a crack, leaving me to believe Cory is hiding.

"It's nice and warm in here," Stella says, following me through the door. After a few minutes, she begins to say, "So where were you today?" I can tell by the look on her face, she's annoyed with me.

'Why is she so nosey?' I think, as I heave off one shoe, that hits the closet door making a loud thud. I giggle under my breath, from the visual of Cory possibly being startled.

"Well if you must know, I was with Cory all day. And before you say one word, I don't care, I like him." With a long pause, I see Stella glare at me with a disapproving look. "I'm not sure what the big deal is, anyway? Plus, he's nice to me."

"Have you not listened to anything I've said this whole week? He's Madame Moyers son. If she finds out you are befriending him, she will probably give you ten lashings in the basement." I watch as she paces over to the fire and sits in the chair.

The memory of that vile room comes into focus, with Stella mentioning the basement, and I begin to feel sick, as the juices in my stomach rise to my throat. Cory must have sensed my pain, fore I experience sudden calmness.

"Wynter, are you okay? What is it?" Stella inquires.

"I'm fine, don't feel well, is all," I say, and I sit on my bed. "Have you ever been to the basement?" I swallow hard, from the bile continuing to float up my throat.

Stella went sheet white. "Why do you ask?"

"Because Madame Moyer brought me to the basement a few days ago. She wanted to *'show me'* where people go who break the rules. It's horrible, and I would rather not remember it." The image of JC hanging in chains continues to stay at the front of my mind.

Stella comes to sit next to me, pulling back her hair, to reveal scars of her own.

I gasp at the sight of it. Pink and rose colors of her flesh intertwined with white lined scars across her back and neck. Some areas of the skin untouched, while others lay ridged in marks. Some wounds are scabbed over, like it happened a few months ago. It reminded me of JC, only Stella's injuries have healed.

"How long ago?" I ask, still fighting the bile in my throat, my heart heavy for Stella.

"About six months ago, I was caught outside the grounds," she says softly. "Madame Moyer came home early on a nice spring day. We were in between school recesses. I was caught outside the rose garden. But apparently Madame Moyer thought I was too close. The next thing I know, I'm given ten lashings and a night in a cold cell."

"You mean the overgrown garden near the entrance to the gate?" I ask curiously.

"Yes, the one and only."

"That's appalling."

"Rumors have it that it was Lady Sara's garden," She went on... "And no one is to ever enter, let alone be near it. It's been locked up for years. Apparently, Madame Moyer wants to burn it to ashes, but Sir Daniel won't have it."

Trying to play it off that I'm hearing about the garden for the first time, so I ask, "Sir Daniel?"

She continues, "When Lady Sara died, Sir Daniel inherited the compound through her death. Deep secrets lie among these castle walls, and so many yet to be discovered. I lay in bed at night hearing eerie sounds of footsteps that roam the halls outside, the moans heard beyond doors, and the babies that cry."

"Footsteps? You mean the shadow walkers?" I ask.

"Yes, how do you know about them?" Stella questions.

"You're not the only one who hears about gossip Stel," I say.

She seems to look surprised by my comment, but brushes it aside, continuing, "It is rumored, that the only way you live, being caught by a shadow walker after nine, is if you're marked. Then they keep you as their mate for life."

"Who told you that, Stella?" Beginning to think what Cory commented on earlier isn't so farfetched after all.

"Nora, she's one of them now. Roams the halls at night. Rosie told me the story once. Much like you, she had a mind of her own. Curious, she ventured out, hearing a sound that didn't seem right. It's then, that the shadow walker took her for his own. Rosie was heartbroken for a long time. Sometimes I wonder if that is the reason she stays."

"Stays? But I thought once you enter you can never leave."

"This is true, with one exception," Stella replies. "If the one who governs passes away, the help are free to stay or go, as they please. Rosie is the only one left from Sara's court. The rest have died. Everyone here now, are of Madame Moyer's hiring."

"Stella, how do you know all this?"

"When you have lived within these walls as long as I have, you become accustomed to the gossip."

"I still do not know why I am here. Have you any gossip about that?" I ask, wondering if I can get more mysterious details from her.

"I am sure you will find answers. I'm sorry, I don't have more to tell you."

"Stella, would you please tell me about the baby cries in the night?"

"Ah…the crying. Well, one day, things changed. You see, this story takes a tragic twist I'm afraid."

My eyes widen, wanting more gossip, as she tells her tale.

"What happens to them?" I finally ask again.

"I don't know. The babies are born, then taken away. No clue what happens to them."

"Taken, to where?" I ask stunned.

"Adopted, I imagine. If you haven't noticed, this is an orphanage." She pauses, as if she's worried. "I shouldn't be telling you this."

"Stella, I don't understand. This is an adoption facility, what's so abnormal about babies being adopted?"

"Wynter, this isn't the orphanage you think it is. Those babies you hear, are bred."

"Bred? You make it sound like this place is a puppy mill for humans."

"That's exactly what it is." She looks at me with terror in her eyes and I know she has more to tell.

Her harsh comment begs me to question, "Stella, you can't be serious?"

She gets up from the bed, and walks to the fire, looking into it for a long while, then turns to me saying, "Couples who can't have children, who are not eligible to go through the proper channels, come to Madame Moyer. She has a vast gene pool catalog file. A couple picks the kind of baby they would like, and Madame Moyer selects a likely genetic match. Giving the couple an album to choose from, the adoptive parents choose a picture of the biological parents. From there Moyer summons them to the castle. Once the woman is confirmed pregnant, the male donors are free to leave. The mother lives here the entire pregnancy and the hosts are paid handsomely."

After picking my jaw up off the floor, I ask. "Okay, wait, I am trying to wrap my head around this. You mean, Madame Moyer genetically matches parents to make offspring for adopted parents on the black market? Why not go to a clinic?"

Stella shrugs her shoulder and adds, "Other times, young teenage mothers come to live here, and Madame Moyer finds proper homes for the unborn child. Those girls have their babies adopted out through proper channels and paperwork. That's how Moyer can hide from the black market. She hides behind a legitimate adoption agency." Stella pauses, for a few seconds, taking in a deep breath, then, she makes eye contact and smiles. Not a happy smile, but rather a grim one, saying, "Let that sink in for a minute. And another thing, if at sixteen you haven't been adopted out, you become a pawn in her scheme."

"What do you mean pawn? You're not suggesting that she turns the girls into hosts, are you?" A question that I can't believe is even a question to be asked.

"That's exactly what I mean. She's careful about whom she selects. Some girls are jailed like prisoners, never to see the light of day, only through their bedroom windows. Once she is done with them, she feeds the girls to the Shadow Walkers."

It takes me a minute to catch my breath, I begin to feel hot, and my stomach starts to churn with knots. "Are you suggesting that Madame Moyer, my grandmother, is breeding humans for food?"

"That's the speculation, yes," Stella answers.

'Madame Moyer is one crazy witch,' I think to myself in disgust.

"So, what does she do? How does she get the girls to submit?" And as quickly as I say it aloud, I remember the blue eyes. *'Of course, that has to be it. This is how she uses her power. To influence people to cave to her will, by her hypnotizing evil eye.'*

Stella shrugs her answer, followed by, "The girls say they don't remember anything. It's as though they are suddenly with child and no clue as to how it got there. There have been cases where some have awoken in the cells below the manor, while other times they black out finding themselves locked in their rooms. I fear I have said too much to you. If anyone finds out I told you all this, I'm as good as dead. *They* won't forgive this."

"They?" I ask.

"The eyes and ears of Storm River Manor." Stella's eyes are dark and solemn, as though hope is gone, from inside of her.

"Stella you have my word." Then I remember that Cory is still in the closet listening, hoping he wouldn't do the unthinkable and report back to Madame Moyer.

Is this her plan? To take my body and use it? What the hell? I bounce from my bed, and exclaim, "We must plan an escape, Stella. Leave this place as soon as possible! I have a funny feeling why I am here now. I'm her next target."

Stella peers back at me, unaffected by my fervor, saying, "She has eyes everywhere. Even when she's gone, with staff reporting to her at all hours of the night. In fact, someone will probably report that you were not anywhere to be found for hours today. Surely Madame Moyer will question you. Wynter, they are planning something big." I watch her cup her hands together in worry.

"Yes, I know, a birthday party. Madame Moyer told me in the basement that my eighteenth birthday is going to be *'exciting.'* She said, plans are already in the making."

"Wynter, I think when she comes back next week, she's going to follow through with her scheme."

"We must find a way to get out of here, Stella. I mean it. We must find a way. Think. You have lived here a while. Is there any pathways you know of? Secret pocket minutes, where one can find a window of opportunity to escape?"

"Don't you think I would have done that already, if I knew of a way to leave? And keep your voice down," she whispers. "We may be able to talk freely in this room, but the hall outside can still hear."

Stella walks to the window peering out into the darkness, "It is rumored that dire wolves roam the night sky. Of course, no one has ever seen them. Only heard them. If you are caught on the grounds at any point unaccompanied, they will attack." She looks down at her feet. There's a long pause. Taking in a deep breath, looking at me, she says, "There is no way off this compound other than death."

"I see now. Perhaps you're right and there's no escape," I reply. On the inside I'm raging mad. *'Where are you?'* I say to the voice inside my head. *'I'm not going to let Madame Moyer think she has the upper hand.'* But the voice stays silent.

I've seen the dogs Stella describes, but I don't think now is the time to tell her that. But, perhaps it's like Stella indicated, one must be accompanied, and Cory was with me today.

Stella walks to my door. "I've said too much, and I should leave. Besides, it's almost nine."

I nod at her, not knowing what else to say. We hug each other goodbye, and I watch her walk down the hall disappearing around the corner.

I hear the creak of the closet door, and see it open out of the corner of my eye. "Thought she would never leave," he says.

"Startled momentarily, I swing around to glare at him. "When were you going to tell me all the little secrets about this place. Huh?"

"Shh - quiet, do you want others back in here catching us together?" he says as he put his hands out to gesture me to calm down. "What do you want to know? I'll tell you everything."

"Is it true? I mean what Madame Moyer did…? Um, let me try again. I mean… is it true that all of this is a cover up for the black-market baby mill?"

I watch Cory lower his eyes. I don't even need to know his answer; the truth is written all over his face. "Yes, all of it. It's true. But not in the way you think," he answers.

"And the legitimate adoptions?" I ask. "Another one of her cover-up's?

He nods. "It's also true, as are the host adoptions," he says. "Moyer has some kind of hold on each and every person who lives within these walls. But Stella doesn't know much about the garden. Only that it is off limits to go in. She doesn't know about the family history either."

"And the dogs? What dogs? I have only seen the pack of wolves released at night."

"It's just like Stella said, they only come out when one is unaccompanied."

"So, they're invisible?" I add.

"Yes," he replies. "But you cannot see them. They are undead. Invisible to the naked human eye. Rather, they are of spirit form, and one must have the power to see the undead, to see them."

"I gather you cannot see them as well, then?"

His silence, leads me to believe he too, is blind by the undead dogs. So, I press another question, changing the subject. "Do you know her plans for my eighteenth birthday?"

"No. Only that you are to come into your power, soon, and anyone witnessing changes, are to report back to Madame Moyer."

"Changes?"

"Yes. For example, your hair. Have you seen it lately?"

"What about my hair?" I ask confused and walk to the mirror to see it has turned from black, to a light brown. "I don't understand. All my life I have had black hair. Blair mentioned it would lighten. I didn't believe her." Witnessing right before my very eyes, the obvious color change, I turn around looking back at him pleading for an answer.

"Wynter, do you want to know the truth?" Cory replies, stepping closer to me. "Because, what I am about to tell you, rather, show you will change the way you see life forever." Taking a solid stance, he firms a glare I had never seen before. Not even when Cole pretended to be him. It's a look, that gives frightened intrigue. If I want to know who I truly am I might as well suck it up, so, I nod at him in response.

Cory walks over to shut off the lights, when he turns around his eyes glow bright blue.

I gasp in alarm, not expecting to see such a sight so quick. I mean, I've seen Cory's eyes become bright in the light, but never in the dark.

"Your eyes are much brighter at night," I mumble, trying to stay composed. The memory of the blue glowing eyes in the hall that day comes to the surface of my thoughts.

"First let me remind you, of my innate abilities," he begins. "They go way beyond the normal human capabilities. I can see you from miles away and hear your heartbeat no matter where you are. Remember that *'rule,'* well it sort of manifests in us. Our senses become keen, more protective, and it doesn't matter where you are, we can sense your location. All I have to do is focus on your face and my mind finds you."

"Innate abilities you say?" I wonder if this is what the Storm family means when coming into their gifts.

"You know I would never hurt you, right?" he assures, walking to the center of the room, like he's preparing me for a revelation.

"Yes, I know." I feel my heart calm, and my head simmer in emotions, as Cory begins to explain. His breathing becomes heavy, and I can see him straining to keep in control of something, as I watch him crack his neck from side to side. The hues from the flames in the hearth give reflective hints of light, as I watch his face change before me. Moving closer I see Cory's nose and forehead crinkle to a scowl, while black veins become vivid under his gray skin, like I witnessed in the library. His mouth forms fangs from his gums.

He moves closer to me. Seeing him up close I say, "Your face. It's changed."

He touches his cheek, giving a grim smile. "This is who I am. My true form. Who you will become soon, should Madame Moyer grab hold of your gift."

He gazes at me with depressing posture. I can see him still as Cory, but he's physically changed before me. The sadness in his eyes tells me everything I need to know.

"This comes out when I become angry, provoked, or sad. Eventually I learned to control it. Now, I can at least anticipate when I start to transform." After a few moments, Cory recoils back to his human form. "Are you ok to talk about it now? I mean…now that you know the truth?"

"Will I become that?" I ask, astonished.

"Honestly, I don't know. But don't worry, it's not something that will happen before you turn eighteen. Unless of course something catastrophic happens. We won't truly know, until your birthday."

"Is this why you keep telling me I must control my emotions, because my transition can be let out early?"

"Yes. And the proof is your hair color. Every time you become enraged, it will change to a lighter shade, until it's white like mine. You must find a way to control the inner anger, you have inside you, the wrath that's hiding for the way you feel about everything you have learned thus far. If you don't, it will consume you, allowing the evil to take over.

Once you turn eighteen, natural human abilities will become intensified. Hearing, seeing, strength, and I am sure your favorite, —running faster," he says, winking at me. "Every Storm has been cursed with these abilities."

He walks over and throws another log on the fire. "It's getting late and I need to go before they come looking for me. I don't think we want Madame Moyer's attention brought to the forefront." Before he leaves, he says, "Lock the door behind me, will you?"

"Sure." I nod, watching him shut the door. As I stand here alone, staring into space, I try to make sense out of all the information I have been given this evening.

'So, I'm to become one of them? A monster?'

'No,' the voice comes from silence.

'Where have you been? Why does it seem you only show up when you want to? It seems you're never here, when I appear to need you the most.'

'I'm here now. Ask any question you like.'

'I can ask, but will you answer?'

'What's your first question Wynter?' the voice says, sounding calm, and not all seeming irritated by my flippant attitude.

'Who are you?'

'Someone who watches over you.'

'Why do you come and go as you please? Why do you ignore me?'

'That isn't easy to explain. Except that, I come and go. Busy working, preparing.'

'Preparing for what? Are you not a ghost inside my head possessing my thoughts?'

And for the first time I hear a laugh come from it. *'Dear heaven's no. I come from far away, able to penetrate the minds of anyone. Even Moyer's should I want to. However, hers is dark, and horrid. I would rather not see the treacherous things she has done.'*

'Why am I here?'

'To fulfill your destiny.'

'My destiny? Is that your comeback? I had a life before everything happened. I want it back!'

'My sweet, I can't turn back time. We must only go forward. Learn from our past and pave a way for our future.'

'There is much work for you to do. It's late and you must rest. You have had a hard day.'

24

Lies, Truths & Secrets

Time seems to fast forward, and I find myself waking in my bed. Not remembering how I got here, I look over to see the clock saying six in the morning. I rush to get ready for the morning chores. I don't want to be late and have Stella make up for my lack of laziness.

When I reach the laundry room the cart is ready as it usually is every morning, but Stella isn't anywhere in sight.

I don't see Stella in school this morning, either. It's then I realized something is wrong. She's missing, and nobody seems to be looking for her.

Cory assures me he's keeping his superpower abilities on high alert and will let me know if anything changes. It's as if she vanished within the walls of the manor.

That afternoon after class, Cory walks me back to my room, reporting he hasn't heard a thing regarding Stella. I begin to fear something terrible. The confessions Stella talked about last night springs to mind.

"Can't you get into her head, like you do mine, and the others?"

"It's not that simple. She too has something protecting her."

"What is it!" I yell aloud in frustration. Not towards anyone in particular.

"Wynter, please try to at least make an effort to control your emotions," Cory says.

"You say that like it's easy to do."

"I've had years of practice. It will take you time."

"Well, how do you control yours?"

He sits down in the corner chair. "As I explained before, I can hear heartbeats and feel your emotions. If you learn to control your feelings, it might fool others into thinking you're not in fear of them. Overtime it becomes a white noise."

"What do you mean?"

"I mean, if you try to remain calm, perhaps your heart wouldn't race so fast. Therefore, misleading the ones who can hear it into thinking you're not afraid. Evil preys on fear. It's the number one way they sense it. Like the night Cole caught you in the hall, for example. Your heartbeat was loud and clear, sending fear among the shadow walkers within the halls of the manor."

"Then the other heartbeats must have rung louder than mine?"

Cory nods. "If I were to look in your eyes and compel you; I would see straight into your soul. For example, I can read what you're thinking by the pictures you see. But your, soul? It would tell me everything about you. All your secrets whether good deeds or bad."

"Is that how you can calm my anger, fear, sadness?"

He nods. "But I don't need to look in your eyes to do that. That's the difference between the compelling Moyer and her crew do, versus me. What I have is a gift that no other has. I mean, it may be similar, but it's never exact. I send calming auras to your senses."

"So, you can hear how I feel all the time, by my heartbeat?"

"Yes." And he moves closer to me, making eye contact.

"Does that mean you know what I feel now?" Trying not to blush.

He quickly looks away, breaking contact, ignoring my question and begins to walk over to the corner of the room. "I can feel many emotions."

I change the subject and ask another question. "Does Daniel have the same…gift?"

"Daniel can hypnotize. He can freeze the body to stone. He's very dangerous and Moyer has turned him into a killing machine. Never give him eye contact. The last person that got caught in his trap was a servant girl. She had a pitcher of water in her hand for the flowers in the parlor, and Daniel was angry she entered the room without knocking. Caught him making advances at one of the maids. His eye contact was so quick she didn't have a chance to look away."

"You mean Chad's betrothed?" I ask.

Cory looks at me with sadness, and nods. "Yeah, how did you know?"

"Nora told me."

"I see. Well, Moyer didn't favor the fact that Chad fell in love with a servant girl, and the speculation is she had Daniel remedy the problem."

There's a long pause before Cory speaks again, "Wynter, have you ever felt danger? Or perhaps sensed something not quite right, but couldn't put your finger on it?"

"Yes, all the time." My mind traces back to when I started to first remember the déjà vu episodes.

Cory says nothing, just stands there giving me a slight grin from the corner of his mouth.

"Wait, are you saying those are already my gifts, that hasn't come to the surface yet?"

"That's exactly what I'm saying. But you see, yours will be different than mine. Although we are cousins, and share the same great-grandparents, I come from a different bloodline than you. We share one common trait. We are a Storm. And a Storm senses when something is either right or wrong in the universe. But like little babies learning to walk and talk, from the magical side of things, we do not earn the powers until the age of eighteen. It's then that we are taught how to control the power. As we age, we become stronger."

"Wynter I'm going to tell you something that may be very hard to grasp, but perhaps I should try and start from the beginning. Rather the story I know. Then maybe it will help you understand?"

"That's as good as any place to start, I guess," I say, smiling at him.

"As you figured out, Blair is my mother."

I nod at him patiently waiting for him to continue.

"The Storm family have deep dark secrets, so deep that I don't even know them all. Moyer is a regular mad scientist. For centuries she has concocted mutations from all sorts of species. But the one species she is drawn to the most, is the Storm family line."

"Why?"

"That's the golden question,' he says, coming to sit down on the edge of the bed. "I don't have the answer."

"How are you a Storm?" I ask sitting next to him.

"Blairs father is Derek."

"Mr. Derek? The teacher? That means he's really your grandfather?"

"It's not something Madame Moyer wants rumored. Most people are of the assumption he's my cousin. She prefers it that way."

"Why pretend that Moyer is your mother? Why the façade?"

"Because if word got out that Moyer is running an illegal genetic lab under the castle, we would all be free," he jokes. "It's the real reason, she has us all trapped. If anyone crosses her, she won't think twice about killing anyone. Blair still raised us, and

Cole and I grew to always know her as our mother but were to refer to her as Blair. Bad business Moyer said."

Cory gets up and walks to the door. "Come on, let's get out of here and go do something?"

"Like what?"

"I hear you like books? I don't think I showed you all there is that a library has to offer, have I? Or perhaps ice cream?" he teases.

I laugh at his comic gesture. "Lead the way my friend."

Later that night, Cory escorts me back to my room. My mind scrolls through the day's past, wondering how we will pull off our escape. Hoping to ask Stella more questions proved to be uneventful.

"I'm worried Cory. Stella wasn't at dinner. Have *they* gotten to her?"

"I would have known. Nothing has come across my senses."

"Well, can't you use your mind to locate her?"

He laughs at my remark. "Wynter you make it sound like my brain is a homing device. I can't just say, 'show me Stella,' and poof she appears in my mind."

I look at him with concern. "Yet you can find me, no problem."

"You're different. You're marked." And he gives me a mischievous grin. I don't play back and wrinkled my forehead in protest.

"I will snoop around, ok?" he says finally. "I need to go do my rounds before someone catches me not at my post. Lock the door."

I look at the clock to see it's eight realizing I might have time for a quick shower and I gather my things.

When I get back to my room, I see Cory in my room waiting.

"Hey, there. Did you forget something?" I ask. Setting my things down onto the bed. I move over to the dresser and take the towel off my head.

"Yes, I did. I realized there's something I forgot to say to you."

"Oh yeah, what's that? Did you find Stella?"

He cocks his head to the side, as if to seem a little confused. "Stella?" he questions. "No. I haven't found her."

"Then, what is it?"

"You know too much, Wynter. I have no choice now." His voice gives a low growl, and I clue in, something is off.

I drop my brush to the floor. "It's you!" I cry, "You're not Cory. You're Cole!"

He backs me in the corner next to the fireplace and I have no place to go. His fangs begin to extend, as I watch them protrude from his lips. Opening his mouth, he hisses, and his skin starts to change color, like I observed in the library during the altercation with his brother.

He lunges toward me, and I lose my footing, falling to the floor. It all happens so fast that before I have a chance to react, he has me pinned beneath him and I can't move. With his fangs drawn-out ready to take a bite, I think to myself, *'Life is over.'*

He hisses aloud, "First in sight, first in right dear brother,' and right as he's about to sink his teeth into my neck, his whole body stiffens. I witness Cole's eyes go dim, and his skin change back to normal, as he falls on top of me. I try to push him off but he's too heavy, so, I shimmy my way sideways. It's then, I see a stake has been driven to his back, and I look up to see Cory standing there, with his eyes glowing bright blue. His skin changed to gray, and black veins bulging from his body; I see a different kind of Cory. It's a side of Cory I haven't seen before, a side of anger, a side of rage, a side that comes out when provoked; reminding me of a predator, protecting his mate. He pushes Cole to the side, allowing me to scramble to my feet.

"Are you okay?" he hisses, in fury.

I can't emit a single word. Nothing comes out. So, I nod, then an uncontrollable tear rolls down my cheek.

"Come on, let's get you out of here. Grab some clothes, for the night. You're not safe here while Moyer is away."

'Ironic,' I think. *'She's the demon I'm running from, yet Cole is the one who's dangerous.'*

25

Running

I stuff my backpack with random clothes, not even thinking about what I'm packing.

"Hurry, we must move fast before the others come running," Cory says with urgency. Then, hauling my book bag over my back, Cory says, "Climb on, it's faster." And with lightning speed we are downstairs within seconds.

"You killed your brother," whispering in his ear while still on his back.

"No. He's...how do I say, 'put on ice,' for the moment. Nora will discover he's late for patrol and come looking for him."

"But I saw you stake his heart, from the back."

"And when Nora removes it, he will be pissed."

"Cory Storm, you have some major explaining to do."

"I know, but for now, we need to get you out of here and far away as possible from my brother."

Cory and I run to the library to find it empty, except for a couple servants dusting the drapes and cleaning the windows. The fire is lit as usual and the place looks tidy. No sign at all that there was a big fight between brother's a few days prior. "The library, it's still open?"

"No. The maids are cleaning. It's done daily after the doors close." He guides me to the back of the room behind the counter where a wrought iron door sits. It's like looking at an old-world gate, with a lock from ancient times. Grabbing a skeleton key, hidden from under the counter, Cory places it in the lock.

"Moyer has tried for years to open this door. But the magic is too strong for her to come inside." Then he turns the lock, opening it.

"Yet you have a key and it opens fine," wondering to myself if this is another good versus evil.

Crossing the threshold, he shuts the door. Peering through the bars we can see the library. I watch as the maids continue to clean appearing to be unaware of where we are. "Can they not see us?" I ask.

Cory shakes his head no. "Remember when I told you earlier that Moyer can't find the key to open the portal gates?"

"Yes," I say, looking at him confused.

"Well, just like the necklace, she can't see the hidden key either." He holds it in front of my face, to see, saying, "The door has a one-way image, too. We can see out, but they can't see in."

"Come on, let me show you the Hall of History."

"The hall of what?" I follow him down the narrow aisle, with books on either side of us. "What is all this?" I ask, pointing to the shelves of literature.

"It's all the history, of the world we live in."

At the end of the closet, we come to a green steel door with books shelved from floor to ceiling, and all around the frame.

"So many books," I say.

"More books of history," he says, smiling.

"I'm curious, if Moyer can't penetrate these doors, how are you able to?"

"Remember when I remarked earlier about my watch, and your necklace; that only the purest of hearts can see, and evil cannot?"

"Yes, I remember."

"Well, it's kind of like that. Except one small detail."

"What's that?"

"Only people who have come into their power can enter. So, either you have developed earlier than normal due to the recent circumstances, or you are much stronger than any of us, and holds greater power."

"Meaning?" I ask.

"Meaning, the prophecy must be true, and you're the one to destroy her once and for all."

"So, you're saying that only people who are good, and have come into power can penetrate past the protective shield?"

"Now, I think you're getting it," he says smiling at me. "You ready?"

"Ready for what?"

Cory slips the key once again into another lock, and the door opens wide, "Behold the Iron Door of Secrets." And as he inserts the key, words above the door light up.

I tug at Cory's arm from the sight of it all. It looks like an ordinary door until the key is put in. Another protective illusion to hold back evil, I imagine.

We walk in a circular room with many doors aligning all the way around the area. It is like stepping into a sphere. Each door having a sign above it. One door stands out to me more than all the rest: Ladorielle. "I have seen this name before," I say, pointing with my finger in the direction of the doorway.

"You have? But when? Has anyone ever mentioned it to you?"

"Not that I know of, no. I'm drawn to it somehow."

"That passage has been locked for hundreds of years. Since before I was born. Or Chad and Blair for that matter."

"What do you know about it?" I ask, glancing back to Cory, hoping he has an answer for me.

"Only that it is the home of the Storms. Blair doesn't teach it in school. The books on Ladorielle are back at the cottage, in the loft."

"I remember now…I had a dream one night. A family was running from something bad."

"Who was it they were running from?"

"I—I don't know. A ghost maybe? It wore a black hooded cape and had glowing blue eyes. Much like everyone here at the house."

"Not a shadow walker?" Cory asks.

I know immediately he's trying to picture the thing in my mind. "Show me the family in your memory, Wynter. Who did they look like?"

I try to picture everyone. The children, the women, the man calling himself Ian. "It's hard to remember all their faces," I say.

"I don't recognize any of them Wyn, I'm sorry. Are you sure you heard them say Ladorielle?"

"Yes, I am certain."

Cory turns to the center podium in the room, where lies a closed book. "Perhaps we can get some answers here?" he exclaims.

"Wait," I blurt out and touch Cory's shoulder. "There was a maid. She looked a lot like Rosie."

"Can you show her to me, in your mind?"

I concentrate on her like the others but her facial features do not appear clear. "Other than the pointed ears she looks exactly like our Rosie," I say.

"I'm sorry Wyn, I can't make out her features to be sure. I will say, that the castle I see in your mind, is the perfect match of the painting in the foyer where the King and Queen are pictured."

"Ladorielle…they have a monarchy?" I ask, trying to figure out how all of this connects to me.

"Of course. Most other worlds do. I mean you will find the occasional democracy world, but very far and few between."

Cory proceeds to open the book on the podium and says, "Come, I want to show you this book. The uniqueness of this volume is a pen." Holding it up for me to see, I watch him as he writes, *'Sara's cottage in the woods.'*

He must have noticed the confusion on my face, because he laughs aloud, and with-in seconds, I watch the ink disappear on the page. Then the book, all on its own, begins to flip through the leaf of pages, finally settling on 127, with a door behind us, opening.

I can see through to the other side, where a chair sits in the corner, and books line the walls.

"Quick, before the portal closes," he calls out. Taking my hand, we step through the passageway across the threshold to the other side.

I look around the room to see we are in the loft of the cottage. Shelves of books line the walls from one corner of the loft to the other. One window pokes through the copious of literature, and if it were daytime, I imagine it would let in a large amount of light. Under it, is a seat for two with pillows accenting.

Like in the Hall of Secrets, a pedestal stands in the center of the room, with a large book lying atop, closed. My curiosity gets the better of me and I walk over to try and open it.

"It's locked, and I haven't the key," he says, raising a brow. "All I know is I've tried to open it."

"What do you suppose we do? How are we to port back?" My worry triggers him to calm my nerves with another one of his stare downs.

"It doesn't matter right now. You're staying here through the weekend. Or until Moyer gets back to Storm River. She's a monster that needs to be dealt with, I agree, but with her here, my brother will not dare to cross her."

"So, what? He doesn't think of the consequences? I don't understand?"

"Let's just say, the will in him is weaker when she's here, than when she's gone." He tilts his head, saying, "Can't say I didn't see this coming."

"What do you mean?"

"It all started when you became marked. Moyer knew it too. Yet she left anyway. It's almost as if she was hoping that Cole would sink his teeth into you first, before your birthday. Making it easier for her to take your gift."

"Cory, I don't understand any of this."

He nods. "I know. Let's go downstairs and I'll explain. We'll make a fire, warm the place up, and I'll tell you all I know." I smile back at his reassurance.

"It's freezing in this place," he says, dropping his backpack on the floor.

"Where did that come from?" I ask stunned, not noticing him wearing the book bag, before.

"See, the neat thing about magic, I can hide things well," and smiles modestly.

I tilt my head at him, giving a look as if to say, 'spill it.'

His cocky grin widens. "Remember when I told you the day, I met Isalora here in the cottage when I discovered this place?"

"Go on." I say, folding my arms, waiting for him to continue.

"Well, she taught me an invisibility spell. Any object is invisible to anyone except the one who casts it. Like this cottage for example."

"I'm beginning to understand this is a great source of leverage to have in beating Madame Moyer at her own game," I reply.

"Precisely. Except Isalora's magic, is much more powerful," he adds. Cory grabs the pack, and I follow him to the floor below. He continues to ramble on, "I had already decided to bring you here tonight. My brother happened to be faster than me. When I came back to your room—"

"You were coming to tell me to pack," I interject.

"In a matter of speaking yes."

A slight wind bleeds through the cracks of the window frames, creating a whistling sound, that makes me jump. "Do you think a storm is on its way again?" I ask, as I veer through the glass window, seeing the shadows of tree branches wave in the moonlight.

"Perhaps, but it won't be an issue. We have dry firewood stacked over there," he assures, and points to the corner. "Please, sit. I'll get this place warm in no time."

Staring at this beautiful young man, I watch him prepare the hearth for heat. Patiently waiting, as he begins to build a fire.

Turning to look at me he asks, "Do you have that dragon lighter on you?"

"Umm, I think so." I check the coat pocket of my jacket and toss him the lighter. "Here you go."

He lights the edges of the papers hidden under the wood. "I have so many questions; I don't know where to start." I say, watching him work the flames.

"I know," he says, poking the fire as he speaks. He looks back at me and stands. "You can ask as many as you need to, until you feel comfortable."

I nod at him. Pressing my lips tight, I say, "Cory, back there…you stabbed your brother and stated, he wasn't dead. I saw him die before my eyes. What was that? He had fangs of a monster. I mean, what you showed me in my room yesterday, and what I saw in Cole is like seeing two different sides." I try and reason with a rational mind, but nothing comes to the surface. I can't explain it away. I've seen Fran heal right in front of me. I've seen eyes glowing blue, and shadow walkers that roam the halls at night. I've even seen Nora change her eyes from yellow to brown and her skin turn to scales. Now this. Stella mentioned vampires, but I didn't believe her. Is that who these shadow walkers are? Vampires in disguise?

I hear Cory speak softly, in such a low voice I can barely hear him. "Wynter remember when I pointed out, there are many things that happen here, strange things that can't be explained away? Well my brother and I are one of those phenomena's."

"Okay?" pausing to gather my thoughts. Then I ask, "Like that thing you did with your eyes in my room, earlier? Or when your skin changes grey and veins appear? You mean there is more?"

"The glowing eyes are a Storm family trait, but the fangs…well they come from the blood of Vampires."

"Come again?" I cry out.

"Up in the loft are books upon books of what happened long ago. While Sara was still alive, she wrote of the dreadful happenings of Storm River Manor when things here began to change. I recommend you take the time and read this weekend. It will help you catch up. Besides, you will need the knowledge if we are ever going to get out from the grips of Madame Moyer."

"That doesn't explain what you just sprang on me? Vampires do not exist Cory."

"Despite what you might think, we do…"

"What? Are you telling me you're one of them?"

"Surprise."

"Not funny Cory."

"Are you afraid?"

"Surprisingly no. I know you won't hurt me, otherwise you would have done it already. All I know is… every time I ask you a question, it leads to more questions. My head is spinning right now. All this information is too overwhelming for me."

"I can understand that. You've been left out of the loop all your life. It's been for your protection really. The less you knew the less likely Moyer could find you." He glances up above to the loft. "Most of your answers are in all those books up there. We don't have to talk about this now. It's late," he says, coming to sit next to me on the couch.

"Perhaps I should dive into them tomorrow?" I say, smiling back at him with tired eyes.

Cory changes the subject. "There are two bedrooms back there," he says, pointing down the hall. "Which one would you like, left one or right?"

I follow him as he shows me the rest of the house. I hadn't seen it earlier when we were here. The bedrooms are not large, but not tiny either. There's plenty of room for a dresser and chair in each. "This one will be fine," I express, and I set my backpack on the ground by my feet.

Then I remember something. "Cory." I turn around to face him just as he's about to walk out of the room.

"Yes?" he answers, raising a brow, having his hand on the knob and about to shut the door.

"What about school tomorrow?"

"I told Rosie you were ill, not feeling well and not to bother you until Monday."

"And she believed you?"

Cory's eyes glow blue. "I have ways of convincing people," he chuckles. Then closes the door.

I have a hard time falling asleep as I toss and turn thinking about today's events. My mind keeps reeling with the information in my head.

26

Cabin Fever

I awake in the cottage, to the morning crisp air of winter, and my breath can be seen in front of me with each exhale. It's cold, and I realize I've forgotten my robe. Peering over at my bedroom door I notice it's opened a crack and can see the entry to the other bedroom is still shut. The smell of burning coals coming from the living area, brings my senses to the forefront, that I should start a fire.

I throw on my coat and venture out into the hall toward the living room. The house is quiet and the only noise I can hear, is the crackling of ice against heavy branches outside. A few whistling sounds come through the panes of the window.

I begin to refresh the coals, that still burn in the hearth and decide to throw on another log, hoping it will warm the place soon.

Last night is the latest I have stayed up since coming to Storm River Manor, and I think all this new-found information has overwhelmed my circuits.

"Perhaps I'll find a book to read until Cory wakes," I say aloud. I look up above at the loft, admiring the rays of light coming through the window. "He did say I should dive into some reading."

The first book I find, is a journal, so I take a seat, in the corner of the loft. There, I begin to step back in another time.

Looking at the title: Sara Deagon, I turn to the first page.

In the year July 4724

This has me confused. 4724 is nearly three thousand years ahead of our time. I'll have to ask Cory about this later. I read on…

Mother has fallen ill, not sure if she will see the light of the next day. My sister Isobel and I wait patiently for the herbs to take hold in her system. We fear it is too late and the venomous poison within her body has taken over. With Sarmira destroyed we are completely confused as to how this has happened. Bryce had slain her as she took her last strike on his beloved Petra. My healing ability was no match for Sarmira's wrath. I could not save his beloved. She lies on the alter ready for burial now, along with father. I fear our mother is soon to follow. Leaving me as queen. I am no ruler. I'm not ready. Oh, father why, did this have to happen.

Sara

The front door swings open, startling me from my reading, with Cory walking through it. He has a large knapsack to his back, my boots around his neck, and one suitcase in his hands.

"What's all this?" I ask, calling over the balcony. "I thought you were in the bedroom sleeping?"

He stares up at me, grinning. "I thought you could use a few things," he remarks, dropping the luggage to the floor, unwrapping my tied boots from his throat and swinging a backpack off.

"Quite the load you have there, Cory." My eyes wide with surprise. "Did you remember—"

"Yes." He interrupts me, pulling my rabbit from the inside pocket of his coat.

I smile and come down from the loft greeting my stuffed Charlie. "Unbelievable Cory," I say smiling. "You never cease to amaze me."

"What, vampires can't be charming?"

"Stop." And I nudge his side.

"Ouch."

"Oh, that didn't hurt," I say to him.

"I suppose not. I was going for a dramatic effect. Apparently, it didn't work."

"Ha-ha."

I watch Cory pull out items from his pack. "Emergency gear," he says, pulling out clothing.

"So, you brought socks?"

"One can never be too prepared," he says, laughing. "There will come a time, when we finally escape. We need to be ready."

"Is that why you brought me a suitcase full of clothes?"

"Mmm, here." And hands over my bag.

I huff a breath of astonishment. "Did you see Cole?"

"No, he was gone."

"That's quite a risk, Cory. Are you not afraid that someone might have seen you roaming around?"

"Don't' worry, nobody saw me."

"What did Derek cast, another one of his illusion spells?" I ask.

"Didn't need to. I simply drank from my invisible elixir. No one knows I'm here. Nor do they think you have left the manor." He reaches down deep inside his pack and pulls out a couple paper sacks. Tossing me one of the bags, he asks, "Hungry?"

I open it to see an assortment of fruit, packaged snacks and a couple sandwiches. I pull a banana out and begin munching. "You have really thought of everything haven't you?"

Cory winks at me and sets his lunch bag on the kitchen table. "I try. But there's still the problem of how to handle Moyer," he says.

"Yeah, I've been thinking about that. I started reading Sara's journals."

"Good for you. You will be up to speed with me in no time," he jokes. Then takes the apple he has in his hands, stabs it with his fang teeth, and carries his garments to the back bedroom. I can hear the faint sounds of drawers opening and closing. Giving me a sense that perhaps sooner rather than later, we will be living here and not the manor and this weekend getaway is permanent.

I grab my tote and lug it to my room. "So, I found something a little odd, when I began reading Sara's book," I begin to say.

"Yes, I'm sure you did. You may soon discover a lot of things will seem strange to you," Cory says from the other room.

"Sara said she's writing in the year 4724. How is that even possible?" While I wait for his answer, I heave the large case onto my bed and unzip it.

"It's a different time. Different galaxy altogether. In fact, scientists here on earth haven't even discovered Ladorielle's universe." Then I hear him pace back to me. "Have you come to the part where you read about Arik and Derek?"

"Briefly. Most of it came from a dream a few nights ago."

"Tell me please, what was it about?"

"I think it was the whole Storm family. They all were escaping from something. Something big." We sit on the end of my bed, and I catch him up to speed on what I know, what has happened to me in the last few days since I have been here. Hopefully, Cory will be able to fill in the blanks for me.

We talk all that day and I read up on many juicy details of the scandalous Storm family.

Later that day, right before the sun is about to go down, I look up from my reading to hear Cory say, "Hey, do you want to take a break?"

"Sure, what do you have in mind?"

"A walk down by the river. I want to show you something."

I grab my black hooded coat and put on my boots and follow him through the trees down to the water. Ice has already started forming around the edges of the shore.

"This is beautiful," I express to him.

"I like to come here during the summer months and fish. It's peaceful out here. My mind gets to think."

"I'm surprised Moyer doesn't know about this place."

"Oh, she does. But she doesn't come here anymore…not since the fire."

"What happened?"

"She discovered the Storm family's plot to oust her out. Sara was weak from the poison in her body. Fran began casting, her illusion spell. So, on the outside of this cottage, it looks like it burned to the ground, but on the inside, all is untouched."

His comments prompt me to remember the day when my family and I tried to escape capture. The day our house burned down.

"Can you imagine if Moyer had my power?" Cory states.

I huff at the thought and say, "What do you think Cole had?"

"My theory? That he can read minds. You know the term you keep hearing, 'eyes and ears watching?' Well, except for a select few in the house, everyone's thoughts seem to be read."

"Is this why my dad always made me wear the necklace?"

He nods in agreement. "Yes, and my watch, along with the other jewelry."

"Other jewelry?"

Cory adds, "You wear one of three lockets made, by Ailbert Storm. The other two, belong to Fran, and Blair."

"I remember my dad telling me, Fran had one, but we didn't know who had the third."

"Before Sara died, she put a spell on all the jewelry her family wore to shield evil, should anyone try to penetrate one's soul. The whole family suspected foul play but couldn't prove it. That day the house burned down, it divided the family: those loyal to Sara, and those loyal to Moyer.

"Knowing Sara, ill inside, they all watched as the house burned to the ground. She thought, by killing Sara it was finally over. Moyer would now be the matriarch. And so far, that seems to be the case.

"Jeoffrey, Fran and your mother, were captured. At the time Moyer didn't know your mother was pregnant, with you." Cory pauses, as if he has more answers. "I don't have all the details, Blair told me the story once. It's a painful memory for her. She blames herself."

"Sounds like Blair was close to Sara, too?"

Cory nods. "The only mother figure she has had in her life really. When Sara died, it was like losing a parent." He bends down to pick up rocks and I watch him skip them across the water. "Sara was an extraordinary woman, Wynter. You would have loved her. You could say, Lady Sara was the *'mother to all'* at Storm River Manor.

Moyer ended up killing most of the entire Storm line, apart from Derek and Daniel. Although they, too, ended up perishing, in other ways."

"What do you mean?" I ask.

"They sold their souls to Moyer in exchange; she would leave the remaining Storm family alone. You can see how well that worked out," he says in a sarcastic tone. "Remember the night you told me, you had the dream of The Storm family centered in the foyer and Drelanda fell ill?"

I nod as he goes on. "That was the day Sarmira came to the Kingdom of Ladorielle: an evil underworld queen. She followed Ian's family undetected. The Storm family thought they had escaped her wrath. But it was short lived. Sarmira found a way to squeeze into the Storm family lives. All the while Sarmira was preparing the perfect plan."

"Sarmira? Who is she?" I ask, wondering how this dream I had, is connected to everything.

"An evil sorceress driven to spread hate through the world and rule. According to Jeoffrey, you're last on her list. Once your powers are stolen, she will be released to rule forever. Nothing can stop her after that. She will be able to seek out anything, jumping from planet to planet consuming life."

He went on, "Sarmira blended in well, possessing Maura Moyer, until the day Rosie caught her. When Moyer was down in her basement lab creating concoctions, she was very much still married to Arik at the time. He caught Moyer there with a vampire. She had strung it up in Valiancium steel chains, a metal so strong there isn't anything that can break it other than melting the steel. By this time, he's angry and moves to get the girl down. Moyer catches him and strikes with a fit of rage chopping off two of his fingers. Shocked by what she did to him, he's caught off guard. He tries to fight back but she uses black magic. Something he didn't see coming. Rosie had been watching from the corner steps and sees the ring still around Arik's severed fingers that lay on the ground. She watches Moyer take her hands, and wrap them both around Arik's neck, breathing in deep, taking in his every breath. Rosie observes quietly, while she watches her lord's life be taken before her very eyes. When Moyer's finished, she throws his lifeless body to the floor, taking the blood from his amputated fingers before the Vampire's feet and bleeds them out into test tubes. Not at all noticing the ring hidden on one. Eventually she catches Rosie peeking out among the stairwell and warns her never to speak of what she witnessed if she valued her life. Then ordering Rosie to clean up the mess before someone detects an issue."

"Surely the others' caught on to the scathing plan?" I reply in downright disgust.

"Ultimately, yes. But it was days later, when people noticed Arik missing. It's then that Derek came down to discover Drena still hanging there."

"The vampire?" I ask.

Cory nods. "Derek brings Drena to her feet. She's weak and near death. Moyer walks in on them, and begins the same ritual as before, only this time he makes a deal with her. His life for Drena's."

"Why would he do that?"

"Because Drena was with child....His child."

I sigh in a breath of shock. "You?"

"No, she ended up losing the baby later. Well you can imagine what Moyer thought. She immediately began to use Drena as a test subject."

"Wait a minute, hold on a second. I thought vampires can't reproduce?"

"Another myth, Wynter. Remember most vampires were human once. And like humans they don't lose everything. They may not look like they don't age on the outside, but the inside still does. See, if someone is turned at a young age, they still have all the working parts so to speak. Moyer figured this out, and for the next thirty years she used Drena while she was still viable."

Then he grins a mischievous smile. "Why do you think most vampires drink fresh human blood in the first place? For our health?" He laughs. "It keeps us youthful looking."

I grab my throat at the thought of Cory doing that to anyone, including me.

"Don't worry you're safe. I prefer the essence. It's the one downfall I have. The one thing that I can't control. Anyway, Moyer killed Drena, after she became useless to her scheming plans."

"I thought vampires are supposed to be strong and fast? Able to withstand a surmountable amount of strength. Another myth?" I ask.

"No, that part's true. Remember the valiancium steel I told you about? You don't need a lot to weaken them. Moyer is supplied with it. She has the steel melted down and makes ankle bracelets. Every one of her creations has one." I watch as Cory lifts his pant leg to reveal a cuff around his ankle.

"Cory?" I cry out in complete shock.

"So, you see, we are all trapped here. You, my dear Wynter are the only one, who is not under her thumb and a select few of the orphans. Moyer needs some of them to stay human."

I think of JC. Cory answers me without me having to ask.

"Yes, she too is a vampire. It's why she didn't care that she hurt you," he says.

"And that's why you think, Moyer left me unprotected? Because then I too would be weakened at the hands of her every beck and call? Weak from her, in more ways than just getting my power."

Cory gives a grim smile. "Now do you understand why I have gone to such lengths to keep you safe?"

"Yes. I get it now." I pause to think, to absorb what Cory has confessed. This is some insane information. "Are you saying she's growing hybrids?"

Cory nods. "Still is, yes. Those babies you hear crying; are her homegrown little vampires. The only difference is, she's blended the Storm gene of the necromancer."

"And that is what I am. Half necro, half vampire." Blair is my mother." He pauses to look down at the water a moment.

"A necro…what?" I ask.

"During the great battle of Ladorielle, a brave knight, by the name of Bryce Storm battled Sarmira once, his wife, and beloved was found near death. She lost her fight with Sarmira. When Sarmira was about to take Petra's essence, Bryce came swinging, defeating Sarmira. She shattered into millions of shards and piercing anyone near her. Bryce fell to the ground, nearly lifeless. That's when Petra gave the last of her life to him. Healing him with her energy and killing herself."

"Shocker huh? Bet you didn't see that one coming, did you?" He says. "Petra was a necromancer. And she hid it from Bryce. Her desire to lead a normal life outweighed the life of magic. Now you know, where your line comes from."

"My gawd Cory, I'm so sorry. And what about your father?"

He takes in a deep breath. "I don't know who my father is."

"I'm sorry to hear that Cory," whispering. "And Blair? She's a Storm? She's a necromancer too?" Is this what you mean by all Storms having the glowing eyes?"

"Yes. The glowing eyes of a necromancer can compel the soul into doing anything they wish the host to do. They can cast memory stamps, making people forget who they are, and they feed off the essence of life, keeping them young. Blair's a hybrid vampire like me. Same as Derek, Daniel, Chad…."

"And my father?"

"No. He and your Aunt Fran escaped before the Storm castle was consumed with Nytemires."

"Nytemires? Is that what you call yourselves?"

"Yes."

"Derek made your dad promise to give Blair, the necklace when she came of age, to be protected."

"So, she was raised good?" I ask.

"Yes. Sara raised her. Which is why if you are ever around Blair, and someone speaks of Sara, 'the vampire in her' will become vile with hate. She blames Moyer for Sara's death."

"Chad said she grew ill?"

"More like poisoned. Sara wore her ring, that protected her, so she was never bitten. Moyer figured out another way to dispose of her."

I take in a huge sigh. "So. What's the plan Cory?"

"That's the loaded question isn't it?" he jokes with dry humor.

Speaking of a plan, he says, "Here we are..." as he points to a grate under a bridge. Behind it, a dark tunnel. "This leads to the basement. Thought you should know it's here. It may come in handy for the future."

"That leads to the hell hole within the manor?" I ask, surprised.

"Indeed, it does. I have thought for years this can be the way to save all the children. Bring them this way. They can't use the portal inside the manor or see the cottage. But if we can somehow find a druid in Ladorielle we can group port them back, like what you saw in your dreams." Cory turns looking down at the rushing water as it spills down a waterfall a few yards away. "It's the only hope I have left."

"We can do this Cory. What's the strategy?"

"To keep you from being bitten, long enough to gain your gift by your birthday."

"So, why doesn't Moyer just jail me. Or better yet have Cole hurry up and do the deed?"

You must remember, no one knows, Moyer is Sarmira, only Rosie. Blair doesn't even know. This is going to have to take careful planning, if Moyer catches on it can devastate all life on this compound. Besides, Moyer - rather Sarmira - will not risk her years of planning. If Blair knew about Sarmira, she wouldn't have the patience to wait. The reason I know, is because Isalora told me. There are still rules within the house, that must be followed. You're a Storm. And Storms are to be held to certain standards. If the rest of the house caught on that Sarmira has possessed Moyer, there would be a revolt. A divided faction so to speak. Sarmira is the one who wants your power, Moyer is merely your grandmother being held captive, much like the rest of Storm River Manor. The exception is, Moyer's soul is bound with Sarmira's. Once Sarmira has your power, all bets are off. Which is why we must figure out how to escape before your birthday."

"Sure, no pressure." I roll my eyes.

We head back to the cabin, where I ask a million more questions.

"Cory, you never did explain how old you are?"

He sighs, "That's complicated."

"I'm sure I can keep up," I reply.

He takes in a breath, and says, "I'm two hundred and eighteen years old."

"I'm trying to wrap my head around all this. It's all so confusing." I pause for a minute, then ask, "What's a nytemire exactly?"

"Well, necromancers go back centuries; on Ladorielle thousands of years. The people of Ladorielle age differently than humans do, too."

My heart begins to pound, attempting to grasp the concept. "My head hurts trying to do the math," I say.

He laughs. "Try not to over think it too much."

"Well, I do. Here you are telling me you're few hundred years old and I'm almost eighteen."

"I see your point. For whatever reason, reasons not yet explained, after I received my gift at eighteen, I stopped aging physically. Perhaps that will be for you as well, but there is no way of knowing, without time."

I stare at him a moment, trying to absorb the absurdity of it all. "So, your saying you have been here on earth for over two hundred years?"

He smiles at me. "Two hundred and eighteen to be exact."

"And your theory is, that once I turn eighteen, my aging process will slow to a near halt?"

"That's the theory," he replies. "Here's another confession: your life has been hidden from Moyer for seventeen years, and during those years, the Storms have been trying to hide you. Bouncing you from one location to another. The childhood you think you know, is a mere illusion to keep you safe all these years," he confesses.

"This is way too farfetched for me to believe." I remember growing up with my dad and my aunt Fran taking care of me. I remember everything about my childhood and fleeing to Seattle from Florida a couple years ago," I cry aloud, protesting Cory's admissions.

"You remember exactly as intended to. For the past sixteen years you have been living on Ladorielle. Until you saw Blair that day…in 'Florida.'

"How do you know that?"

"Because I was there, with her."

I stop walking, and stare at Cory in shock, beginning to put it all together. "The hooded figure in Florida. That was you?"

Flashbacks of that day at school, when I saw the figure, by the building, and then near my home, come to the front of my mind. Before I have a chance to say a word to Cory, he says, "Yes. That was me…and my brother. I was the one at school, and Cole was the one you saw near your house.

"That morning when you went to school, I warned Jeoffrey that Moyer had taken another souls power. I didn't know what the power would be, but she was close on your tale, and this time she would probably catch up to you all."

"So, you knew I was coming, before you read dad's letter?" I question.

"Yes," he says. "And, like we discussed before, I had to be careful leading you to the clues."

"And this business about Cole marking me? It's not really accurate is it?"

"No. He can't have you, even if Moyer's law is invoked."

"Because you saw me first," I say to him.

He nods. "Exactly. But don't worry, I'm not my brother. As I mentioned before, I believe people have the free right to choose. I want someone to love me because they do, not because some stupid necromancer law."

"And so, this thing about being a vampire; you don't seem to fit the stereotypical mold."

"None of us nytemires do. What do you think, that we all live in coffins and drink the blood of our victims, like vampires?"

I wrinkle my forehead. "Well, yeah. Isn't that what you do?"

"Not exactly. I agree I'm different than most, but there are similarities."

"Like what?" I inquire, waiting to hear more.

"I eat food like you. I may not need as much per se. If we eat a fresh animal kill, we can go weeks without eating human food."

"So, what? You don't drink human blood?"

"Oh no, we do. Isn't my brother a witness to that?"

"Suppose that is a wrong frame of questioning on my part," I voice back.

Cory laughs. "Wynter, I choose not to kill humans. That's not to say I won't do it. Anyone who comes within a foot in harming my family, I won't think twice."

"Have you killed a human before?" His silence is deafening, when he doesn't reply, and I think back to the night in my room when Cole was about to finish me off.

I realize Cory sees my thoughts and says. "Brother or not I won't let him harm you, or anyone else. As long as my heart beats."

"Your heart, beats?"

Cory laughs, again. "Wow, Wynter. What a way to ruin a perfectly good moment."

"Hah, sorry."

"Yes, our hearts beat like any other. "Truth: We drink blood, run fast, have exceptional hearing and eyesight. Oh, and while the stake to the heart would kill anyone, it will freeze a vampire, until it's removed."

"We also sleep but not nearly as much as you of course." He pauses as if he thought of something sarcastic. "And contrary to what you might believe, if you haven't noticed we walk in the sunlight."

"I've read so many books about vampires. You're not like any of the myths."

"You catch on quick," he says in a sarcastic tone.

"What about garlic?

"It's great on pizza."

"What about being seen in a photo?"

"Have you not seen us in photo albums? I have a camera somewhere, back at the cottage," he scoffs.

"You know, you're quite the smartass." I smile at him ready to punch his arm, but don't. "Last night, that's why you staked your brother? You knew it wouldn't kill him."

"It bought us time, didn't it?" he says.

I nod in agreement. "So, I imagine you're immortal too?"

"Essentially yes. "Fire is the only way we go down."

I thought occurs to me and I blurt out "Cory that's it!" I raise my voice. I think I know why Sarmira is raising such a brood of vampires. And I think I know how we can defeat them."

"You forget one thing. It won't kill Sarmira. Her human body perhaps, but she will turn back into the wraith she is, and we are back to square one."

27

Rosie

The next morning and afternoon we spend reading book after book, up in the loft. Cory explains to me the necromancers are sorcerers that dabble in black magic to raise the dead, and only a handful of them resist the evil power. The Storm family is one house who found their deity in doing good magic. They refused to bow down to the underlord having Sarmira as their queen. When Sara's kingdom disobeyed, Sarmira went after them with a vengeance.

The whole family exiled to Ladorielle, finding peace. For a few centuries until the day a wraith came, peering in on the unsuspecting family by a river. It's my dream, that left me clues to the past. The wraith chased the Storms to an entirely different universe, hoping that they escaped for the final time. But it was short lived. According to Sara's journals, Sarmira followed. That's where Maura Moyer met her fate.

"Cory?" I say looking up from my reading.

"Yes," he says, nose still in his book.

"How does Moyer know I'm the one?"

"I don't know that she does. What I do know, she wants your power. It's valuable to her and the only way to get it, is at midnight, on one's birthday."

I change the subject slightly. "Stella told me you and Cole fought over a girl once."

He dips his head in agreement. "Yes, it's true, we did. But not in the way that you think." I can tell he's uncomfortable, telling the memory. Hesitating, he finds a voice, laughing aloud, but not a laugh of happiness, rather a laughter of unpleasant recollection it seems. He comes to sit down next to me on the sofa.

"Here's the short version," he says, pausing. "The 'whys' will have to wait." His facial features hint that this isn't a pleasant subject to begin.

"A pure necromancer feeds from the power of essence of a human. The babies you hear," he grows to a soft whisper, "are bred from the Storm bloodline. She combines our blood with that of vampires, werewolves, species from Ladorielle; constantly working to make the perfect creation."

"I—I don't understand, I'm just—"

"The girl Stella told you about," he interrupts, "was bred from one of those living within the house. Raised to fight alongside with all the other evil beings. But she had a pure heart, a soul that would not accept the horror. Much like you, Wynter. In fact, she stood against Moyer and her heinous crimes. You see, with each child born, they are raised still with innocence in their hearts. At eighteen, the power within them is revealed, matured. Moyer, sends the teens to the chambers the day before their birthday, compels them, and at midnight, sucks the essence of magic from them. The strong ones survive. She then changes them."

"You mean, to a vampire?"

"Yes, or if you are not born a nytemire like Cole, Blair, or me, she blends them with other species like Nora."

"This must have been what my dad and Fran questioned the day of the accident. They mentioned something about her gaining another power. They seemed to catch up to us quickly. Fran had no warning, like she usually does."

Cory goes on, "Last week, an Elvin druid was stripped of his power. Well, at least it was rumored he would be. No one knows what their power is until the day they turn. He was a pure blood. Both his parents are druids; porters one might call them. They can jump from one world to the next without having to use a portal chamber. All they need is a rune to that world. Moyer managed to nab him while his parents explored Scotland years ago. There are spies working for her everywhere in the human world, going undetected. When he was kidnapped, he was the only child of course. So, she had to wait years for him to mature."

Remembering the nightmare from a few nights ago, I confess to Cory, "In my dream, I saw a woman they called Elena, pull from her pocket a stone. She began to move her hand, circling around it until a bubble formed around the group. Within seconds after that, they disappeared."

"You're describing the druid's talent from Ladorielle," he replies.

"So, Moyer's a predator?"

"In a matter of speaking, yes. You see, she breeds these world species blending them with other species."

"But why?"

"To become powerful. To breed an army. To destroy…you. She has been preparing centuries for war." He breathes in a deep breath. *"Your war.'* The war you will lead when the super blood moon comes this winter."

"Me? But I'm—nobody. I'm just a teen who loves music, reading and running."

"You're harmless until after you turn eighteen. She wants your power first. Once she has it, she will kill you."

My heart pounds, beginning to make me hyperventilate. Suddenly I can't breathe. I feel faint like I'm about to pass out. My blood races through my body and I become dizzy. "Kill me?"

"I'm not going to let that happen."

"Cory, we can't stay in this place forever, she will come looking for me."

"I know."

"If what you say is true? And I have something of value to her? She won't stop until she gets what she wants." I look towards the corner where the coffers lie in the floorboards and say, "What do you suppose is in the leather jewelry box? You know we haven't tried to find the key."

"I'm hoping there will be a clue in one of these books we are reading," he says, and gets up to add a log to the fire.

We continue to read through the rest of the afternoon and we discover the great war that happened thousands of years ago all started because of forbidden love. Sarmira is only smidgen of the real mystery, but she is now the root cause on my fate.

Later into that early Saturday evening, Cory bursts through the cottage front door, after chopping more wood, and says, trying to catch his breath, "We have to go. We have to go, now!"

"Cory what is it? Is everything okay?"

"No, everything is not okay. Moyer's arriving this evening. She's going to be looking for you and will be angry!"

"How do you know?" I say, closing my book.

"Exceptional hearing, remember? I overheard Blair talking with Casey in the barn. We haven't much time. Grab your coat. But first drink this." And he hands me a teardrop shaped bottle. "It's an invisibility elixir. It will allow you to reach your room undetected."

I hesitate, a second, then swig it down. It tastes bitter, like sinking your teeth into the rind of an orange after brushing. I look around feeling unchanged. "Did it work? I can still see my hands," I cry out.

"Of course it worked, look." He turns me toward the mirror hanging above the mantle, with Cory the only one showing in the reflection. I watch as he too chugs down a second bottle and disappears.

"Are you ready?" he says, grabbing my hand.

"I guess so." And we leave the cottage. Climbing on Cory's back as before, he speeds to the front door of the library. "How is it, that I can still see you?" I whisper in his ear.

He smiles. "The caveat to the elixir is you can see others who are invisible too." Setting me to my feet, he opens the back door gently, whispering, "Follow me up to your room. I don't want to take any chances."

When we reach my corridor, we see many people in the hall. Most of them are other orphans. But one stands out different from all the rest. It's Nora. She leans up against the wall with a grey glow surrounding her. People would walk by and seem not to notice her standing there. Her arms are folded, and she looks to be waiting for something. I notice Cory pulling me back behind him. It's at these times I wish I can read his mind.

"She can see you. And Cory." I finally hear the voice that has been dormant in my head for days. *'You certainly pick a fine time to show up.'* I say in a sarcastic tone.

'Yes well, I had other business to attend to. I knew you would be in good hands with Cory.' It says.

'Oh really? Did you know Cole tried to sink his teeth into me the other night?'

'Apparently you're still you, and not a nytemire.' It says, sounding pleased.

'Is that all you have to say?'

Cory and I hang out in the very corner spot where Cole found me the first night, he caught me. I tap his shoulder, and Cory glares at me, as though to imply, 'wait.'

'Stay put, Wynter. Until Nora leaves,' the voice says.

'Can't you do something?' I say. And as if she knows what to do before I even have to say the words, I hear a commotion from

the next corridor. It is long enough for Nora to be distracted. Giving us the chance to sprint to my bedroom door.

"Well, that was fun," Cory murmurs.

"I sink down to the edge of my bed. "What's that grey cloud around Nora?"

"Her invisibility mist," Cory shares.

"And only we can see her?" I ask.

"Yes. Remember when I revealed the advantages of the invisibility elixir? One of the perks, is others also can see who are invisible."

"Ah, I understand now." Then it dawns on me, "That's the eyes and ears watching me, isn't it?"

"My goodness Wynter, you catch on quick," he jokes.

"It's starting to all make sense now." Thinking back to the day when Nora caught me in the wrong corridor, and she appeared out of thin air. Or when she was suddenly behind me, as I walked to breakfast, and slammed me against the hall wall.

Cory nods at me. I can tell he's seeing the pictures in my mind. "Now you know, why Moyer knows what happens every minute, of every day." He paces back and forth across my floor, as I watch his facial expressions. His concentration amazes me, and I wonder many times what he's thinking when he does that.

"So, what do we do now? I ask with concern. "You're stuck here in this room with me."

"Go with the flow. Pretend like nothing has changed. Moyer has expedited her plans. I hear people arriving now."

"You can hear this far from the foyer?"

"Yes. And I hear footsteps coming outside your door." He pauses as if he is tuning in as to who it is. "It's Rosie. She's come to check on you. I see her holding something."

"How—"

Cory slips into my closet again, and hides. With a knock at my entrance soon to follow.

Rosie stands there budding a smile. "How are you feeling dear?" she says, holding a plastic bag. She steps into my room and looks around. "I have strict instructions to give this to you," she says, and hands me a sack.

"What is this?" I ask, looking in the bag to see garments folded nice and neat.

"The family crest attire. You will find every Storm wearing one, today." She pauses and looks around my room. "Have you been up long? Cory says you haven't been feeling well. Yet your bed is made."

"Play it off. Tell her you feel better today. Give her an excuse like reading, or something," the voice says.

"I've been up for a while. Reading," I fib.

"Without a fire to keep you warm? Dear child what is going on? Do not lie to me. I'm the one person in the house you cannot lie to. I can see it. Your aura speaks when you do not tell the truth."

"That went well didn't it?" I reply, to the whisper in my head.

"You know when someone is lying?"

Rosie smiles, "I know all truths, even the one Cory told me Thursday."

I hold in a breath of shock, not knowing what to say and sink back down onto my bed, dropping the bag in my hand to the floor.

"Ever since you arrived there have been dishonest auras popping up all around everyone," she says, walking to the fireplace to start a fire. "It's freezing in this room, child." She crumbles the paper throwing it, along with splinters of wood in the hearth. "You can come out now Cory, your aura cannot be missed when the closet door is cracked open."

He opens the door and walks out. Before he has a chance to say a word, Rosie pops up from the fire, placing the poker back in the stand, and says, "You may have gotten away with this little escape," - pointing her finger at the both of us, - "but you won't when Moyer finds out. Do you have any idea how much trouble you have given us all?"

She moves over to him and stands. Much shorter than he, but she has a bite in her tone. "Listen here Cory; there are some things you need to tread more lightly with, and you should know that I, of all people, am on your side here. How do you expect me to cover for you if you don't tell me what's going on?"

"Yes, ma'am." Is all he has to say.

I, for one, am shocked, if not floored, by hearing Rosie's disapproval.

"Now that, that is cleared up," she says smiling. Turning her attention onto me, she continues, "I assume Cory has taken you to a place where things are hidden and safe and you now know much about the Storm family line. Use that knowledge, because you my dear, are going to need it. Regarding those garments I gave you, the grounds will increasingly become crowded. The guests need to distinguish who is a Storm, and who is not."

I pull out a cardigan V-neck sweater with a large gold shield stitched in a shape of a teardrop, with crossing swords in front of the armor. Words in another language stitched above the crest saying: Taigh na Stoirme

"House of Storm," Cory says. "It's our family crest.

"Something doesn't feel right. Why am I wearing this?" I ask concerned.

Rosie steps around Cory, toward me, taking the sweater, and holding it up to my chest. "I assume Cory has told you of the nytemires. They all have a craving for blood, my dear. You are not one of them. This sweater will tell everyone you are off limits."

I watch as Rosie takes off a gold band from her finger. Placing it in her pocket. "Come erase my mind Cory," she says.

"But Rosie—no."

"Do not argue young man. She mustn't know where you have been. It's your duty to protect it, leaving no choice. You must remove my thoughts. I'm not protected like you two are."

Cory does as he's told, and I observe as his eyes begin to glow. He tells Rosie she will have no memory, of our conversation, and that I was ill all weekend and stayed in my room. Then commanded the memory remain locked until he unlocked it. He turns her facing my bedroom door, then races back to my closet, this time shutting the door tight.

I watch Rosie turn around and she smiles. At first, she looks confused and then her eyes grow big. She places her hands in her pocket. Her body language says it all. She puts her ring back on and says, "Tell me if the clothes fit, will you? You're free to roam the grounds my dear…and try to stay out of trouble." Then Rosie walks out of the room shutting the door behind her.

"What is that all about," I say, hearing the closet door creak back open.

"Moyer keeps her around, untouched for her gifts. What I didn't tell you, about that day when Rosie caught Moyer; they made a deal. Rosie would remain loyal to Moyer, if she left Rosie alone. Giving her the freedom to be herself. Rosie became an asset to Moyer. She has the ability to know when someone is lying or hiding something of secret."

"That's why she made you erase her memory? To protect you, because of what you know, and what I know?"

"Yes."

"And the ring?"

"Sara gave it to her. Rosie is after all, her lady's maid. She's caught between loyalties. You, and Moyer."

"But if she can see my aura, what's to stop her from telling Moyer?"

"Sara," he says, softly. "You're a direct descendant. You take precedence over Moyer. Rosie, like myself, and many others, will not overstep our loyalty when it comes to Sara and her bloodline."

"So, what now?"

"We both prepare for company." And he nods towards the bag, still on the floor.

It isn't too long before Cory and I are dressed and ready to greet guest's downstairs. Outfitted in this ridiculous uniform I hesitate as we descend the stairs together down the formal flight of steps.

My heart is heavy, and I don't know what to say or think. So many faces, some staring at us, others ignoring what's going on around them and continue to gossip.

Evil blood runs through the Storm bloodline, generations deep. I'm still trying to wrap my head around the fact, that Moyer is centuries old. It's something that plays out in legends, not in real life. Any normal human being would think this to be insane. Apparently, I'm not normal. I have seen things that the human realm cannot possibly understand. Peering through this place with new eyes, and what I know now. Each person I see, looks normal. But what lies beneath? Is every one of these people I see a vampire, concocted by Moyer sick creations?

We walk the manor nonchalantly trying very hard not to draw attention to ourselves, making our way to the foyer bench, and sit.

I observe Chad escorting guests to their perspective rooms, along with Daniel, Derek and a few other attendants, realizing that the orphanage has turned into a five-star hotel resort. The parlor's changed to a gathering spot for wine, liquor and chatter.

The people arriving seem to have class status, too. Men in suits and ties, women in nice dresses. Suitcases at their side waiting for attention.

There must have been fifty guests or more. Quite honestly, I didn't think that many rooms were in the manor. Every guest set forth to the grand staircase before coming back down to enjoy themselves among the fun.

"They all look and seem like ordinary people, to me," I voice out loud. Not expecting Cory to answer.

"Each and every person who enters here, has some sort of magical gift, or supernatural ability about them. Look there, for instance," he says, pointing with a nod of his head. "That's Mr. and Mrs. Rauls from Scotland. Mrs. Rauls is said to have blood ties with Madame Moyer. A distant cousin."

"Does she have similar powers, like the rest of us?" I ask, glancing at her stature, as I watch one of the attendants take her coat and hat. Another bellhop nearby takes their luggage placing it on a cart trolley.

"No, but her hearing is exceptional." And at that very moment she looks our way turning up her nose, siding a grin. "Better than mine even," Cory whispers in my ear.

Mrs. Rauls is indeed a chatterbox. She stands there for what seems like an eternity, babbling on and on about this and that. Finally, one of the servant's escorts both her and Mr. Rauls up the grand staircase.

Once attention is dropped from us, Cory takes my hand and squeezes. He matches my gaze, nodding with a smile, and before I have a chance to take one step, we are in the library.

"Wow, you're quick," I whisper.

"All in the wrist my dear." He winks.

People are standing everywhere chatting among themselves, in the library engaging in warm conversations. A lot of laughter fills the room. One thing that does speak loudly in my thoughts though; not a child in sight and the heaviness in my heart begins to pound.

"Not now," I hear Cory say under his breath. "You must calm your emotions, or you will attract every supernatural in this household."

My heart continues to race, whispering back at him, "You say that like it's easy to do?"

"If you ever plan on defeating *her*, we must control it now. I've had years of practice. It will take you time."

"Well how do you control yours?"

"I try to think of something else," Cory says, with a slight, but firm smile. Then he breathes in deep, and I begin to sense calmness. Something he hadn't done in a while. "I've been trying to avoid doing this. To wean you. I won't always be around. How do you feel now?"

I try to think happy thoughts. "Is this the only thing that's going to get me through this right now?" I ask. "I'm concerned that I won't learn in time. That I'll have every vampire in here after my blood."

"Remember, they cannot harm you, but they can hear you. Keep the fear away. We all…including me…feed on it."

My eyes widen with surprise. Not having the words to say anything. It's like my tongue is jammed behind my teeth.

Cory chuckles. "I'm not immune to the temptations that vampires have. I've had years of practice and learned to control it. Besides, like I told you before; you're mine anyway." He gives me a mischievous smile. I can't help but smile, back. Thinking he knows, how I truly feel about him. And, as if he read my mind, whispers in my ear, "I've known from the first day, you saw me in the library."

My stomach flutters, and if he hadn't pacified me, I'm sure my heart would be racing right now. I see him point with his eyes at the camera on the ceiling, and grabs my hand, leading me away from the lens.

We dash behind the desk. Cory grabs the skeleton key in his pocket, that he hadn't put back from underneath the counter, and opens the iron door behind us.

"Well, that was fun," Cory says.

People on the other side of the door are seen moving about, continuing to talk amongst themselves, oblivious of the invisible one-way gate to the portal.

"What are you doing, Cory? Why have you taken me here again? We can't go back to the cottage. She will find out."

"I didn't bring you here for that. It's the only place in this castle where I can freely do this." And he pulls me to him, gently kissing me. His lips are soft, warm and inviting. Not at all what I expected. I invite him in with the wetness of his tongue, barely touching mine tasting his sweetness. His hands caressing my back as he holds me close, pulling me closer to him. Our lips linger together, for what seems like minutes, rather than seconds.

'So, this is it,' I think to myself. *'The chase is over, he's captured my heart, and I have fallen into his.'*

28

Stella's Not There

"It's nearing dinner time, Moyer will be looking for us soon," he says as we make our way out of the library. Guests continue to file into the foyer. "Just so you know, I'm not letting you out of my sight." Taking my hand, he leads me into the dining room, where I hear many voices chatting amongst themselves.

"Cory, I don't see Stella."

"She's probably around somewhere," he says.

"So many people," I whisper. Round tables have been set up along the sides, with floral center pieces. The long tables where the children sit, are decorated with table runners and place settings. It is like looking at a grand dining room prepared for a holiday feast with family and friends. Each seat has its own name.

"Assigned seating," he murmurs. "On rare occasions, today being one of them, Moyer will have a grand party celebration. Through the week until your birthday."

"Through the week?"

"Instead of her going to Scotland where yearly events take place, she's brought Scotland here. I have no doubt it's because you are her grand prize and she wants to show you off." He pauses, looking at me. "What's wrong, Wynter? You look like you have seen a ghost."

"Nothing. It's fine. I'm fine, Cory." Trying to play off my bewilderment. *"How are we to escape? Moyer will catch onto us for sure, now,"* I say to the inner voice.

"No, she won't. Stick to the plan. Do not lose focus."

"So, where have you been, all day?" Stella says, coming up from behind me.

She startled me so much, I jumped. "Hi there, how are you? I was beginning to worry."

"Me? What about you? You're the one that has been cooped up in your room all weekend long. How are you feeling?" she says, sounding legitimately concerned. I don't have the heart to lie to her, but feel there is no choice, but to. I must keep her out of the family drama as much as possible.

"I feel fine," I say, as she glances to Cory standing next to me.

"If you will excuse me, ladies." He bows and takes his seat at the head table.

Stella squints her eyes. It leaves me to wonder if Moyer has somehow put her up to the prodding of my whereabouts.

"We should look for our seats," I propose, trying to change the awkward moment.

"So, where were you, really…?" Stella whispers. My heart sinks to the bottom pit of my stomach. She isn't letting this go, I thought. And before I can answer her, the chimes of the bell rang out ahead, with Daniel grabbing everyone's attention.

I rush to my little corner table, hoping to be unnoticed. I discover many more tables than I originally realize, along with many more guests, near my table and the Storm's. Each tabletop appears to be marked with a different color. I hear Daniel announce each setting as a *'house of such & such'* with all members of that group bowing before everyone in the dining hall.

When it comes time for my name to be called, all eyes look towards me with curiosity, and I glance over at Cory who nods, gesturing me to stand. Many faces smile an evil grin, while others glare with disgust. Some stand out more than others, whereas a hand full of guests whisper to each other and snicker softly. Chills cascade across my skin. Again, Cory nods, signaling that I may sit down. His brother Cole sitting next to him glares at me with malevolence.

I'm prodded and poked with veering glances, and murmurs. Moyer seems to lavish in all the mysterious wonder from the guests. Thankfully Cory helps me through it all, with his glancing innuendoes. When I picture something in my mind and he answers me with facial expressions, it helps some, but I can't wait to leave.

Later that night Cory escorts me to my room. My mind rolls through the previous days' wondering how we will pull off our escape. Hoping to ask Stella more questions proves to be uneventful.

Cory starts a fire when we arrive in my room. Then reminds me to lock the door, and he leaves to patrol the halls.

I find a book, and snuggle up to the warm fire, but it's short lived. The knock from my door wakes my exciting thoughts, that is about to dive into a story.

Thinking it's Cory, I don't bother to ask who it is, turning the knob and swinging it open.

"Stella? What are you doing here? It's almost nine."

"Can I come in?"

"Sure." I step aside and shut the door. "Stella is everything okay?" She looks scared, I see it in her eyes. "What's wrong?"

Something isn't right. I can feel it in my gut. Like the time Nora had been here, the first time I arrived. Her monotone aura gives me the first clue.

"Stella you look tired, come sit down in the chair by the fire. Are you okay?"

"Yes, fine? Why wouldn't I be?" she says, with a grim smile. Her eyes are withdrawn, appearing sunk in with grey patches showing lack of sleep. Not sure why I didn't notice at dinner, but she does seem to appear ill. I don't know if I should ask what happened. But from my previous experience I gather she's been compelled. Someone wants information and I'm beginning to feel nervous she's in my room.

I touch her shoulder and she flinches. Thwarting me into thinking she's hurt, yet her drone stance might cover any pain she's in.

As I look closer at her face, she sheds a tear. Almost like her soul cries but not her flesh. "Stella? Are you hurt? What did they do to you?"

She turns her head as if to snap out of it, causing me to motion myself backwards onto the floor. "I'm fine, Wynter, why do you keep asking me these questions?"

"Hey, you're the one that knocked on my door, remember?"

"Oh. That's right, yes. I did, didn't I?" She calmly sits back in her chair, smiling. Then without any warning she says, "I never knew how much my life would change after the train accident. I didn't know that by being brought here, it meant never leaving." She stares at the fire in front of her. Gazing into its flames as it crackles from the sounds of burning wood.

"At first they make you feel welcome. Like a part of their family. It isn't until you have been here a while, that you begin to feel the change."

She glares at me with her eyes. They are black as coal and this time they look evil. Her pupils are so dilated that I can't see her irises. "Isn't that what's going on with you Wynter? You're beginning to change?" she says, tilting her head sideways, widening her eyes. "I had so much hope for you. Now all is lost."

"Stella you're not making any sense. What's going on with you. Who's done this to you?" My feelings take over, and I grab her arms, shaking her.

"Stella snap out of it!" I scream. And as if that triggered something, she recoils backwards in her chair, looking around.

"Where am I?" She glances at me, and realizing where she is, says, "Wynter, how did I get into your room?"

I hug Stella, saying, "You don't remember anything?"

She shakes her head. "I can't recall. The last I remember is sitting down at dinner."

At this point I don't know what I should or shouldn't say. There's no telling what would freak Stella out. After she gathered her senses a bit, she got up from the chair and paces my floor, pulling at her lip. Appearing to be deep in thought, I finally interrupt her. "Stella, what's wrong?"

She stops in her tracks, staring back at me. "It's just that…the last time this happened, I was in this very room." She pauses as if afraid to say anymore. "They must be listening."

I nod, feeling a little queasy. "There is something that doesn't add up for me."

"What's that?" Stella whispers.

"Everyone I have ever interacted with, indicate, once one enters here one never comes out."

She smirks a smile, keeping silent, prompting me to inquire, "Stella, what's wrong, what are you not telling me?"

"Nothing…why would you think something is wrong?" she probes.

"I can see it on your face. It's like you're afraid of something, or someone."

"No, it's fine. What else would you like to know?" she asks.

Without warning my door is forced open, jolting us both backwards with terror.

"That's enough Stella, I'll take it from here," Moyer says, as she pulls Stella toward her, lifting the girl's feet from the ground. I can hear Stella gasp for air, and her face shriek with terror.

Madame Moyer chants a spell aloud, and her eyes begin to glow. Bright blue hues protrude from Moyer's sockets, her skin turns grey, and veins black like the twins in the library.

I watch as I see Stella's life begin to be sucked from her small body. As she hangs in the air, her head tilts backward, and her flesh darkens like Moyer's. Then without warning, a shadow in a hooded cloak lunges forward, sinking teeth into Stella's neck. I can't tell who it is, as it feeds on her blood, drinking its fill. Then I witness Stella go limp, and it turns to face me, grinning with blood dripping from its fangs. It's the face of Cory, only I know better. The eye's told me it's really Cole. Stella falls to the floor, unconscious. Her lifeless body lay there, unmoving. I know she's dead, for her chest is still from breath.

"Why!" I scream. "You're both mad!"

He smiles. "No, just thirsty. I must save my main course for later. She's merely a snack," he says, gurgling a laugh. "Fear not my love, once it happens, you will have no memory of your old life."

I reach to smack him, but he's too quick, grabbing both my arms behind my back. Moyer steps forth giving a wicked smile. "She knows too much, I see that now." Glancing in the direction of Stella's lifeless body, she says, "Seems you now know more that you should. Whatever shall we do with you?"

My chest heaves up and down. The rage in my blood boils, showing the heaviness that festers within me. "You won't get away with this."

"Oh, my dear, but I already have. And one by one, I will begin to eliminate all you care about. Blair comes to mind... well I can't kill her. Cory either for that matter. Although torture still doesn't ever get old."

"What have you done with them?" I bellow back at her. I feel the veins in my body begin to burn, and the grip that Cole has on me goes numb.

Raising an eyebrow, Moyer looks amused. Cackling she nods to Cole to release me. "They are fine, both patrolling the grounds." She pauses looking me up and down. "You, on the other hand, will be prepared for grooming. The plans are set in place and the party is about to begin."

"Grooming?"

She simply grins, evilly, breaking her glare, calling, "Rosie!"

'We must find a way to escape,' I think to myself, hoping this time the voice is there listening to me.

"I have a plan," I hear it say.

"Nice for you to show up," I reply.

"I've been busy planning," it says.

"Yes, Madame Moyer," I hear Rosie say, as she comes running into my room, ignoring the body on the floor.

"Prepare the staff. We are having a welcoming party Monday evening, for Wynter." Then she focuses her eyes on me again saying, "And bring Stella back to her room, where she can rest."

Astonishment crosses my face, "You mean—"

"Dead? Oh, my dear heavens no." She smiles wickedly. "She's one of us now. Like you will be once I have what I want." Raising her hand for Cole to follow, she leaves my room, slamming my door shut.

Cory must have seen my terrified mind and within minutes he's at my door.

"I don't want to be alone in this room tonight," I say to him.

He doesn't say anything. No need to, all he has to do is see the pictures in my mind to know what happened, and I fall asleep, laying on his chest.

29

The Power of Truth

I hear rattling sounds that wake me from sleep. Looking over at the clock, I see it's 11:30 at night. Listening to Cory's heart beating, as I lay on his chest, I watch as faint hues from the burning coals leave shadows of tree branches waving on my walls.

A loud pounding comes from the other side of my bedroom door, followed by twisting on the door knob. I realize that is what must have woken me. Another forceful thrust comes from the other side, jolting Cory from sleep. With the room so dark, I can't see his reaction, but what I do know, he's nervous. Silently he slips into my closet, putting fingers to his lips, and motioning with his other hand to open the door.

There she stands, the devils Spawn of Satan, wickedly smiling, and eyes aglow, holding an oil lamp in her hand. "You seem to not understand that breaking the rules will not be tolerated. Why is your door locked?"

"I feel safer that way." *'Was that the excuse I gave her?'*

She cackles loud, "Safe? You have no idea how unsafe you are, Wynter. Follow me."

Now I know why Cory was quiet, fleeing to the closet. Who knows what she would have done. She glides effortlessly across the marble floor, passing each room until she stands before the stairwell to the basement. Déjà vu sets in as I remember JC hanging from the ceiling. I know now where we're going, and it sends chills throughout my whole body.

"Remember, No fear. She can see it. So, stay strong," the voice says.

I step forward, as Moyer leads the way spiraling downward to the pit below.

When we hit the last step, Madame Moyer lights a second oil lamp hanging beside the doorframe. It's still dark and musty, like I remember, sending gagging messages to my stomach. The filthy air touches my tongue with every breath I take in.

Edging the corner as I follow, once again seeing the wrought iron bars with dozens of cells lined in a row. This time Moyer opens the gate and we pace through, where I see each jail cell floor, covered with hay. The dampness in the air smells of death.

She turns to glare at me, "I know I have brought you here before, but it seems, JC wasn't enough influence on you. Perhaps I might be able to change your mind? I can be patient to a point. But after hearing of your scathing escapades, I feel we must take it up a notch."

She slowly walks the passageway, showing me each chamber. Many people putting out their dirty hands, through the bars, moaning. One woman, cries repeatedly, "I'm sorry, I won't do it again," as if it's the only words she knows.

"Please observe," and she brings me to a chamber, where in the center is a chair mounted in the middle of the room. Straps hang over the side, and a machine in the corner is lit up with a dozen dials or more.

I hear a familiar voice from behind us say, "Excuse me Madame Moyer," and she turns to face Casey standing there. "The boy is ready."

She grins maliciously. "Looks like you will see firsthand what is in store for you this week. Please do sit down." And motions me to sit in a corner chair.

"That power of yours will mature at midnight on your eighteenth birthday." She comes to stand next to me, her hands cupped in front of her as if to be waiting for something exciting to happen.

Casey brings a blindfolded boy, to the chair. Taking off his mask, I observe that he's not much older than me and stares back with pleading eyes.

As Casey straps him in, like you would a prisoner on death row, I suck in a breath.

"This should be a good learning lesson for you. I can't wait to see your reaction," she says in an enthusiastic tone.

Once Casey finishes securing the boy, he pulls the machine in the corner, to the chair. Capping the lads head with a gray metal crown, with wire hanging out, he's hooked up to the monitor. I see his eyes widen, and his body stiffen. I hear heavy breathing fill the room and realize it's his.

"What are you going to do with him?"

"Watch my dear and you will find out," she says, coyly.

Casey turns on the machine, "Ready when you are, Madame Moyer," Casey says. His fingers tracing to the far dial.

She steps forward. "No, start him slowly. I want Wynter to observe every painstaking process that goes into all that we do here."

Casey moves his hands to the nearest dial and turns it. I watch as the boy, stiffens his whole body, pushing his torso upward in pain. He screams in agony."

"Again," she calls. "This time move to the next dial, I want to see her watch him suffer."

Moyer is a monster. No, that's being too kind, she's a fiend of malevolence. A spawn of the devil himself. A minion of his creation. I squirm on the inside watching her direction as she instructs more and more torture on the teen.

Finally, Moyer raises her hand, as if to say enough, steps forward and grabs his chin. "My dear Casey, I do believe we almost killed him." She tosses his head from side to side, then lifting his eyelids. "Ah, there is still life in him. Good. Never want a gifted power to go to waste. She slaps his face lightly to wake him from his unconscious state. He moans softly, as he comes to. I barely see his eyes open, when Moyer's eyes, begin to glow bright blue. He opens his mouth as if to feel yet again more pain. His skin turns grey and his veins bulge as I watch her fiercely breathe in every breath of his air. Pulling from him the very life that exists of his soul. He flails in convulsions again. She continues to suck his essence, until leaving him lifeless in the chair.

I cringe and realize I just viewed a person die right before me.

A cold breeze wisps through the air and touches my skin, giving me goosebumps. The voice inside me says, *"He is with me now. As you can see, she must be stopped.*

Casey unleashes the corpse and lifts him over his back disappearing out of the chamber.

Moyer paces to the doorway, saying, "I will be hosting a lavish party for you this week. Eighteen, it's the right of passage for you." She smiles, but it isn't a warm smile. I don't trust it one bit. I know it will come soon, when I'm to be in that same chair. Her evil plans are driving me to revenge. With each step I feel the power within me gaining momentum, and I feel a burning in my stomach like never before.

"Now you're getting it. Yes, turn that fear into anger, but don't let it control you."

"You will discover more than I care for you to know, Moyer says coolly. "It's inevitable, I realize that. Just like I know that Cory has shown you the cameras."

"Cameras?" I ask, trying to play dumb.

She cackles. "Oh, my dear, you have much to learn about trying to fool me." As we walk out of the cell and into a familiar large room, that still hangs ropes, nooses, chains, shovels, hooks, and machetes. So much stench fills the room. The same red stained workbench sits against an adjacent wall and my eyes fill with disgust. A torture chamber of unimaginable repugnance. My thoughts fill with dread, my emotions scrambling to recover. I want to scream from the madness before me. Why is she showing me such painful wickedness, again?

"Because she needs to weaken you. Prepare you for this week," the voice answers.

"No matter. Now that you know, I'm always watching you," Moyer says, bringing me back from my thoughts. "Perhaps you will think twice before going off somewhere without permission. It seems you have grown quite fond of the boy, strolling out onto the grounds, like you own the place."

The rage begins to lose focus in my mind, and fear coming back, at the thought of her harming Cory. "Oh, don't worry. I won't harm him…yet. He's much too valuable. But she on the other hand," she says, as she points to a figure naked hanging by the wrists, and feet dangling, "will possibly change your mind from ever disobeying me again!"

Casey teeters forward to the body, turning it to face us. There hung Blair, her frame beaten so badly her skin no longer the same color, but black from bruises. Her face nearly unrecognizable. Her throat slit, with pools of blood puddle below her toes. "You killed her?"

"Oh, my dear no. Are you kidding? If I did that, who would teach you your studies?" Then she peers deep into my eyes, as if to compel me, only this time her eyes don't glow. "If you ever cross me again, this is only a fraction of what I can do. She and her sons are mere pawns in the grand scheme of things. I will not hesitate to destroy anything and everything near and dear to your precious little heart." I look over Moyer's shoulder to see the necklace hanging from Blair's bloodstained neck, glowing bright red. A hue of light I know Moyer can't see. Proof of what Cory conveyed earlier, that evil cannot break through the protection.

"Blair can be replaced, there are many more where she came from. The twins too," she says. "I would rather not kill any of them, and it would inconvenience me greatly, but if it means keeping you in line, it's a tradeoff I'm willing to take."

Tears begin to well in my eyes and I try to control my emotions, but the pain I feel in my heart, begins to beat with fury. There isn't a word left to describe the vile existence of Madame Moyer.

She backs away from me and straightens her posture. "Casey, get her down. I think Wynter here, gets the point."

She looks at me, as if to approve of her little soirée this evening. "Clean her up and give her a bath, then throw her in one of the cells. Let her reflect on her sins."

"Can you imagine what happens to the ones who try to escape?" she scorns, "Well, I am sure you saw the workbench around the corner. I imagine the thoughts you were planning earlier of running away are no longer an issue?"

"What?" I look at her in shock. That isn't something I shared with anyone. I hadn't even mentioned anything out loud. My mind wanders, thinking of when I let my thoughts out. Trying to reflect if I had cited anything in passing. Then I remember the conversation Stella and I had in my room.

"Oh, come now, Wynter, I know about the questions you ask Stella, the sweet conversations you have with Cory. I even know about the little note you burned in the fireplace that your father wrote, so that no one would know. You play me for a fool?"

"I-I h—how," I stutter. Looking up at her with panicking fear.

She maliciously smiles at me and says, "You will not foil my plans. You will prepare for the ball Monday night, and you will be on your best behavior. Do I make myself clear? Fore if you do not, I will not think twice about killing you, after I take your powers Thursday night."

Tears stream down my face, my cheeks flush, and my body fills with anxiety.

"Brave the Storm, dear Wynter. Believe in your abilities. She can't harm you as long as you wear the necklace."

"I'd rather die than let you take my gift from me!" I scream.

Moyer glowers, lunging for my throat, only to be shocked with electricity, jolting her slightly backwards. The surprising look on her face, tickles me on the inside, bringing me more confidence.

"That's right show her the power, you have. She will recoil, trust me," says the inner voice.

"No! It can't be. Isalora is dead. You have no power to protect you."

"What was that?" I ask the voice talking inside my head.

"A mere touch of what your power will be once you turn eighteen. The necklace, also known as, Keeper of the Amulet, is in the Protection of the Sword and will always be with you."

Moyer seems to grapple in thought, as to how I sent electricity through her veins. I watch, as she looks at her hands, and balls them into fists.

"I know you are here Isalora," she hisses. "You've somehow managed to find the undead plane of immortality… haven't you? We shall see who will win this game. You may have won this little battle, by getting inside your daughter's head, but you will not defeat me!" she screams aloud and charges for the stairs. "Casey see to it that Wynter finds the way to her room and lock her there until I return."

"Daughter?" I ask the voice. But there is no answer that comes back to me.

"Yes, Madame." Casey cowers, tilting his head in confusion. "Where shall I tell Chad, you're going?"

"To cast a spell to the Portal of Hate. I need to talk with Vothule The Soulreaper. He's the only one who knows how to break that wretched spell." She stalks up the spiral staircase disappearing, leaving me standing here with Casey.

I feel nauseous thinking about the way Moyer's mind works. With everything I witnessed, I don't know what to expect. One thing is for certain, Moyer is after blood… No, my soul. *"Who are you?"* I ask, the voice. As I turn to watch Casey clean Blair up with what looks to be a blood-stained rag. She lies lifeless on the table, revealing every beautiful part of her badly bruised and scarred body.

The voice continues to stay silent. But Casey's words brings me back to reality. "She's not dead, if that's what you're thinking," he says, as he wrings water over her stomach removing the dried blood from her skin.

"How is that possible? Her throat is slashed, nearly decapitating her."

I turn away as I see him reposition her head and wipe her face. More blood seeps through the gaping wounds oozing out beneath her neck, making more of a mess. I try not to look as I unintentionally peek out to see red liquid drip to the floor. *'How can anyone have, any blood left in them after that,'* I think.

Casey grins, showing how deformed his features really are. His head is larger than average size, disproportionate to the rest of his body. He isn't small, and lean, but rather muscular in the arms, chest and legs. From the back he looks like a body builder.

"Right now, she sleeps," he says, interrupting my thoughts. "Her body regenerates slowly. Not like your mother's or Fran's did."

"You knew them?" I ask, astonished by such incredible news.

"They were the Lord Storms children," he answers. "He was my master. Until…" - He peers at me, looking up from what he's doing. "Would you mind grabbing that jug over there in the corner please?"- Pointing a few steps away.

I grab the container and hand it to him and witness him pour the entire liquid over Blair's lifeless appearing body. Bubbles begin to form around each gash where a whip pressed through her skin. I look at him in amazement.

"It's just alcohol. Kills the germs." Then he continues his tale. "…Until the day Sarmira arrived and shed darkness upon the Storm family dynasty."

"Darkness…Dynasty?" I question, as he continues to clean every crevasse of her body.

"Have you not figured it yet girl?" he stops. Staring straight into my eyes, he resumes, "You're the last pure blood left."

"Pure blood?" I ask, taken aback by his claim.

"All hope of the worlds of magic, whether it's good or bad falls squarely onto your shoulders. If anyone is to defeat her, it's you, My Lady."

"Worlds? You mean more than one?"

"My dear child, has no one told you yet?

"Tell me what, Casey?"

"That you come from royal blood."

"Yes, Cory told me yesterday, but he didn't have much to tell. Only that Moyer wants my power, then plans to kill me.

"She wants your power yes, but kill you no. She plans to breed you. Turn you into a genetic experiment. Take your royal blood and genetically alter to make magical powerful hybrids."

I try to control the bile coming to the surface of my mouth, from this devastating information. I stand here silent, barely able to continue listening to his horrid words.

By this time, Casey has placed a towel over Blair to dry her, grabbing a brush in the process, and begins brushing her hair.

"With your powers stolen, there will never be any chance for her to be over powered. While in the process, she grows amazingly fierce, evoking chaos onto the magical world, the galaxy, and even earth. Imagine if one being had the ultimate power, a power more than God, or Satan?"

"Nobody is that powerful," I say, finally able to work past the bile that stains my mouth.

"Nobody yet. Face your fear child. We are all counting on you. The universe depends on it."

"How on earth am I to do this alone?"

Casey ignores my question, and I watch him blanket Blair, covering her from head to toe.

"You're not alone. You have me." The voice says

"Is Casey, right? Is what he's saying, the truth?" The voice doesn't answer back.

"My Lady, I will escort you to your room now," Casey says. We leave Blair lying on the table, as I follow him to the stairs.

"What will happen to her?" I ask.

"Nothing child. She is regenerating. What one might consider…rest," he replies.

"Will she remember anything?"

"Only until Moyer slit her throat, bleeding her dry."

"How is she still alive?"

We reach the top of the stairs, and I can hear nothing but the silence in the halls and the whistling of the wind howling outside.

"Because the only way to truly kill her kind is with fire."

"So, what now?" I ask, wondering how any of us is going to survive such wrath of pain that is yet to come.

"I take you to your room as instructed, where you wait for Moyer's return."

I cringe the thought of her coming back. It does settle my heart a little to know that the necklace is more than a compelling shield.

We reach my corridor and around the corner, where he brings out a ring of keys.

"What are those for?"

"Madame Moyer says, to lock you in your room, until she returns. I cannot go against her wishes, no matter how much I disagree with them."

"Why not? Am I not a descendent of the Lord of Storm?"

"Indeed, you are My Lady, but she has cursed a spell, that my will, cannot be broken. She is who I must obey, no matter the cost." He pauses, tilting his head, looking at me with sad eyes. "Only you can break the hex she has on this manor and the people who live in it."

"Before you go, one question please?"

"Yes, My Lady?"

"You never finished explaining, how she is still alive?"

He smiles, his lopsided grin. "You mean Blair? Because she's a nytemire of course. But you already knew that. And with that he shuts the door, locking me inside."

30

The House of Storm

I find Cory sitting on my bed, with his hands in his face. How am I going to tell him what my evening experience was, what was done to his mother, or about who I am. Lastly what her plans really are? How am I going to keep it together? I feel like I'm about to bust at the seams and bawl like a baby.

He turns to see me standing here. "Hey, there you are," getting up from the bed. "I'm amazed I didn't hear you come in."

"You're still here?" I say, in surprise, and before another word escapes, tears of anguish fall from my cheeks. My heart races, in turmoil and my mind can't form thoughts that lead to my tongue.

Cory speeds to my side, in a matter of a half a nanosecond. "Are you okay? Did she hurt you?"

I shake my head no. He wraps his arm around my shoulders, and says, "Come sit down."

I try to bring the words to my mouth, but nothing comes to pass through my lips. Feeling Cory's body stiffen like a board, I know I don't need to say anything, he's already reading the pictures in my mind.

"Everything is going to be fine," he says, tucking a lock, behind my ear. We lay down together, his hands caressing my hair, my head on his chest, listening to the soft sounds of his heart beating, where I find myself drifting to sleep in a wet pool of sobs.

The door shutting wakes me from my pleasant sleep. I look around to see that I am in my room and Cory is gone. The window is wide open, and it is freezing. My whole-body shivering, head throbbing with piercing pain, the covers are at the end of the bed, and I'm still dressed from the night before. I look over at the clock to see its morning. The sound of birds sing outside, as I peer in their direction to see the sunlight escaping through the trees.

A light knock at my door startles my body. "Wynter, are you in there?" says a familiar voice.

My mind races to collect my thoughts for a moment. "I'm fine, come in," I say, forgetting I'm locked in my room. "Wait—"

And my door swings open with Nora standing there, holding a zipped-up garment bag and boxed shoes. "Hi there, Wynter, may I come in?"

"Sure," I say, thinking, *'she sounds pleasantly chipper this morning.'*

"I've come to bring you this. Rosie's orders, as per Moyer. She wants you to wear this to the ball," she says, and I watch her go to hook the bag to the back of my closet door.

"Thank you, Nora, anything else?"

"No, just that breakfast is in an hour." Then she gets an awful expression on her face. "Gawd Wynter, what's that smell?" She peers towards me. "And you look like hell."

"Thanks." I smile, realizing that I'm in desperate need of a shower. "I should probably get ready then and head for breakfast. Thanks for dropping the dress off." Working my way to pushing Nora, back out my door.

"Oh, I almost forgot, Moyer has unrestricted you. You're free to roam the manor but remember to wear your clothes Rosie gave you yesterday. As she leaves, I see Cory come up from behind her and I watch the two of them hiss glances at each other.

Slight fear enters my soul, seeing him. It's like he knows something. Sliding into my room quickly I shut the door behind me.

"Cory, your scaring me! What's wrong? Unless you're Cole. I can't tell anymore." His fists are closed tight and the muscles on his jaws clenched.

"I'm sorry, I didn't mean to scare you," is all he says.

"So, tell me, are you Cole or Cory?"

"Wait, you don't believe me?"

"Cory, you are acting like your brother, what am I supposed to think? It looks like you're ready to kill someone." I tilt my head and fold my arms. "And aside from all I have gone through, I frankly don't know what to think anymore."

"I'll prove it to you." He smiles, raising his wrist, revealing the watch.

"No, sorry, that isn't going to cut it anymore. Cole has on the same one. Remember? You're going to have to do better than that." I cock my head to the side a little more.

My mind goes to Blair hanging in chains, and the death of a poor helpless soul strapped in a chair.

I watch Cory, as he tightens his lips. "I don't know what makes me angrier, Moyer bleeding my mother dry, or my brother impersonating me." He looks into my eyes. "I'm so sorry you had to go through that. I had no idea." He steps closer to me, but I put a hand up.

Stopping in his tracks. "You still don't believe it's me?"

Tears begin to well. "I don't know who to believe anymore. You said nobody can see the enchantments of the jewelry we all wear for protection. How did they find out?"

His eye's turn to sadness. "I don't know. I'm just as perplexed as you." Then he says, "My brother cannot read thoughts, of the minds of other souls. That is a gift only I have, at least, that I'm aware of. How else can I prove to you it's me?"

Shaking my head, I shrug.

"Think of something else," Cory says. "Something that you have never told anyone. A secret only you would know."

'What can it hurt,' I think. So, I reflect to the day we left Washington, when dad told me the story of Sara and Ailbert. I look to my window, to see my favorite sparkling gem dangling in front of the glass—

"Labradorite," he says to me. "It's the glue that keeps the Storm magic protected."

I run to Cory, tears flowing down my cheeks, hugging him tight. "It is you."

"Of course, it's me. Didn't I already tell you that?" he says, and he hugs me back.

After I finish sobbing, getting it all out of my system, I say, "So, what do we do now?"

"Do the only thing we can do. Find a way to stop her. And I know just the place to go, to prepare."

That evening we walk together downstairs to the dining room for dinner.

Ahead of us is Stella waving. "Careful what you say to her," he whispers. "She hasn't any memory of what Moyer did to her."

"Is she a vampire now?"

"Yes, not a nytemire. She was human, before she was turned. A nytemire must be born of necro blood," he reminds me, in a soft tone.

"Where have you been?" Stella says, "It looks like we missed out on Friday for movie night. I have no idea how I slept the whole weekend away."

"It's good to see you, Stel," I hesitate, not knowing what else to say. She sounds like she has no recollection of the last few nights.

"Excuse me," Cory says, "I'll leave you two to chat." And I watch as Cory takes his seat at the Storm table.

"What's that all about?" Stella asks rolling her eyes toward Cory.

"What? Cory?" I ask.

"I see the way you two look at each other. Can't fool me Wynter," she replies, spatting out a snarl under her breath.

"It's nothing. We're cousins, remember? Can't we be friends?"

"I see," she sneers again, not at all sounding pleased that I'm hanging around him.

"I've been walking the grounds exploring with Cory," I say, hoping I can assure her.

Stella's frightful eyes give me a clue that she's not at all happy about it. "It's ok, Blair gave me permission to." I smile.

"What? But—"

Before I can answer her, the chimes of the bell rang out ahead, with Daniel once again, voicing announcements.

Afterwards, ceiling lights, light up like a stage does in a performance, with blue rays beaming across the room, like all the other times before. In unison, the kids begin to pick up their forks and eat. Knowing the outcome before, I know this is my cue to play the part. Pretend I'm also pacified like the others. I veer over to see a few words exchange between Blair and Cole. He appears angry as the two whisper, and she looks as if she's completely recovered from the basement.

Then Moyer enters the room, glowering in my direction, whip in hand, looking ready to pounce.

Deep in my soul I know she knows I'd been with Cory. Her eyes glow with fury as she glides my way. I concentrate on my food and pretend to ignore her presence. She stops and peers down at me with daggering eyes. "It has been reported you have been on a weekend adventure, Miss Wynter."

Playing along with the soothing atmosphere as the rest of the children in the room, I don't respond.

She slams her hands down on the table. "Look at me!" she yells, glowering into my eyes.

I stop eating and stare back at her, unmoved by her advances. Cory said to show no emotion and it will make it difficult for her. Fear drives her power, so fear she will not get from me. A glowing light emits from her pupils and again, I see a face, not like the face of her, but a face of another, peering back at me. After knowing who this really is before me, it's presumed that Maura is the trapped image behind the pupils of Moyer's stare. Maura opens her mouth as if to be saying something, yet I cannot understand her mute voice.

"I will ask again, where did you go?" Madame Moyer says, in an undertone that sent shockwaves through my veins. I can tell she is trying to intimidate me, but I stand my ground.

"I walked the fences, around the perimeter of the manor, until I reached the river," I state. "There I sat, reading a book. Lost track of time."

"I see," Moyer replies, slapping the wand in her hand. Her tone clearly sounding like she doesn't believe me. "And where is this book? Do you know what happens here to people who try to deceive me?"

I control my pounding heart, not to give way to my fear. Cory should be proud. Pretending is going to be hard, I must fight this urge to give in. I place my hands in my pockets. Trying to keep in the rhythm of the rest of the pacified room, when I feel something under my vest. It feels like a book. Not questioning how it got there I pull it from under my garment. I can't explain it, nor do I care, and I lay it on the table for her to see.

"So, either you had that in your pocket the whole time, trying to manipulate my authority, or there's magic here at the manor. Which is it!" she shouts.

"Leave her alone!" Cory yells, standing up to face her from across the other side of the room. *'What is he thinking? Cory please sit down,'* I think.

Moyer stiffens and bolts so fast I don't have time to react. She flings him to the ceiling, holding him there with some sort of invisible force, one can't see with the naked eye.

"You dare challenge me, boy?" she screeches. Extending her hand and twisting her fingers, to form into a fist, it appears her magic is choking him of breath.

I see Blair, Chad, Derek and Daniel all get up, pushing aside their chairs, hissing as they make a fighting stance circling the front area of the dining room. The rest of the guests stand as well taking sides of either Moyer or the Storms. All the while the rest of the room remains unaffected by what's happening. The kids continue to eat their food, staring either at the walls or plates in front of them, as if they are unaware of their surroundings. If a fight begins, the children would certainly be in the crossfire.

I hear Blair say, "I'll gladly fight to the death, before I allow you to kill my son, Moyer. Take your hands off him, now." Her eyes begin to glow, along with the rest of the Storm family.

Cole remains in his seat, smirking. I watch as he sips a glass of wine, peering an evil grin, then cheers his goblet towards me and drinks.

It's the first time I have heard Blair openly admit in front of everyone that either of the twins are her sons. This is a side of Blair I haven't seen before. Changing my initial thoughts as to who she really is. Cory mentioned that it's all a façade. To keep Moyer at bay.

I see the amulet dangle from her neck, the red hues of light exhume from her body. Apparently, Moyer doesn't see her light shining bright. I'm immediately reminded of my dad mentioning the third necklace as lost. It's not lost at all. Blair has had it the whole time.

'Play the part and act accordingly,' is the first thought that comes to mind. Is this what Blair, Cory, Chad and Derek are doing? Moyer is smart enough to figure it out. No, I feel in my gut she knows who is on whose side. She's evil, but she isn't stupid.

The rest of the Storms move around the front table as if to prepare for battle, all hissing like vampires ready for a kill. Each of them eyeing the other, growls coming from the throats of them all.

Moyer asks Cory, "What are you doing? You dare to defend the likes of her?" I can sense the squeezing of her fingers, around Cory's neck, as the pressure increases. My body seems to mimic the same feelings as what Cory feels. The pressure beginning to coat my throat. Is this part of a power Cory explained earlier? My ability would slowly grow to full force, should something provoke it?

My neck feels the constricting pressure and I feel as though I cannot breathe. Anger begins to fill my head and a surge comes over me as I witness my necklace start to glow. I begin to imagine the pressure around Cory's neck be released. Focusing on pushing the power away I envision Moyer's concealed aura, releasing him from her grasp.

"Drop my son!" I hear Blair hiss a scream, that sounds louder than the first time.

Cory tries to answer Moyer's question, but her grip is too tight. Another hiss comes blaring out, only this time it's Chad.

"Oh, please son, do you dare challenge your mother?" she exclaims.

"Leave him be. Wynter is a Storm like the rest of us. We will not allow you to kill blood, mother," Chad intervenes. The hues of his aura glows green. Can she not see the colors before her?

I feel the pressure of Moyer's power release from Cory's neck. Her strength is far greater than mine. Sweat beads across my forehead but I'm not going to allow it to distract me.

She looks around, dropping Cory to the floor and laughs out loud. So loud that the castle vibrates from her rumbling mouth and the force pushes us all backwards.

"Well, how convenient is this? You dare challenge me children? Your own matriarch?" she screams.

Thunder begins to rumble outside, and I know this is not going to end well. Cory is slumped over in the corner, grasping for breath as he tries to gather his composure back.

The orphans still eat their food, emotionless as to what's unfolding. It's as if all in the room are pacified except the Storm family, and the other Houses. Even the maids continue their task of pouring beverages to those with empty glasses and clearing plates for those who have finished their meals.

The rest of the vampires and guests crouch around the room or rise in the air. Hovering everywhere ready to strike anyone who makes the first move.

'*So, they can fly too,*' I think.

"You cannot defeat me!" I witness Moyer's eyes power a glow brighter than usual, as she begins to laugh louder. She roars as loud as a thunderstorm, then moves her arms in front of her body, clasping her hands together in a fist. Releasing her bonded hands, she flails a magic sonic boom through the air, thrusting everyone against the walls.

I find myself on the floor, my head throbbing with pain, when I feel something wet oozing down the side of my face and realize its blood. I look for Moyer, but she is nowhere in sight. The evil witch has disappeared.

Hearing some children cry, while others lay silent, I look around. The pacification has dispelled, replacing muffled sounds of pain. I know I will be ok because of the healing abilities I possess, but what about all the others? So many children lie on the floor unconscious. I look to see Stella is breathing, however, the child next to her is clearly limp without life.

"Cory, Blair!" I scream, scrambling to the girl appearing to be no older than five, laying on the floor with blood oozing from the back of her skull. Checking for a pulse, I cry out, "She's not moving and so small. Just a child," I sob. "How can *she* do this to innocent children?"

I hold the little one gently, as her dark curls dangle freely in the air. Looking at her peacefully sleeping face, tears begin to flood my cheeks. Her skin is smooth and soft like a young one's would be. No breath exhales from her body, as she lies limp as a doll in my arms. I look around the room to see many more laying lifeless on the floor.

Derek and Chad check on the injured ones. Some of them crying, while others whimper for Rosie and Blair. Servants assist the dazed children out of the room while other hired help bring linens and ice packs, for others still on the floor.

"Come on," Cory says, putting out his hand. "Let's get you out of here, I'll walk you to your room. They have it under control."

My tears continue to fall on the child's face in my arms. "I'll take her, Wyn. Don't worry, the child is in good hands," Blair says softly. "She's at peace now." I place the small orphan in Blair's arms, and get up to go with Cory. Although tears stream down my cheeks, the rage within me grows. *'I want her dead.'*

When we finally arrive in my room, I simply want to crawl into my bed and fall asleep. I feel drained of energy. The horror and power I witnessed this evening puts everything into perspective. Moyer is evil to the core. How can anyone defeat such wickedness? I'm beginning to realize why the cabin is protected from her malice. Why Dad and Aunt Fran kept me away, kept this secret from me. And why the Labradorite amulets are so important to wear. If she can physically do such harm to others with that power she possesses, I can only imagine what she can do inside my head. Reliving the memory of all those children lying on the floor, is only the beginning to the wrath she can execute. I know now why she must be stopped, why she must be drained of every ounce of power within her iniquitous spirit. According to my dad, I'm the key to her destruction. What I observed today cannot go unpunished. She must be stopped. The lost lives of innocence are unacceptable. *'If you are listening, whoever, or wherever you are, I accept my fate.'*

I sense Cory starting a fire from the sounds of crinkling paper and throwing of kindling in the hearth. Ignoring the noises, I find myself drained and drifting to sleep.

31

New Ability

The next morning, I wake to the buzzing sound of the alarm, and roll over to slam it off. At this point all I can think about is breakfast. I quickly race to the bathroom for a shower and change for school. I've been here a week and I already feel like I have been here for a month. I'm not exactly looking forward to the week after the experience of last night, but I know the only way to destroy Moyer is to get my hands dirty. I'm ready for a fight. Killing innocent children is where I draw the line. Knowing of what Moyer is capable of, I know we must be careful. Perhaps Cory and I can find an end to her existence once and for all. I don't care if she kills me. She must be destroyed. No one should ever have so much power that it extinguishes the lives of everyone around them.

I make my way down to the kitchen to see the cooks working over the stove, and maids serving up food in the dining room to a sparse number of orphans.

It's as though nobody remembers the fateful night before.

"They don't recall anything," I hear someone say, over my shoulder. It's Chad, and he looks calm. "You have discovered her wrath firsthand, my dear. I doubt it will be the last."

"Where is she? I want her dead." I know I'm no match for her, but would she dare kill me? I have something she wants. Do

I dare push the envelope, to give that wicked witch what she deserves?

"Seems your powers have excelled a bit," he says, smiling at me with a bow. He steps down into the dining room and glides to his table in the front. There he sits, and picking up his paper, he begins to read.

I follow him, obviously my aura spoke of annoyance. "It's not evolving new power, it's anger, Chad. She must be stopped!" I can feel my cheeks flush red the more I think about her. The more I think about those poor children lying on the floor, lifeless.

Chad doesn't flinch once, as he reads his paper. It's as though he's ignoring me: like I don't exist in his reading world of the morning news. "She's not here," he finally says. "Left this morning and will not be back until the evening. Tread softly my sweet niece. I know that's anger in your heart, the revenge will eat away at your soul. You mustn't let it get to you, else you *will* fail."

If only he can see the red flames I have inside. "How can you ignore what happened last night. Just…just sit there reading your… whatever it is you're reading and not do something about it?"

Chad chuckles, shaking the paper erect, so he can read the top column. "When the time is right, it will all come together. Do not be hasty….Now, if you please, I would like to read my paper."

Fury flashes before my eyes and my gut burns, trying hard not to scream at him, when I hear Stella call me.

"Hey there Wynter, I didn't see you walk in. Will you sit with me?"

Like shutting off a faucet, my emotions dissipate, and I turn around bringing a smile in her direction, "Hi Stella, how are you?" I don't want to give her any hints of my rage, because if she truly doesn't remember anything the night before, it is best she not know.

I sit next to her and a maid brings me my plate of food.

"How are you feeling today Stella?" Worried that she might have hit her head real hard from Moyer's sonic boom.

"Fine, although my noggin hurts a bit, patting the back of her skull. "You?"

I nod. "Fine," I say, taking a bite of food, lying through my teeth.

She smiles back at me, chewing. "I see your hair has changed?"

"Huh?" I look down at my locks to see my hair has turned a dark blonde."

"My hair seems to be lightening. Not sure why," I lie again.

After breakfast we pile into the classroom. Many of the desks are left open. The students don't seem to notice the others are missing - or care that they are.

I see Cory sitting at his desk with his head down, not at all himself. His hair is a mess and he looks to be in pain.

"Hey there, Cory?" I say as I sit down. Stella follows behind me and takes her seat.

He stays quiet, and nods. Never looking up to make eye contact. I turn around in my seat when I hear Mr. Derek come into the room.

"Good morning class," he says. "Please open your books to page twelve and begin reading." He appears unfocused, like something is on his mind. Blair pops through the door and gestures him over. They glance toward me and then follow out into the hall.

I turn to Cory. "What is going on?" That's when I notice Cory's lip is split. He looks up at me with a grim smile. His cheek is bruised, and there's a large gash across his brow. "What the happened to you?"

"Got into a little brawl is all. I'll be okay. This is what happens when you stand up to *her*. She pulled me from the dungeon this morning. I was much worse an hour ago. Trust me. I don't heal as fast as you do."

"Oh my gosh Cory, what the hell?"

"Hell is right. I lived it last night." He squints in pain, as he changes positions.

"Are you okay?" I want to help him, yet I feel helpless. I can feel the numbness in my body take hold, a warm feeling flowing through my veins. If only I can heal him from this pain.

"Not really. Couple cracked ribs, and a little weak from bleeding out. Going to take time to regain my energy."

"Bleeding out?"

He nods, turning his neck to show me the slash. "Quickest way to weaken a supernatural like me is to bleed them dry of blood. It lowers my heart rate, to a mere murmur. One is at the mercy of whoever is in control at that point. Remember Blair?"

Tears well up in my eyes, and my face turns red with fury. "We have to stop her."

He nods. "Indeed, we do." And he shifts his body to get comfortable, then screams in pain, as a bone breaks through his chest, sending blood gushing everywhere.

"Cory!" I scream, as he falls to the floor. I don't know what to do, so I place my hand over the wound to see if I can stop the bleeding, when my hands begin to glow with light, healing him before my eyes.

The classroom hovers around witnessing, *'Now everyone knows I have powers,'* I think to myself.

Blair and Derek come racing in to see children talking excitedly.

"Class to your seats please," I hear Derek say, as Blair runs to Cory's aid.

"What did you do?" Blair says. Her eyes becoming wide from seeing the bloodstained shirt Cory wore.

"No. It's fine. I'm ok." Looking up at us, then to me, he says, "She healed me. The pain is gone."

"What?" Blair exclaims, staring at me in surprise. "You healed him? But how?"

"I—I don't know."

"How do you feel? Any pain at all? she asks, Cory.

"No, nothing," he replies, as he gets up to stand.

"Come, let's get you both out of here," Blair says, grabbing Cory's arm, we head for the door.

"Blair," I say.

She turns to me. "Yes?"

"Everyone saw. What's happening to me?" I ask.

"I know, don't worry. Chad will take care of it." She looks at Derek. "Can you handle both classes for the moment while I get him?"

Derek nods, giving a thumbs up. "Okay class shows over, back to work," I hear him call out as we leave the classroom.

We make our way back to the doctor's office.

"Cory sit over there," she says, pointing to the examination table. "Now Wynter, I want you to show me what you did to Cory back there."

"It's okay, Wyn. This is a new power you have come into. We are all a little alarmed because normally this doesn't happen until you turn eighteen." Cory says, adding, "I see your hair has lightened, too."

"I know, it seems like every time I have an emotional break down it lightens a shade."

I hesitate a moment, then come over to him. "Um, maybe you should lie down?"

He tilts his head. "Sure."

I take my hands, and move them over his body, as we watch the golden glow play off my fingers.

"Astounding." Blair says, "Cory can you feel anything?"

"I feel a warm numbing sensation come over my body. Like hot cocoa warming my veins on a cold winter night."

Together Blair and I watch Cory's face come back to normal complexion and his split lip disappear.

"What does this all mean?" I ask.

Cory sits up, feeling with his hand the area of his body that once held wounds. Now only a faint scar exists where his rib poked through the skin. "Do you think anger caused such power to form early?" he says, glancing at Blair.

"Quite possible," she says looking him over, then to me. "It means, Wynter, that you have the ability to heal others. I'm not sure what brought it on, but it's showing itself loud and clear."

"Yet I couldn't save those children."

"You see here young lady," she cries out, jerking my shoulders toward her and looking me straight in the eyes. "There is nothing, and I mean NOTHING, you could have done. You can't raise the dead, child. Do you realize the amazing ability you have?"

I stare at her, as tears begin to form in my eyes. I want to scream at the top of my lungs, but I know it wouldn't do any good.

"Listen to me!" she continues. "She will not beat us down; do you hear me?" She shakes me to answer. "Wynter do you understand? She hasn't beaten us. We will stop her, but we must plan carefully. If she figures out that we're on to her, she'll put the wrath in us that we may never see the light of day again. Moyer must not find out."

"Yes, I understand. Blair, I want her dead, more than I have ever wanted anything in my life."

Blair hugs me tight. "I know, believe me. I know. It's time we set the strategies in motion for escape."

She releases our embrace and says, "You two are excused for the day."

"So, now what?" I ask looking back at them both.

"Now we prepare," they say in unison.

"The party, it's tonight. She will be expecting us," I say.

"And, so we shall attend," he says grinning. "I have a plan, remember?"

Cory leads me to the portal in the library. Once hidden on the other side of the gate he says, "I can see it. Your color is blue. The same blue that is declared to be in the prophecy. Wynter, Moyer knows. The ball is her cover. She plans to capture you tonight and hold you until your birthday. When you retire for the evening, instead of going to your room, I want you to hide here in the library until I get here. We must leave tonight. You remember how to hide from view of the cameras, right?"

"Yes." What about everyone else? The kids, Blair, Derek. What about saving your brother?"

"They will all have to wait. Saving you is priority. There's no saving them if you're stripped of your powers, or dead."

"Where are we to go?"

"The cottage. It's the best place to be: protected by magic."

"Cory, I feel like this is a trap."

"It's going to be fine," he says, trying to assure me.

"Wait." Pulling at his hand to hold off opening the door. "There's something else."

He turns to look at me, and I say, "When I was down in the basement, while Blair hung from chains, Moyer tried to strike me down."

"Come again?" Cory's eyes began to glow.

"But she couldn't touch me. Something in the necklace pushed her back." I pause as I see his skin become translucent,

"Cory, there's more, something else happened. Moyer called out Isalora, referring to me as her daughter."

His eyes stopped glowing, his tension eased a bit, as if to be in shock. "What?"

"You're right about one thing, I am the last bloodline alive on earth, but I'm apparently the lost princess of Ladorielle."

"Casey." Cory sighs. "Sometimes when Casey speaks, he tells of story's, that are passed down as legends."

"Then how do you explain the voice in my head?"

"What voice?"

"The voice that has been speaking to me since I got here."

Cory begins pacing the tight closet isle, putting his finger to his lips pulling at them.

'Tell him, 'Nyta.'

'What?'

'Trust me. He's the only one who knows that name, with the exceptions of your father and Fran.'

I do as the voice requests and blurt, "Nyta." I watch Cory stop in his tracks.

"What did you say?" turning to me in surprise.

"Nyta?" I repeat to him. "The voice said you would know."

"Aye, I do." Cory nods. "What I didn't tell you that day when I met the wisp…rather Isalora, she said I would know the battle begins, when I hear the name Nyta."

I take a step back, sucking in a breath. "This is it then? We escape or die tonight."

"Yes." And he pulls me to him. "Remember to stay calm. A pounding heartbeat calls to them all. Anger makes you more powerful, and fear weakens you. You must keep your emotions in check tonight. I know what to do now. Stay close to me and follow my lead."

We sneak back out from behind the gate into the library and follow into the foyer, where we see more guests arriving.

Rosie finds us standing near the hall bench and instructs me to go upstairs to dress the part, as Jeoffrey's daughter, wearing the gown, Nora brought me the night before.

"Don't worry, I'll come get you in a few hours." Cory says walking me to my door. She won't try anything until after you have been properly introduced."

I smile at him. "Is that supposed to make me feel better?"

He raises his eyebrow. "No, but perhaps it will prepare you for anticipation."

32

Formal Introduction

When I arrive in my room, I find my dress is out and hanging above the door frame of my closet. *'I really should invest in smuggling a key.'* Someone obviously went to great lengths to have it out prepped and ready for me to put on. It's a deep purple taffeta gown accompanying a black velvet jacket, with a petticoat attached to a second hanger, along with a corset. *'What is this, eighteenth century?'* White stockings hung around the dress and black heels sit on the floor. I don't think I have experienced anything like this in all my life. Wondering if the whole house will be dressed in the same costume attire.

'Dress the part,' I hear the voice say in my head.

'I don't know how to put any of this on.' What a mess this is going to be. I hear a knock at the door, startling me from my thoughts.

"Wynter, it's me, Nora. May I come in?"

Thank goodness, maybe she had some pointers, and I rush to open it.

There she stands, dressed up a bit too, only her dress not as extravagant as mine. "Are you ready for your debut?"

"Not exactly." Widening the door for her to step in. "Do you have any suggestions on how to put that on?" I ask, pointing at the dress hanging on the closet.

She smiles coolly, saying, "Indeed, I do. Rosie sent me up here to help you." And for the first time I see Nora, in a different light. It's like as if she's suddenly in her element, knowing what to do, and when to put on what. She has the knowledge to see to it that each detail is executed in precise precision, all the way down to the last strand of hair. I literally looked like an aristocrat. A noble lady. After she's finished, Nora giggles.

"What's so funny?" I ask.

"The expression on your face. It's priceless."

"I look like a big purple grape in heels."

She laughs louder this time. "It's not often we get to dress up like this. As for me, I'm excited. It's been centuries."

"Centuries?"

Nora pauses. I imagine, realizing she's disclosed too much, she turns away, saying, "That was a slip of the tongue, now, wasn't it?"

"Don't worry, I'm not at all shocked."

"You're not?" Nora says, moving back to face me again.

"I know about the nytemires."

"I see." She pauses, then says, "So I suppose you know all about me then?"

"No, not exactly," I reply, firming a smile, as I look in the mirror to see my hair pinned up, appearing almost platinum. "My hair will be white soon."

"Yes. It's lightening faster than any other Storm's has in the past." She comes over to me, showing her eyes, as they turn lizard looking, her skin changes to scales.

The alarm on my face shows through to the reflection in the mirror, and she says, "Don't worry, I'm not going to hurt you tonight."

Looking back at her through the mirror I say, "I wasn't expecting that from you. Is all. You caught me by surprise."

"I know. Believe me, it isn't intentional. I wanted to show you what I look like in the light. You said nytemire, earlier." Pausing to sit down on the edge of the bed, she adds, "I'm an Iknes Shaw."

"A what?" I say to her turning around.

"Half human, half snake." She huffs an irritated breath, "...and now vampire, too."

I move to the corner chair to sit, trying to find the proper way to be seated, and find myself having a giant hoop flung up into my face. "How am I supposed to sit in this?" I cry out.

I hear Nora giggle, before saying, "Stand up." And I do as she instructs. "Now, feel for the second rib on the back of your skirt, and lift." She smiles as she watches my quandary. "There you go."

"Gawd, Nora. You really had to wear these all the time back in the day?"

"Imagine what it's like trying to go to the bathroom dressed in one?" she says, snickering.

"Umm yeah, that will be a problem."

"Not to worry - you will figure it out. Just lift the skirts up."

"Let me guess. A genius invention from a man's point of view?"

She giggles again. "The original designs, yes."

Once I finally become comfortable in the chair, Nora continues her tale. "I'm one of Moyer's experimental subjects," she scoffs. "Years ago, she used Rosie's body as a host to grow many kinds of species, until her age became an issue."

The thought of Moyer using people as pawns, festers inside me, but I keep cool, listening. All the while devising a plan of my own.

I was born, half human, half snake. Or should I say, half elf. I'm not even human. Much like you. Anyway, Rosie was allowed to raise me as her own. I was very curious. Still am, for that matter. But things changed when I went snooping around one night. Like you, I went out beyond the doors after nine. I thought I was going to die that night, but instead, he kept me for his own."

"Cole," I say.

She shot me a look of surprise. "You knew?"

"Yes. The day I re-broke my leg, when Cole impersonated Cory, he told me you and he were an item. I don't understand why he would still chase me, when he already has you."

"Don't be so naïve Wynter. He's a man."

"Nora, I'm not interested in him at all."

"I know. It's why I haven't killed you yet."

"What?"

"I was hoping Cole would listen to reason, when he saw that Cory already has you marked first. Everyone in the house knows it, too. Yet, for some reason, Madame Moyer doesn't control Cole's advances towards you. It can only mean one thing. She wants you turned, before your birthday. Cory won't do it, so she won't stop Cole from coming after you."

I try to control my beating heart, while the burning sensation begins to flow again within my veins. *'Stay cool.'* "Why are you telling me this?"

Nora pauses for a long time, then says. "She plans to strike tonight. Going to the ball is a trap." She gets up and walks to the door. "I've expressed too much to you this evening. My advice," she says, as she opens my door to leave, "be careful." And she begins to shut the door behind her. Another knock startles me, as Cory stops her. "Nora, thank you." He bows at her, and he steps inside.

After she leaves, I say, "You heard my heartbeat, didn't you?"

"Yes, but you controlled it much better this time."

I tilt my head at him. "You sent her here?"

He smiles, as if to seem proud that he accomplished a goal. "Testing you, to see how well you do under pressure."

"So, you know about Nora, and her past?"

"Yes, we all grew up together, as children."

"Wow Cory, what else do you have hiding in that brain of yours?"

"You don't want to know," he says, laughing.

"So, tell me. Is what Nora saying, true?"

"What's that?"

"That we are walking into a trap?"

"Not if I can help it. We stick to the plan. Remember, I will find you wherever you are."

"Is that supposed to assure me, knowing there are going to be vampires everywhere I look?"

"They won't hurt you. It's Cole who we have to look out for."

Putting out his arm for me to take, he says, "You ready my lady?"

"Really Cory. Do you have to be so formal?"

"Ah, humor me. It's not often I'll get to act ceremoniously." He smiles, flashing his gorgeous white teeth adding, "You look absolutely stunning."

"Thank you. You're not too shabby looking yourself." Taking his arm, I ask, "Any clue why we are dressed like the eighteenth century?"

"Every once in a while, Moyer throws a ball. Never on a holiday of course. Usually during the summer. Guests fly in from all over the world to attend. The attire is always eighteenth century. I had expected nothing less from her. Promise me you will try to stay composed?"

"Only if you promise to stay close."

"Fair enough," he says, with a chuckle.

"May I ask, why are we being introduced? Isn't the dining room introduction enough?"

He laughs again, at my ignorance. "We are Storms of course. Moyer does not like embarrassment. People would talk if they saw you, knowing you have white hair like mine now, scurrying around unannounced."

We walk out the door and begin down the hall toward the French doors. "Oh, something I forgot to mention, we will be walking through the main corridors." He smiles. "Play the part, my sweet Wynter."

We walk down the second set of doors, before Daniel stops us at the top, guiding us to the line taped to the floor. Cory and I stand there waiting for our names to be called. "Just a few more minutes. Remember to smile," he says.

I hear Daniel begin, "Announcing Cory Storm, of the house of Storm and son of Madame Maura Moyer, and Wynter Storm of house of Storm daughter of Jeoffrey Storm."

"Here we go," he says softly.

33

The Ball

We descend the grand staircase together, with ensuing eyes watching, followed by gasps and whispers, as we slowly make our way to the bottom of the stairs.

"So many elegant people," I whisper. Women in beautiful dresses, fans in their hands, men in aristocratic attire, some wearing knickers. Servants are dressed in black formal wear, serving champagne, and hors d'oeuvres. I can hear in the distance a band playing in the ballroom a few steps away. A pianist is playing classical music in the corner of the foyer, on a grand piano.

People are laughing and talking to one another, with many of them, having white blonde hair. It makes me think that everyone is wearing a wig.

"I fear we will be stopped by someone soon, if we do not quickly move away from this room," Cory says. Taking my hand, he escorts me through the crowded guests, leading me toward the ball room. It's a grand sight. There are tables decorated in white linens, and flowers hang over the sides of large vases near the stage and each doorway. An orchestra plays a Minuet, while we stand there watching couples dance elegantly.

"So, what do you think?" he whispers in my ear. "Have you ever seen such a sight?"

"No, never."

He bows. "May I have this dance, miss?"

"So formal, Cory." I giggle. "Oh, I don't know, I can't dance like that."

"Sure, you can," he says, "just follow my lead." He smiles. Taking my hand, and as if something innate in me takes hold, I begin to dance with him like I had been doing it for years.

We dance and dance as people watch intently. We skip around the ballroom floor, until we become tired, and parched.

"I feel warm Cory; may we find something to drink?" I ask.

"But of course," he says leading me to a table filled with refreshment choices, pouring me a glass of punch. We make small talk for a while. He introduces me to distant cousins across the pond. I can't help but consider that this a ploy to satisfy their curiosity.

"Cory, lad, it's good to see you, son. How have you been?" I hear a gentleman who is about Cory's senior ask.

"Stanley! They let anyone in, here don't they?" Cory chuckles. They hug, as though it has been a long time. Then the man glances abstractedly in my direction.

"Who is this blue-eyed beauty, Cory? I must say, you have done quite well, indeed."

Cory smiles. "Stanley I would like you to meet my cousin."

"Oh, come now, she can't possibly be. She's much lovelier than a Storm bloodline such as yourself," he teases.

"Pleased to meet you sir." I curtsy at him, role playing the part.

"My dear, how delightful it is to meet you. You are a form of beauty I have not seen in twenty years or more." And he kisses the top of my hand.

At a loss for words, I smile and nod.

"Aw, come now, Stanley, you're making my girl blush. Although I do have to agree, with you. She's captured my heart." Cory beams.

"I see, being cousins isn't keeping you two apart? You know, people will talk." He adds.

"Since when has a Storm ever shied away from gossip dear uncle?" I can tell Cory doesn't care what people think.

"You don't say, well, who am I to judge?" If I was in my sister's position, I would want to keep her myself, I can't blame her for matching you two, no matter how close the bloodlines. Where is she by the way? Have you seen her yet?"

"She's around somewhere," Cory says.

"Hmm, yes. If you will excuse me." He bows. "It's a pleasure meeting you Wynter," he says, and he walks away.

"Madame Moyer's brother?" I ask.

"Yes. Usually this party is at his large estate back in Scotland." He smiles. "Did I mention Moyer has a brother?"

"No, you seem to have failed to tell me that part," I say with sarcasm.

"The Storm bloodline is very large; most people here are Storms. Moyer is the family matriarch. Some reference her as their queen and are very loyal to her views and values."

Cory continues telling me stories of his experiences growing up until, a bell rings out in the grand foyer. "Ladies and Gentlemen, may I have your attention please?" I hear Daniel say. Then he clangs the bell again, to grab everyone's focus. "May I have your attention, please," he says again, this time louder.

Thank you all for coming today to celebrate such a wonderful holiday. It's so great to see so many familiar faces. Family and friends, it is with great pleasure that I introduce to you Madame Moyer, Lady of Storm River Manor."

At the top of the grand staircase stands Madame Moyer in a red velvet and silk gown. It hugs to her body, revealing every curve of her silhouette form. She looks young, and not at all old, leaving me to wonder what soul she killed tonight, in order to appear that extravagant. She doesn't look like a grandmother at all. Not a wrinkle in sight. As she descends the staircase, I can feel her eyes watching my every move, as she zooms in on my location in the crowded room of spectators. Her smile is wide, and her eyes sparkle as she greets each guest, making her way towards us.

"Shall we go now, Cory. She's spotted us."

"I know. It's too late. She is coming now. Remember what I said earlier. I won't leave your side."

I nod in response.

"Good evening, you two, I hope you are enjoying yourselves. Come, Wynter, I would like to have you meet Dr. Kimble. Don't worry Cory, I promise to bring her back in one piece."

I can feel Cory soothing my senses, as he stands a small distance away, not taking his eyes off me.

"Dear Philip, I would like you to meet my granddaughter, Wynter. Darling this is Dr. Phillip Kimble. His practice is very similar to Storm River Manor, but in Europe. If ever you decide you would like to visit, his compound is quite lovely."

"You're too kind," he says trying to sound flattered. "My, my Maura, where have you been hiding her? I dare say, Madame she is a gem indeed. Will you be putting her on the auction block tonight, by chance?"

'Auction block? What?' I say to the voice.

'Stay calm, no need to worry, you will not be going there tonight, if I have anything to say about it.'

"I would pay handsomely for her of course." As he grabs one of my hands and kisses it gently. "I haven't seen the likes of her in centuries. She very much looks like her mother do you not agree?" He smiles, revealing straight yellow stained teeth.

"Yes, indeed I believe she does, but Phillip, my dear she isn't for sale...." She gives me a smug look, then glances back to Phillip, "At least not yet."

"Such a shame," he says in a disappointing voice. "What I can create from the likes of her."

My stomach churns at the thought of being sold like property. Is this really a conversation these two people are having right in front of me?

Moyer laughs. "Yes, well we do indeed have plans for her. Soon, Phillip, very soon. Perhaps, we may have a future soul for you in a few months. Shall I put you on the list?"

"Indeed, do, Madame." He smiles at me wickedly.

"Fabulous, Phillip," she sneers. "In the meantime, there are plenty of other souls to choose from to whet your appetite until the time comes."

"Intriguing indeed, Maura. I shall wait, for her to bare a soul in the future. Lovely eyes as those, who can ever resist such fruit, as she?"

"Will you be joining us this evening for the auction?" Moyer asks him.

"Aye, I have my ticket waiting to have it stamped."

"Fantastic."

Dr. Kimble turns to me, again taking my hand, kissing the top. "My lady, I am looking forward to seeing you again." There is evil in the depths of his eyes and my gut tells me to stay away from the likes of him.

Within seconds, Cory is next to me. "Good evening Phillip, good to see you again. How's business?" Cory entangles his arm around mine, pulling me tight to his side.

"Oh, my dear lad, I didn't realize," he sneers, and glances to Moyer. "You didn't tell me she's already marked. I see now why you say a soul will be here in the future for the taking. I'll be looking forward to it." He sips the champagne he's holding, and says, "If you will excuse me, I'll leave you now. Moyer, it is a pleasure to see you again, please let me know when to expect my package."

Moyer turns to us both, giving a smug smile, saying, "As you can see, I have big plans for you both. Do not disappoint me." And she walks off.

The thought of being someone's piece of meat; property to do with what they pleased, makes me want to hurl. "Cory, I think I need to sit down."

He squeezes my hand, as if to say everything is going to be fine. But I don't feel like everything is going to be fine. "Will you excuse me, I need to freshen up. And, honestly, my stomach hurts so bad that if I don't get there quick, there's going to be a mess to clean up in front of all these people."

"Sure, but I'm walking you to the restroom," he insists.

I can't get to the bathroom fast enough. I find a toilet just in time before everything comes up. I take a couple deep breaths and splash my cheeks with water, before I ready myself back to the party. Meeting Dr. Kimble is one of the most unpleasant experiences I'd ever experienced. It's going to take time for the shock to wear off. What I really need is fresh air. Moyer's plans are vile and grotesque. My thoughts are, we leave for the portal right now. As I leave the bathroom to seek Cory outside to tell him we cannot wait any longer, I'm caught from behind, and a cloth placed over my mouth. I breathe in to scream, which sets my fate.

34

Reverie

My room is dark when I wake, and a faint glow of amber coals give off any illuminating light in the room. My memory slips away from me, as I try to figure out what day it is. My gut tells me something bad happened, but I don't know what it is. I look at my clock, but it doesn't show the time. Replacing the numbers with odd shaped letters.

I look around my room to see two shadows with glowing eyes in the corner. Guessing one is Madame Moyer, and the other probably Cole, I wait for them both to appear from the darkness, but they remain still. Staring at me.

"I know you're there," I exclaim. I see your blue eyes. Not hard to, when you hide in the dark like you do."

Silence comes from their end. Not one slight movement, even when I acknowledge them. Then, in my next breath I feel an unexpected surge of power pushing me towards my pillow, forcing me down. My head fills with a haze of random voices, and my eyes lose focus. I can feel my body trying to fight the impulse to sleep as it comes upon me with a heavy weight.

"Careful what you say out loud. Moyer has put a memory stamp on you. She only can do it while you sleep," the voice says to me.

"So, I'm asleep?"

"You're fading in, and out."

"What's going on? I thought she couldn't reach me when I have the necklace."

"She has outside help from Vothule. She is channeling his power. The necklace is no match. They are combining their powers to get to you. You must resist, at all cost. I will be here to help you. She cannot harm me."

"I can't fight it. I'm too weak against their powers," I reply back to the voice within me.

My eyes fight to stay open, yet with each resistance I give, comes more force from the power that invades me. I feel myself drift back into unconsciousness, and find myself landing in a meadow, where the wind blows soft, through my hair. The smell of roses brush my senses. I'm in a place I've never been before. Looking upward to the sky I see three planets that looked like they would join very soon. Odd sounding birds chirp above the tree tops. I feel peace, love and tranquility. Yet this strange place feels familiar.

"You're on Ladorielle," the voice echoes to me.

More voices in the sky speak, like gods looking down on their humans. Sounds of thunder rumble in my ears with each word.

"You can't keep her under for long mother, it's too dangerous," in a voice that isn't Cory or Cole. The sounds of Chad's voice carries through my senses.

"My dear son, she'll be fine. She's having a peaceful dream, back on Ladorielle."

"When will you wake her? Is this necessary?" he asks.

"Your nephew got too close. He loves her and will try anything to save her. There isn't time to play with young love. It will risk foolish impulses. He's lost under her spell and his loyalty is with her now. Did I tell you, they plan to escape?"

"How does she know?" I ask the voice within my head, but it remains silent.

"No, but why?" Chad asks his mother.

"My dear son, you have much to learn. Tell me if she wakes, I must find Cole, before it is too late."

I feel the cold winter air nip at my cheeks, and the roses that are in front of me begin to wilt before my eyes. Petals drop one by one to the ground and before I have a chance to pick any of them up the wind blows them from my reach, to an enchanting garden ahead.

"No, not there. Stop," says the voice.

"Who are you?" I ask. "Are you the one they call Isalora?" Again, my question goes unanswered.

I take a few more steps forward, to the plot of greenery ahead.

"You must not venture any further. Stop before all is lost." This time it's a woman's voice, that sounds like Aunt Fran.

I twirl around, to seek the voice behind me. "Is that really you?"

To my right peripheral vision, in the distance under an arched gate leading to a weeping willow, a ghost-like image reveals open arms to welcome me. A second image appears, this figure larger than the first."

"Come, come sit with me my dear child," he says.

"Dad! Is that really you?" I don't walk, I run to him.

He looks the same as the day before the accident. I held nothing back, darting into his arms. "Oh, father I have missed you so much. Are you real?"

He laughs lightly. "In this world, I am as real as it gets my dearest."

I begin to cry. "Shh now, my sweet, don't cry. No matter where you are, we're always with you."

"Aunt Fran is that really you?"

"Yes, my dear, it's me." She smiles and hugs me tight."

"How are you in my dream? If you're here, then—"Tears well up. "Then it's true. You're really gone from the real world."

Dad says, "We're not gone. We have never left."

"Are you the voice, inside my head? Has it been you all along?"

"What voice?" Fran says, sounding confused.

"No, that would be me." And we all turn to see her standing in a field, dressed in white chiffon.

"Isalora." I hear Dad say.

"My child, she may have defeated us in human form, but she did not defeat our spirits. Alas, that is the form that she must be defeated in after all," the woman in white says.

"What do you mean?" I ask, looking at this woman, memorized by her beauty. It's like looking at an angel with wings. Her aura so bright that I must squint to see her.

It took a few seconds for me to absorb her words.

"Are you saying Moyer is more powerful in the spirit form?" I question.

"Moyer? No, she is a mere host for Sarmira."

"Then what Cory revealed is true, Sarmira is Moyer?"

"Yes. I must warn you all. We are under Moyer's control what you say out loud, she can hear. She can hear your dreams, even control them, if you let her. When you feel your dreams changing, fight back!" Isalora says.

Then she looks up towards the sky, as if to acknowledge that whoever is there is listening. "You hear me Maura? My daughter is a fighter! You may be able to control the human world, but I control the spirit realm."

"Daughter?" I whisper, glancing at her in shock. "You're my mother?" Lightning strikes in the distance. Rain begins to pour down, spatting against the ground.

"Yes." She smiles at me, her eyes soft, gazing back. Then loud thunder rings out again, rumbling the ground beneath us like an earthquake.

"Come with me everyone," Isalora yells, as the wind kicks up and the thunder roars.

We all race to sit on a bench, under a Gazebo. My dad and Aunt Fran embrace in a hug with Isalora.

Aunt Fran, I have one question. "Are you Drelanda?"

She nods her head, saying, "There is so much that still needs to be told."

"So, the poison, when you became ill, as a little girl, your body healed, right?"

Fran nods, saying. "Yes."

"My sister," Isalora says, "and my dearest Jeff. I have waited so long to see you both again. We must hurry, there isn't much time."

I begin to speak. "How— "

Isalora shakes her head, pointing to her temple.

"You want me to think it, not say it." I think to myself.

"She can't touch us here in our thoughts," she says.

Dad says, *"Do we have a plan?"* He looks at Isalora with concern.

"Moyer is planning to destroy all good magic. You're the key to it all. You and Cory must find a way to bring Cole back from the evil that has taken his heart. She can only be destroyed in the spirit form, and the three of you must find a way to defeat her."

"Tell me what I need to do." I say to her in my mind.

"You have much training ahead of you. Moyer has you in a coma. She plans to wake you, right before your birthday. You must fight to wake up." Then pauses, looks around at the weather and says, *"You must travel to Dragonscale, and find the Sword of Valor. It was used to strike her once long ago, when your great-grandfather pierced her heart shattering her into a million pieces. What we didn't know then, she followed the Storm family line seeking revenge, killing each line that was a direct descendant of the Deagons.*

"You my dear are last of the Deagon line. The only one left to destroy her once and for all."

"Who are the Deagons exactly?"

"Descendants of the dragon. My family line. The line, that your great-grandmother, Sara comes from.

"What Casey told you, is true. You're a princess, yes. But not of the Storm bloodline, rather, you're the lost princess, of Dragonscale."

She stands up, and looks towards the dark black sky, with the lightning bolts cascading down. "We haven't much time, before she finds you again. She will soon pull you from here and place you somewhere else," Isalora says aloud.

Thunder explodes, and the lightning flashes before us. Fierce winds kicked up, rain smashes down, making it hard for any of us to concentrate.

"She's angry and will change your dream soon. I will find you. She can't hide you from me in here. Remember to keep within your thoughts, do not speak out loud, she can hear you otherwise," Isalora tells me with her mind.

And within a blink of an eye, I'm moved to somewhere pitch black. I can't see anything, and the feeling of nothingness surrounds me. I feel death, and cold chills; goosebumps cover my body.

I hear screams of agonizing terror, in this pit of darkness. My eyes bulge from their sockets fighting to see any spark of light in front of me. I hear the lashings of a whip, hitting bare skin. There's an echo of flesh splitting and screams of pain that ensue afterwards. A figure in the far distance can finally be seen. Like someone turning on a spotlight. I see someone hanging there tied by their wrists. Reminding me of JC. A second figure shows up with a whip in their hands, freely lashing at the hanging object in front of them. Then more screams and it's becoming clear the man doing the whipping is Casey.

Like from a picture set, I stand there watching with anticipation. Then as if I'm on a movie projector, I fast-forward, flashing right in front of the figure that looks very familiar.

The face is unrecognizable, like the memory of the accident seeing Aunt Fran and her face peeled off from her skull. Who is it? I can't tell.

They are stripped of all clothing and I can see they're male. Bruises on his skin, red lashes across his back, neck slit wide open. Streams of blood trailed down his legs, dripping off his feet to a pool of blood on the ground.

Blue eyes of evil fixate on him from the darkness, and as I watch Casey change whips. This one has tiny jagged spikes at the end of the straps. Another lash, and then another, rips through the skin of the hanging man. He screams in agony. With each ripping sound it sends brutal pain to my sensory. As if I, too, can feel this person's pain.

"Stop it!" I scream. "Stop! You're killing him!"

"Wyn-ter, I-Is that you?" The voice hanging in chains says, as Casey slashes him again.

"No!" I scream. Immediately recognizing it as Cory.

Casey ignores me and keeps going, whip after whip. Slash after slash. Until the screams were no more, and pure silence follows.

"Casey can't hear you." Isalora says.

"Why am I here?" I move slowly towards Cory. Blood dripping off his body.

"To scar you; control you. To make you concede to her will."

"Never!" I say out loud. "Do you hear me Sarmira? Never! I will never yield to you!"

Casey then moves the limp body, throwing it to the side. I'm brought to full view only to see it's no longer Cory, but me.

"No!" I scream in terror when I see a mirror image of me. Face puffy, hair dried with blood, body overwhelmed with lashings, and then I begin to feel the torture. Scars begin to appear on my arms as I watch the blood drain from my body, before my eyes. Bled like the corpse on the ground in front of me. Falling to my knees, I cry in anguish as I feel every ounce of pain inflicted. The ping of pressure penetrating my skin as I feel it split open. The agony is so real that I can't bear it any longer."

"Fight!" I hear Isalora say. *"She is feeding you an illusion. Fight!"*

I continue to scream in pain. *"You must learn to control your emotions,"* I hear Cory's voice, say to me. *"It's a trick. Fight it, Wynter. Fight!"*

I try to push through the fear and anxiety. She hasn't beaten me, yet. I try and think of all the evil she possesses.

"You can't hurt me here Sarmira!" I scream.

"That's my girl. Shout back at her. Stand your ground." I hear Cory say, this time.

"You hear me?" I shout again. "You can't trap me in here forever!" I stand up and face myself. I look at her. My eye's see a dead girl lying there.

"Face your fear, Sarmira feeds on it. Give her a taste of her own medicine. Fight it, Wynter! You let her win, and she's got you."

Isalora says to me. *"Tell her the power of three is within you. Do it now."*

I repeat the words, "the power of three is within me."

Then the body before me disappears. The blackness around me gone and I find myself in a green meadow where it went on miles all around me. No trees, just green grass as far as the eye can see.

"Good, you confused her. She is planning a new approach. Be on guard," Isalora says softly.

Then she appears in front of me, gesturing to take her hand. *"Come, let's go. You did well."*

We appear inside the cottage. It's as I remembered it. A fire is going, feeling warm and real. I sat down on the sofa with her. I'm about to speak, when Cory walks into the room.

"Does he see me?" I say to her.

"Wynter is that really you?" Cory says with excitement. "Ah this is just a dream. Another illusion."

"Cory, it's me," I say aloud. *"I can read thoughts in my dreams. Can you hear me?"* I then say in my mind.

"Yes." He reaches for my hand.

I went to him without any hesitation. His warming embrace, giving me the security, I need. It feels real. Not like an illusion.

We sit on the sofa, holding hands. I stare at him, knowing it's a dream.

Cory says, *"The night I waited for you in the hall. Someone appeared behind me knocking me out. When I came to, you were gone. Wynter, she has you in a cell in the basement. You must wake up. Remember that day I showed you the river? The tunnel? I want you to go there."*

*"If, I'm in the basement how am I to get to the tunnel? "*I ask.

"There is a bench in your cell, if you can move the stone, it leads to the underground tunnel. Moyer doesn't know about it. But you must

wake up Wynter. You must fight! You turn eighteen tonight at midnight."

"What happened Cory? Are you dead too?" I ask.

"No, I'm back at the cabin, looking at you as if I'm seeing a ghost. I escaped, trying to free you. I was nearly killed by the hands of one of Moyer's men. I don't know how I was able to lose them, but someone else is out there. Someone else knows, and they are on our side. I was near death, drifting off to the land of no return, when I woke in the cabin, healed. I have learned much in the day and a half you have been gone." He pauses a few seconds, *"When you wake, I want you to focus, giving me pictures in your mind. I will find you. I will get you out. I promise."*

There's a loud thunder and a flash of lightening and before Cory has a chance to speak any more, he disappears.

35

Eye of the Storm

A hard surface lay underneath me, as my eyes try to focus. At first, I see fuzzy images then slowly everything becomes clear, and I notice the wrought iron bars in front of me and my body lying on hay.

I hear voices in the distance, and I try to stay under the radar, as I listen to what they are saying.

"Have you found him yet?" one male voice questions.

"Not presently, no, my lord," says another voice.

"That's not good enough, we must find him before her birthday. Moyer will not be pleased if you fail her again."

"We have looked at every square inch of land. He is not anywhere to be found."

"Well look harder. He is not going to leave her here to rot. Perhaps it's time to send the dogs out. Now get out of here."

"Yes, sir. I will round the others and we will hunt him down, sir." I hear footsteps fade away as the man leaves.

Whimpering sounds in the cell next to me, channels the cries of a young child. Echoes of dripping water trickle down the back wall and gnawing noises can be heard in the next cell over. The thought of rats nearby disgusts me and I push the images out of my head. I need a clear mind, for Cory. Goosebumps begin to appear all over my body and I can't tell if it's because I'm cold or the rats.

"How is our birthday girl doing?" I hear her say.

"Just fine, not a sound from her yet. Perhaps you have killed her already," the man says scruffily.

"You fool, she is awake!" she retorts. I hear her feet step towards my cell. "Well, well, my dear child, so you are finally stirring, I see. Having lovely dreams, are we?"

I ignore her. She doesn't deserve the time of day with me. I'm not about to give that satisfaction to her.

"The silent treatment will get you nowhere, dear," she scorns. "No matter, you don't need to speak, just listen. We will find Cory and when we do, your precious hope for escape will be gone. No, you will not be going anywhere. That cell is your room now. I suggest you make the most of it." She stalks off, saying a few words to the man guarding the jail area, then I hear her steps echo, as she paces up the spiral stairs and disappears.

Moaning can be heard in the distance, along with chains clanging, and vile stench fills the air. Screams begin as I hear a whip hitting skin. More shrieks echo, bouncing off the stone walls. I want to tune out the noise but can't.

Then I remember the hole near the bench. Before venturing a look, I check around to see who is watching. I'm sure she has a camera on me. I needed to be sly about the hiding spot or she would find it. Wondering a second whether I should fall asleep to find Cory and warn him. Perhaps he already knows what to do? Then I recalled one important thing. The voice inside my head.

'Are you there?'

'Yes.'

'What do I do?' I ask.

"Wait on my signal and then I want you to start digging out the stone under that bench." Isalora says.

Is Cory on the way?"

"Yes, he knows. He sees your pictures. But before you start, I see someone coming."

"Is she awake?" I hear a familiar voice ask.

"Why do you ask me? Go see for yourself," the jail guard says, while sharpening his blade in his hands.

"Oh, you're useless, why does mother even keep you around," Chad replies, and he stalks over to my cell. I feel him stand there a few minutes before hearing him say, "I am not sure how, but I will get you out of here, Wynter." His voice is firm, giving me assurance that not all the Storms cave to Moyer's evil tendencies. It isn't clear to me if he's truly intent on rescuing me, or it's a ploy to get me to talk. I don't have the same trust in Chad as I do with Cory. He throws me something and it hits my back.

I hear the blade wheel stop. "So, is she or is she not awake?" the guard says, through his slithering mouth.

"It appears she's asleep, though I don't know how in this filth. When did Moyer say she would return?" he asks.

"Around five pm this evening."

"That's in four hours." Chad says softly.

"Eh, what's that, you're mumbling?" the guard says.

"Nothing. Nothing at all, I'll be back to check on her in a few hours. Tomorrow is her birthday after all," Chad replies. I can feel his eyes staring attentively at me. I don't dare make a peep. Is this his way of saying, that now's my chance to escape? Does Chad know about the secret passage way? Why else would he subtly say aloud when Moyer would be back. Is this his way of giving a timeframe?

"Yes, indeed. I do love birthday celebrations. She will be a perfect sacrifice for the good of the cause, don't you think?" the guard says, as I he sharpens his blade.

"Not If I have anything to do with it," Chad says under his breath.

"What's that? Boy, you need to speak up to an old man who's deaf. I can't hear your dad-blasted mumbles."

"I said, yes birthday celebrations have everything to do with it. We must waste no more time." Chad whips the cell bars with his leather stick, making my body recoil. I know now, he's warning me. I also know, he saw my body flinch at the rattling of the cell bars.

Once I hear the wheel blade turn back on, I hear Chad speak, "You haven't much time, use what I threw to you." I hear him step away, closing the outer gate, beyond the cells.

Turning over I pick up the object Chad tossed at my back. I am realizing it's a pocket knife much like the one Cory had the day we found the coffer. Tucked in between the blades is a paper. Opening it, I see it's a map of the tunnels under the manor, leading to the bridge outside, where Cory showed me that day at the cottage.

'So, he knows about the passageway?'

'Another story for another time,' Isalora says. *'Quickly now, we haven't much time.'*

I begin to inch my way under the bench, and with Isalora's guidance she shows me which stone is loose. I work at the grout for what seems like hours rather than minutes, until I'm able to loosen the brick. I wriggled it for a good few minutes before it comes free. It falls backwards in a hole behind the wall, making a crash sound on the other side. A rather loud noise, too, and I hope that the man outside the cell doesn't hear. Once I know it's clear I tried a second brick. It moves much easier than the first and breaks free, finally giving me the room, I need to slip through the opening.

It's not until I try to fit in the tiny slot that I see I'm still dressed in my gown. There's no way I'll fit through there with all these garments on, so I slip off my undercoats, hoping that will be enough. I ponder as to which way will be easier to poke through, head or feet and decide I don't care at this point.

'Breathe,' I say to myself. *'Just breathe.'* I clear my mind giving Cory a picture of what I'm about to do. Going feet first my body dangles, bracing for a long fall, I take a leap of faith and let go, hitting inches from the ground.

I look into complete darkness at my surroundings. I hadn't any light, and at this point I'm going down a tunnel blind.

'I can't see. Which way do I go?'

'The opposite of the light behind you,' she says.

Only the faint light from the hole above allowed me a glimpse down the long tunnel. It looks like the tunnel is circular in shape with a shimmer of light on the ground leading the way. My guess, water is surrounding my feet and toes. At least hoping it's that and not something horrid. Not wasting another moment, I make my way down the long, wet, dark tunnel to seek what waits for me at the end.

Squeaking sounds of rats bounce off the walls, echoing down the dank tunnel. I hate rats, they are so disgusting. My feet are soaked from walking in water. The thought of freezing to death comes to mind, so, I begin to pick up my pace.

'Save your energy, you have a ways to go.'

'Okay, lead the way out.' I say to her.

Soon I came to a crossroads, where the tunnel split in three directions.

'Which way now?' I ask.

No light at the end of any of the tunnels. Only from the way we came, where the hole still lights the way back to hell. Suddenly I feel a brush of sensation like someone taking my hand, but no one is there. Urging me to push forward, not turning either way.

'Is that you?'

'Yes, but it takes a lot of energy to do it, so don't expect it all the time,' she says.

I trust my instincts and keep moving. By now the stench and filth has numbed my senses so much that I don't seem to notice the smell any longer. My fingers are cold, my face feels frozen to the touch, but I'm not going to give up. I need to keep moving. If I stop, I know I'll freeze to death. I keep reminding myself of the horror Madame Moyer has done; of the awful manipulations she's gotten away with. Those memories drive me to push onward. Anything is better than that cold cell Moyer put me in.

'How long have I been walking? I'm so tired.' I say, trying to stay focused.

'Keep moving. It's not far now," Isalora says.

I begin to hear running water, like a water fall. Is it true? Am I near the end? I want to run to the sound, but I don't have the strength. My toes are so cold that I can no longer feel them.

'How much farther? I feel so weak. So cold.'

Finally, I come to another crossroads. When I look right, I see darkness, but when I look left towards the sounds of water, I see a light at the end.

"This way Wynter." And I feel her tug at me again. Grabbing my hand, like winds of a song, leading out to safety.

I follow the sound anxiously, trying to pace myself from running. The stream of water becomes louder with each step I take. I can hear birds chirping, as their songs echo through tunnel walls.

"Almost there. Freedom is not far behind," I hear Isalora encourage me.

The light becomes brighter and brighter the closer I get to the outside world. I can hear the wind kick up and whistle through the passageway, and the water sounds became louder with each approaching tread, bringing me hope. *'It isn't going to be long now. I'm going to be free. Free of this hell hole!'*

I'm frozen from head to toe, and all I can think about is getting out of these wet clothes and near a warm fire. I imagined a cup of hot cocoa in my hands and a warm blanket around me. My teeth begin to chatter, just thinking about it.

At last, one final step to freedom, when I look up to see the wrought iron bars on the tunnel opening, looking sealed.

"Oh, please no! Please let the gate be unlocked, please." I say aloud, knowing no one is listening.

My hands grasp the black iron bars and franticly try to budge them, but it is no use. They are tightly bound to the cemented tunnel. I have nothing to pry them open, no key, and certainly have no strength. I feel completely hopeless, a lost cause. Escape from my hell above, only to be still trapped within the bonds of another hell below.

I hear the dogs howl, echoing through the damp tunnels, making me think, Moyer must now, know I have escaped. They will find me and bring me back, to the torture and torment.

My cries went unheard, my tears untouched. Is this to be my end? I have no more strength to fight. My body is cold like ice from the wet clothes I wear. My head is sick with devastation and grief. I can't hang on anymore. I must sleep. I'm too tired to battle this any longer. I give up.

I feel the cold wind brisk through my hair and across my face. I know Isalora is trying to keep me awake. I can't help it, I finally fall into a dreaming sleep.

'Wynter, wake up, you must not give up. Fight!' I hear her say.

'I can't, I have no energy, I'm cold; I can't feel my fingers, my toes.'

'Wynter, he's coming for you. You must stay awake. He can't see you if you sleep. And Moyer will find you if you do.'

I doze in and out of consciousness and no longer can differentiate whether I'm dreaming or awake.

I hear voices of both Cory and Isalora. *"Wynter, wake up. She will find you,"* I hear them both say together.

It gives me some strength. Enough to open my eyes. Then a chilling breeze brushes my face. My eyes feel heavy, and I begin to shut them once more. I try to think where Cory is. To tell him I'm under the bridge, where he said for me to go. Please hurry, I feel like I'm going to die.

A loud sounding crash, bangs against the iron bars, jolting me awake, enough for me to open my eyes once more. "Cory," I whisper.

I can't keep my eyes open and feel my body drifting and moving slightly. Like I'm about to leave my frame.

Then I hear him say, "Can you walk?"

I don't have the strength to speak, but I saw his face, *'you came for me.'*

"You're safe now," he says. That's all I need to hear, and my body stops fighting sleep.

36

The Gift

My life up until now is based off a lie. Everywhere I turn, I find new stories, new truths. When is the real truth going to step up to the plate and reveal itself? I keep thinking my birthday is coming yet I feel I'm between worlds: a world where I can do nothing, yet able to do anything if I keep pushing through. Now that seems quite out of the ordinary doesn't it?

Will I finally wake up and find myself in a garden again, dreaming within a dream, or truly wake up in a cold cell? How do I know anymore? My state of mind is fried, and the truth lies somewhere in between this alternate reality. All I know is where ever I am it feels safe. Safe from her, safe from evil. Am I sleeping? How do I know?

When I open my eyes, I see the smallest specks on the ceiling above me. I smell a fire burning, and hearing it crackle lights my senses. My ears begin to ring, hearing every sound imaginable. Even the birds outside chirping sound as if they are right next to me in this room. Senseless voices start humming in no order, saying random words. I feel my body floating back to reality as it escapes my dreamlike world. Voices? There are too many for me to decipher.

I don't feel any different, except maybe I'm a year older, and for the new brash of five senses Cory warned me about. The sun shows bright through the window, and I realize I'm in the bedroom at the cottage. I can see fresh snow has fallen overnight.

I wonder if Cory is awake. Not knowing when my power would show its abilities, I sit up and ponder whether I should get dressed or lay back down and snooze. I still feel weak, and my feet ache, although my body is warm underneath my feathered comforter. It's then I notice a silhouette of a woman, with her back to me, looking in my closet. It takes a moment for my newly sharp eyes to take focus. A stranger in my room?

She doesn't seem to notice I'm awake, staring at her. My curiosity gets the best of me. "Who are you?" I ask, and I watch her fall forward in the wardrobe, as if I startled her. My hanging clothes swivel, and a thud sound comes from my closet wall. She quickly gets up and pivots back through the doors.

Looking at me, while straightening her attire, she says, "You can see me?"

I cock my head to the side, raising a brow. "Um yeah. Why wouldn't I see you?"

Her hair is black, cascading down over her shoulder in ringlets, eyes green as emeralds. Smiling at me she moves closer. "Unbelievable." Sliding next to my bed she reaches out to touch my face. "You can really see me?"

Startled, I retract my hand away. "Yes, who are you, and why are you trespassing? Did Cory let you in?"

That comment seems to break her trance of amazement. She stiffens her posture and says, "It seems you have come into your power. How exciting is this?"

I take a closer look at her and realize there is something recognizable about her. Her voice although different, feels like I have heard it before.

"Why do you look so familiar?" I say softly.

She smiles. "I've been waiting a long time for you to see me."

A knock at my bedroom door breaks both of us from our curiosity.

"Wynter, everything okay?" Cory questions from the other side. He doesn't wait for my response, and bursts through the room, standing there like he sees a ghost.

"Isalora, it's really you. Isn't it?" he asks, gliding closer into the room. I can see when he looked toward her, he is able to see what I see.

Widening my eyes in surprise. "You're Isalora? But—how is this possible? Can you see her too, Cory?"

"I can, but only through your eyes. If you were to shut them right now, she would disappear. I can see her through you."

My memory must be playing a joke on me. At the foot of the bed I see both Isalora and Cory standing there. My eyes try to focus on the two figures through my pounding headache.

"Wynter, this is your power. This is the gift you're given. No one has been able to see me without having to use magic," Isalora says.

"What are you saying? That I can see ghosts?" She doesn't need to answer me. Deep down I already know. "So, this is it?" I'm annoyed. "This is the big great power I'm to get at eighteen? No reading minds, moving objects, seeing the future, just able to see ghosts?"

"Wynter, it's a huge power," she says. "I don't think you quite understand." She seems worried, like somehow, I'm missing the point. And perhaps I am, but how is the 'great' power supposed to defeat Madame Moyer?

"Sarmira can only be destroyed in spirit form. Otherwise she roams the universe as an apparition, always searching for another host and possessing the new body as she does with Maura Moyer's."

I'm beginning to realize that this is a power only for those who can see the dead. "So, what you're saying is, because I can see you, I can see others who have passed over as well? Like dad, and Fran. So why can't I see them?"

She overlooks my questions and says, "Yes, you have the power to see the undead. It's what your father and I suspected all along. That you would be the undead mystic. A seer with the power to destroy Sarmira. It also means you can see right through to Maura, to the aura within her. I suspect that the next time you lay eyes on her you will not see Maura's face, but the face of her intruder, Sarmira.

Cory is standing still giving me a look like he's about to come unglued from our one-sided conversation.

"So, he cannot hear your words?" I ask looking from him, to her.

"No, only you." She pauses a few seconds, "Cole's the one who could do that."

"What is she saying," I finally hear Cory say, sounding frustrated.

I smile over to him. "That we must find a way to destroy Madame Moyer."

"Tell me something I don't know," he says, in a sarcastic tone.

"Alright," looking back at him, not sure how to conform the right words, so I just say it. "Cole is the one who can read minds. Rather, would have been able to if his power hadn't been taken from him."

"I see," he says, nodding. "So, my theory's right. Can he get them back?"

Isalora answers, "I don't know. Nobody has ever had an opportunity to find out if it's possible."

I shake my head at Cory, and glance back to Isalora. "So, what now?"

"We find the Sword of Valor." Isalora says. "The last time anyone held it was when Sir Bryce Storm weld it, killing Sarmira. At least he thought, but we now know he killed the host, and not Sarmira."

"This is driving me mad, not being able to hear Isalora speak," Cory says, clenching his fists. "Can't she do a temporary spell or something?"

"She says, she can, but it will leave her weak. And unable to travel with us on the journey we are to go on."

"Journey? What Journey?" he asks.

"To where the Sword of Valor was last seen," I answer.

"How do you propose we do that? The book of secrets is locked. You are not suggesting we go back to Storm River Manor, are you?" His tone sounding a bit nervous.

"No." I smile back at him with a mischievous glance, and say, "Meet me in the living room," and I jump out of bed.

When I skip out into the hall towards the hearth in the front room, I stop in my tracks to see two familiar faces. My heart races to think about what I'm seeing before me. Can it be true? Are my eyes deceiving me? I turn around to see Cory smiling wide. Isalora is quiet and stands there as if oblivious to what I see standing in the middle of the room.

I know they all can see the confusion on my face, and I rub my eyes. "Okay, explain please, I'm confused. I see all of you. I'm still dreaming, aren't I? And If I am not dreaming, and I am truly awake, then what is exactly happening here? Cory, do you see them too?"

"Yes, of course," he says, grinning. Like he's amused to see my perplexing reaction.

"Right, you see them through my eyes," I say, remembering they died, and my new power 'sees ghosts.' I see Cory shake his head, no.

"Wynter, Happy Birthday!" They all say together.

"Are you real, or is this a dream? Because if it is, I don't want to wake up."

She shakes her head no, and he opens his arms. "We are not ghosts," Dad says, and I run to them, forgetting that my speed has been upgraded to nanoseconds; nearly knocking dad down to the floor. Thankfully he is stronger than he looks.

"How is it that both of you are alive?" I finally ask, after I wipe my tears.

"Well," Dad begins, "that's a long story."

Cory and Isalora come to join us by the fireplace and we sit. There, he tells the longest tale ever told to me.

This isn't the plan I had for a birthday. I'll bet Moyer is furious that I got away. And what about Chad. Will she blame him for my escape?

There are limits a person can take. It's time to heel my emotions and seek revenge later. All that is in me, all that is whole, with every desire I have, leads to destroy that evil monster for good. I'm impatient with wanting revenge, but it will have to wait. Tomorrow will be saved for retribution. Today, I will celebrate my new power, my new endeavors, my new-found freedom away from hell.

Epilogue

"It's taking too long Cory, they should have been back by now," I say to him with worry. Now is the time to gather all the coven together to prepare for the fight of our lives. For the last three days I have been working on how to maneuver my new-found powers. Isalora has been my teacher of history; reading as much as possible up in the loft. Fran has helped me with my healing ability, guiding me through the white noise of all my senses. Dad takes me outside where he teaches me combat, and how to wield a sword. But my biggest hurdle of them all, is the projection: to be able to lift the spirit out of my frame. It leaves me tired and weak afterwards. Cory says, it will take time to master.

"Everything will be fine," I hear him say to me. "You forget Francesca has the ability to see someone coming. She will always be one step ahead." Coming by my side, he gazes out the window with me, looking at the cold river rushing down the stream.

"Aunt Fran's premonitions didn't work out too well when we got into the car accident a few weeks ago, now did it?" I retort back.

"That was different, Moyer had help from the druid she imprisoned, and the spell she made Blair concoct.

I sigh in frustration. "Can't you see them?"

"No, they are too far away."

"I knew they shouldn't have gone alone," I say impatiently.

"Stop worrying, they will be fine. Besides you know the plan, if they don't return, we stay the course no matter what."

"I know, I know," I voice, pacing back to the couch, but all I can do is worry. My fear of losing Aunt Fran, Dad, and Isalora, sets a stage of flashbacks. "I feel my family is whole again. I can't bear the thought of losing them a second time."

"Listen Wynter, look at me." Cory sounds worried.

"No, I don't want you to sooth my feelings again, it's not going to change anything. It's just a big fat band-aid on my mind."

"Please, look at me…" I feel his heart heavy with concern. It's strange how I can understand now what he meant by reading heartbeats of others once I developed my gift. I think he can't handle seeing the images I have in my brain of losing them again.

Reluctantly I stared back at him, into his deep blue eyes, patiently waiting as the emotions began to pacify me.

"Better?" he asks.

"Better." Smiling back. Wishing I didn't give in so easily.

"Perhaps we should practice your projecting? It might get your mind off the others and you need to be strong when facing Moyer."

"Cory, all these new changes are overwhelming me. I run faster, hear better, see clearer. I mean, yesterday I discovered my own strength and about broke the door off its hinges."

He chuckles at me. "In time you will learn to control it."

"How long did it take you?"

"Oh, I don't know, couple months maybe."

"Great. The evil of the underworld is out to seek and destroy me and you tell me it took a couple months. We are doomed!"

"Relax, we are not doomed," he says, snickering. "Just try. Small steps. Push yourself to the fireplace. Close your eyes and concentrate. You can do this."

I sit down, shutting my eyes, and concentrate on seeing the fireplace in my mind. The pressure in my head begins to build with each straining thought. I can feel my veins pulsate as I try to focus on the location of the mantel a few feet in front of me. I begin to feel my body lift, and float overhead. For a split second I'm closer to the hearth, hearing the wood crackle, and the heat consume my senses.

"That's it Wyn, you're doing it," I hear Cory say, and my concentration severs.

"Ah sorry. I blew it didn't I? Try again."

"No Cory, I'm getting a headache."

"Maybe this is all too much for you. It's only been two days since your birthday." His words are challenging, making me feel like I'm quitting too soon.

"Okay, one more time," I say, beginning again. But before I have a chance, Cory blurts out, "Wait, I see them, Wyn, they are in range on their way back.

"Do they have him?"

"No, it doesn't look like it." Cory goes silent.

"What do you see?"

"Hang on. Something's wrong."

The anticipation is killing me. "Well are they all together. Are they okay?"

"No. It appears they are being followed. Francesca is showing me pictures, and she doesn't see him. The advantage of my gift is, that I can see peripheral vision. It's Dexter, hiding many yards away."

"What does this mean? I thought she can see people coming?"

"She can, but she's not looking for a human to follow them. Her visions are skewed. I imagine that is Moyer's plan. Anticipating that Fran won't look beyond the scope of a supernatural. Which means, Moyer will find us if we don't warn the group soon." I see the urgency in Cory's eyes. It's a look of worry. "Wyn, you need to warn them. I know you can do it."

"You mean project? Cory, they are too far away. I can barely get to the hearth from here, let alone a half a mile away."

"Sure, you can. All you need is concentration, and quiet. You will get to them much faster than me. You must do this, or we all will be found out. Remember the tunnel?"

I nod. "You mean the one under the bridge?"

"They are just above it, on the other side of the trees from there."

I stand up against the mantel, gathering as much warmth from the fires as I can. I don't know why, but for some reason when I'm near fire I find my power is exemplified.

"Will you hold me up, if I become weak?"

"But, of course." And he comes to my side.

I start concentrating on the tunnel, working a visual in my mind. My veins become warm, and I feel a burning sensation across my skin, as my spirit lifts from me, once more. Soon I'm soaring above the clouds, like I'm in a dream flying. Looking around I see trees topped with snow and the river rushes towards the water fall. Trying to focus my ears on listening through the cold wind that passes through my featherweight body, I hear voices arise in a short distance from the bridge.

Realizing the voices are Fran and Isalora laughing, at dad's corny jokes, I move closer to find where they are coming from. I hear them, but can't see them, so I try to shout as loud as I can, "Stop!"

My voice goes unnoticed, so I yell a second time. "Stop."

"You hear something?" Isalora says.

"What, the whistling of the wind?" Dad laughs.

"No, I heard something. It sounded like our daughter."

"Stop!" I say once more. Pleased that mother heard me. "Go back! You're being followed"

"What is it Isalora. I can't hear anything." Fran says.

"It's Wynter, she's projecting. You can't hear her because she's in spirit form. But I can, and she can hear you too, through me. We are not alone. Fran, scan the area. Someone else is here."

"You may go Wynter. We will take it from here. Be home soon," Isalora says to me.

As though my body has been away for hours, I feel a rush of power slam back into my frame. Thankfully Cory is here to catch me else I may have hit the floor.

"Here, come lie down on the couch. You did great." Cory leads me to the sofa where I lay down. My head burst with pain and I feel sweat bead across my forehead.

"The pain, it hurts so bad," I holler. "Can I take anything for this?" My head feels like it's going to explode with pressure and I can't seem to think. Even the slightest sound feels like a freight train passing two feet from my ears.

"It's a side effect I'm afraid," and Cory passes me a pill and water. "Here, this will help." Even the sound of Cory's voice echoes, within the walls of my pounding skull.

"No talking please. Just no talking." I barely get out a word from my mouth, as I swig the miracle drug down my throat.

It isn't too long before the group arrives safely back at the cottage, and still resting on the couch, I hear Cory say, "Did you find Cole?"

"No," Francesca says, her voice sounding disappointed. "But thanks to Wynter's successes at projecting herself, we are still safe. There is no time to waste. We must prepare to leave within days. We need to find a way to get Cole back. We can't complete the circle of three without him."

"He's my brother. I know he is in there somewhere. We can't give up."

I sit up, burrowing through the head pain, saying, "We are not leaving anyone behind, Cory. We will find him."

"So, tell me more about this projection you did Wynter," Fran says, coming to sit down next to me.

"Well," I begin, looking at Cory, and he nods to go on, "It's Cory's doing really. He encouraged me to try."

"It sounds like your abilities are getting stronger. Faster than any of us. Took me months just to filter out my visions," Fran says.

"It's time we prepare," Isalora says, and she walks to the corner where both coffers lie in hiding, pulling up the floorboards; bringing out the box that hid behind the hearth back at the manor.

"That's some hiding spot," Fran says.

We all grin at her in surprise. Isalora takes the small chest to the fireplace, setting it down.

"Wynter," Isalora says, "would you mind handing me your necklace?"

I hesitate to follow her instructions. "My necklace, but won't that leave us vulnerable? I mean, Moyer will find out where I am."

Isalora smiles. "No, my sweet. You're safe as long as you're under the protection of this cottage."

I unclasp the chain and hand Isalora the heirloom. We all watch in suspense, as she unclasps something from the locket, releasing the attached sword. Cory and I both glance at each other, and I begin to say, "Is that the k—" and before I can finish, she releases the locked coffer.

She smiles at us, giving a pleased smirk, knowing the key was hidden right under our noses, the whole time.

She takes out a brown leather binding. "This is my spell book. Take it with you on your quest." Handing it to me, she says, "It will be useful on your journey."

"What do you mean quest?" I ask.

"To Ladorielle of course. To find Dragonscale."

"Are you coming with us?" Cory asks.

"No. The visibility spell renders me too weak. And I must be at full strength when we fight Sarmira. It's either become one of flesh so I can speak to all of you freely, and you can see me, to prepare you for what is to come, or I remain a spirit and go on your journey. I chose the former. Besides Ladorielle is not ready for me yet."

Underneath the book, is a letter and she pulls it out, unfolding it.

My dearest Ones,

If you are reading this letter the prophecy has begun. Look to the pages for the truth:

The power comes from within, revealing to all what's hidden....
The final step, before three can be one....
Look to the west, under the sun....
When the wolves descend, and the moon has begun...
It is there, what you seek to be revealed...
The fate of all, is then sealed...

"Give this to Dragonscale," Isalora says.

"Who is he?" I ask.

"The great ruler of Ashengale, and king of the dragons."

"One more question." Looking at Cory, dad and Fran, knowing we are all as curious, I ask, "How are we to get there?"

The next thing I know, she pops up in the loft. "Why here of course. How else would you get there?"

"But first you must prepare for travel," she says. You are to leave by dawn tomorrow. There is not much time before the Super Blue Blood Moon rises next month.

The following day we are all packed and ready to go. Cory and I grab our bags, throwing them over our shoulders and I tuck the brown book into the pocket of my jean jacket. Dad and Fran behind us waiting to follow. Greeting Isalora at the book she opens the clasped hardcover with the same key that unlocked the coffer.

It flips open automatically as if it knows where we want to go.

"No pen?" I ask confused.

"No pen needed, this book knows where to take you." And as if her words mattered, a portal opens where the window sets in the east.

ABOUT THE AUTHOR

Emmy R. Bennett lives in Northern California with her husband, two children and their dog. She also has two adult children living out of state.

When she isn't at her desk writing, she's spending time with her family, gardening, crafting, or reading.

Emmy grew up in a Lutheran household. Although she's strong in her faith, she believes everyone has the right of free will, in their beliefs.

She loves to study genealogy and her family line has been traced back to the Vikings. It's one of the many inspirations from which she's drawn to write.

Made in the USA
San Bernardino, CA
13 December 2018